The Chronicles of the Accursed: Volume 1

Dawn of Darkness

Inscribed by Agrith Dragonflame

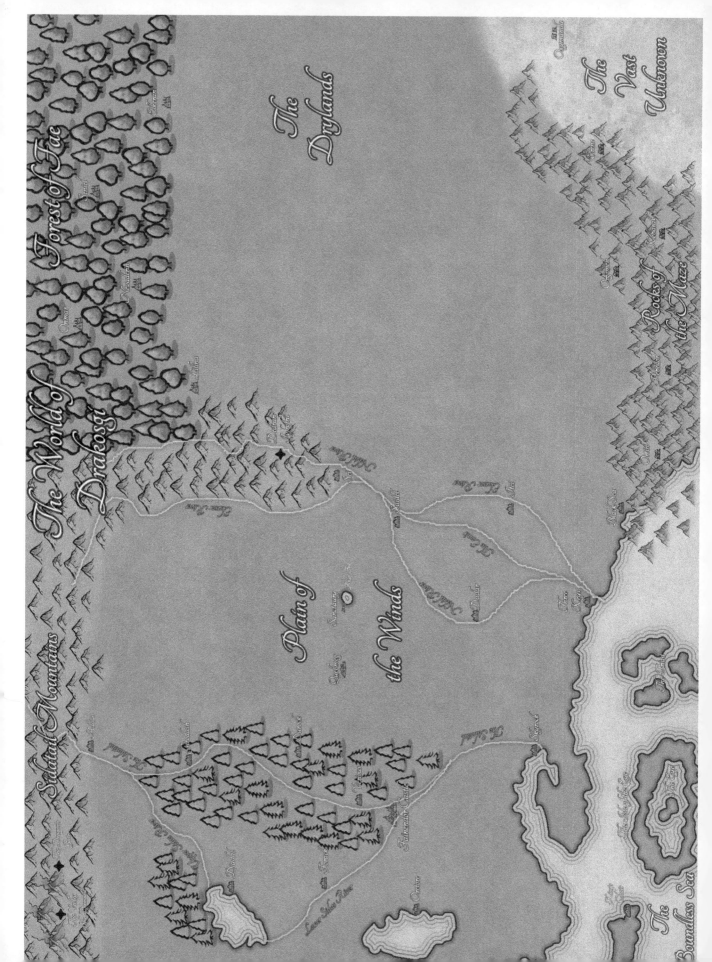

Within this Tome

Prologue

Dane

All this from one dragon, was the thought that ran through Sir Firrik's mind as he gazed at the smoldering, bloody ruins of the village. The light from the newly rising sun painted the wreckage with an orangish-red wash, making the scene somehow all the more gruesome, *All this destruction from one dragon. Adrian was a flourishing village. Numerous people, prosperous mine. It was expected to be one of the wealthiest towns in the kingdom short of the ports. And one dragon managed to destroy it all. In only one morning, too. Damned beasts…*

The knight grimaced and gave a cough, an armored hand futilely waving to drive away the still drifting ash and choking stench. The stench… it was like nothing Firrik had ever come across. It was as though someone had burned a steak over a wood fire that was fueled by some sort of sickly sweet perfume while also being used to burn brimstone-laced charcoal and forge metal. But more unusual than that was another sickly scent interweaving through it all. A scent that defied any sense of normality by smelling naturally artificial. Firrik found himself grimacing yet again as a thought came to mind, *This is the smell of when even death burns.*

"Sir," Firrik turned his gaze about to focus on a soldier who was approaching. The man pulled himself into a salute, his armor jingling with his every move. Beneath his helmet and, quite hidden, cropped hair, the man's piercing blue eyes seemed to bore into Firrik.

"Neros. Report," was Firrik's reponse to the soldier's approach. As he spoke, the knight knelt and began running a hand through the ash.

"We are trying to be as thorough as possible, but-"

"Nothing," Neros took a startled step back at Firrik's blunt, one-word interruption. However, the soldier was fairly quick to follow up with a nod. Firrik heaved a low sigh and got to his feet. After a moment to sweep his gaze across the destroyed village, the knight's gaze caught on something. He cautiously stalked over to a pile of scorched stone.

Lying among the rubble was a mostly unscorched, though very scraped and bruised, body. From it's garb of a red woolen dress and small size, Firrik guessed they used to have been a young girl, though her head was lost amidst the fallen stone that likely ended her life. She had a withered, crumbling bracelet around one wrist, with an identical one lying on the ground nearby. Firrik knelt again and gently picked up the brittle bracelet, his gauntleted hand passing the girl's bloody and scrapped foot. Turning it over, the wreath of flowers looked so fragile in his metal grip. He gazed at it, his expression passive as he murmured, "A flower bracelet... Neros? You were sent here once. Adrian observed the Zenith Festival, did it not?"

"That is correct, sir."

"That explains the lack of armor or weapons," Firrik mused, rising to his feet, "After all, wielding such things upon the day of the festival is akin to begging for a misfortune in the future."

Neros nodded, barking a false laugh, "Ironic, huh? They bore no arms for a good future, yet got slaughtered because of it."

"Indeed. Neros, I want you and your men to begin searching the village center. I suspect you'll find scraps of what used to be a festival. Keep watch on the skies. The dragon may return."

"Yes, sir!" Neros replied, his expression morphing at Firrik's words. The soldier spun on his heel, his head regularly darting up to gaze at the skies above. Firrik watched the man go, then shook his head, eyeing the bracelet.

He slowly returned it to the body, tucking the flowery accessory into her empty hand before turning away.

"Firrik, sir!" another man called out, his voice thin and echoing in the broken village. Despite the few words he said, each held a note that sounded just a little too loud. Like someone trying to whisper in a silent room, "We found something!"

Firrik paused for a moment, then raised his head to see the source of the voice, a pale-skinned young soldier under his command named Rendrich. Rendrich's shaggy hair was rapidly shifting along to the gesturing he was making towards a ruined house with one crumbling wall still standing. The young man's waving was hurried, each swing of the arm just a little too fast for simply drawing attention. Even so, Firrik opted to ignore the man's oddity. Rare would be the person who wasn't unsettled in a place like this. Turning his gaze to the ruin, Ferrik considered it even as he began making his way to Rendrich. He had noticed earlier that, among the shattered housing and broken streets, only that house had anything of note standing. Every other house and structure was destroyed with not even a pitiful beam or sorry-looking stone to mark them. Only ash and death. The state of the charred and sorry-looking structure alone had attracted his attention enough to send a few men to search that place in particular, but, now that he paid a little more mind to the place, he heard something. Amidst the hollow sounds of a listless wind hung the piercing notes of a thin cry. Something was alive there.

"What have you found?" Firrik asked.

"We found a child. Young, only a few months old. It was lying amidst a pile of wood and ash, but you have to see it," Rendrich replied, his tone fast and laced with the discordant echoes of a feeling that was almost primordial, yet always so fresh.

Firrik pondered this revelation. What child could survive a dragon attack that even grown men couldn't escape? Of course, there was an easy way to get that answer. The knight began to make his way towards where the younger soldier had been almost desperately gesturing, prompting Rendrich to to turn and begin leading the way, his gait both rushed, yet meticulously planned. As had been requested of him, Firrik followed Rendrich, though, much like the younger man, Firrik took care to step around the numerous non-descript chunks of flesh, the disembodied and bloody limbs, and the bodies of the fallen. They had suffered enough. Even so, it was rather difficult to avoid all the bodies. There were just so many… As the pair drew nearer to the crumbling wall, another one of Firrik's men, Gordrin, strided towards them, his movements stiff. The newcomer was unlike many of Firrik's men, if only because he was bald, was a giant, and possessed unusual pink eyes. The mat of scars he used as arms were cradled, no doubt holding what had to be the child in question. Without a word, for he had lost his tongue long ago, Gordrin showed Firrik the child.

Firrik's breath caught in his throat. The boy, as it was clearly a boy, was unscathed. His clothes, if he had any to begin with, were ashes, but the boy itself was not harmed. But that was far from the only unbelievable aspect of the boy. On the boy's face was what appeared to be a scar, but this scar was not just a simply healed injury. Not with that shape.

"Sir," Rendrich said, "It looks like-,"

"A dragon," Firrik broke in, "Aye, it does," indeed, an intricate dragon had been carved into the boy's head. And truly, it looked as though someone had taken a knife to the babe's head, rather than a hot iron. More curiously still was that it did not seem recent, in complete spite of the boy's age. Firrik scowled as he realised this, "Whoever put this on him… Hmm…"

"What should we do?"

"I will take the boy to my home and raise him. He will be raised as the son of a knight," Firrik stated, his voice firm. He did not know who this child's parents were, but to allow this to happen to their own child… Whoever the parents were, they did not deserve a child.

"What will his name be? If there was anything that revealed who this was, the dragon's fire already destroyed it."

Firrik thought for but a moment before deciding. He found his eyes drawn to the boy's peculiar scar before providing Rendrich with an answer.

"Dane."

Chapter 1

The Bandit Lord

Dane drank some water from his waterskin before looking around. His gaze swept over, yet lingered on, the forest that lined the path he had been traveling. If he had to describe it, he would have called it serene and beautiful. The pleasantly green leaves rustled slightly in the soft breeze that blew by over the delicate, yet determined grasses and shrubs below. The clear skies above and the silent stillness that was broken only by the gentle breeze that drifted by. Earlier during his trek, Dane had spotted a doe and her fawn watching him from deeper in the trees. It was so peaceful, he almost wished he could spend a little more time here. But that would have to be another day. He was traveling to Girodash to serve as a guard for a merchant's caravan, at his father's behest. The pay was certainly good, but he was aiming to be a knight over exceedingly wealthy. As his father said, 'A true knight is loyal to his lord without question and beloved by his people both young and old.'

Still, Verious to Girodash was no easy stroll. He had been on the road for three days and was expecting to travel for three or four more. Barring trouble, of course. The road to Girodash may be through a serene wood, but beauty didn't always mean good. A wood-lined path was an easy place for an ambush. Still, it had been proven safe to Dane more than once, despite recent rumors of bandits and marauders.

Even so, the young human was on his guard. Dane had set up camp in a hollow space to the side of the road, well out of the way of chance encounters. While it was still quite early, the rather exhausted knight-to-be had spent most of the day slogging through mud, which unfortunately sapped his strength long before Sehero had the chance to set. He glanced at a nearby puddle, in which the world stared back at itself. It had rained the day before, hence the mud in the first place. Of course, Dane had traveled through the rain as well. Traveling through rain had not been pleasant, but it would take more than that to stop him. He had a mission and he could not disappoint. He could not afford to disappoint.

While he looked at the puddle, he couldn't help but study his own face. His brown hair was a little dirty, but his equally brown eyes gleamed. His face appeared lean in addition to its rather strange appearance. It had sharpish angles, but not so sharp as to appear inhuman. His ears tapered very slightly, and below the head those ears were attached to was his rather fit body, one that looked like it belonged to a routine runner. Despite all of this, by far his most notable feature was the dragon-shaped scar across his face. The tail curled around his left eye, its main body cut across his face from his left eyebrow to his right. Its head curled back down to the right of his right eye, just above his cheek. Its wings were folded on its back. Even more peculiar was that faint amber glow it possessed. Dane had no knowledge of how he got it, or what could have given it to him. It certainly wasn't the result of a brand, the scar wasn't precise enough for that.

Dane frowned as he studied the scar. It had been the source of much ridicule back at home in Verious, a small town situated half a mile from Fainendor Castle, home of King Aridor. The children, now young adults like himself, used to constantly teased him about it. Whenever he had the chance to play with them, they always used it as a reason that he should be the bad guy in whatever game they were playing. Even today, some people appeared uncomfortable around Dane. Some even called him dragon-lover, usually trying to insult him. Of course, most didn't do so to his face. He was the son of one of the King's knights, after all.

He looked up towards the sun, known more commonly as Sehero, as he thought about the dragons. Dragons. They were so often depicted as fierce and powerful, but also evil and cruel. Raiders of wealth and thieves of families. Yet, for reasons he couldn't explain, he thought they weren't entirely evil or cruel. That something was wrong when they were thought as such. But why did he think that? Stories of destructive dragons and their evil ways were abound everywhere. There was nothing, nothing at all to show them as good. Well, save for one, anyway. Maybe it was that one...

Dane was startled from his thoughts when he heard rustling. A breeze was blowing, of course, so it was only natural to hear something. However, a light breeze blowing in a single direction did not make leaves move so rapidly back and forth. No, that would only have happened if something was moving in the bushes. Dane glanced around his camp and reached for his sword. It might just be an animal, but it might not be. Better to prepare himself.

"Hello? Who's there?" Dane called into the forest. The only response was a bird calling and the rustle of leaves moving normally to the wind. Whatever had been moving had stopped, but they had done so too late to avoid alerting Dane.

"I know you're there! I heard you!" Dane called again.

"Heard us, you did? Then you have some mighty fine ears," said an armed man as he stepped out of the bushes, followed by two more.

Dane wasted no time in sizing up the men, his eyes darting from one to the other. They were of average size. One had an axe, while the other two wielded swords. Their armor seemed piecemeal, with no two pieces fully matching. The strange mismatched armor and weapons led Dane to believe that these were bandits, but not that great of ones, given their equipment quality. But they were wearing armor, at least. That at least made them somewhat successful.

Dane spared a moment to take stock of his situation. He had a mail hauberk, he rarely travelled without it, but he was not wearing it. Fortunately, the human preferred to travel wearing his gambeson, so at least he had that. It wouldn't stop his foe's blades, but it might lessen some of the blows for him. As for weapons, he had his sword and shield available, but no other weapons besides the dagger at his belt. And it was a three-on-one. Nevertheless, Dane stood and readied himself into a more combat-favorable stance, his shield up front and blade to his right side.

"Come now! Let us negotiate before you get ready to fight!" the well-armed bandit said, his voice uncannily smooth. It was almost eerie how such a rough-looking figure sounded so elegant.

"Very well," Dane replied, "what do you have in mind?"

"Simple. Hand over your gold, weapons, supplies, and other goods, and we will take you to the nearest village, Durock, I believe, and not kill you," he gestured to the east.

"No," Dane responded flatly. He hefted his shield, making a clear point.

"Very well. Prepare to die at my hand, the hand of Lord T'Rostok!" Dane scowled at those words, *Lord T'Rostok? I don't know of any lords or bandit leaders by that name. Must be new.*

As though his words had been a signal, one of T'Rostok's companions rushed forward and swung at Dane with his axe. Dane raised his shield and blocked the rather haphazard swing, hearing the thud as the axe hit wood. Dane countered and, much to the surprise of everyone present, lopped off the man's head. It became very quickly clear to Dane why that was as the axe began to weigh down his shield. The axe was struck.

T'Rostok motioned to his remaining man, who rushed forward at Dane. Dane struggled to defend himself against the attack using his weighed down shield, but managed. He attempted to counter, only to have his own sword blocked in return. Dane swept his blade into a low stroke, but the bandit spotted the attempt and managed to intercept. However, Dane spared a thin smile as he noticed that momentum lay with himself. Taking advantage of this, Dane jabbed forwards with an attempt to disarm the bandit. The attempt was unsuccessful as the bandit managed to parry it sloppily, but it proved to be his key mistake. Dane noted the horrible parry and wasted no time in capitalizing on it. It would mean death otherwise. Dane stabbed at the bandit a second time, and, sure enough, he narrowly missed hitting the man as they clumsily managed to knock the thrust aside. The bandit attempted to copy him, only to fail as Dane parried with the grace of a skilled swordsman. The man stepped back, panic overtaking him as he recognized that he was severely outmatched. Unfortunately for him, Dane didn't give him a chance to run.

Dane launched his assault, consisting of two more quick thrusts. The first was barely avoided with a clumsy parry, but Dane had been planning on that. The bandit had no time to recover from his first parry when the second thrust rocketed forward, spearing him through the heart. Dane roughly pushed his former foe's body off his blade, letting it fall to the ground before turning to T'Rostok. Dane reached around his shield in an attempt to swipe with his sword, trying to knock the axe off, but found no success, "You are no lord. You are nothing but the leader of a petty band of thieves. Do you still want my money?"

"You killed two lesser men. But you will not best me! I am Lord T'Rostok!" T'Rostok bellowed as he rushed forwards. His weapon, a great blade that had to be gripped in two hands, flashed as he chopped for Dane's head. Dane raised his shield, still weighed down as it was, and blocked. The block proved to be a rather illuminating experience, as it revealed that T'Rostok was far, far stronger than Dane himself. His shield had nearly been split in two from the one blow. The only good thing was that the axe was gone. Not that it helped much as Dane tossed his ruined shield aside before countering. T'Rostok blocked the attack easily with the flat of his sword. The move looked almost too easy for the self-proclaimed lord. Dane scowled and opted for a backhanded slash at T'Rostok's waist, only to be met by a quick maneuver that Dane couldn't quite follow. He might not have been able to follow what T-Rostok had done, but he was able to see the results. Dane could only watch as his sword flashed through the air and landed a few feet away. The knight-to-be was shocked, given T'Rostok still gripped his blade with two hands.

"You made an effort, but you are clearly weaker than you make yourself appear. Now, must I kill you? Or shall I take your goods without you stabbing my back?" T'Rostok asked, casually swinging his blade.

Before Dane could give an answer, there was the sound of vibrating material, similar to a drum, and a blur the color of the brightest gold coin slammed into T'Rostok's back. Dane didn't question what had happened, instead scrambling for his sword. When he turned back to face T'Rostok, he saw what the thing was.

It looked a lot like a lizard with a line of spikes down its spine. A sort of diamond-shaped tip to its tail. Two pairs of wings that looked similar to a bat's sprouting from just behind its shoulders as well as back near its hips. A long neck, kind of like a snake that ended in a vaguely triangular head with backwards-facing, off-white horns. It was a *dragon*. It was also small, about the length of Dane's arm. Maybe a dragon hatchling? Whatever type of dragon it was, it was in trouble.

T'Rostok was furious. Before Dane could do anything, the bandit had spun about and swung his sword. Dane saw the sword hit the dragon, but not where. Not that it mattered to Dane. He charged forward and stabbed with his sword, hoping to at least distract T'Rostok. As it would turn out, fortune smiled upon him. T'Rostok had begun to turn just as Dane made his move. This proved to be the bandit swordsman's fatal error as the sword found a rent in T'Rostok's armor, possibly from a past battle. The padding underneath was far from enough to stop Dane's sword, which went through T'Rostok's back and out his chest, though it failed to pierce the bandit's breastplate. T'Rostok looked down, but there was nothing to see as Dane pulled the sword out from the bandit's back. The self-proclaimed lord staggered before toppling sideways, leaving Dane looking down at his dead body for a moment to ensure he was truly dead. That moment ended quickly as he spun about and rushed over to find out the fate of the dragon.

The dragon was lying unconscious a couple of feet to the left of T'Rostok. T'Rostok's blade had found the dragon's side and opened a gash from the dragon's shoulder to its belly. It was a long wound, but not deep. Not that it made much of a difference to Dane. The young warrior was rather inexperienced in the arts of the healer.

As expected from someone inept at healing, Dane had no idea what to do. Fortunately, it was not long before he remembered that the bandit had mentioned that Durock was nearby. If he recalled right, that farmer he'd spoken to a while back had said that a renowned healer lived in Durock. This particular healer was beloved by commoners because of how little she requested in return. As it happened, she was also particularly favored by farmers for her supposedly stellar work with animals. He could only hope that she knew how to help a dragon. Firstly, he had to get the dragon to her while it was still alive.

Dane dug a bit of cloth from his bag to attempt to slow the bleeding. To his surprise, when he pressed the cloth onto the wound, the dragon's blood, of all things, began to burn the cloth. The cloth was crumbling to ash as he watched. Turning his eyes to his own hands, Dane noticed that the blood had done nothing to them, despite them being soaked in the stuff. Perhaps it just didn't affect flesh?

Either way, Dane gathered his equipment quickly, using the puddle from earlier to wash off as much of the dragon's blood as he could first, then set about picking up the dragon. He found that the dragon was light for its size. Despite it being the length of his arm, it was lighter than a similarly sized lamb. Even so, it took him a few moments to find a comfortable position to hold the creature that made sure that his hands staunched the wound. With the dragon relatively secured, Dane set off to Durock, leaving the bandits' bodies unmolested.

Chapter 2

Draco

Much to Dane's relief, he found that Durock really hadn't been that far away. Lightweight though the dragon was, it was certainly still very far from weightless. Of course, there was also blood all over his hands and starting to burn holes in his leggings and gambeson from his attempt at staunching a wound longer than his outstretched hand, which unfortunately did not improve matters. When the walls of Durock began to loom overhead, he realized that he had to make a decision. If he had learned anything from what people thought of dragons, it wasn't good. Letting the dragon be seen would similarly be bad. Not that Dane entertained high hopes in sneaking in. Though he wasn't wearing it, mail was really bad for stealth. Even carrying it in a pack could make too much noise. Despite his poor odds, Dane found himself concluding that his best option seemed to be sneaking in.

As with any human settlement, the area around the walls had long been cleared away. With no option, Dane opted to simply approach slowly and as low to the ground as he could. The approach was nerve-wracking and Dane was almost certain that someone was going to call out and challenge his presence at any moment. But no one did. In fact, there didn't seem to be anyone on the walls or on patrol. To his surprise, Dane even found the guards' posts empty as he slipped inside the walls.

After what had to be a quarter of an hour of creeping on the outskirts of Durock, jumping at every sound, Dane finally saw his target. A small building sat on the edge of town bearing a sign that read, 'The Rejuvenated Dawn,' Despite the inn-like name, that was the apothecary, where the healer supposedly both lived and worked. If Dane was remembering what the farmer had said right. Which was no guarantee, as he realized he couldn't remember the healer's name. Was it Katherine or Katerina? Maybe Kataria? None seemed right.

Upon reaching one of the building's doors- one where it was unlikely anybody could see him, thankfully- he knocked on the door, to his chagrin causing the dragon to momentarily lose more blood. Pressing on the wound once again, he anxiously awaited the healer, wondering if she was already asleep. Fortunately, he didn't have to wait long.

"Knock, knock, at the door! Who wishes to see me?" a voice called out.

"I am Dane of Verious! Are you not the renowned healer of Durock?"

"Yes, yes I am. Tell me! Why are you here? Your voice tells me you are tired, but unharmed and healthy. So who, or what, did you bring that needs healed?" the voice asked. It sounded feminine and definitely on the older side.

"It is better that you see for yourself!" Dane answered, astounded by what the healer could discover simply from how he spoke. No wonder she was a well-renowned healer.

"A secret! I love a good secret! Worry not! No one will know about your secret. Come in! My name is Kathenirin! Come in! Come in!" The door opened to reveal a kindly old woman with wispy grey hair and a smiling face. She but glanced at what Dane held before bustling Dane inside, seemingly oblivious to the fact that it was a dragon.

She had him sit down before saying, "Keep your hands staunching that wound. I'm not sure how you can do it, but normally your hands should be ashes at this point," she paused before adding, "Did you find the long lost recipe for the Freefire Potion? Can make anything it is put on immune to even the hottest heat. But no, if you had, you would have put it on a cloth so you could bind the wound instead of using your hands. Not certain the potion would affect dragon blood, though. Most likely, it would not."

"No, I haven't found the Freefire Potion, whatever that is. I don't know how I can do this." Dane said as he looked up from his hands at the old healer.

The healer stared for a moment before saying, "Dane of Verious, indeed! Why didn't you just tell me that you are from Adrian?"

"Adrian? You mean the Forsaken Village? No one has been from there in almost 20 years. Ever since it was destroyed."

She laughed before leaving, saying, "Stay there!" As she strided down the hallway, Dane began to wonder about what she had said. From Adrian? Adrian was dead. Gone. Turned to ash. More popularly known as the Forsaken Village, it was now full of dragons. At least, that's what the stories said. But even so, Dane couldn't be from Adrian. Dane's father, Sir Firrik, was from Verious. His mother was from Bearitor, near Verious. Adrian was about a good three or four day journey from Durock, let alone Verious or Bearitor. She must have made a mistake.

"Tell me!" Kathenirin said as she reappeared with a basket of supplies, "How does the Dragon-Marked come across a young dragon that should rightfully be too young to travel alone or even leave his parents' aerie?"

"Dragon-Marked? Are you insulting me about my scar?" Dane asked, more confused than angry. Dragon-Marked was a new one, but why would she insult him when he was a customer?

"No, not insulting. Just acknowledging you are most likely the boy from a rather obscure prophecy. So obscure that no one really knows all of it, that I know of," she said, pulling out a hooked needle and what looked like thread, "You are going to have to sew the wound, I can't touch his blood. The prophecy, as I've heard it, states that a creature shall come, bearing the mark of dragons. Supposedly, they would end the suffering between the races of dragon and men. Naturally, most people believe you are to exterminate the dragons, thus stopping any suffering, because there would be no dragons to cause suffering among humans and humans couldn't cause suffering among dragons if there were no dragons. He's lucky, the wound looks long and nasty, but nothing major was damaged. We can just stitch the wound and that should be all," she handed an odd-smelling paste to him, "Put that around the wound. Make sure it gets beneath the scales. It should deadened the pain a little. Helps with keeping an unconscious dragon from waking and spewing fire everywhere."

"Now, listen carefully or you might sew the wound wrong. Line up the edges. Yes, just like that! Now poke the needle through there. No, like this. You are going to have to try to work around the scales, my needles are not going to go through those. That's it. He is going to squirm, this is uncomfortable, you know. Tie off the thread about there. You want plenty to stitch the wound, but not too much," Kathenirin said, watching Dane carry out her commands. She held a small piece of leather as well as a needle, which she used to demonstrate what she wanted the clueless warrior to do, "Keep it tight. No, like this. Good, good. Now punch the needle through there. That's it. Just keep stitching like that and he should be fine," Kathenirin watched as Dane quickly caught on and began to stitch mostly without instruction. He was stitching quite well, for a man. After many long minutes of silent stitching, in which the healer watched Dane's actions like a hawk and the unconscious dragon squirmed quite a bit, Kathenirin nodded.

"Good! That should be all you need. Poke it through one more time. Now tie it off like you did in the beginning. Keep it decently tight… There we go!" she finished, studying the stitching, "A bit clumsy and crooked, but it should be fine. For a man, you sew rather well."

"Kathenirin-"

"Let him rest for a day or so. He should be fine after that! Should be careful not to open the wound for a while, though. We can't bind it, unfortunately, so this will have to do."

"Kathenirin," Dane exclaimed, "What do you know about that prophecy?"

"Well, what I told you. That's about it. Assuming what I heard is true. Of course, there is your ability to withstand the touch of the blood, but whether or not that is part of being the Dragon-Marked, I can't say. Now, it is late. You may as well stay here for the night. Pick up the dragon. Watch how you do it, you don't want to reopen the wound. Now come along."

"But-"

"It's getting late! Just come and spend the night! You will be fine."

"But how do you know all this? About the prophecy, I mean," Dane pressed, only for Kathernirin to give him a vague wave.

"Do you think a simple village healer gets to be as renowned as I by sitting at home doing nothing? Now, enough questions. The dragon, as well as yourself, needs rest. Come."

"Very well," Dane surrendered and began to follow Kathenirin.

ΩΩΩΩΩΩΩΩΩΩΩΩΩΩΩΩΩΩΩΩΩΩΩΩΩΩΩΩΩΩΩΩΩΩΩΩΩΩΩΩΩΩΩ
ΩΩΩΩΩΩΩΩΩΩ

Dane opened his eyes to the view of an unfamiliar roof above him. For a moment, he considered where he was. He was… Yes, that's right. He was in the apothecary and house of Kathernirin in Durock. With a dragon, no less. A *dragon*, of all things. There weren't many dragons in the kingdom of Havmare anymore. Actually, aside from the dragon in the house with him, Dane could only think of one other dragon… In any case, he hoped that it wouldn't delay him for too long. He did have to get to Girodash. Soon enough he found himself wondering what the dragon would do, or why it had helped him.

THUD!

That would probably be the dragon. Dane guessed that it was probably awake and not happy about being somewhere it didn't recognize. Rising from the bed, he made his way towards the door. Might as well try to calm the creature down. For a moment, he wondered what the dragon was like. He would love to get to know the dragon. If he could spare the time.

Dane stepped into the hallway just as there was another thud. The door next to his almost seemed to bulge in slightly. Remembering from the night before that this was the dragon's room, Dane reached out and opened the door. Apparently, the dragon had been about to ram the door again, to its dismay. As Dane swung the door open, it zoomed through the doorway and nearly slammed into the wall, managing to use the floor to stop just in time.

"Ah! Are you okay?!" Dane asked, silently cursing himself for not saying anything first.

"Stay where you are!" The dragon grunted as it pushed itself into a more stable standing position, its golden eyes burning with anger, "I should burn you to cinders for capturing me!" The dragon's voice was rather adorably high-pitched and squeaky while still maintaining an accent that put heavy weight on abrupt sounds. A word as simple as 'capturing' sounded more like 'K- apT- uring.'

"I've done nothing to you," Dane managed to say, however, he was unable to even get one more word out as the dragon's gaze sharpened and the gold-scaled creature spoke again.

"You are the human I saved. The one who is marked. Who are you? Where are we?"

"My name is Dane and we are in the house of a well known healer who helped me stitch up that," Dane replied, pointing to the jagged stitching amidst the scales of the dragon's left side, "Who are you and why did you help me?"

"I am Draco and I helped you because I saw your scar and that you were about to die. Why else?"

"Okay, but-"

"That scar. It marks you. You must come with me. We must leave now."

"Okay, but-"

"I don't know anything about you, so don't try anything. Let us go talk to this healer, then get underway."

"Okay, but-"

"Come!" Draco called as he headed down the short hallway, his pawsteps resolute for such an adorably small and cute hatchling.

"Okay, but-"

"Ah! You're awake!" Kathenirin said as she appeared from the end of the hallway, "Greetings! Tell me, dragon, what is your name?"

"Draco."

"How are you feeling? Not too hot or cold? No unexpected pain, or unusually excessive pain?"

"I feel fine."

"That is good," she paused, then said, "You're not sure about me. That is why you are saying very little to me. I assume you wish to go to the Lake of Light? You may do so, if you want. However, you must take it with caution. You don't want to reopen the wound, after all," Draco didn't respond, "Dane, if you two must go to the Lake, as the dragon will doubtless try to take you there, then I suppose you will need some help. Keep an eye on Draco's wound. That goes for the entire trip. I don't like it that you two are leaving before his wound has healed, but so long as you are attentive, he should be well. Just keep an eye on it and if it reopens, stitch it up with what I have here for you. You must use this, normal thread would be burned through in an instant. Moreover, attend his injuries well. Should the flesh about the wound begin to swell and leak a liquid that is not blood, it may have grown infected. He'll need a healer's hand and skill then."

Dane nodded and accepted the offer, putting the bundle Kathenirn handed to him in his pack where they were easily accessible. He looked back to Kathenirin and noticed she had something else. It was long, but wrapped in cloth. It almost looked like a sword. In fact, Dane was sure that it was a sword.

"I was given this long ago and was told that I would know what to do with it when the time came. That time has come. I give it to you," she unwrapped the object, revealing an intricate and ornate arming sword, "This is *Verachodairgin*. In the language of the elves, that means Dragonforged, for this blade was forged by man and dragon in days gone by. It will never break nor dull nor even scratch, for what is that the face of dragonfire and magic?"

"Thank you, I don't know what to say," Dane said, shocked that Kathenirin would give him something like that. Like the arming sword he had, its hilt was just long enough to be wielded comfortably in one hand. The sword was as beautiful as it was sharp. The blade was fairly long and Dane could see a peculiar pattern, as if the blade was a gout of fire. The hilt was shaped to look like the blade was protruding from a dragon's mouth, with the dragon's open mouth acting as the crossguard. The dragon's eyes were rubies and the pommel was pointed, similar to the tip of Draco's tail. The handle was wrapped with wire that almost felt like leather.

"Hmm. I suppose I should warn you. It seems to me that Draco and you are connected by fate, or destiny, if you will. Many creatures are bound by fate, but a scarce few find their fates intertwined so irrevocably. Such individuals are called Companions or *Feminatenas Gerato*, which fittingly means 'Fated Companions.'"

"But, how can he be my… Companion? I've not seen him before yesterday!" Dane exclaimed.

"Some live their entire lives without ever meeting their Companion, should they have one."

"But how do you know?"

"Whatever he might say, most creatures wouldn't risk their lives like he did. A hatchling so soon left from the aerie risking death and worse for an utter stranger? Surely you are no fool as to not realize this is not a normal affair? Companions, however, are doom-driven to one another. To aid one another in their times of need and walk alongside them. It is as if they know that the other is important, if you will. Ever more, Companions bear a dark fate. It is said that, should one die, the other left a mournful shell. Condemned to a miserable, sad life. If they do not merely kill themselves. A painful affair, to be sure. Such that I will say this to you now and as many times as I must: *Ve kens deret frokior!* 'Do not let him die!'" Kathenirin pressed.

"Hmph. I may be young, but I am far from helpless. I will look after Dane as much as he after me. If not moreso. *Hasi Ove neverin.*" Draco said, surprising Dane.

"Pride goeth before the fall, young Draco. *Frotikelo rotese kirin neh.*

"*Frotikelo ors iv reilstelsier Oeren,*" Draco replied.

"So be it, yet watch well your step, lest you wade into the hornet's nest. But now is no longer the time for talk. *Draco ve jeg.* Go, Dane. Before the guards take up their post again in the morning. There is a time where nothing of evil heart can enter the walls of Durock, as was long ordained. However, this protection fades come the light of day. You must go before the guards stand ready. I believe that I do not need to tell you what will become of a dragon and their allies if found."

"No. No, you do not," Dane found himself murmuring as he obeyed Kathenirin's order. As he pulled the door open, Draco spoke.

"Follow me," Dane sighed as he watched the dragon push past him and began to make for the east, clearly not taking 'No,' for an answer. It would seem that Girodash was not going to happen.

Chapter 3
The Words of Magic

"Draco, what were you doing near where T'Rostok and I were?" Dane asked Draco, wanting to break the silence that had dominated the journey since they left Durock. They had already been on the road for around an hour now and Draco hadn't said a thing. Dane was starting to question Kathenirin's statement about the two being destined companions. Draco had so far seemed to be entirely uninterested in Dane, aside from Dane's scar, that is.

"I was cursing my luck," Draco said, his voice rather plain and blunt for such a statement, "I just so happened to hatch a few days ago and my memories returned to me."

"Returned? How could your memories return if you never had any?"

"It's a long story, but since it seems that we are going to be on the road for a while, I'll tell you. It's not as if it will help you against me. First, answer me this question: How long has it been since the attack on Adrian?"

"Twenty years. I was born around that time," Dane answered, "You know about it?"

"'Know about it?' Of course. I, out of anyone, should. But I am getting ahead of myself. Two and thirty years ago, I first hatched. I was a reckless youth, often troubling others. An ogre was sent to reign me in when I had but a few years. It near broke my neck, but inevitably achieved little, save make me angry at the ones who sent it. Still, it would drive me to seek out creatures who were not dragons. Simply put, that would lead me to decide that I wish to be less like those that scorned me. Which resulted in me being a… helpful dragon. Or as helpful as a dragon can be. I did my best. Unfortunately, a dragon isn't exactly what you'd expect to help you and I sometimes ended up causing more problems than I solved," he gave a short mirthless laugh, "That, and some didn't like my 'attitude' and refused my help. Your kind in particular can be quite ridiculous about it."

Draco paused, considering his next words, "It was when I had but twelve years that I heard of a dragon that was terrorizing a village. That would be Adrian. I went there as fast as my wings would allow. I may not see much of humans, but assaulting one of your villages is a dangerous affair, even with a reason for it. Humans like yourself tend to be rather vengeful. Overly so… That aside, once there, I found the dragon. When I tried to hear his reasons, he ignored my words. I suspect that he had none. I chose to forego further conversation and simply attack the other dragon. As would be expected, our fighting caused us to destroy many buildings, kill many humans. I remember as I clawed at the other dragon, my tail whipped around and caught a human female in the head. Her child went flying into a wrecked house. I am certain they are both dead," Draco paused, but continued speaking soon after, "I couldn't do anything, in the end. When the dragon finally realized that he couldn't best me, he resorted to magic. His spell was wild and uncontained, desperate and cruel. I cannot claim to know what his intent was with the spell, but his magic was… less than pleasant. It forced me into a younger state, into an egg. To add to it, it sealed my memories so that I remembered nothing, thus preventing me from trying to hatch too early," Draco hesitated yet again, "I have no knowledge of what he did to my egg after that, but I can guess. Our eggs can hatch at many different times, but higher… ah, what's the word… You humans use it when talking about hot and cold…"

"Um, temperature?"

"Aye, Temperature. That's it. Human is such a strange tongue, the words are easy to forget. Anyways, higher temperatures and the presence of plentiful prey can cause dragons to hatch earlier. I assume that the dragon left my egg in a cold place with little prey, as I would be less inclined to try to leave. Cold temperatures make hatchlings slow and tired. It does much the same to unhatched dragons as well. But I do not know why he would have moved my egg so that I would hatch and regain my memories a few days before you would arrive nearby."

Dane scowled for a moment, his thoughts evident on his face, "You're right about that. It does seem odd. What person, or dragon, would do something like that? Dragon eggs are difficult to damage from the outside, if the stories are true. Even if he did it so you would hatch into a vulnerable youth to make it easier to kill you, it doesn't explain why he left it for so long or why he let you hatch without interference."

"As I said, I cannot explain it myself. Though something was different about this dragon. His scales were black, a color that has only appeared but rarely. That and his eyes were red, which has never happened, save for dragons with red scales. Even so, there was still a difference. The red of his eyes held a strange, malicious feel to them and almost seemed to give off its own light. It was unnatural. He also spoke strangely, almost to himself whenever it wasn't gibberish or crazed laughter."

"There's a children's poem that I know, I don't know where it came from and I don't know much of it, but it has something about black dragons." Dane offered.

"There is? What is it?" asked Draco, glancing at Dane, both his voice and gaze colored by his intrigue. As the dragon made his question, his tail drifted from its previous side-to-side motion to being near motionless.

"Dragon armored bloody red, burning people, now they're dead.

Dragon silver, falsely shine, false friend taking wealth of mine.

Dragon bright and shiny gold, dragon risk to trust I hold.

Dragon black, evil at heart, may never meet or world depart."

Dane nodded to himself, for a moment, as though reassuring that he had spoken the poem right, "That is what I can remember."

"Humans don't have a high opinion of dragons," Draco observed. Though his voice seemed to be plain and level again, Dane saw through the deception this time. The dragon wasn't pleased about that.

"Dragons have been destroying human villages, towns, and even a city since it all started at Adrian. Before as well, though not as frequently. Regardless, it makes sense that dragons are disliked. Even ones with scales of gold."

"... So by failing to defeat that dragon, I've loosed a beast driven to destroy your kind," Draco said, his displeasure changing to a hint of an unexpected emotion. It also seemed to be bitter.

Dane looked at Draco before saying, not expecting that reaction to a simple poem, "Such things have existed before, if the stories are right. Some even say that we ought to have been annihilated entirely. Humans have the tendency to survive, and tend to strike back when their enemies think they are down. Don't worry. They- that is, we- should survive until we stop this mad dragon. We always do."

"That's… reassuring," Draco paused before saying, "Dane? Thank you. For keeping me away from the memories that… Are less than pleasant. From my failures. I should mean nothing to you, yet you have helped me. Twice."

"It doesn't matter who you are. You are clearly a good person and needed the help. You even saved my life first. As for your memories, I was not keeping you away, but teaching you how to face them. That was one of the lessons taught to me by my father, Sir Firrik. Perhaps one of his more valuable ones. Though most of his lessons are valuable."

"He sounds like a wise man."

"He hates dragons, he saw the destruction at Adrian," Dane murmured, his gaze drifting away from Draco.

"He saw the battle?" the dragon eyed his human companion. However, Dane merely shook his head before replying.

"No, he saw what was left."

ΩΩΩΩΩΩΩΩΩΩΩΩΩΩΩΩΩΩΩΩΩΩΩΩΩΩΩΩΩΩΩΩΩΩΩΩΩΩΩΩΩΩΩΩΩΩΩΩΩΩ ΩΩΩΩΩΩΩΩΩΩΩ

Draco's mind was a mass of conflicting emotions. He had failed. He had fought against someone he could not afford to lose to, then lost. Dane's statement about humans was calming, certainly, but it did not change that, in the end, Draco had managed nothing.

Dane, meanwhile, was also lost in his thoughts. Specifically, he was considering what Draco had told him. That Adrian had been destroyed by not one dragon, but two. Draco and that strange black dragon, *Who were they? What did they-*

Dane was broken out of his thoughts as a voice spoke. It sounded familiar, but strange. Almost like he was listening to someone he knew speak in a large room that echoed, but didn't echo at the same time. Not that Dane could really understand the voice. Turning his head about, he called out to Draco, startling the dragon out of his thoughts, "Did you say something?"

"I did not. Why?"

"Because I thought I heard something."

Draco met Dane's gaze, his brow ridges furrowing, "What?"

"It almost sounded like words. I think one of them was 'nothing,' Though I will admit that I'm not quite sure. It was very muffled and... distorted, I guess," Dane held the dragon's gaze, then turned back to where the pair were going.

Words like this? Draco wondered, suspicion touching his thoughts. It couldn't be...

"Yes, they sounded exactly like that! How did you say them like that? Or yelling them, I should be saying." Dane asked, oblivious that Draco had said nothing out loud.

I'm not saying them, I'm thinking them. Draco said, using his thoughts, though he didn't try as hard as before. Still... This was an interesting development. Perhaps it could be useful.

"Ha! Right. I can't read people's minds."

Then look at me.

Dane looked at Draco. Draco once again merely thought his next sentence, his mouth remaining distinctly closed, *See? I told you.*

"But- but how? Can you hear me?" Dane said before seeming to concentrate. While Dane looked amusing, Draco noticed a resounding nothing happening.

"Nothing."

"Can all dragons do this?"

"Not that I know of." Draco said, shaking his head and rustling his wings. His tail paused for a moment, then returned to its careful drifting, "Unless they do and just don't talk about it? I wouldn't be surprised if that was so."

"Could this be something that comes from being bound by fate? What did Kathenirin call it, being Companions?"

"You can't do it. I doubt it," Draco stated rather bluntly. Dane found himself studying the dragon. It had almost sounded like Draco was attempting to cut the conversation short.

"Strange."

"That it is. I never would have thought it was possible without magic. Like those supposed frost dragons."

"Frost dragons?"

"Aye. Dragons who are said to possess a breath of ice, instead of fire. Some dragons up north are supposed to be able to do that… And are very cold to the touch. Never actually met one myself, but that's how tales are."

"Strange," Dane said again. He might have said more, but never got the chance.

"Not as strange as a human talking to a vile dragon!" a voice rang out, its tone accusatory and mean-spirited. Upon hearing it, Dane swung around. Behind them stood three men with naked blades. The man who must have spoken stepped forward, "Now, why don't you step away from the dragon and lay down your weapons and no one gets hurt."

Follow his instructions. I have a plan.

It was still very strange, hearing Draco's thoughts. Nevertheless, Dane obeyed both Draco and the armed man before him. He slowly drew *Verachodairgin*, then laid it on the ground. He did the same with his dagger. Then, hands raised to clearly show that he was unarmed, Dane slowly stepped away from Draco. Once there was a few yards of space between the two, the apparent leader of the three men spoke.

"Good! Now, what are you doing here? And why are you traveling with such vile creatures as dragons?"

"*Dragon bright and shiny gold, dragon risk to trust I hold.* That is why."

"An old, crazed poem! It means nothing. All dragons are evil!"

"This one has not wronged me," Dane replied.

"He is biding his time, waiting to strike when you least expect it!"

"No."

"No?! No!?! You dare ignore me!?! I am Lord Destrios! Lord of Forack!" the man postured, pointing his blade at Dane. The weaponless warrior smiled.

"You are not. Forack is a fortnight's journey southwest. I am in more danger from you than from my friend here." Dane said coolly, stunning the man. Out of the corner of Dane's eye, he saw Draco begin to move. The man who called himself Destrios, as well as the other men, were fortunately too focused on Dane after what he just said to notice Draco.

"What-?"

"I also happen to know Destrios and know that he would listen to the person he was confronting before deciding judgement, even if the person travels with a dragon. You also do not look like him."

"Lies!" the man spat.

"Are they?" Dane challenged, "Prove to me that you are Destrios. Who is Destrios' most trusted advisor? And don't lie, I know exactly who they are."

"His… advisor?" the man's answer would have revealed that he had no clue, even if Dane didn't already know the answer.

"Wrong."

"Wha-? How would you know!?" the False Destrios demanded. He wasn't able to get an answer as one of his men shattered the conversation with a worried call out.

"Lord! Where's the dragon?!"

Before anyone could move, Draco blasted out of the nearby bushes where he had snuck off to while Dane distracted the men. The dragon slammed himself into the chest of the False Destrios, who stumbled and fell over. Before the False Destrios could get to his feet or even make sense of what had just happened, a sword appeared from nowhere and stabbed into his chest.

Dane, who had regained his sword while the False Destrios had recovered on the ground, withdrew the weapon from its current place in the fallen man's chest and charged at the two remaining men. Draco took to distracting one man while Dane went for the other.

The man flashed his blade up, as if to take off Dane's head, but then brought it down to cleave Dane at the waist. Dane saw through the feint and brought his sword down, easily intercepting the attack. Dane winced as he did so, realizing that he had sloppily blocked edge to edge. Even so, Dane didn't miss a beat, striking back and catching the man's hand. He swiftly attempted to follow with a backhanded blow. However, his foe saw it coming and managed to block. The man, now angry and having difficulty holding his sword, grabbed it with both hands and raised it to chop at Dane's head. Even as he did so, he gasped. A clattering sound erupted from around his feet as his sword slipped through his nerveless fingers. Dane gave the man a hollow glare as he withdrew his sword from the stab that had finished his opponent. Once it was free, the foe before him crumpled to the ground. Not that Dane was really paying attention. He was too busy gazing at his blade in wonder.

Verachodairgin was clearly superior to any sword Dane had ever wielded before. It had easily passed through the man's armor as if it was paper, requiring only a little effort from its wielder and leaving behind naught but melted metal and charred flesh. Almost as if the blade had been resting in an unfathomable blaze. Not only that, the edge was still perfect, despite the fact that any normal blade would have normally taken some damage from merely striking armor, let alone using the edge to block his opponent's strike. Dane shook his head and turned to see Draco using his fangs to rip out the remaining man's throat. The man's sword was impaled in a nearby tree.

"I would have rather not fought these men, if only because I wasn't in the mood to fight," remarked Draco, "Your kind are, as usual, quite keen on battle."

"Not all, but many," was all Dane could say, awe just barely tinting his voice. Draco noticed this, but decided against commenting on it. It was only right, after all.

"Aye. Many, indeed," Draco said, "You asked the man who Destrios' most trusted advisor is. Who is it?"

"A silver scaled dragon named Foren. Foren hides himself to avoid causing unwanted attention and questions. Actually, though I've heard about him, I've never seen him. To most, it is but a rumor. If Destrios himself hadn't told me that Foren exists, I'd likely believe the same. Even so, if Destrios would listen to anyone, it would be Foren. Which would make him an oddity, considering most people's feelings about dragons, regardless of how friendly. But few people know the truth about Foren… Destrios says he is wise and trustworthy, if nothing else."

"That is the life of a dragon in human lands, now. Secrecy and hiding. *Ove rekilek dairgin frozesul hasi veo ketik.*"

"Those words. What do they mean?" Dane asked as he started to continue onward. As he did so, Draco gave Dane a look that was best described as a mixture between intrigue and surprise.

"You don't know?"

"No. Only what Kathenirin told me."

"Then I shall teach you," Draco stated. He spread his wings and, with a short run-up, threw himself upwards. Dane watched as Draco's wings caught the air, allowing the dragon to fly, even if he was flying level with Dane's head. The human found himself curious as to how Draco was able to fly at all. Weren't dragons supposed to be older before they could do that? He opted against questioning it, deciding to first continue their current conversation instead.

"Really?"

"Indeed. This language may do you well, if you happen to be fortunate enough to be talented at magic. Even if you are not, you can start training with magic and grow stronger. But I would prefer to teach this language while teaching you of magic. It makes it much easier."

"Very well, let's start." Dane replied.

"I will decide when we start," Draco said, a pride and strength belying his size in his voice, "First, one of the most basic spells is holding something in place. While you can manipulate the spell to in turn manipulate what you want to achieve, simply saying '*Tred*' will work for now. *Tred* means 'Hold.' Just focus your will and say '*Tred.*'"

"Focus my will?"

"Commit yourself to the task. Ah, how can I explain? Have you ever wanted to do anything, no matter what got in the way?"

"Yes. Plenty of times when my father taught me."

"Good, it is much like that," Draco tilted, allowing himself to circle above Dane. It kept him from inadvertently outpacing the human, but also felt rather amusing. That he could both travel with Dane and fly circles about him at the same time, "Imagine that you want this spell to succeed, that you will put everything into making the spell work. Then try to cast the spell."

Dane nodded, considering what Draco had said. Then with a deep breath to steady himself, Dane cried out, *"Tred!"*

Nothing happened.

"Try again," Draco replied. His two-word statement was quite straightforward and rather heavy.

Dane did exactly that. He was used to trying something and failing. Just like all the times before, the first failure only made him want to succeed more. However, as he was about to speak, he realized that he probably also needed something to stop. Without a second thought, he decided to try to hold Draco in place.

"Tred!*"* As the word rang out, Draco gave a startled cry. Or rather, Draco attempted to give a startled cry that was cut off abruptly as he stopped. His wings, body, legs, everything suddenly stopped as soon as Dane had cast his spell. Draco was essentially hovering in the air, not moving an inch.

"I'm sorry, It worked but… Sorry."

"What… are… you… sorry… about?... Focus… your… will… and… say… '*Frotred*'… Release… me." Draco struggled to say as the spell held his mouth closed. It was as though someone had clamped an iron muzzle onto his snout. And everything else. Regardless of what he was moving, his body struggled to even move a centimeter.

"Right. *Frotred!*" Dane said, his face tightening in focus. Almost without a warning, Draco was freed and dropped like a stone. He barely managed to stop himself from slamming his face into the ground, well aware that if he didn't know what Dane was doing, his face *would* be in the ground.

"Good! Good," Draco exclaimed as he managed to steady his flight, "It took me most of a day to manage that. That being said, I was quite young when I learned. Though it would have been nice if you had warned me. Now, to hold something specific, you can specify that thing. For example, you could say '*Akron ve tred*' to hold an incoming sword in place or say '*Draco ve tred*' to specifically hold me. Go ahead, try it. I'll be fine this time."

ΩΩΩΩΩΩΩΩΩΩΩΩΩΩΩΩΩΩΩΩΩΩΩΩΩΩΩΩΩΩΩΩΩΩΩΩΩΩΩΩΩΩΩΩΩΩΩ
ΩΩΩΩΩΩΩΩΩΩ

"How about we take a break for the day? All these spells have left me tired!" Dane exclaimed, bent over with his hands resting on his knees. Draco, who had finally allowed his claws to touch the ground (of his own accord), turned his gaze over to Dane, watching as the human heaved a sigh before pushing himself back upright. The dragon gave a huffed breath as his tail made what seemed to Dane to be an amused twitch.

"Absolutely. You are straining your will and physical strength with every spell you cast. As I said earlier, you can only do what you have the will and energy for." Draco replied, his wings rustling as the dragon sought to move them into a more comfortable position, "Remember though, specifying what you want the spell to do puts less strain on your will as it requires you to focus less on what you want the spell to do, but it takes that same amount of energy regardless of how specific it is."

"Then what happened to that crazy black dragon's spell? You know, the one that turned you into an egg? You told me you didn't know what the spell was supposed to do. Wouldn't you know if he told you what it did when casting it?"

"The one that regressed me into an egg, you mean. Still, you would be right. That was particularly strange. He didn't explain what he wanted, but said a poem. If you wish, I could tell you the poem," Draco had barely finished the offer before Dane nodded in response, "Very well," Draco paused for a moment before beginning to chant,

"Time is lost and youth is gone,

Turn back clock and repair lost,

Cast away what not belong,

To seal away by fire and frost."

Dane considered the poem for a few moments, then admitted, "I can't make any sense out of that. It almost feels like something is missing."

"I think the same. My guess is that, due to his madness, the dragon couldn't focus on whatever it is he wanted to do and thus the spell essentially lost control and did whatever it could within the boundaries of his words. Assuming he had a plan to begin with."

"Really? A spell can do that?" Dane asked, eyebrowed raised in surprise.

"Indeed. If you lack the focus to keep your spell focused, it can do almost anything within the guidelines of your words. If you lack the willpower, you are unable to cast the spell to begin with. Finally, if you lack the energy, it consumes all the energy it can, kills you, and you die in vain."

"It *kills* you?"

"Aye. Why do you think I've been making it clear that you make sure not to cast a spell if you are too tired or can't focus?" Draco sighed, his head drifting back and forth in the dragon's way of shaking his head, "I cannot decide about you sometimes."

With that statement, the pair returned to walking in silence (or flying low, in Draco's case) for a couple minutes before Draco suddenly spoke, "Ugh… I smell wolves. We'll need to keep an eye out, they don't like invaders in their territory," though he didn't mention it, Draco also got a vague sense of being watched, but decided that it was probably the wolves. Not a notable cause for alarm.

Dane nodded, "I know. I am a hunter, among other things," the human hesitated, then stole a glance at the sky, "Sehero's getting low. We should find somewhere to rest for the night."

Draco grunted, his gaze drifting to follow Dane's, "Hmph, fine. But keep watch for wolves!" With that announcement, the two searched in silence. While they soon found a location, it didn't quite ease their situation. Both were a little worried about the night to come and didn't notice the shapes hidden amongst the trees. At least, one of them didn't.

Chapter 4

Secrets

Draco struggled. There was nothing else to do. Someone or something had hold of him and he couldn't get free. Just what was it? What was strong enough to hold a dragon? He felt like he should know, but he just couldn't remember… He heard struggling somewhere behind and roughly to his left, where he guessed Dane was being held. How did he know it was Dane? He wasn't sure, yet hearing it convinced him to struggle harder. In spite of that, the unseen creature, or creatures, he didn't know, seemed like they couldn't care less as they began to drag him somewhere.

"Draco!" Dane yelled, still struggling, "Don't drink! Draco! Don't drink!"

For a moment, there was a bit of confusion. Then, Draco was just able to see Dane, not being held and armed, standing off to the side. He was watching as though helpless. If there was more to see, Draco didn't have a chance to as his captors plunged his head into water. *Draco!* Draco struggled to get his head above water, but the creatures were too strong. *Draco! Don't drink!* Draco struggled, but he felt weaker and weaker. His strength was fleeing rapidly, unnaturally so. The dragon's lungs needed air, yet he had barely been in the water for a few seconds. Right? *Don't drink!* Draco couldn't hold his breath any longer. He had to do something. Anything. *Draco!*

He drank.

Draco woke with a start, his wings, tails, and legs flailing. He froze as Dane's voice rang out, "Whoooa there, Nellie! You're twisting and turning like a bucking horse, Draco. What kind of dreams did you have to get that?"

Dane was crouched next to Draco. But that wasn't what Draco noticed. The dragon most noticed that the human's voice was cheerful and just slightly teasing. There was a hint of something else, but Draco couldn't quite place what it was. Not that he particularly cared at the moment.

"I-I don't know. I can't remember any dreams." Draco murmured, his expression confused. He was twisting and struggling violently in the middle of his sleep? Because of a… dream?

"Well, it was probably just a nightmare. A bad dream," Dane chuckled to himself as he slung his pack over his shoulder. Draco noticed that the human had already completely packed up the camp around him.

"Maybe." Draco wasn't so sure. A bad dream? It felt like too simple an explanation. Almost like he had seen something. Perhaps something important, but he couldn't remember it. What was it? Something about… about water? That seemed right, but also not… "I feel-I feel as if the… dream was very important."

"Hmm. Well, we will have to go without. Important though it may be, you do not remember," Dane smiled, rising from his previously crouched position.

"I hope we aren't making a mistake."

"We'll be fine. What is there that's a significant threat to a dragon? Now come on, we need to get going."

Draco thought over what the human said, but couldn't help but agree. However, now that he was thinking, he realized something, "Fine… You didn't wake me last night. We were both supposed to watch last night, were we not?"

"Sorry. I must have fallen asleep. I was quite tired last night. Anyhow, we need to get going."

Dane turned and began walking east, the direction the pair had originally been travelling. Draco looked after him and heaved a sigh. Something was off, *Why do I get this feeling that Dane is more than he looks? And the dream, or whatever it was. Why is it bothering me like this? Should it? Should either of these? ... Yes, they should. Something isn't right. It can't be.*

"Hey! Draco! Come on!"

Draco sighed again. His thinking would have to wait. Dane was watching him, clearly waiting for him to start moving. Without any preamble, Draco took off and flew after Dane, keeping low to the ground as was usual. Curiously, Dane started walking again almost as soon as Draco had taken off. He didn't even wait to see if Draco was steady. The dragon would have frowned if he could. This wasn't right. He wasn't sure about it, but Dane seemed to be a little hasty. More so than yesterday, that was for sure. He considered this as they returned to their travels.

Dane has to be hiding something, Draco decided, *But what? What could be causing Dane to act so strangely? Was it a dream of his own?*

With no real answers, Draco opted to try asking Dane himself. However, rather than say the words aloud, he decided to try communicating via his thoughts. He wanted to get somewhat used to speaking like this. It could be very useful. Or perhaps not, it felt exceedingly awkward to speak without actually speaking, *Dane? What is wrong?*

"Nothing. Why do you ask?"

You are acting strange. You are impatient, which, from what I saw of you yesterday, is not normal for you. You normally are cautious. Or so it seemed. Just a few moments ago, you would have walked into a trap if it meant we would get going. So I ask again, what is wrong?

"I just want to stop this dragon, whoever he is, and I don't want to waste time."

"But we are heading to the Lake of Light, remember?" Draco spoke aloud. Speaking with his mind just felt too strange, like Dane could peer into his innermost thoughts. He didn't like it.

"Yes we are. And then we hunt down the dragon. Either way, I want to keep moving. If we dawdle around too much, it might be too late."

As much as it made sense, something about Dane's denial felt wrong. In spite of the ominous feeling he was getting, Draco decided to put the knowledge to the side. Something about the way Dane spoke led Draco to believe that this was something Dane would defend vigorously. Enough so that it was probably more trouble than it was worth. And yet, something about Dane just seemed too… mysterious to let it go. The words didn't quite do Dane justice, but it was all Draco could think of to describe him. Nonetheless, now was very much not the time to try and pry out the human's secret. Though Draco was hesitant to admit it, Dane was right. They needed to keep moving. With a sigh of acquiescence, Draco began to settle back into the routine of the previous day. He was about to start teaching Dane more about magic and the *Kuritik Metol*, the language of magic, when he heard Dane say something. It was almost immediately clear, due to Dane's muttering, that the human wasn't talking to Draco. Curious, and just a little suspicious, the dragon strained himself so he could try to hear what Dane said. The human was talking in a very low voice, making listening in quite difficult. Nevertheless, Draco was able to make out something:

"…cursed as I am, I will not give in. I cannot. Not if it means… that… But I don't know how long I can go on, what with the wolves last night… I-I need…" Dane's voice sank below Draco's hearing, then returned, "…If only my curse was like others and not..." his voice faded again, leaving Draco to ponder what he had said.

A curse? What curse? What does he need? Draco was about to ask when Dane started up again, "I wish I could…" Dane's voice faded out, then came back, "…I wish, but I dare not. I don't know what would happen… No, I think I do know what would happen and it would be terrible. I just can't."

He wishes what? Draco wondered and was about to ask again when he heard Dane grunt and mutter, "Ah, it still hurts. But how? It is supposed to be far faster than it seems to be. Still…" Dane's voice once more dropped out of Draco's hearing. Dane muttered a fair bit before his voice rose to audible levels again, "…healing, that it would have completely healed. Could it be something to do with wolves? No… they do not like me, but it can't be them. It must be something else that is responsible, but what?"

Draco thought about this new tidbit and found himself frustrated, *What healing? He's a human. Humans have no special healing powers, not without magic and I haven't taught him such spells yet. I* can't *teach him any such spells. Even so, he has already shown that he knows little of magic. So what healing does he have? And wolves don't like him? When? Last night? He was uninjured before and I would have woken if there had been any fighting at all,* Draco was about to question Dane, then hesitated, *No… If I know humans, this is likely one of those topics that he'll either lie about or not tell me everything. Asking will only make him suspicious. I'll have to observe if I want to learn more… Yes, I'll do that. Once I have more to go on, I'll confront him,* he decided. Still, his decision couldn't stop him from wondering, *Just who is Dane? What curse does he have? Why hasn't he mentioned it?*

"Draco? Are you… okay?" Dane asked. He had stopped and was giving Draco a strange look. Draco quickly realized why. The dragon had been circling the same spot for the past few moments, even though Dane was well ahead of the spot.

"What? Oh! Aye. Aye, I'm fine. Merely lost in thought," Draco rushed at giving Dane an answer. Perhaps a little too fast.

Dane nodded slowly. In spite of the dragon's reply, it was clear that something had distracted Draco. The human found his thoughts turning to worry, *Draco knows something. Did he hear me? Please don't have heard me. Telling him, it might drive him away. I don't want to drive him away.*

"I was just worried."

"Thank you." Draco's reply was rather formal as he caught back up to Dane. As the dragon hurried toward him, Dane noticed that some was off. He scowled, trying to work it out with little success. Then, like the flash of a lightning bolt, it came to him. Draco was bigger. The young-looking dragon was almost certainly longer than Dane's arm. Despite it being only one day since they had met, the dragon had already grown a significant amount. Dane stared for a moment before he decided that it was more funny than disheartening that he hadn't noticed earlier, "Draco, you're growing."

"Aye, I am. It is only natural. Didn't you notice?"

"Ha ha! No, I didn't. I'm not sure why, but it seems funny," Dane couldn't help but continue to laugh. Draco just looked at him, then shook his head in dismay, *Humans!*

ΩΩΩΩΩΩΩΩΩΩΩΩΩΩΩΩΩΩΩΩΩΩΩΩΩΩΩΩΩΩΩΩΩΩΩΩΩΩΩΩΩΩΩΩΩΩΩΩ ΩΩΩΩΩΩΩΩΩΩ

"Draco?" Dane called out. The pair had been walking for only an hour or so, but Dane couldn't help himself. For some reason, Draco had decided not to continue his lessons, leaving the pair to walk on in silence.

"Hmm?"

"Where is this Lake of Light?" Dane asked, relieved that Draco had spoken instead of remaining silent or grunting. The dragon seemed to like silence far too much for Dane's tastes.

"I don't actually know. Legends puts the *Arun Fril,* or Lake of Light, somewhere in an eastern direction. At least from here," Draco admitted, "I only know that we have to find it. That you have to go there."

"Then we could spend forever searching for the Lake?"

"We could, but I don't think we will."

"That's… rather depressing." Dane said, his expression melting into something akin to ponderous as he continued to walk, "But I guess yo- what's that?" Dane interrupted himself to point at a strange-looking furry shape on the ground.

"Let's find out."

As they approached, Draco found himself able to recognize what it was. It was the body of a wolf. To the dragon's side, but very much out of his sight, Dane's brows knitted together more and more as they got closer. As though in worry. And for good reason. The wolf was lying there with a little blood around it. It was covered in injuries that obviously should have left more blood, yet the location was oddly absent of the red substance. Equally strange was that the body was alone. Even if it was a dead body, it was still a wolf. Wolves usually travel in packs… And mourned their dead.

"Dane. These are claw and teeth marks. Some animal did this. But these are so large and the only scent nearby is that of wolves. The only wolf that could do this…" Draco broke off, staring.

"What is it, Draco?" Dane prompted, his tone carrying an odd hint to it. His eyes flicked between the dead wolf and Draco.

"The only wolf that could do this," Draco repeated, "Is a direwolf."

"A… direwolf?"

"Wolves that are large, cunning, and intelligent. And usually… aggressive. Aye, aggressive's the word. Very dangerous," Draco stated, his voice holding a measure of disgust to it.

"Oh… dark wolves. I know them as dark wolves," Dane murmured, his tone still carrying that odd hint to it, "But if there was one here…"

"So you do know of these creatures?"

"Yes. I… do. Very dangerous, as you said. But why didn't we get attacked?"

Draco found himself considering this new development, *Dark wolves? Direwolves are known nearly universally as direwolves. In Human anyways. And Dane did say he was the son of a knight. No, Dane has to know that they are called direwolves. But if that's so… why did he lie?*

"You've never heard of the name direwolf?" Draco pressed, studying his human companion.

"No. I've learned of dark wolves."

Draco scowled, *He appears calm, but… No. He's worried about something. I'll have to press it. He is keeping too many secrets. Has told me too little,* with a deep breath, Draco began prepping his will. The spell he was going to cast was one he had never had reason to before. After all, who in their right mind would normally lie to a dragon? A fully-sized dragon, that is.

"*Dane ve tolkest sekelas!*" Draco spoke, his voice taking a tone similar to a commander ordering their troops. As he did so, the dragon continued watching Dane.

"What does that mean? You need to let me know," Dane said, an expression of curiosity on his face. Or, rather, an expression of curiosity that hid his worry. Unfortunately for Dane, Draco was too experienced to be fooled by something like that. Or so he liked to think.

"It is a spell. Under its effects, you cannot speak anything not true," Draco replied, his voice steady and level, but harsh, "Dane, did you know of the word 'direwolf?'"

"I said no," Dane replied. Draco would have smirked if his muzzle could have actually done such a thing. Clever boy. That might have gotten Draco if he hadn't done the same thing himself when he was subject to the spell.

"That is not what I asked, Dane. Yes or no. Did you know of the name direwolf?"

"N-N-," Dane couldn't finish. Each time he started to say 'no,' his tongue seemed to tangle itself up into a knot, "N-. Fine! Yes! I did! Does it matter?" he cried, anger searing his words, "Is there really an issue with my calling them dark wolves?"

"No, but you were hiding it and it made you suspicious. Why did you try to hide it?" Draco asked.

"I-I-. Agh! I didn't want you to know. I've encountered direwolves before. It… It turned out rather nasty," Dane admitted, his eyes drifting away from the dragon. He seemed uncomfortable. Or was he embarrassed?

Satisfied that Dane had told him the truth and that he had gotten all he wanted to know, Draco made a chuff to draw the human's attention, "Listen. The spell to counter this one goes, '*Dane ve tolkest frosekelas,*'" Draco gave a faint nod as he finished the phrase, "There. You should be fine now. Go ahead, speak a lie."

"I am a dragon," Dane said, wary of the spell stopping him. As the phrase left his lips, he relaxed, "Now can we keep going? I think we wasted enough time with this. And don't use that spell on me again!"

"I won't if you don't lie to me," Draco snapped back. He was quite sure it was far from a waste of time, but the human was right in one part. They did need to keep moving. Anger supporting his steps, Dane began to walk onward. After a brief pause- during which the dragon found himself considering Dane's anger- Draco began to follow. Then he immediately froze again as the realization struck like a bolt of lightning. He had Dane under a spell to speak the truth! It had been the perfect moment to ask after the curse. And he'd forgotten about it *and* told Dane the counterspell! Silently cursing himself over the mistake, Draco wondered how he'd forgotten in the first place. He didn't usually forget much. Maybe it was the magic egg business. Yes, that must have been it...

Chapter 5

Jel Nersirit

The forest-lined path soon gave way to open plains with the path itself splitting off north and south. Naturally, rather than follow either path, Draco went straight east, off of the path entirely. With the trees no longer obscuring everything, the land was visible for miles. There wasn't much aside from grass, the occasional tree, and small, scrubby bushes. The only animals that could be seen were shaggy, brown-furred creatures with horns that resembled cattle. Dane couldn't remember what they were called. Actually, Dane didn't think he even knew what they were in the first place.

Now that there were next to no trees, the soft breezes morphed into rather significant winds. Draco found himself struggling against a headwind almost as soon as they left the forest. He had to watch for the near constant gusts of wind that would send him tumbling towards the ground or uncontrollably hurtling upwards. Though it didn't do him much good. Young dragons were unfortunately not equipped to successfully overpower nature.

"Draco, I could walk slower so you could walk on the ground," Dane offered after Draco nearly slammed into the ground for the third time.

"I'm fine. I used to fly through winds stronger than this," Draco replied, his voice and sharp as a blade. Unfortunately, that sharpness was dulled a fair bit as he was hurtled upwards like he had five times before.

Dane waited for Draco to make his way back down before noting, "You were bigger back then, right? It would have been easier for you. Right now… It might be safer if you walk."

"I said, I'm fine!" Draco exclaimed, glaring as Dane. He didn't get to glare for long as the wind blew him downwards. This time, the dragon wasn't able to save himself from getting plowed into the ground, carving a fairly good sized trench. When the dragon recovered his sense of where he was, he found himself with a mouthful of dirt and Dane watching with an unreadable expression, "Not a word," Draco said after spitting out the dirt. His tail lashed from side to side, striking both sides of the trench, "Not one word."

Dane nodded with silent amusement, but commented, "Watch yourself. That wound is starting to ooze again. I really don't want to replace the thread again, you big baby," before he started to walk on. Draco growled at his comment, but didn't offer a response. Instead, he climbed out of his handmade trench and began following Dane on foot. Mere moments later, the dragon began to grumble about how awkward travelling on foot was and how slow. Dane smiled to himself, having decided that it was only for his pride and opted to say nothing, leaving the dragon to his moaning.

After about half an hour had passed, all of it spent walking, Draco perked up, "Do you feel that? The wind is dying down. With any amount of luck, it will stay like such for a little while."

Dane frowned and shook his head, "I wouldn't, if I were you."

"Enough," with that one word denial, Draco took to the skies. For a moment, everything seemed fine. Then the dragon panicked as he was sent skyward. Dane watched the dragon's mishap of a flight, then sighed. He watched the dragon steadily descend, only to be greeted to the dragon grumbling, "What manner of plains are these?" Draco grumped as he hurried back to the ground. He was not going to tempt the wind again, "It better not be what I think it is or we have a problem."

"The Plain of the Winds, I think," Dane answered, "If you had asked, I would have told you. I thought you knew."

"Of course. Of all places, we would be here," Draco groaned, ignoring Dane's comment, "How are we here? Here!?"

"At different parts, the wind blows in different directions, though always away from the center. Supposedly, the winds don't blow in the center," Dane pointed out. Draco offered the human a glare in return for his "helpful" comment.

"I know that! But we shouldn't be anywhere near the *Jel Nersirit*."

"*Jel* means land. What is *nersirit*?" Dane asked, curiosity dancing along his tongue. Draco sighed, his tail twitching from side to side.

"*Ner* is wind. *Sirit* is ever. Everwind."

"So… It means, 'Everwind Land?'"

"Aye, but this should be to the south! We are off track!" Draco exclaimed, stomping the ground with a forepaw. His wings momentarily flared out before the dragon remembered that he was in a *very* windy area, "Yet, it feels like we aren't. This should not happen!"

"Draco. How good is a hatchling's sense of direction?"

"Fairly good, but not infallible… I see. You think my sense of direction is not what it used to be?"

"Exactly. We may be going the right direction, but you can't quite place the locations," Dane guessed. Draco didn't give a response, instead staring at everything that wasn't Dane, "Or we are going in the wrong direction altogether."

"I don't know exactly where it is, but it should be east, somewhere," With that statement, Draco began to walk onward, Dane soon dogging his footsteps. The human didn't do so without a sigh, however.

For a time that neither cared enough to know how long it was, the pair travelled in silence. The silence was broken when Draco finally ventured to ask, "Dane. There was something about the wolf we found. The little amount of blood. The size of the wound. It just doesn't fit. There is something else. There has to be."

"I wouldn't know what it is. But I think you may be right. I can guess that it was dragged from somewhere, but beyond that…" Dane punctuated his observation with a shrug.

There was a momentary pause, then Draco surprised Dane by asking, "What do you know of wolves, Dane?"

"They travel in packs. They hunt together and are rarely alone. They stay away from humans. Their packs are their families. They are loyal to their packs. They live in dens. Not much else."

"Wait. What did you say?"

"They live in dens?" Dane said.

"No, before that." Draco prompted.

"They are loyal to their pack?"

"Before that."

"Their packs are their families,"

"How do you know? You can't have met that many wolf packs," Draco asked, his eyes narrowing.

"I've had to do a number of things while growing up. Hunting was one of them," Dane responded, though he wasn't looking at Draco, "Naturally, I learned a fair bit about animals. Wolves included."

Draco glared at Dane, his still narrowed, *You are lying to me. A hunter tends to learn such things? I think not. Just what is it with you and wolves? What are you hiding? … But you are just going to dodge my questions, aren't you? I'll have to wait for now. Until you cannot escape,* the dragon nodded to himself, content with his decided course of action. All that remained was to keep moving.

Unfortunately, with Draco confined to the ground, continuing to move was a rather slow affair. Something Draco was keenly aware of, especially given his near constant grumbling and complaining about it, "Curse these winds! They're slowing us down!"

Dane nodded and chose to respond as amicably as he could, "They are the reason few have been to the center of the Plain of the Winds. But, once we do get to the center, we will have a tailwind wherever we go. Though it is said the wind gets stronger as we get closer to the center."

"That is what I am dreading. Stronger winds. I'm so small, a strong enough wind might blow me away," Draco exclaimed, "I am not going to be blown around like a feather."

"Then maybe we should do something about your size," Dane replied rather bluntly, "Your size problem aside, I've actually read a little about the winds here. Nearer to the center of the plain, it is said the winds are a whole different strength of wind. Old texts call it 'The Wind with the Force of Endless Gales.' The winds are said to be as loud as a lion's roar, maybe even a dragon's. A full grown dragon, that is."

"Oh, ha ha, Dane. Aren't you funny," Draco said, his voice dripping with sarcasm, "Don't you have something better to do?"

"That would be accompanying you. You're leading me to this Lake of Light, remember? I would have nothing to do with this, otherwise," Dane pointed out, "I'd be on my way to Girodash. Or at Girodash, most like."

"Hmph."

As was predicted, the winds only grew stronger as the pair progressed onward. Naturally, the winds became progressively louder as well. It swiftly got to the point where Dane was distinctly unable to hear Draco speak aloud.

We should stop here for the night. Look, there is a large rock over there, we can use it for shelter from this infernal wind! Draco's thoughts reached out to Dane. The human simply nodded, fully aware that Draco would not hear a word if Dane attempted to say anything. The two dragged themselves to the rock and ducked behind it. Dane was rather relieved that the boulder-like rocks had begun to appear. They were great to take cover behind to get something of a break from the oppressive wind. Even now the rock broke the wind, causing it to lessen and the noise it birthed to slightly abate.

"I think we are getting close!" Dane yelled. Even with the help of the rock, the wind was still deafeningly loud.

What? Speak louder, was the response Dane got. With a relatively silent sigh, Dane tried again.

"I said, 'I think we are getting close!'"

I should say we are. I wish there was a better way to speak to each other, Dane grumbled mentally, *I hate being unable t-,* with any warning, the dragon's mental communication cut off.

"Draco?" Dane yelled, concerned that the dragon had stopped so abruptly. He had been looking to the right, peering around their current stone sanctuary in a vain attempt to try to see if he could spot their destination. It also meant that he was looking away from the dragon, though he was quick to turn back. He was greeted to the sight of Draco lying on the ground with several cracked scales and a trickle of blood on his head. Lying next to the unmoving dragon was a fist-sized, slightly bloody rock, "Drac-!" Dane was unable to even finish his exclamation as something struck the side of his head and everything vanished.

Chapter 6

The Quel'meg

Something was happening. In front of Dane, three shadowy figures of similar size were struggling against each other. Well, that is to say that two of the figures were struggling with a third figure that stood between them. The third figure was quite large… but it seemed familiar. Dane started to move, to do something, but soon stopped as he noticed the sword at his throat. He couldn't see what held it, but that didn't change its presence.

"Draco!" Dane yelled, desperately trying to find a way out of this situation. He wasn't sure why he had yelled the dragon's name, yet it seemed imperative that he did, "Don't drink! Draco! Don't drink!"

Don't drink? Why did I say that? And is that Draco? How? Draco is nowhere near that size. He couldn't be anywhere close to that size right now… But I have to get out of this, a thought crossed Dane's mind. It was hopeless. An act of desperation, but… it might be his only shot.

He watched as Draco's head was plunged into a lake. He didn't recognize this lake, but he suddenly had a bad feeling. A very, very bad feeling. With nothing to lose- Why did he think that?- Dane took a chance, stepping back and lashing out at the unseen holder of the sword. To his surprise, no one was behind him. Nor was there anyone to his side or in front of him. In fact, there wasn't even a sword to his neck. Dane's mind reeled, attempting to process what he had just occurred. He got nowhere before the figures pulled Draco from the lake and left him upon its banks. Draco laid there, not moving an inch.

"Draco? Draco!" Dane called, "Draco, wake up! Dra-!"

Suddenly Draco began to move, as if Dane's words had roused him. He rose, his legs seeming weak as they shook violently. Even so, he managed to get to his feet and swung his head to look at Dane. Or would have looked at Dane if the dragon's eyes weren't closed. They opened, allowing Dane to stare into Draco's blood-red eyes.

Dane gasped as he snapped awake, sweat soaking through his tunic. Rising in a seated position, he looked around hurriedly. Nothing was there. He was in a small hut that looked like it was built next to a rock wall. What wasn't solid rock appeared to be made of earth, with a couple of empty square windows covered by woven grass screens and a wooden door. Accompanying the scene was an odd, low wailing sound. There certainly weren't any lakes. Dane froze, taken aback as his thoughts settled. Why was he looking for lakes?

Much more importantly, Dane finally noticed that Draco wasn't there, either. He leaped to his feet, panic surging through him. They hadn't stopped in a hut. Where was he? Where was Draco? "Draco? Draco!" Dane called, "Can you hear me?!"

"Si kor lihs!" an unfamiliar voice cried out, surprising Dane.

"W-what? Who said that? Where are you? What *did* you say?"

"Lij frok!"

"I don't know what you are saying!"

"…Sit down!" the voice said, a heavy accent obscuring his words. To Dane, the words had sounded more like, 'Sits tone,' Uncertain what was going on, Dane did what he assumed the speaker had meant and sat down.

"What were you… doing… with dragon?" the voice asked. Now that he was paying attention, Dane could place the voice as being on the other side of the door.

"We are travellers! We were travelling together!" Dane said, his voice somewhat desperate, "I'm sorry if we invaded your home. We were just passing through, I swear upon my-"

"Dorimok. We will find way to… remove… spell from you."

"What spell? What are you talking about? Where am I?" Dane asked, slightly miffed at being interrupted.

"…You are in… village… of Quel'meg. We are… inhabitants… of… Plain of Winds, you call it? We live here."

"We're still in the Plain of the Winds? People live here? I thought-"

"Enough. Why you travelling to sacred place?"

"The sacred place?" Dane asked, "What do you mean?"

"Center… of… Plain of Winds. Why were you go there?"

"We were going east. Our destination is somewhere to the east… At least, Draco said that it is," Dane explained, his uncertainty dancing in that last sentence.

"…Come."

"What? But-?"

Without warning, the door swung open and a bald man stepped into the hut. He was quite tall and muscular. He was garbed in what looked like hides that concealed most of his body. What skin Dane could see was pale, very pale. His face was just as pale and supported a stern, hard expression.

"Come," he said, a glare clearly sitting on his face.

With nothing to gain from arguing, Dane chose to simply obey the man's command. As he stepped outside the hut, the first thing he saw was Draco being dragged from another hut. The dragon looked unharmed, aside from the broken scales on his head. Dane was almost certain that Draco would complain about that later. If there was a later.

The two were taken to what appeared to Dane to be the center of the village. The village was situated under a massive stone overhang. Holes dotted this overhang and some had water trickling from them. Adding to the rather strange feeling Dane got was the haunting wail that seemed to constantly be sounding. It was the same wail that Dane had heard before, though he couldn't place where the wail was coming from.

Sitting in what seemed to be a simple chair was a sandy-haired, dark skinned man who looked even more muscular and fit than the one that was leading Dane. Next to him was a weathered, white-haired old man leaning on a stylized staff that was hung about with hide strips and intricate carvings. Next to the old man sat a short, old looking woman with light brown hair and dusty-looking skin. The rest of the village formed a circle around the place. Dane noticed that most of the rest of the villagers had much healthier looking skin. Most distinctly, they were not pale and most were almost dark-skinned. There was also a big cat next to the old woman, but Dane didn't have much time to consider it.

"Sit," the pale man ordered while shoving Dane forward.

Dane looked around. He didn't see anything to sit on, so he sat on the ground. Draco was dragged next to him, allowing Dane a cursory inspection of the dragon. Dane was relieved to see Draco breathing, if unconscious. Of course, that didn't change the fact that they were in the middle of a ring of villagers that Dane was uncertain as to whether they were hostile or not.

The pale man stood next to Dane and Draco, glaring at them, until the muscular man in the chair said something Dane couldn't begin to understand the meaning of. The man joined the circle, leaving Dane, Draco, the seated muscular man, the old man, and the old woman as the only people not part of the circle.

"You must forgive Jascor. He does not trust outsiders," the muscular man said with a thick accent, though it wasn't anywhere near as bad as Jascor's, "This is the village of the Quel'meg. I am Chief Nesik. Who are you?"

"I am Dane of Verious, son of Firrik," Dane replied to the chief's question. He noticed that, as he spoke, some of the people were whispering to each other and pointing at him. However, Dane didn't pay them much attention as Nesik spoke, dominating the outsider's attention.

"Why were you traveling to the sacred place?"

"At the behest of prophecy, or so I was told. Mostly, I am travelling there at the request of my companion," the human warrior gestured at his draconic companion.

"Hmm. Come here. Let me look into your eyes," Nesik said, waving Dane over, "The eyes are said to be windows to the soul. Whether they are or not, I find you can learn a lot about a person from their eyes."

Dane didn't even take the time to consider defying this chief. Something about him just seemed powerful. Not too different from Dane's own father. With that thought in his head, Dane stood and walked towards the chief. Nesik leaned forward and began staring, directly meeting the outsider's gaze. A second passed, then two. Dane stood, discomfort starting to spawn and grow as the examination grew longer and longer. Yet, in spite of the length of time, Nesik looked on. With no real idea what was going on, Dane chose to remain still and wait. His patience was rewarded as, after what felt like a short eternity, Nesik drew back, caution on his face.

"Hmm. Yes. I see. Very well. You are… intriguing. Strong and cunning, yet something about you sets me on edge… No matter! Tell us your story. Begin when you met… *that*," Nesik said, gesturing towards Draco.

Dane was about to speak when a wave of what could best be described as nervousness washed over him. He was not one to be struck by such, but he quickly realized almost at once that he was trying to talk for both his and Draco's lives. It wasn't the first time that he had spoken for someone on their behalf. However, it was the first time that his and the other person's lives were on the line. And that he was doing such defending to someone with as powerful a feeling as this Chief Nesik. Unfortunately, this only caused him to completely mangle his words. Instead of, "Well, I met the dragon whose-" Dane's words sound more like, "Well, er, I-uh net theragon roos-"

"Hmm. I assume you meant dragon, but it sounded much like something rather familiar to me," Fortunately, Dane found himself being interrupted by the old woman's musing, "Wouldn't it be interesting if the dragon's name was… but no, that's not right. He's a he, isn't he…? Scales aren't the right color, anyway."

"If Dane could continue?" Chief Nesik asked gently. His voice had taken a strange tone, as though he was attempting to be assertive, yet was also trying to avoid angering the woman.

"Yes, yes. I was rambling, wasn't I? Go on. Continue."

Dane breathed a sigh and steadied himself. In a voice that was mostly calm, he began again, this time speaking in words that were actually understandable, "Right, I met Draco, that's his name, during a fight. I was fighting against a bandit who was trying to rob me and I was losing. As the bandit was about to finish me, Draco attacked from seemingly nowhere and distracted the bandit, allowing me to kill him. It was one of the strangest things I'd ever seen-"

"Really? That's strange to you?" the old woman interjected, "You may be surprised at just how stranger life can be, especially for heroes. I know of those who are destined to forever combat dark forces, generation to generation, but though their names are simple and same, their own heroics doom them… But ignore me. Carry on! Carry on."

Dane did so, though more wary of the old woman. He told of carrying Draco to Kathenirin and of meeting the healer. He spoke of stitching Draco's wound, then starting on their journey. He started to speak of Draco teaching him magic when the woman broke in again.

"You can use magic, travel with a dragon, and wield a sword like that. You are very much like him. I wonder what your fortunes would be," the woman said almost wistfully. The large cat next to her seemed to look at her before turning back to Dane. It seemed like it was watching him, more so than a normal cat would. Somehow, its presence unnerved him.

"May he finish?" Nesik asked, giving the woman a look that seemed like it should be speaking volumes about her. However, whatever the look should have said about her, it told Dane absolutely nothing. If anything, that alone brought Dane to worrying about the strange woman. Just who or what was she?

"Alright, alright! Go ahead and finish," the woman gave a semi-dismissive wave of her hand. Dane didn't need to be told twice. Hurriedly, he told the rest of the story, from when Draco started teaching him magic to them being ambushed by the Quel'meg, "After that, I woke up in a hut and was told to follow Jascor… You already know what else happened," Dane finished with his eyes on Nesik, but he was most wondering if the strange woman would say something. She didn't seem interested in doing as Nesik nodded and stood.

"Hmm. Very well," Chief Nesik seemed to consider something for a moment, then he looked up at the people around him and ordered, "The dragon is dangerous, we cannot let it live. Hurry now, it's waking up. Dane, however, is free to leave."

"WHAT!?" The order of execution came as a shock to Dane. Had he said something wrong? Just as shocking as how quickly four other tribesmen grabbed Draco's legs, tail, and head, clamping his mouth shut. At the same time, Jascor hefted an axe that Dane hadn't unnoticed. Where had it come from? Still… its presence meant… They had been planning to execute Draco from the start.

From his restrained position, Draco could only glare at Jascor. He didn't do so for long as he shifted his gaze to look at Dane, *I knew I would die eventually, but not like this… I suppose I have only myself to blame. Damn my ineptitude…* Draco allowed his thoughts to communicate as Jascor stopped and raised the axe. Draco closed his eyes, as though he had accepted his fate or merely did not wish to see it. However, the dragon soon found out that someone was very much not going to just let that fate happen.

"Hold! Hold!" Dane said, surprising the chief and the gathered assembly by rushing forward and placing himself between Jascor and Draco, "If you wish to execute Draco, you must kill me first! I need him alive!" Dane declared, spreading out his arms in the nearly universal gesture of, 'I won't let you do this.'

Dane! Don't be a fool! Draco was glaring again, though now at Dane's back, *They are going to let you go! Stop this nonsense before you get yourself killed! You must stay alive!*

"Trok," Chief Nesik said, his hand raised, "Dane. Dragons are dangerous and deceptive creatures. They are not above exploiting those they can and charming those they cannot. And killing those who are not useful. We are trying to free you of the spell we believe Draco has put on you."

"He hasn't casted a spell on me," Dane replied, his voice certain and rather blunt despite the unintentional lie.

"It wouldn't work anyways," the old woman spoke up. She studied Dane, especially his face, as she continued, "The spell would continue after death, most likely. Even if you killed the dragon, Dane would have likely attempted to kill us to get revenge, resulting in them both dead and who knows how many of us. If Draco was at all clever about his spellcasting, that is."

"Thank you, I think?" Dane managed, surprised at the woman speaking on his behalf.

"Oh, you are most welcome. I haven't seen such a stir among the tribe's people since the last chief died in his sleep. You've caused quite a ruckus. Ruckus. What a wonderful word, don't you think?" Sure enough, the tribespeople were whispering, pointing, and even arguing as the events played out before them.

"Umm," Dane blinked, confusion taking up his thoughts. The woman's statement was easy to understand, yet it just didn't seem to make much sense. Dane was quickly returned to the situation at hand as the chief spoke.

"Are you certain of that?"

The old woman chuckled, "Nothing's certain, love, but you have to take a risk sometimes. Dane certainly seems trustworthy. So why not take the risk on him?"

"Hmm…" Chief Nesik looked between Dane and the woman, then offered a slow sigh, "I suppose we can keep an eye on it. If we watch it well, It shouldn't cause too much trouble. Especially if it is as Dane says… Very well, release the dragon."

The tribesmen let go of Draco without hesitation. Jascor, on the other hand, stalked over and said something to Nesik. Though Dane couldn't understand him, the pale tribesman sounded rather angry. Nesik offered an answer in the same, incomprehensible language. Instead of ending the discussion, as Dane had hoped, the answer only caused Jascor to argue by saying something else. Nesik gave another response before cutting Jascor off mid-sentence.

"Enough. We shall speak no more of this. Dane and Draco shall be our honored guests as long as they are here. As long as they cause no trouble, they should not be harmed," Nesik noticeably stressed the words 'no trouble,' his eyes drifting over to pointedly stare at the dragon.

Dane nodded and offered a low sigh before he looked over to Draco, "I suppose we should rest before we continue on. Plan our next move?"

Jascor whipped his head around. Draco, now able to clearly look at the world around him, was somewhat surprised that the pale head didn't fly off its neck, "Continue on?! No, you go back. No one defile sacred place!"

"Jascor. I will deal with this," Chief Nesik waved Jascor away as he was about to argue, "Enough," the chief turned his attention back to Dane and Draco, "I am sorry, but we can't let you go to the center of the Plain of the Winds. It is sacred to us."

"But it is not sacred to us," Draco replied, his voice not quite a growl, but very close, "We must go there, it may, however unlikely, be the location of the Lake of Light."

"Lake of… Light?" the old man murmured, interest dancing upon his wizened face.

"What is it, old man? Do you know where it is?"

"Old man? I am Resken, shaman of the Quel'meg tribe!" Resken declared, his gaze locked on Draco, "I have not heard of a Lake of Light, dragon, but I do know there is a shining lake in the sacred place."

"Then we must go there!" Draco said firmly, "We must go to the Lake of Light!"

"No! They cannot! Would be disgrace to-" Jascor cut himself off as Resken raised a hand.

"No. I feel it would not. There is something about you…" Resken said, peering at Dane. He muttered under his breath before turning to Nesik and saying, "Let them go. The Guardians will stop them, if they be not strong and pure," Dane almost shivered. *Pure*. And the muttering. Dane thought he had almost heard a word that sounded like 'doom.'

"Also…" Resken approached Nesik and began whispering to him. After a brief conversation that seemed more like it was questions and answers, Nesik gave a nod.

"Very well," Nesik turned back to Dane and Draco, "Go. Rest for the day and we shall send you on your way," before they could respond, he added, "We will give you some food and water. I believe your supplies were rather depleted."

"That they were, but I don't need as much as you might think," Dane replied, then gave a little laugh, "I was going to have to catch something soon. Probably without telling Draco. If I told him, he'd probably end up doing it. Then he'd end up grumbling about it despite it having been his choice."

"I have no doubt he would! Ha ha! If that is the situation, then come! Rest!" the chief paused as a thought crossed his mind, "Hmm… Come to think of it, perhaps we should prepare a feast? The gods know, we've needed something to enjoy ourselves with!" Chief Nesik laughed, nodding to himself, "Yes, that is what we shall do! Come! Let us celebrate with a feast! A feast for the arrival of a legend-to-be!" His sudden change in attitude would have caught many by surprise. It certainly left Dane flabbergasted. However, the villagers themselves took it in stride. Their chief made his decisions and followed them wholeheartedly. Dane could only look around as the villagers erupted into a cacophony of excited talking.

"I don't grumble that much," Draco grumbled in response to Dane and Nesik's conversation, his gaze drifting over to lock onto Dane pointedly, "I've never been to a feast. Feasts have never really interested me and most do not prepare enough food for a dragon and its other guests combined."

"Well then, perhaps you should try it this once! You may like it! Come on, let's go!" Dane laughed, the excitement in the air filling him. He was about to begin going somewhere, only to realize he didn't know where to go. However, that was quickly rectified by the chief waving at the pair to follow. Dane made to follow Nesik, leaving the dragon to stare after him.

"Hmm. Why not?" Draco said to no one as he began to follow Dane, releasing a sigh that held far less resignation than it sounded, "I suppose it might be interesting."

While the dragon made his decision, Dane was smiling and "speaking" to a young child. Naturally, Dane had no idea what the girl was saying, but she certainly seemed excited about it. When she had finished speaking, she took off, prompting Dane to chuckle merrily as he watched her go. However, despite his mirth, Dane had one thought on his mind, *Legend-to-be? I am no legend. Where is this prophecy taking me?*

Chapter 7

Wolf in the Shadows

"You are the dragon-marked one," Dane started as the words erupted behind him. One hand unconsciously darted to where his weapon should have been, only to find nothing. Naturally, he had been stripped of his blade before he had woken up and it had yet to be returned. Without a weapon to protect himself, Dane slowly turned. Behind him stood the old woman from earlier.

"Umm. Y-yes, I su-suppose I am," Dane said, giving a weak smile.

"What? Can you not speak well? You did seem to have difficulty earlier."

"No, it's not that. You just surprised me," Dane replied. While he was certainly not lying, that was far from the only reason. Nesik may have given the feeling of power, but this woman… She exuded an aura of mystery. Enough that Dane found himself uncertain how much of a threat she was. Being unable to ascertain whether he should be threatened by her or not unsurprisingly set Dane on edge.

"Surprised you? Then your hearing is terrible. I made enough noise for a dwarf to hear, even while forging!" The woman exclaimed, one hand rising as emphasizing her words with a wide gesture. As she did this, Nesik caught sight of the elder's movements and began to approach, accompanied by another, much younger woman.

"Wise One. Let him enjoy the feast. You should, too. You haven't been to one in years, by your own words," the chief said, a smile on his face. He held out a hand for her to grasp.

"Hmph. Very well. I suppose I could enjoy the feast. Though when did feasts involve games and plays?"

"Quel'meg feasts do! Come! Please, enjoy yourself!" Chief Nesik chuckled, then nodded to her, "You rarely do."

"I make my own fun without the tribe. That's because there is nothing to enjoy myself with! You Quel'meg enjoy yourselves as much as a toad, no *frog*, can fly!" the old woman grumped as Nesik led her away. In spite of her words, there was no hesitation on her part.

Dane watched them go, then turned his attention to the woman who had been accompanying Nesik. She was dressed in a tunic with voluminous sleeves as well as breeches, rather unusual for a female. Her feet were protected by a pair of leather wrap sandals. Dane did not have much of a chance to consider anything else as the woman spoke, "You are Dane, no? I am Vreena."

"Yes, I'm Dane." Dane replied. Somewhat unconsciously, he noted that the woman appeared slim, yet also quite fit, "Vreena isn't a Quel'meg name, is it?"

"No, it isn't. But I have a question for you. Why do you follow the dragon? You do follow him, yes?"

"Well, not really. We are travelling together, he just somewhat knows where we are going."

"The Lake of Light? That was where you were going, yes?" Vreena pressed, her eyes seeming like they were going to shoot out of her head and bore into Dane's.

"Yes. There is some prophecy that says I must go to the Lake of Light. So here I am."

"A lake of light. I wonder what that would be like," Vreena nodded, then tilted her head back and looked skyward. Her expression was ponderous, as though lost in thought. However, she was not the only one.

Dane was also deep in thought as he noticed that the graceful, yet sharp appearance of her body seemed familiar. But how? She was lean, yet fit, sure, but he didn't know her. Her face was like none that he remembered. Even so, he was sure he recognized something about her. Her face was an odd, yet pleasing mesh of angles and curves. In fact, it was rather beautiful. Framing that face was her hair. Blonde, but an odd shade of blonde. If Dane had to describe it, he would call it both bright and pale. Still, it seemed to fit her startling green eyes. All of it made her seem timeless, such that Dane couldn't begin to guess her age.

Even as Dane came to his conclusions, Vreena shook her head and turned to speak to him. As she did, Dane saw that her ear, momentarily revealed by her shifting hair, was pointed, more so than Dane's ever could be. It came as quite the surprise to Dane. To think one would be here of all places.

"A lake of light… Wherever it is, it must be splendid, no? Just imagine…" Vreena mused aloud, eyes on Dane.

"Ah, yes. It must be. You-Your an elf!"

Vreena blinked in surprise. Curiosity touched her face as she replied, "Half-elf, but how did you know?"

"Your ear. It appeared from under your hair for a moment," Dane answered, awestruck. A half-elf. An actual half-elf. All he knew about them were that they were more elvish than a normal human, but more like a human than typical elves. That, and a lot rarer than both. Unfortunately, that was where Dane's knowledge hit its limits. While there was only so much he was able to learn with his own problems getting in the way, it never failed to annoy Dane.

"Really? No one else notices my ears. Usually people who are familiar with elves realize I'm a half-elf," Vreena studied him, her eyes looking as though they were attempting to probe his secrets, "I'm guessing you have not met any elves, given your assumption."

"No, not yet, anyways. But I might."

"If you are traveling, then it is possible, though unlikely," Vreena looked off for a moment, then turned back to Dane, "What do you know of the other kinds?"

"Other kinds?" Dane parroted back, surprised at how quickly the conversation changed.

"Dwarves. Elves. Halflings. Wolfear. Those who are not human."

"Not much, I know dwarves are experts in anything stone or metal and live in or near mountains. I know little of elves, besides their affinity with nature and magic. I've met quite a few halflings. They are quite the friendly bunch. And rather small, too. As for wolfear… I've seen a few, but have never really talked to one. You don't see non-humans all too often in the Kingdom of Havmare. As far as I know, there is nothing stopping them from coming, but they just don't. For the most part. Anyways, the merchant I was supposed to guard was a wolfear, according to my father. I know that they are basically human-like wolves and live in tribes. Little else."

"That information would work for a common farmer, but not for a noble or child of a noble," Vreena almost seemed to chide him.

"I am the son of a knight," Dane attempted to verbally counter. Vreena did not look impressed.

"No, you are not. You can't be. You have elvish blood, though likely from a distant ancestor. Most humans with elvish blood are nobles. Who is your father?"

"Sir Firrik of Verious."

Vreena looked stunned, as though she had not expected that name. She blinked, coming to terms before pressing Dane, "You cannot mean Firrik Windblade! The exemplary human knight whose blade is said to match and best many an elf! He is nigh a legend among elves."

"I do not know about a Windblade, but he is the greatest knight beholden to King Aridor," Dane answered, "One of the five Royal Knights."

"You are ignorant of your so-called father's title, then. Not something I would have expected from a human. Your kind are usually very particular about titles."

Dane gaped at Vreena. To say that was paramount to a challenge. It was an insult to his honor, "I would not know of those titles, if he had them, for no one used them. He *is* my father, whatever you say about him."

"*Iv tivekevis al orsal frogroir.* Enough. You must know it would not be wise to travel to *Arun Fril* with Draco being so young. While you wait for him to grow more, I can teach you of the other kinds and creatures, common or not, that share this land. If only that you don't die by an unintended insult to someone," Vreena's words were haughty and carried a tinge of arrogance. Enough that Dane felt fit to prove he wasn't as stupid as she seemed to think.

"I am not deaf. Though the knowledge would be useful, we are only staying for the day. And Draco is only young in body," Dane replied, internally pleased that he remembered enough of the language to understand her. The half-elf, however, merely scoffed.

"However old in mind, one must have the body to match, no? That will take more than one day. And you know some of *Kuritik ko Metol*? Good. Meet me tonight, here, and we can begin," Vreena turned and walked off, "Do not disappoint."

Dane stared after her, slightly bewildered and discomforted. He shook his head in a vain attempt to settle it, then glanced about to see what Draco was up to. Fortunately, it was rather easy to spot the golden-scaled dragon speaking to the shaman, Resken. With nothing better to do for the moment, he came to the decision to see what Draco was doing. As he drew near, he managed to hear the shaman say, "I might be able to help. But only if he is willing."

"I'm sure he will be. Ah, Dane! Come here," Draco called out when he saw Dane, "This is Resken, remember him from earlier? He is a spellcaster and is offering to teach you a little of magic, if you agree. Probably more than what limited amount I know. Refuse if you wish, but it would do us good to wait a while longer."

"I would like that. We need to wait here anyways, for you to grow a bit, according to Vreena. She's that half-elf over there and has offered to teach me of the 'other kinds,' Well… it was an offer, but I don't think I have a choice to refuse," Dane replied, still uncomfortable about the earlier conversation.

"Ah, yes. Vreena is a good teacher and student," Resken murmured, a faint smile touching his lips, "She knows much, though few know she is a half-elf. I wouldn't speak of it too much. Meet me tomorrow at my hut. It is over there," Resken gestured to a simple-looking hut with an intricate design carved into the door. With that done, he walked off, meeting with a slender man who handed him a stone cup. Draco and Dane could only watch the shaman as he wandered off, sipping the drink.

"I guess I have some tutors, then," Dane said, now even more bewildered. He wasn't exactly sure what had happened. How did he just get two complete strangers to randomly become his tutors?

"Aye, I should think you do. Now come! Let us enjoy this feast!" Draco exclaimed, a note of excitement touching his voice. He began to saunter toward the slender man, catching the smell that he believed was the drink the man was handing out.

Dane shrugged, still uncertain about… everything. How had his life led to something like this? Still, he let himself follow the golden dragon. After all, Draco was right. In times like this, it was best just to go with it.

ΩΩΩΩΩΩΩΩΩΩΩΩΩΩΩΩΩΩΩΩΩΩΩΩΩΩΩΩΩΩΩΩΩΩΩΩΩΩΩΩΩΩΩΩΩΩ ΩΩΩΩΩΩΩΩΩΩΩ

The feast seemed more like a party to Draco, but he wasn't one to complain. In fact, he was rather enjoying it. There was just so much going on that was all interesting in its own right. The musician, to name the one example that Draco could think of. Not that he could put much thought behind such a question or answer. The feast had already extended well into the night and Draco's will against the mead had long since broken. Unfortunately for Draco's common sense, he knew nothing about the drink.

Why have I never tried mead before? Draco wondered, but couldn't find an answer. Not that it was possible with the mead clouding his mind in a happy daze. He staggered towards… somewhere. He wasn't sure were he was going. Not at all surprisingly, he managed to bump into the side of a hut. He stopped and stared at it for a moment, wondering why the building had bumped into him so rudely before turning away and wandering off. Not even a minute later, Draco had already forgotten about the building.

As he wandered, Draco found his gaze constantly sweeping over the area. Eventually, it settled on a figure standing off a little ways from the rest. It took him a moment, but he finally was able to give a name to the figure. Dane had told him it. Vreena. He thought so, at least. Maybe it was Vrena? Or Venra? Veenra?

What is she doing over there? I should find out, Draco decided, tearing his attention away from the topic of the… elf? No, half-elf. Yes, the half-elf's name. He stopped moments later because he noticed something else. On the edge of the village, there was a dark shape. It looked familiar to Draco, but he didn't know why at first. Then it came to him. The shape was that of a wolf… Wolves… Draco didn't like wolves… No… Not wolves… Something about wolves… and a friend… He wasn't sure, but he definitely did not like that wolf thing being there.

That wolf… it's looking at Ve… Vre… at her. Why? Wait… now it's looking at me. And now her again. Something's off about it. It looks too… big, Draco thought as he watched the wolf, his befuddled mind unsuccessfully trying to grapple with the mystery. Finally, after a few minutes, he realized the wolf was too big because it wasn't a normal wolf. It had to be a… yes, a direwolf! Or some other magical wolf… No, there wasn't any. Right?

As he continued to struggle against his unruly thoughts, Vreena turned and also spotted the wolf. She stiffened, then cocked her head, as though she was puzzled. Draco watched her study the direwolf before she raised her arm, perhaps about to make some form of gesture.

At that moment, a dancing couple spun in front of Draco. He managed to dodge around them with a stagger, but ended up running into another couple. He attempted to apologize, but stopped midway through because he had forgotten what he had been going to say, which only annoyed them more. Eventually, he managed to make his way through what resembled an apology and was able to turn back to Vreena. Fortunately, both she and the wolf were still there. However, Vreena's hand was slowing to a halt, as if she had just finished some hand motion. She was also a little closer to the wolf than before. The wolf looked at her for a moment more, then spun around and fled. Vreena didn't move, instead opting to stare after the fleeing wolf. Draco took that time to begin moving over to Vreena, inadvertently bumping into another couple, which he chose not to apologize to. He also seemed to forget that he had a tail, as he somehow knocked a plate out of a person's hand and set off what might have been swearing in the Quel'meg tongue. Despite that, he made it to Vreena without causing too much trouble. Aside from the person whose plate he had knocked on the ground. They were still at it with whatever they were saying, except they didn't seem to be talking to Draco. He assumed, at least.

"A direwolf. Here. Direwolves prefer places they can hide easily and ambush their prey. Such as a forest. Why is it here?" Vreena asked aloud.

"I do not know, but I want to know why it did not attack. If it wash a direwolf, shen it should have attacked," Draco slurred. It was strangely difficult to talk for some reason… Draco wasn't sure why, but that didn't matter right now.

"Ah, Draco. Welcome. Have you seen Dane? He was supposed to meet me here."

"No, not shince I got him Reshken as a… a… what shpellsh are called. I know it, but I don't know what it ish."

"Hmm. That direwolf. It didn't attack… Not that it had a reason, but it also has no reason to be here, either," Vreena said, completely ignoring Draco's statement, "Nor did it approach. If it's friendly, why did it not? If it isn't, why has no one been attacked?"

"Could it not trush ush?" Draco questioned, his thoughts running as fast as they could.

"That is possible. In truth, that's probably the likeliest reason. If it is friendly," Vreena decided, "But is Dane usually late? I expected him to be here."

Draco thought he heard a note of contempt in her voice, but decided it was just his imagination. Not that his head was at all reliable at the moment... Why was that? Draco wasn't sure... ... Wait, yes he was. It was mead... ... He was... What did humans call it? He wasn't sure... ... Nonetheless, he managed to answer Vreena's question, "Not in the time we've been togesher. But before, I'm not sure. Poshibly."

"Wonderful. I get a lazy, stupid, late human as a student. Just what I needed," Vreena snarled, "I'm goin-" Vreena was cut off as a loud snarling came from the direction the direwolf had vanished.

Vreena's eyes widened, "The direwolf! We must find it!" She rushed off toward the sounds. Draco gave a moment's confused thought that, for some reason, turned to him thinking on how horrible it would be to have an off color scale. He managed to remember that he was going to follow Vreena and managed to do so, but the thought of that scale...

The darkness of night quickly swallowed the village behind them. As they passed the stone overhang that the village was mostly situated under, the sound of the wind returned. It almost seemed aggressive, as though it was seeking some kind of vengeance. Draco found himself stumbling on foot after Vreena, not that he could fly in his condition. He'd already managed to nearly fall over three times. And he was on four legs!

They soon found the source of the snarls. Or, rather, what it had left behind. Lying before the pair was the injured remains of a wolf pack. While there were four wolves still standing, the shapes of three more were lying on the ground, not moving. As the half-elf and dragon approached, the remaining wolves started to growl. If Draco was sounder of mind, he would have noted that the wolves had begun to move as though they expected an attack.

"*Verichas ve jeg! Fronerk Oasve! Froireakas kirin neh!*" Vreena cried, one arm sweeping outwards. At her words and gesture, the wolf pack paused.

Much to Draco's befuddled surprise, the pack began to back away. Very, very warily, the wolves faded into the darkness.

"What happened here? Was it the direwolf? But why would it do this?" Vreena mumbled under her breath as she knelt next to the nearest body.

Draco meanwhile, just stared at the mess. He couldn't place it, but something was off… What was it? "It cannot have gone far, it mush have been… in- … insh- … inshur- … hurt," Draco's mind suddenly came up with his answer as he finished speaking. The scene looked familiar! But… why? Why did this look so familiar to Draco? This looked like… like… like something… that friend… some about…

"That doesn't explain why. Why was it here? Why did it not attack the village, but a wolf pack instead? What is going on here?"

Draco stared at her dumbly, before shaking his head, "I'm not sure. But it doesh not sheem good. I shink?" Faintly, he felt as though he was being watched, but disregarded it as soon as he'd felt it. He was much too focused on the semi-angry half-elf before him.

Vreena sighed, shaking her head, though with far more dismay than the dragon, "Enough. I was to be waiting for Dane and you are in no shape to hunt down a direwolf. Let us return. With any fortune at all, Dane will be there!"

Chapter 8

Unveiling the Unknown

"Wake up! You had not the decency to show last night! Rise, now!"
Dane's eyes opened to the sound of someone charging into the building that
he had been allowed to sleep in.

Dane groaned, confusion dancing over his not quite open eyes. He
wasn't expecting to be suddenly woken up. Not right now, "Okay, okay. That
isn't you, Draco, is it?"

"*Neheren al froseres.* I am Vreena! Now, wake up!" Dane pushed
himself up as he managed to fully open his eyes to see Vreena glaring at him.
She did not look happy. Not at all, "You are lazy! You did not come last night
and you would sleep in today! Lazy!"

"No. Not lazy," Dane replied, shaking his head in a vain attempt to
clear it, "I have spent quite some time traveling. It's quite exhausting, you
know. That, and last night was far from the best night I've had."

"What? I could not find you at all last night! What were you doing?
You were supposed to meet with me!" Vreena stormed. Her voice, despite her
anger, did not rise above a consistent growl. Despite that, the sound won
Dane's near undivided attention. He knew that sound very well.

"I'm sorry. I had other things to deal with," he managed to say.
Moments later, it became clear to him that it was the wrong thing to say.

Vreena stared at him in astonishment. Several seconds passed as she
just looked at him, as though expecting him to say something else. When she
realized he was not going to, the half-elf was very quick to attack his excuse,
"Other things! You just came here! How could you have 'other things!' No

one knows you here! And how would last night be 'far from the best night' you've had? It should have been a fairly good night. If you were at the feast. Just what were you up to?"

"Ah. Well…" Dane realized she was far too suspicious. He had let too much slip. He had never been interrogated like this immediately after he had woken up. His head wasn't clear enough. Not yet… Nevertheless, Dane was quick to come to a solution. Albeit poor and risky, but a solution nonetheless.

"Come over here, I have something to tell you." Dane managed, reluctance tugging at his every word. He'd rather not say anything at all, but that opportunity was long past. At this point, he had no choice but to say something to her. In his own negligence, he had gone too far, "It should explain everything, but I can't risk anyone else hearing. And don't tell Draco, whatever you do. Please."

Vreena's face held an almost painfully suspicious cast to it, but she nonetheless offered a nod, "Very well," she drew closer, only for Dane to beckon her closer still. Suspicion still clouding her eyes, the half-elf approached, soon moving close enough that she would have been able to hear Dane whisper. And whisper Dane did.

Dane's words were hesitant and halting. The words of someone who was both nervous and who was far from fluent in the language. Even so, Dane managed to say, "*Oeren… verichlun karak.*"

The statement had a profound reaction in the half-elf. She practically leapt back, hand darting to the hilt of her blade. As she did so, Dane's own hand strayed towards his dagger. "You- You can't be. You *can't* be," She stammered, eyes locked on the human before her.

"I am."

"Then, you-"

"Yes."

"So each time Ephala is full..." Vreena trailed off, her hand falling away from the hilt of her blade. Though the aggression had leaked out of her stance, Dane still had a hand by his dagger.

"No. Every time Merani rises. Or if I get too emotional," Dane answered, "The latter times are the worst."

"Ah. Then the-"

"Because of me. They don't like me, typically," Dane easily predicted her question. While he had never talked about his... condition with others, he could guess what they'd say. If they talked about it, that is. It was rather lucky that Vreena wanted an explanation as opposed to wanting to kill him. Almost refreshing. Hopeful, even, "Probably because I smell like an invader to them."

"I- I'm sorry I've been so rude. If you are not lying, and you do not seem to be doing so, then you have struggled through far more than I could have anticipated. Now I know why you have learned so little. Why you... Why you were unable to come last night," Vreena's voice was quiet. Her face was empty, yet thoughtful. The face of someone who was imagining something, but didn't know what they were truly imagining, "Please, allow me to offer my apologies for my ignorance."

Dane laughed dryly, "I've suffered through far worse for far longer. Don't worry about me," he paused, allowing his hollow laugh to die, then murmured, "It can be such an effort, learning included. I must try not to get too frustrated, but it's not always that easy. When I was younger, it was far too easy to get frustrated. Far too easy to nearly... I trust you know what I mean. That aside, I've had better control over myself in the recent years. Enough that my father and I have been considering finding a proper tutor for me. Though I'm still not certain it would be safe for them," as Dane voiced his concerns, his hand finally drifted away from the dagger. Neither of the two noticed the movement, however.

Vreena was quiet for a moment. She was looking Dane in the eye, as though searching. She apparently found whatever she was looking for when she nodded and replied, "You have my sympathies, but you still have much to learn. If you will have me, I would like to try."

"Are you quick of foot or strong in magic? I don't want to hurt you, in case… You know," Dane asked her, accompanying his question with a vague wave of his hand. Vreena laughed, a sound that was best described as a flute accompanied by falling pieces of glass, and gave him a faint smile as she offered her answer.

"Not as much as a full-blooded elf, but I am in both. Now let's begin."

"Very well," Dane nodded, his expression both concerned and excited.

Vreena smiled as she tossed a small plank of wood at him, then pulled a small stack of parchment out of the depth of her sleeve. Dane chuckled to himself, amused, as she handed the parchment to him. She also grabbed a quill and bottle of ink from the other sleeve, "Now, you should try to write this down. I do hate repeating myself."

"I can write fast, does that help?" Dane asked her, accepting the ink and quill.

"Yes, I don't have to slow down. That's good. Now, you will probably most deal with dwarves. Dwarves are well known for being hardy and strong. They are also short compared to you or me, but don't mention that to them. They are a bit touchy about their height. Though usually because they are offended that you might think them to be lesser in any way than actually because they are short. Most are well trained in the working of stone and metal, though it is in battle and war that dwarven culture specializes. When in battle, dwarves favor axes and hammers, as, in their own words, 'they don't require any difficult or fancy techniques.' Which, along with their discipline and highly militaristic society, might help explain why their soldiers are among the greatest to walk this world. Dwarves love being straightforward. Such to the point that, if you are not providing anything useful to a conversation, they are known to call you out on it. As expected from a military-minded people, much of their culture relies on warfare and physical strength. Rather surprisingly, dwarves also feature a dislike for magic. There are dwarven spellcasters and their existence is necessary, but they tend to be few and viewed with suspicion by the rest of their kind. Rather inexplicably, as their spellcasters are often among the longest lasting. Of course, when war is unavailable, dwarves also have a love of the 'work of the hand.' That is to say, they have great knowledge and interest in craftsmanship. Dwarves have a tendency to live in mountain ranges, usually under them, though they are rumored to have a great city far away. Supposedly, they do not require sunlight to survive."

"Next are the elves. In a physical sense, elves are often thin, slight, and beautiful. That being said, their most well known physical ability is that they are fast, far faster than most humans. Though they are only a little stronger than humans, they have far greater energetic potential, as the elves call it, and can continue doing almost anything long after humans would have collapsed. This makes them superb spellcasters, though they are known for favoring druidry. Uniquely, other races have been known to claim that elves can bend time to their whims and have even shown proof for it. In spite of this, the elves themselves have been unable to prove this and have been known to question the truthfulness of such claims. Above all, elves admire beauty and are known for being aggressive advocates of it. As for homes, elves favor forests. Especially the Forests of Fae. Mostly due to such places being their ancient refuges. Elves are known to live by what they refer to as the Three Worldly Blessings. These are Beauty, Nature, and Deed. As you might expect, elves thus put a lot of faith in the truth of a person's appearance, their interaction with the world around them, and their actions."

"Halflings are a small and peaceful people. They look much like short humans, being about as small as a dwarf, though possessing what can seem to be limitless stamina. Because of such, dwarves and humans tend to favor them when hunting for slaves. That aside, know that halflings have a thin, gangly appearance to them, making it easy to differentiate a dwarf and a halfling. The best known and most easily identifiable feature of a halfling is their unusually hairy feet. They get the nickname 'furfoots' from it. As a people, they prefer to live in little houses that give the feeling of a farmhouse. Or even holes in the sides of hills. Both are very homely, I've been told. In general, they are quite kind and usually open to visitors. Most enjoy jokes and often make jests about their own height. They may seem like a peaceful race and that is because they are. While they can fight, halflings prefer not to and do not often take sides in war as a race, though they may individually. Even that is rare. Unfortunately, that makes them rather easy to subjugate. When it comes to magic, halflings are quite accepting if a little pragmatic. In fact, most halflings know how to cast basic, practical spells. While they tend to favor the same lands as humans, they have a love for the serene and picturesque. However, they are far from a calm and collected folk. Most notably, they are known for their fast paced music and their celebrations, which can be a bit too much for most."

"The wolfear are, as you well know, wolf-like beings whose shape resembles that of a human or elf. They are agile and quick on their feet, as well as being light and on the smaller side. They live in familial pack-like tribes, much like regular wolves. Also much like regular wolves, they excel at teamwork, multi-person tactics, and endurance. When it comes to battle, they favor light equipment, relying on their natural agility. They do make for rather accurate archers, interestingly enough. Wolfear do not appear to have a racial preference regarding battle. Some tribes are highly aggressive while others are quite peaceful. Something wolfear do appear to share as a race is their sense of honor, which appears to revolve around their families. Speaking of their families, wolfear are highly defensive of them. In fact, they are known for being so defensive that they frequently refuse to let a non-wolfear enter their villages, nor are outsiders allowed near their 'birthing dens.' It is believed that these birthing dens are where wolfear children- which they call their pups- are born and raised. As far as magic is concerned, some practice it, some do not. Some tribes mention magic as corrupting, though they never explain why. Nor does it stop the wolfear in the tribe from using magic. They have been known to hold grudges and keep them strongly. Never offend a wolfear."

Vreena paused, watching Dane, then remarked, "You are quite quick with the quill. Very impressive. Now, there are some important other creatures to know about. Such as the phoenixes-"

ΩΩΩΩΩΩΩΩΩΩΩΩΩΩΩΩΩΩΩΩΩΩΩΩΩΩΩΩΩΩΩΩΩΩΩΩΩΩΩΩΩΩΩΩΩΩ
ΩΩΩΩΩΩΩΩΩΩ

"Now the last and rarest creature I have for you right now are the people known as the dragonborn. They are sometimes referred to as the draconians or dracon. Dragonborn are said to be descended from dragons. Maybe they are, maybe they aren't, but what is known is that they are scaled and strong. Their scales are said to be just as varied in color as dragons and they can easily overpower a human and are even stronger than dwarves. But little is actually known about them, mainly due to the belief that they are only legends. No consistent proof has been brought forth that dragonborn truly existed, even by the long-lived elves. Some consider them as a form of demigod. Not really a surprise, as they appear in all sorts of stories. In such stories, they are either portrayed as monsters or grand warriors. However, whether evil, monstrous, or good, they are always displayed as greatly powerful and some are said to be able to battle dragons single handedly," Vreena's mouth might as well have been blur, such was how fast she was speaking. Dane could barely keep up. His hands had a few splatters of ink where the speed of his writing had flicked ink onto them. Still, his haste was rewarded with allowing him to write down almost everything Vreena said. Even if the parchment was ink-splattered.

Vreena nodded as she studied the inky mess that was Dane's hands and notes, "This is basic information on many creatures that a noble should know. And yes, if I understand human standings right, a knight is a form of minor noble. You ought to know this."

"Vreena! It is time for the midday meal! Also, Resken wishes to teach him now," a voice groaned from outside the hut, "Ugh. My head. Could I ask you a question? How much mead did I drink? Ugh."

Vreena stepped out of the building, offering Dane another nod, "I will see you tomorrow, Dane. We will continue on some more precise information on those creatures. As for you, Draco, it was somewhere near a barrel. Enjoy your headache."

"A BARREL?! Ow, too loud. Too loud," Draco moaned as Dane pushed the door open. The dragon looked truly terrible. He looked dead on his paws and almost regularly made pitiful sounds that sounded like a cross between a groan and a growl. It almost reminded Dane of… No. It reminded him of nothing. Dane swiftly turned his mind to more situationally apt thought.

"You still have a headache? How are you not dead?" Dane question, his disbelief manifesting in his voice.

"Speak softer. I'm a dragon. We are much sturdier than humans. Uhh."

"It would appear so," Dane said, shaking his head in utter disbelief. He additionally reminded himself not to underestimate dragons. It would seem that, even young, they were far from frail.

"Ugh."

Dane walked to the center of the village, taking care to soften his steps so as to not bother Draco overly much. As he had been told by Vreena just earlier, the Quel'meg preferred to eat in one big group. The only exceptions made were those who wished to talk to one another in private, those who were unable to come- usually because they were distracted by their work- and outsiders, such as Dane. Dane, however, made the decision it was better to do as they did. Some, such as Jascor, clearly didn't seem to like him. He preferred to not anger them, if at all possible. After collecting the food that was offered to him by the Quel'meg's cook- a thin women with a piercing gaze and eternally pursed lips- he sat down. Draco must not have been hungry, as Dane watched him lay down nearby and cover the sides of his head with his paws while closing his eyes. The position brought the image of a dog to Dane's mind.

"Dane. Come with me," ordered Resken, surprising Dane. He hadn't noticed the old shaman approach, "We will discuss magic in my hut. Bring food if you wish."

"Very well. I hope you don't mind, Draco. Are you going to be fine?"

"Uhh? What?" Draco mumbled, "If Resken's here, just go with him and leave me alone," the dragon had not moved from his previous position, "Curse mead for tasting so good, yet feeling so bad…"

Dane grabbed his carved stone plate with its smallish portion of, as the Quel'meg called it, beffula meat and followed Resken. Resken led him to his hut on the edge of the village. The shaman stood by the entrance and gestured for Dane to enter before entering himself.

The interior of the hut wasn't very impressive. It consisted of a sleeping mat, a few chests, a small table with bottles, scrolls, and a book on it, and a small three-legged stool that looked to serve as a chair. Resken was standing in the middle of the hut, watching Dane.

"Greetings, Resken," Dane said, offering a pleasant bow.

"First, while I am your tutor, you shall call me Master, understood?"

"Yes, Master."

"Good. Now, tell me what you know of magic," Resken asked, his tone blunt and exceedingly straightforward. It almost brought a shiver to Dane's spine. There was no emotion in the manner than Resken was speaking.

"Well, I know that it requires focus, will, and energy."

"Basic knowledge for a mage. Very well, let us begin."

Dane began to extract a sheet of parchment and a quill as well as a bottle of ink, only for Resken to hold up his hand, "You will have no need of that. You are interested in the practical use of magic. While a deeper understanding is better, you need only write down and memorize the necessities. I will tell you when I will require writing tools. Is this understood?"

"Yes, Master."

"Good. Magic is, in basic terms, the manipulation of energy and material to achieve a purpose. However, magic is very flexible. How a purpose is achieved varies from spellcaster to spellcaster. I will teach you three most common ways to call upon magic," Resken spoke much slower than Vreena. It was easy for Dane to keep up and pay attention. Especially without the writing, "First is the one you know of, that which spellcasters call 'magecraft.' Magecraft is the use of pure thought, focus, and will to direct the energy in one's own body to achieve a purpose. As such mages possess the most flexibility of spellcasting, being able to cast a spell to do almost anything. It comes at a risky cost, as they are most prone to losing control of their spells and can wreck the most havoc when they do. They also tend to accidentally kill themselves should they be too ambitious with their spells."

Resken paused, seemingly waiting for Dane, who opted to speak, "I would guess mages are carefully watched."

"No more than any other spellcaster. Now, the second is wizardry or witchcraft. A wizard or witch relies on objects to focus their magic for them. They provide the energy and will, but the object focuses and refines it. Some magical objects also provide the spell, but these are rare and usually very obvious, They are typically ornate. That said, they merely guide their wielder to perform the spell in the most efficient and effective manner. Setting that aside, the energy used for these spells is a mysterious energy that permeates the air, land, people, and everything else in this world. It is referred to as mana. Intelligent creatures naturally draw this mana into themselves and, as wizards or witches, can use it to fuel their spells. What mana actually is… that I don't know. No one seems to be able to identify what mana actually is. Some wizards have questioned if it is actually energy. The nature of the source of their magic aside, wizards and witches boast extremely powerful spells, especially since using all their mana does not kill them. This allows them to cast awe-inspiring spells with little to no risk. They also have the most control over their spells. However, they cannot cast spells without a focus and are very limited as to the spells they can cast, as certain objects are only effective for casting certain spells. For example, a branch is useful for spells involving plants or nature, but quite ineffective for fire or death related spells. A focus also determines the limit of a wizard's magic strength. The previously mentioned branch would most likely only allow very weak magic, though nature and plant magic would be noticeably stronger. Because of the nature of foci and mana, wizards and witches are required to be more particular on what they say to cast their spell. They create more structured spells that can be finely prepared for their specific focus. Often, they write these down in a spellbook, though an mentally proficient wizard can memorize all their spells. However, all of these advantages run into the difficulty that they cannot create a spell in a moment. Not unless they are truly exceptional and have a deep understanding of their focus."

"The last common form of magic is sorcery. A sorcerer usually uses their magic to summon a physical shade of other creatures to do their bidding. They can use magic without summoning creatures, however, for reasons not yet discovered, this magic must be used on living creatures. That is, only living creatures may be the target for such spells. These spells are called hexes or curses, though they aren't all unpleasant, as the names imply. For example, a happiness curse or a good dream hex. A sorcerer who chooses to refrain from magic beyond summoning creatures is known as a conjurer. Sorcerers also use the energy in their bodies for their spells, but unlike other magicks, they also require mana as well as a specific set of related materials and carefully created incantation. In simpler terms, summoning, curses, and hexes are not spells casted at a whim, but require careful planning and preparations. This does make such magic difficult to cast, but it also means curses and hexes are rather difficult to defend against. It is known for being the most difficult magic to learn, though some say it is easy and that understanding it comes naturally. Further, despite the rigidity of this method, sorcerers have been known to heavily influence its potency with nothing more than their own emotions. As expected, stronger emotions result in stronger changes. It has been called the 'magic of desire' for that reason."

"So Draco has been teaching me magecraft?" Dane asked after taking a moment to consider what he had been told. Resken nodded in agreement.

"Yes. As will I. I am a knowledgeable spellcaster in all three forms of magic that I spoke of, though I would otherwise be regarded as a poor spellcaster. Still, I am certainly capable of teaching you all three. Be aware that I will not allow you to use magic in your native tongue. While it is certainly possible, most of our shamans have found speaking the mystic tongue, known as *Kuritik ko Metol*, encourages thoughtful consideration and discipline. Now, I would know your capabilities. Any questions before we begin?"

Dane nodded, "Are those the only kinds of magic?"

Resken hesitated, then shook his head, "No. They are the main ones. Most of the other kinds, save for dark magic, are minor or unknown to me. And I will not teach dark magic. It is too risky to consider. Now, pick up that rock…"

Chapter 9

Advanced Thoughts

"Hmm. You have certainly proven that you have a grasp on basic magic," Resken noted, considering the answer Dane had just given him, "You show promise… Enough that I believe you are ready for some more advanced knowledge."

Dane frowned, "Ready? In only a few days, Master?"

"You show enough promise. That aside, though the knowledge is advanced, it is quite simple. The key to true magic is understanding."

"Understanding?" Dane tilted his head as he considered what the mage had said.

The shaman nodded and offered a warm smile. Dane blinked, surprise painting itself across his face. Resken didn't seem the kind of person who'd smile. He always seemed so dour and focused, "Yes. Understanding. Magic is very powerful in the hands of even an apprentice or adept. But it is understanding that makes it the versatile force a true master commands. If you understand what a spell does, then you can cast it with less words or cast it in different ways. For example," Resken held up his hand before proclaiming, "*Negdir ve hediar vered ko O.*"

As Resken spoke, Dane watched as a tongue of flame appeared. It curled around the old shaman's fingers, only to be joined by another. Then another. Soon enough, five or six separate flames danced around and between the fingers of Resken's hand. The shaman took a moment to watch the dancing flames, then turned his gaze to Dane, "Fire. Perhaps the easiest of the elements for a spellcaster to manipulate, owing to its status as being the only one of the four that is believed to be pure energy. Now, tell me. What did I say?"

"'Fire, come to my hand.'"

"Yes. Now, what does it mean?"

Dane scowled in thought, studying the flames enshrining the shaman's hand, "Other than an order for fire to gather to your hand, you mean?"

"Yes."

Dane nodded, his head rising and falling in the span of several breaths as he pondered over the fire, "Well... I don't know."

"You don't know."

"I don't."

Resken nodded, a stern look taking over his face, "It is a good thing that you have the humility to admit that you don't know. And that is as it should be. I wouldn't be much of a tutor if you knew everything I had to teach," the shaman raised his flaming-encircled hand and watched as the flames faded to nothing, "Now, what is fire?"

"Energy."

"Yes, in a basic sense. But I want you to give me a more substantial answer. What is fire?" Resken stared at Dane. It almost felt like the shaman's gaze was trying to pierce the younger human's head to see into his mind. It was certainly what Dane would call uncomfortable.

"I'm not sure what you want me to say."

"That is of no difficulty. Fire is two things. Heat and flames. Both exist in fire, yet the heat can warm you without the flames ever touching you. Thus, two parts. Now, how does fire exist?"

"By burning something, like wood," Dane replied, uncertain as to what the shaman was asking. The question was very simple, what more could there be?

"Yes, but that is but a side result. Fire is not unlike a living thing. To survive, it needs food, air, and warmth. The wood is the food and the warmth is from however you plan to light the fire. Depending on your surroundings, something as small as sparks or heat made by two objects rubbing against one another can provide the warmth for a fire. If you happen to be in a rather cold situation, it may require greater warmth. Even the remains of an older fire can do."

Dane nodded, his eyes brightening, "I see. Like tending to animals or a child, you need to make sure the fire's needs are met. Otherwise, it will die."

"Exactly so. Now, how can fire be made?"

"Flint and steel, a tinderbox. Sparks and flames from an existing fire. And… rubbing two objects together?"

Resken offered a faint bow of the head at Dane's answer, "Yes. Remember, fire simply needs heat, air, and something to burn. Air is simple and magic can answer the need for the other two."

"It does?"

Resken chuckled at the question, "It does. Of course, it is unknown as to what it is that fire created by magic burns, but it is burning something. As for the heat… Once a fire has been lit and taken, it has little need for outside heat, it provides its own. However, until that happens, it needs outside help. Now, how can heat be made?"

Dane's brow crinkled into a scowl as he thought over the question. A few moments of consideration later, he had his answer, "Heat is made by rubbing objects together or by striking sparks."

"Yes. But it is more than that. Heat is energy. It is why living things are warm and dead things are not. Life makes heat, though not enough to start a fire. Normally, of course. There have been exceptions. Outside of those exceptions, heat can be made in many different ways, so long as it is possible to create energy in some way. Now, what did my spell mean?"

Dane paused, his expression stagnanting to ponderous. He was silent for a few moments, then he murmured, "You want me to put this together myself, do you not?"

"I do. Take your time thinking it over," Resken waved at the stool, "Sit if you wish. Some have their best revelations while seated, staring at nothing. Others prefer to be active with what they think, be it simply pacing a track or wandering or doing something useful. If you must leave, then I shall permit it, so long as you use this time for pondering my question."

Dane nodded, silently mulling the question over. Without really noticing what it was that he was doing, he began to wander, making his way outside the hut. Resken watched him approach the door, opting to make no sound and observe. Soon enough, the ponderous human made his way to the door and pulled it open. After a moment's pause while he seemed to have some idea, Dane kept going. Resken watched, amusement touching his thoughts as the door swung shut behind his exiting pupil.

"A wanderer. I thought as much... Reminds me of myself... Ah, but that was much too long ago. Now, where was that scroll?"

ΩΩΩΩΩΩΩΩΩΩΩΩΩΩΩΩΩΩΩΩΩΩΩΩΩΩΩΩΩΩΩΩΩΩΩΩΩΩΩΩΩΩΩ
ΩΩΩΩΩΩΩΩΩΩ

Dane's meandering took him on a wandering path through the village. As he failed to particularly care where he was going, his thoughts turned over what Resken had told him. If he could just sort it out, "Fire is energy, but divided into the heat and the flames... It needs heat, air, and something to burn in order to exist... Heat can be made many ways, but you need it for fire… Hmm… And all that explains what his spell truly meant… But what is that?"

With the village's near signature wailing dogging him, Dane's wandering took him past a smallish hut with a flower painted on the door. If he was paying attention, Dane would have marvelled at how beautiful and real the flower looked. What broke the illusion, if only slightly, was that the painted image had begun to fade with age.

"What are you doing here? I thought you were with Resken," Dane started at the voice, rapidly turning about to see Vreena watching him from the flower-marked door. The startled human gave a rather guilty-looking smile.

"Oh, er… I am. He's just had me-"

"Thinking over a question he asked? Wants you to answer for yourself?" The half elf finished for him, a faint smile bending her mouth, "You aren't the only one. Everyone who has had him as a tutor knows of it. It's just how he is."

Dane bobbed his head, He paused for a moment, then hesitantly turned his gaze back to her, "I don't suppose you'd help me, would you?"

"This is the kind of thing that works best if you figure it out on your own, so likey not. What did he ask you?"

"What was the meaning of the spell he casted. He lit his hand on fire with the words, 'Fire, come to my hand,' then taught me what fire is. I'm just not sure as to what it all means."

Vreena nodded at that, the smile still there. She held up her own hand, looking at the palm, "Ah, that one. Yes, I know of it. And I believe I can tell you two things. They are both obvious, but I found it was easier to figure it out when I mulled them over. Anyhow, the first one: You must understand how fire comes to be to answer the question. The second is slightly more obscure. You must also understand the question to even attempt the answer."

Dane nodded once more, his thoughts immediately drifting off with the new knowledge, "Understand how fire comes to be and understanding the question… Hmm… What does 'Fire, come to my hand,' mean and how does fire come to be…"

Vreena raised her hand in farewell as she pushed open the door, "Until we next meet, Dane," Dane only vaguely nodded as his wandering began again.

"Fire is made by heat coming to an object that can burn, so long as there is air… But how does that relate to Resken commanding fire to come to his hand? Hmm…"

This time, he gradually made his way toward the village center. Amidst a small gathering of villagers was Draco. The golden scaled dragon seemed to be bored, yet he was talking rather consistently. Dane's wandering took him ever closer to the dragon. If he was paying attention, he might have heard the dragon give a derisive snort.

"Really? That's a question for human children to ask? I think you asked your own question, rather than her's," Draco drawled, eyes focused on one of the older villagers who, supposedly, translated a little girl's question for him.

"Answer."

Draco sighed, "Very well. Have I ever eaten a human? I have. And before you ask, aye, it was on purpose, but no, they were not good people. They were more monsters than humans. Also, no, I didn't like their taste. Though there was a rather nasty woman… I believe she was a maiden… She had a peculiar taste. I didn't like it, but there could be dragons that do, I suppose. For myself, I've grown a taste for wolf… Hmm?" If Draco had anymore to say, he was interrupted as he noticed Dane passing by, "Dane. Were you not with the old shaman?"

Dane started, finally coming to acknowledge not only the number of people present, but also Draco's presence, "Huh? Oh, yes. I was. But he has me considering a question he asked. I'm just thinking it over…"

Draco snorted again, eyeing Dane, "What's the question? I'm sure I could help."

One of the villagers interrupted Dane before he could even begin speaking, "You receive instruction from Resken? Then no help on question. Find answer on own self."

Draco snorted yet again. He turned his gaze to the man who had spoken and gave a reply that dripped with scorn and distaste, "And? Why should I care? If I feel like answering the question, I will. In fact, I think I feel like I should do exactly that."

"But you cannot. Would make question mean nothing," the man tried to complain, though his voice was weak and lacking in any meaningful confidence.

"Is that it? That's how you'll stop me? What is the phrase you humans use? 'Shall I bring the heat, is it?' Aye, I think that's what it was. As a dragon, I can certainly do that, as it were. Spur some actual action out of you instead of that weak response."

"'Bring the heat…' That… makes sense. Yes, if the call to fire to come was a call to bring heat to that location…" Dane mused, eyes lighting up as his thoughts began to connect, "Yes… That must be it! The question was how he did it… Of course, for magic, what you mean is how you do the spell to begin with," Dane spun on his feet, hurried to return to Resken's hut, leaving a highly confused Draco staring after him.

"What?"

One of the villagers nodded, "Good. He learn it by own self. Is only help we offer."

"Silence, you. What's your next question to me? Before I get bored."

ΩΩΩΩΩΩΩΩΩΩΩΩΩΩΩΩΩΩΩΩΩΩΩΩΩΩΩΩΩΩΩΩΩΩΩΩΩΩΩΩΩΩΩΩΩΩΩΩ
ΩΩΩΩΩΩΩΩΩΩ

Dane soon arrived at Resken's door. Rather than bust in the shaman's home, he swiftly pounded on the door. It promptly flew open at the first hit, leaving Dane standing in the doorway with his fist raised. Resken, seated on the stool, turned his attention from the scroll he was reading, "Dane. You seem quite energetic. You have managed to discover the answer to my question, I would presume. Then do tell me, what did my spell mean?"

Dane nodded, a pleased smile stretching across his face, "Of course, Master. Your spell commands fire to come to your hand, but it's more than that. If you were more of a novice, like me, you would probably describe how the fire comes to your hand. Where the heat comes from, what it burns, if anything in particular. As well as what the fire should do."

Resken nodded, considering his pupil's words. After a moment, he responded, his voice level and rather emotionless, "Is there more to your answer?"

Dane started, blinking in surprise at Resken's response, "Ah... Well... If I had to add more, I'd probably just make it easier to explain. Such as saying that your spell means both what you say it does and how you have it do that."

Resken smiled again, "Correct. I am pleased that you continued to keep to your response after I questioned it. Many have second guessed themselves and believed they were wrong when they were, in truth, completely right. Unless you are proven wrong, it is always best to keep to your answers and beliefs. Do you understand?"

"Yes, Master."

Resken nodded, the smile disappearing back to the shaman's traditional expression of passivity, "Good. Now, I have two more questions for you."

"Two more?" Dane asked, his voice carrying the tinge of fatigue.

Resken nodded again, his eyes sharply peering into Dane's, "Ah, don't fear. These two will be simple. First, did you have help with answering the question?"

"Well, yes. Vreena and Draco helped. They didn't really tell me it so much as helped me figure it out."

"And how might they have done so?"

Dane looked away, anxiety creeping over his visage, "Vreena told me that I have to understand how fire comes to be and understand your question to find the answer. Draco simply used the phrase, 'Bring the heat,' while ranting at another villager, which helped me put the pieces together."

Resken's expression did not change as he continued, "I see. Next is my second question. What have you learned?"

Dane gazed away from Resken for a few moments, before looking back to him, "What have I learned? I learned that I could not answer that question alone, at least, not within the day."

Resken's expression morphing into a look of contemplation, "Yes… I suppose you did learn that. But that was not the answer I was looking for."

"I guess I also learned…" Dane drifted off, before suddenly speaking again with newfounded intention, "I learned how to understand a spell by understanding how the spell does what it does."

"Exactly so. Now, you may go for the day. Tomorrow will bring more questions like today's. Be ready for them."

"Yes, Master."

Chapter 10

Nature's Art

Resken stood amidst an empty patch of ground just next to the shaman's hut. Having been asked to meet with him here, Dane slowly approached. He took a moment to cast his gaze about the small area, but saw nothing of intrigue. Other than a couple of hide and grass training dummies and the shaman himself, of course. Resken was leaning on his staff as he gestured for Dane to draw closer, "Good, you are here. Today, you are to learn sorcery."

"Sorcery. That's the one that involves summoning other creatures' shades, right?"

"That is correct. To an extent. But you are right for today. Today, we are focusing on conjuring, or summoning, a creature's shade."

Dane nodded, "Shall we begin, Master?"

Resken raised an eyebrow, but offered a shallow nod of his own, "We shall, but I trust that you shall exercise patience. Summoning a creature is a very fickle affair. You must know what plane of existence that creature lives in. Anevike Protaodrakos, the Unmeino Fukasa, and the Caelum Sidereum, to name a few. The creature's name is also important, if you are trying to summon a certain creature. That is actually quite important if the creature in question is something powerful, such as a demon or angel. Do you understand?"

Dane mulled over what Resken had said, then offered another nod, "Yes. Except that I don't know what those places are."

The shaman looked over at Dane, then nodded in agreement, "But of course. They are the old names. You would likely know them by the name of Drakosgi, the Abyss, and the Æther."

"So our world was once called Anevike Protaodrakos?" Dane tried the world. It was long and unfamiliar. Even alien.

"Yes. Drakosgi was once Anevike Protaodrakos. Or so some say… That aside, let us begin. You are to summon a pixie from our world."

Dane studied the shaman for a few moments, "Master… how do I do that?"

"Patience. I shall teach you. To begin, you must know the plane of existence. From there, you must create a symbol to represent what it is that you are summoning. While you can create your own, some previously discovered ones tend to work better… Then again, you could always discover a better one. Once you have drawn the symbol, you must call upon the creature you wish to summon. While you can call the creature by name, simply naming the kind of creature is sufficient in most cases. For your first attempt, simply call for a pixie using this symbol," Resken began to sketch on the ground. The symbol he made resembled three leaves attached to the same stem with a circle encasing them, "Of course, it works best when the symbol is drawn without breaks."

Dane studied the symbol, then glanced up at Resken. He found himself hesitating before asking, "What shall I say?"

"You must summon the pixie. Any phrase will do for an unknown creature. If you know who or what it is you are summoning, then a specific incantation is more important. Supposedly, one's emotions also play a part, though I am uncertain as to the true effectiveness of that. Now, summon the pixie."

Dane bent to begin drawing, only for Resken to stop him, "Use magic to mark the sigil in the air. You will understand once you have truly begun. It can be done on the ground, and some creatures are easier to summon that way, but I want to see you do it in the air, if you can."

Dane nodded again and straightened. After a moment to collect himself, he spoke, "*Fril vewetkrek ve hediar vered ko O nive arkelw sir kirin O,*" with a hand steadied by a warrior's will, he began the sketch. His eyes were both focused and distant as light began to shimmer from where his hand traced. The light arced and twisted after Dane's hand until, with a flourish and a smile, the trefoiled leaf glittered within its sparkling circle. Even as it existed, the symbol turned a vibrant, leafy green. Resken studied the symbol and gave a small, hardly noticeable smile.

"Good. Now, call forth the pixie from its own place."

Dane gave no indication that he had heard. Almost as though he were in a trance, he raised a hand, "I speak to Pixie of Anevike Protaodrakos. I ask of you to heed my words. Come forth and grant your strength. Aid me in mine endeavours!"

For a moment, nothing happened. Any other time, Dane might have worried that he had failed. However, he seemed to have no such worry on his confidently smiling face. It soon became clear as to why when the symbol began to turn. Encircled by what was now a wheel of light, the trefoiled leaf slowly crept faster and faster. It spun to such speeds that the leaf became nothing but a shining blur.

Dane stared at the whirling, swirling circle before him. Save for a wince as he felt the telltale feeling of exhaustion beginning to creep in, he made no movements. Then, before he could so much as blink, the circle collapsed in on itself, then blew apart. Harmless glitterings of light fell towards the ground as though they had weight. The shining sparks fizzled out long before reaching the ground.

Dane wasn't focused on the flashy light, but the faintly transparent figure that had appeared and nimbly landed on the ground below where the ex-symbol had collapsed. It was about two feet tall and looked for all the world like a normal human, save for its size, rather spindly figure, and pointy ears. Its clothing was mostly ragged cloth with a couple of rings glittering on its fingers. It- no, as Dane looked, its long, tangled hair gave him the impression that the pixie was a female- glared at him. She proved his impression correct by speaking.

"You summoned me?" the pixie glared at Dane, her eyes appraising. Her voice was distinctly female, but very high pitched. Dane had the briefest thought that her voice was what a rat would like.

"I did," Dane glanced at Resken for a moment, unsure as to what he was supposed to do. When the shaman gave him no sign of a clue, the novice summoner chose the first thing that came to mind, "What's your name?"

"And I should tell you for what reason? I owe you nothing," the pixie snapped, venom coloring her voice in an ugly, almost squeaky, light.

Resken slowly rose from the seated position he had assumed, taking a moment to dust off his legs, "Good. A successful summon on your first try. While not unusual, it certainly isn't the most common… Hmm, I find it curious that you spoke quite formally when summoning. We will address that later. What I want you to do now is successfully control your summon. First task, I want you to get it to tell you its name. Start now."

Dane shot Resken a glance, then turned it back to the pixie before him, "Very well, Master."

"Oh, 'Master' is it?" The pixie snickered, a cruel grin stretching across her face, "I think I'm going to have fun,"

"What do you mean by that?" the pixie snickered just before she leapt with surprising agility and swatted him in the face, "Ow! What was that for?" Dane exclaimed, rubbing his cheek. The slap hadn't hurt, per se, but it did sting. Somewhat.

"Focus. A conjured creature should never be able to disobey a command. If one does, it usually means the sorcerer either gives it too much freedom or the creature is too powerful," Resken rebuked as he watched Dane struggle to control the pixie.

"Pixie! What is your name?" Dane asked. The pixie just laughed. It sounded like an irritating mix between a tinkling bell and a squeak.

"Oh, how beautiful. Do you really expect me to simply tell you? You are going to have to try much harder."

Resken nodded, "She is correct. While I admire that you wish to be nice to the pixie, my instructions were to *command* the pixie to tell you its name."

Dane took a deep breath. He knew what he would have to do. But before he did that, "Last chance, pixie. Tell me your name," the summoned creature loosed a laugh at him before leaping to give him another slap. Much to her utter shock, Dane snatched her mid-jump and made a sound none too different from a growl, "Pixie. I am the leader here, not you. You *will* tell me your name. Unless you wish to challenge me?"

The pixie's eyes widened at the human's sudden change in demeanor. With a hurried gulp she squeaked, "Rilyn of the Neminum, sir."

Resken eyed Dane, his face taking on a thoughtful expression, "Good. Now, give it another command. Remember that, while summons have their own reserves of strength, their shades are manifested by their summoner. Thus, summons draw upon their summoner's strength to heal and recover from injuries and afflictions."

Dane nodded, his head rising and falling in a slow rhythm while he took a moment to think and to release the pixie. As he did, he was surprised to see that Rilyn was waiting for his command. She was also closely watching him, her eyes appearing both wary and expectant. Putting the pixie's current actions out of his mind, Dane pondered both a suitable command and the pixie, *What could I ask? Something that isn't easy. Something that will give Rilyn the chance to question me… or not to… … Vreena mentioned that pixies are magical creatures tha- That's it! Magic!*

Without a second thought, Dane's eyes darted to the diminutive creature, "Rilyn, you must know magic. Would you share any of your knowledge of it?"

The pixie momentarily hesitated, almost as if she was reluctant to give Dane an answer, "You are different from others of your kind. You summoned me, yet you did not instinctively command. When you did command, it became clear that you are one I should be cautious about, yet I feel no danger from you… You have a most strange aura about you, one I feel I should fear, yet I don't… I may do as you will, of my own will, if you answer me this: What are you? There is something about you that I am missing. Something that doesn't fit with what I know."

Dane paused at this, his thoughts racing, *I can't lie or she won't help me. I could just command her to… No, I want her to do so of her own volition. She'll be more willing and teach me better that way. But can I speak the truth to her, with Resken here? … No…* Dane glanced at the shaman as he made his decision.

"Very well. Master, could I speak to Rilyn alone?"

Resken looked on with a neutral expression. Speaking with a voice that rivaled a calm sea, he asked, "I am teaching you to use magic, why do you seek it from the pixie?"

"I want to learn as much as I can, be it magic or not," Dane reasoned.

Resken allowed a small smile and began to make his way to his hut's door, "That is what I hoped. I shall wait inside. Come to me when you are finished."

After the door closed behind the shaman, Dane turned back towards the pixie. He took a step closer and spoke in a low voice, "*Rilyn ve groir. Oeren verichlun karak.*"

The pixie froze, her expression suddenly going blank. As this happened, Dane found himself tensing up. He wasn't sure what he was going to do. Dispelling the pixie wouldn't do away with the fact she knew. However, the pixie's response greatly helped to ease the tension.

"You spoke in *Kuritik Metol* and had your tutor leave so as to keep the knowledge from him. This is a great secret for you," Rilyn noted.

"It is. You will not tell anyone." Dane said, more a statement than question. Whether he knew or not, there was a slight edge in his voice. An edge that Rilyn duly noticed.

"Hmm. Even now knowing what you are, I do not fear you," Rilyn frowned before continuing, "I will not tell anyone, as long as you do not share what I teach you with anyone."

"You have my word. I will not share what I know with others," Dane replied swiftly. Despite how quickly he responded, his words sounded true.

Rilyn nodded, more to herself than Dane, before saying, "Good. Do you know of druids?"

"Druids?"

"Yes. Spellcasters of the forest that learned their magic from creatures such as myself. They call upon the power of nature itself for their magic. It is very common amongst elves," Rilyn dropped to the ground, "Lay your hand upon the ground, like so," Dane nodded in understanding as he laid the palm of his hand upon the ground. Rilyn eyed him for a moment, then added, "Now, look into the earth. Do you feel it?"

"Feel what?" Dane asked, an eyebrow raising.

"Shh. Feel. It is weak in a place like this, but it is there. Look and feel."

Dane decided to humor the pixie. He began looking at the ground. After nearly a minute of silence, he spoke again, "Am I supposed to see-," he began, only to be cut off.

"Look and feel."

Dane silently shook his head, *What does she want me to see?* He turned his attention back to the ground and stared. He noticed that it was all grass, *Of course, it's grass. It's supposed to be... It does feel rather soft, though. Very soft. Does it normally feel this soft?*

Rilyn spoke again, interrupting the human's thoughts, "Breathe. In and out. In... and out."

Dane eyed her, but did as she said for a little while. After several minutes, he gave a smile, *The air is rather calm... And the grass is... beautiful... So beautiful, it almost shines... It- It is shining. The grass is glowing. It- It's pulsing... I can almost feel the throbbing... I can feel the throbbing. It's... like a heartbeat... No... more like a ripple. A ripple splashing on the banks or a lake... It's beautiful... And yet there's... something about this sight that-*

"Yes. You see it now," Rilyn whispered, distracting Dane from his thoughts, "What you see is the blessing of the earth that runs through every living thing. Even that which flies in the sky was once born in the cradle of the earth."

"It feels like a heartbeat. Or a ripple?"

"That is the earth herself you feel. Her blood flowing beneath the ground, nourishing all things. This is the secret of my people and of the forest. All creatures share this blessing, but few humans and dwarves still feel it. Elves can by nature, of course. They keep this to themselves. If this were to be known amongst your kind, it could be used to corrupt or even kill nigh upon anything. If one was capable and understanding enough," The pixie adopted an odd look, somewhere between a grimace of disgust and a scowl of deep thought, "That happened once. A band of humans dressed in darkness tried to corrupt the world. They were stopped by their own foolishness, but not before they succeeded in corrupting the area around the lake they called their 'safe haven.' The place was sealed away out of fear and other humans, better ones, blessed another lake to shine like Sehero. They did so in case there was ever the need to combat the darkness of the Corrupted Waters. Such can be the power of the earth herself. No matter if used for good or ill."

Dane nodded slowly, turning his gaze to the pixie. He started as he realized that Rilyn herself seemed to glow as well. She noticed his surprise and offered a rather pleasant smile, "Everything carries this blessing. Even that dragon in the distance. By focusing just a little and truly *looking*, any can see this. But look to yourself, *Verichlun Karak*, and see what darkness truly is."

Dane frowned at the pixie's tone and looked down, as she requested. He had barely gotten to his hand when he stopped, eyes widening in shock. He had been so focused on the light and pulse, he hadn't noticed that his hand was coated in a curtain of shadows that writhed and squirmed like they were alive. Dane didn't move. He almost couldn't. He was far, far too focused on the shadows. Some light managed to pierce the shadowy cloak that garbed his hand. While they were a mixture of feeble and strong, it didn't matter to Dane. Nor did he have to ask why the shadows were there. He knew why.

"Yes. You see?"

"I-I do. But I never harm anyone. I did lose control years ago, but never since. I… I have killed a few creatures that attack me, but I have never hurt anyone otherwise. I am a good person!" Dane felt a wave of fear overcome him. Was he truly meant to be a monster? A beast? Would he have to live forever under the shadow of himself?

"Perhaps you are. You do seem to be one. But though you may be a creature of darkness, you are no monster or demon. You are a creature of light as well. You are unique. A creature of shadows between the light and the dark. A creature of the dawn and dusk. Of twilight," Rilyn paused, ruminating over what she was about to say, "I have seen others of your kind. By day, they are humans, elves, and dwarves, living their lives. By night, they are monsters that can hardly try to control themselves. Darkness blocks out their light. All of them are like that, even the strongest of will. All, that is, but you. You seem… different. You, I believe, can control it. You can let your blessing shine."

"But what makes me different? Why can I do what others can't?"

"I cannot tell you. Only you will know for sure."

"I-"

"Enough. Let me teach you how to use the blessings of the earth in your favor," Rilyn gestured to the ground, "Press your hand against the ground and focus on the pulse of the earth. Feel it. Let it flow through you. Then, when you feel the moment come, strike! Imagine the earth herself striking your foes! Try on that thing over there. The practice dummy."

Dane frowned at the explanation, but returned his hand to the ground. It took him a moment to settle himself, but he soon felt the pulse of the earth, steady and comfortable against his palm. After a few moments, he had noticed no special moment. He was about to consider giving up, when he realized that he was slowly swaying in time to the rhythm of the pulse.

At first, he stopped the swaying and started trying to understand what Rilyn meant, only to come to no conclusions and the discovery that he was swaying again. He repeated this a couple times, each time a little shorter than the last. Finally, he gave up resistance and allowed himself to sway with the pulse. As he did, the swaying gave him a calm feeling. He found his mind starting to clear. As it did, he began to notice the eddies and even the strength of the pulse, which seemed weak, if he had to put a word to it. Though he wasn't quite sure how he came to that conclusion. The pulse had swirls and eddies, like an ocean current that still somehow fit within the time of the pulse. Dane 'watched' these eddies until they began to fade, almost as if they were matching the pulse. Suddenly they disappeared and Dane gasped. The pulse was… It felt… unbroken and true, if he had to describe it. Sure, it still seemed somehow weak, but it felt so much different to what it was before. Dane looked up at the dummy and allowed the thought of a spire of earth tearing through its stomach. He was not at all sure of what he was doing, yet it seemed to work.

As if on command, a spike of earth, like a little mountain, erupted from the ground and speared the dummy. Dane watched, dumbstruck, as the earthen spike then collapsed and returned to the ground, leaving a newly made hole in what would have been the dummy's abdomen. Despite it erupting from the earth, where it had come from was not disturbed. Even the grass was still there.

"How?" Dane asked, bewildered at what had happened. He looked to Rilyn for some answer, but found her inspecting the dummy.

Rilyn gazed at the dummy for a moment more, "Hmm. Could be a bit more accurate next time. You took out the entire lower half of the dummy. Oh, and your question. The earth was drawn from the ground, but around the plants, leaving them unharmed, aside from being covered with dirt. It could do with some improvement… No matter. Come, let us seek out your instructor and continue your lessons. Do not fear that I shall abandon you, you still have much to learn. So much to learn. Even so… It feels rather strange, but I want to see you grow… Perhaps it is because I now know what you are. Anyways, I will return home when you have no more need of me and send me away. Though I suspect that will be a while," she began to trek off in the direction Resken had gone, gesturing for Dane to follow when he didn't move immediately.

Dane blinked, but started after her. As the pair began to seek out the shaman, he found himself wondering about the darkness that had shaded his hand, *Something was off. The darkness… It felt like… Like it was both soothing and tearing. Like I could trust it and fear it. Like it was fighting itself, trying to tear itself apart,* Dane couldn't help the shiver that ran down his spine.

Chapter 11

Burnt Words

"Greetings. Yes, I know you believe it is not safe for me, but I assure you that I am fine. In any case, I must speak with you. I must meet with you tomorrow."

"You understand? I can't really tell, but I think you do. Can you nod? … … Good. I will see you tomorrow. Can you tell me when it should be safe?"

"That doesn't look like anything related to time. … … Now that looks like a… Ah, I see. Very well. I will see you then."

ΩΩΩΩΩΩΩΩΩΩΩΩΩΩΩΩΩΩΩΩΩΩΩΩΩΩΩΩΩΩΩΩΩΩΩΩΩΩΩΩΩΩΩΩΩΩΩΩΩ
ΩΩΩΩΩΩΩΩΩΩ

CLAK! CLANK! TWACK!

Draco started awake at the unmistakable sounds of battle. Nearly leaping to his feet, he rushed toward the location of the sounds, though he was unsure if he intended to stop it or join in. As it turned out, whichever it was would have become a moot point. It was Vreena and Dane who were battling each other. Each held swords sheathed in thin wooden sleeves that allowed them to spar without cutting each other to ribbons. Even as he watched, Draco saw Dane get past Vreena's guard and give her a solid hit on the arm. Vreena stepped back with a faint gasp, her free hand shooting up to rub the spot.

"A good hit. I didn't think you would be quite that fast," Vreena remarked, clearly not noticing the new arrival.

"What is this? Why are you two fighting here?" Draco broke in, his voice seeming both serious and peeved, "If this is sparring, the Quel'meg have a place for that. And if not, why are you fighting?"

"I wished to test Dane. The Quel'meg do have a sparring field, but it comes with a custom all are expected to follow. You may pick your foe as long as you defeat the foe you were fighting. If you have not yet fought, you may challenge someone as long as you are not challenged. Unless no one else is there, it is possible Dane or myself would be challenged as soon as we got there. Either of us would have to defeat our challenger in order to fight the other. Not the best for testing another's skill with the blade. When challenged, you cannot refuse unless you fought another foe and defeated them. You either fight or play the coward by surrendering and admitting defeat," Vreena explained, walking over to a spot where Draco assumed she had started and gesturing Dane to go to where he must have started in order to continue her test, "If you play the coward, you are forbidden to spar there until the next day. It is also a source of great shame to the Quel'meg."

"Fine, fine. But why here of all places?" Draco's voice still held his annoyance, though it had significantly lightened.

"I met Dane here and there is no reason for us to go elsewhere."

"That and I don't want to meet up with Jascor. He doesn't seem to like me and he supposedly always goes to the sparring fields," Dane added.

"I was sleeping. You could have waited until I had woken. It's still early."

"Sunrise was not that long ago. That and you sleep for a ridiculously long amount of time. Typically around midday, if I let you?" Dane spoke up. He gave the dragon a snide smile then shrugged before continuing, "If we did as you suggest, we'd never do anything."

Draco growled in response, "I really do not care. I wish to sleep. Now find somewhere else to do your sparring," Draco lumbered off towards his usual resting spot next to the guest hut, as the Quel'meg called Dane's temporary living quarters, grumbling something Dane couldn't hear as he went. Whatever he said, Dane was certain it wasn't pretty.

"Perhaps we should do as he asks. Dragons tend to like sleep. Come, I know a good place to practice," Vreena began walking off, removing the wooden sleeve. Once her blade was free of the edge-blocking wood, she returned the blade to its sheath, "Come."

"Very well," Dane followed after her, returning his sword to its sheath as well, "Vreena? I have a question."

"What is it?"

"Draco seems very… alone. Are all dragons like that?"

Vreena nodded. She remained quiet for a while as they weaved past groups of villagers. As they began to near her hut, she answered, much to the surprise of Dane, who had assumed that the nod was all the answer he was going to get, "Yes. Like most dragons, Draco prefers to be alone. However, most dragons do have some association with something or someone else. Treasure, other dragons, or people, whatever their reasons are. Draco seems to care for none of this. He walks a lonely road, though I cannot say if it is the only one he has ever known."

"Draco used to help people. He did have associations."

"Used to. Does he now?" Vreena shot back as she stopped. Now that they were standing behind the hut that belonged to Vreena, she turned to face Dane, "Here we will fight, but allow me to show you something."

Vreena waved at Dane to stay and walked into her hut. Dane took the moment to look over her hut. It was decent sized and rather normal for a Quel'meg hut, made of a wooden frame with a hard dirt-like material making up the wall. And, of course, its painted flower door.Not for the first time, Dane wondered where the Quel'meg get their wood.

Soon after, Vreena returned, holding something. She opened her hand and offered Dane a burned scrap of parchment, "Read this."

Seeing no reason to refuse, Dane gingerly accepted the near-crumbling scrap of paper and, deciphering the ancient handwriting, read,

"...gle act, a dark s...
A cur... lack, de...
...le great, a hero bo...
...sign of dragon w...

A curse, a sou...
...nd hono... rne
...m and evil lie
...ark to die

...r, a mon... ight
A dark sou... den light
Torn apart b... t divide
Yet by twi... rlds col...

...ath, a las...
A kn... h, a woe... act
A si... ct to end... ll
...orn the wo... nal fa..."

Dane frowned at the fragile parchment, before looking to Vreena, "Why show this to me? With it burned like this, nothing that makes sense can be read."

Vreena nodded, "That is mostly true. It is what can be understood that I wanted to show you. '*Sign of Dragon.*' If I am right, I think that refers to your scar."

"My scar?" Dane was taken aback. A hand rose to press against the mark in question, "I mean, yes, my scar is shaped like a dragon, but why would it have anything to do with this? This parchment looks old. Very old."

Vreena nodded again, "It's a prophecy, of course. But that is what I wanted to ask you about. When you came here, you spoke of a prophecy that led you here. Is this it?"

Dane shrugged, shaking his head, "I don't know. I know a prophecy bids me go to the *Arun Fril*, but I haven't actually seen the prophecy."

"You have not? Then why do you go?"

"I… can't say. I follow because I think it is right," Dane responded, his voice uncertain. He took care in handling the parchment as he gave the fragile material back to Vreena, "I mean… Draco did seem like he needed my help…"

"A poor reason. Perhaps Draco meant you harm, yet you would follow him?"

"I know that. But I trust him. I know I had no reason to, but I do."

Vreena nodded yet again as she returned to her hut. Dane stared after her until she reappeared moments later without the parchment, "Draco must know, then? Surely he must know what you told me, yes?"

"…No. I… You know he doesn't."

"So you say you trust him, but you will not tell him that. Perhaps you lie?"

Dane shook his head, "No. I trust him, but would you tell your family or friends something like that?" Dane asked, glaring towards Vreena. Vreena glared back for a few moments, then she seemed to soften as she looked away, "I thought not. Now enough, let us spar."

Vreena sighed, but nodded, "Take your place."

Dane and Vreena each took up positions roughly 10 feet from each other, each returning the sleeves to their swords. Dane raised his sword, holding it diagonally across his body, instinctively raising his left arm as well. Vreena took up a different stance, brandishing her slender sword out and away from herself, the edge facing Dane. Her left hand was low but still by her body.

Dane took the first move, rushing forwards and stabbing at Vreena. She sidestepped with apparent ease and countered with a quick, short backstroke. Dane's blade rose, catched the attack with its flat. He quickly fell back, watching Vreena carefully. The half-elf smiled and began slowly shuffling to the right. Seeing her ploy, Dane began imitating her. As he did, he did his best to note where Sehero was. Vreena shuffled right a few steps more before lunging forward in a startlingly fast upstroke. Dane just managed to knock the stroke aside before jabbing in return. Vreena deftly deflected the strike with her blade's crossguard before returning Dane's stab.

Dane swiped his sword across his front, intent on parrying the stab, only to be surprised as Vreena changed tactics. She interrupted her own stab to change into a slash that struck and stopped Dane's blade. Before he had a chance to muster a defense after the unexpected attack, her wooden-sheathed blade leapt to Dane's throat.

"You are too traditional. Expect your foes to strike in odd and unexpected ways and never allow yourself to be paralyzed, however briefly, by them," Vreena whispered to Dane.

Dane surprised the half-elf when he smiled. In the same whispered tone, Dane invited Vreena, "Look down."

Vreena frowned and did as he suggested, stepping back when she realized that the blunt point of Dane's sword was hovering level with her heart. Dane took a step back a well, his weapon falling to his side.

"My sword was already there from your counter. It was easy to prepare it for a stab in the short time it took for your blade to reach my throat," Dane explained, "I would have no chance of stopping your blade, you are too fast. This was the best I could do."

"Fast I may be, but it would seem like I once again underestimated your own speed with the blade," Vreena replied, her voice taking on a thoughtful note, "Perhaps this is what they mean when... But that will not happen again. I wish to continue," Dane simply nodded and returned to his original position, "Ready?"

"I am," Dane's reply came with a thin smile.

"Then let us begin," as soon as she had spoken, the half-elf was already beginning to creep to the side, to get at Dane's side. Dane mirrored her actions even as he studied her, searching for a gap where he could-

Before he could even finish the thought, he saw the gap he was looking for and leapt forward, his blade arcing into a diagonal stroke that would have cleaved her in two, had the sword been able to. And, more importantly, had it hit.

The half elf backstepped, easily dodging his stroke before attempting to punish Dane with a swift jab. Unfortunately for her, Dane expected the counter and sidestepped. Their attempts defeated, the pair dropped back into warily circling. Dane eyed the half-elf as he cautiously stepped right, mirroring her own movements. Just as he was about to step again, Vreena twisted and rushed forward, perhaps attempting to unbalance Dane with her slash.

Her attack was smart, low and to Dane's left. Right where it would be harder to parry. Dane noted the action and reacted, lightly tossing his blade to his left hand. The move must have surprised Vreena, though she did not falter even as Dane managed to parry the strike. Dane attempted to counter with a stab. Vreena was far from caught off guard. Knocking aside the blow, she struck again. This time was a swift sidestroke that Dane avoided by leaning back. The warrior followed by darting back to evade a potential follow-up. That proved to be the wrong move as Vreena charged, making the dodge worthless. Dane swept his blade between them, attempting to catch Vreena's strike. He was just a tad too fast as Vreena's wooden-sheathed blade darted past his failed parry to tap his chest. Dane froze, then shook his head.

"Good hit. You got me."

"That was a predictable move."

Dane shrugged, a faint grin on his face, "It works normally. You're just too fast. And too skilled, for that matter."

"I've had quite some time to practice with the blade. It would be strange if you could best me every time," Vreena said in response to Dane, "Especially since I now know your fighting style."

"My fighting style?"

"Yes. You fight quick, but hard. Your attacks are fast, but not as fast as mine are. You put more force behind your blows, slowing your strikes down. Further, your movements are very calculated. Very few wasted moves."

"Hmm. I see what you mean. Your attacks focus on short strokes and quick jabs, mine involve heavy slashes and stabs, though mine are quicker than what is normal," Dane shrugged again, "At least, my father says as much."

"That is how you bested me at first, as you know. As you and I have noted," the half-elf gave an amused smile, " Most warriors like you use slower, heavier strikes. You defy appearances in that manner and throw your foes off balance. That and you change your style on a whim. In this last bout, you switched your sword to your left hand to make a more effective parry. That was quite the surprise as well. If my father hadn't done much the same, I doubt I would have known how to react."

Dane chuckled and offered a shrug, "I've had a bit of practice fighting with my left hand. It can be useful… We should rest, that was a bit tiring… That aside, you mentioned that you were going to tell me how I understand Draco, despite him not actually saying any recognizable words."

Vreena offered Dane a smile. A genuinely pleased smile, "Yes. Many creatures that seem to possess the ability to speak can't truly do so. Instead, they make use of a spell that was originally created by a human ambassador to the wolfear. Before the kingdom of the wolfear was destroyed, of course… That aside, the spell requires the creature to at least attempt to speak. Where the creature itself fails, the spell picks up, resulting in it sounding like words we know. Before the spell was perfected, it used to fail to perfectly match the creature's 'voice,' resulting in very odd sounding, yet understandable conversations."

Dane grinned and held up his hands in mock surrender, "Hold on! I haven't anything to write on. Unless you want me to memorize this, can you hold off a moment while I fetch quill and parchment?"

"Yes. Go."

ΩΩΩΩΩΩΩΩΩΩΩΩΩΩΩΩΩΩΩΩΩΩΩΩΩΩΩΩΩΩΩΩΩΩΩΩΩΩΩΩΩΩΩΩΩΩΩΩ
ΩΩΩΩΩΩΩΩΩΩ

"You said that certain materials are good for certain types of spell," Dane said, answering the question Resken had just posed to him.

The shaman nodded at Dane's answer, "Correct. I am gifting you with a rod made of a material called frozen ash. Despite the name and its smoky appearance, they do well with stone-related spells."

Dane frowned, studying the crystalline rod he had been given, "Why? Wouldn't it be good with fire or ice?"

Resken shook his head, gesturing to the frozen ash, "From its name alone, one would think that, but it is a crystal and thus stone they share relation to. Dwarves find it fairly often. But put aside your questions for now. I want you to use air to lift this stone," he gestured to a rock as big as Dane's hand on the ground.

Dane raised an eyebrow, but gave his tutor a nod. He stared at the rock and, pointing the frozen ash rod at it, commanded, "*Sir ve ven nelg!*"

A shimmering appeared along and almost inside of the rod in Dane's hand. At almost the same time, the stone began to rise. However, it did so slowly and with clearly considerable effort. After about a foot, the rock suddenly stopped and hung in the air. Resken eyed the floating rock for a moment, then turned his gaze to Dane, who appeared to be struggling. The pupil's hand was gripping the frozen ash rod in a near death grip, "It is difficult and drains your mana for little purpose. End the spell and simply raise the stone."

Dane managed a nod and the stone dropped. A thud sounded as it struck the ground. After a moment where Dane visibly relaxed, he pointed the rod again and declared, "*Nelg ve veng!*"

Unlike with the previous spell, the rock lifted off the ground with ease. It rose to about level with Dane's eyes before stopping. However, Resken easily noted that Dane was far more relaxed. Very clearly not struggling and no doubt able to do more if the shaman just asked, "Yes, as you know well, that would be a spell with relation to stone and thus is very easy with that rod. But you clearly have yet to encounter the material limit."

Dane frowned slightly, "'The material limit?'"

Resken nodded again, "Yes. A material limit is the maximum strength of spells a wizard or witch can cast with an object of a certain material. Of course, this varies depending on the material, the object, and the type of spell."

Dane's frown continued as he studied the shaman, "Maximum strength of a spell?"

"Yes. Wizards have to measure the power of their spells by some means so that they do not attempt to cast a spell that is too great a power for their focus. Thus they measure spells by certain requirements."

Dane nodded, understanding appearing across his face, "What are these requirements?"

"It depends on how much mana a spell costs, what it is affecting, how much it affects, and how it affects them."

"So if I casted a spell that lifted four large boulders as high as Draco, it would be a powerful spell."

"Fairly. Likely your rod wouldn't focus a spell of such strength. It can be uncertain as to just how powerful a spell an object can focus."

Dane turned his gaze to the still floating stone, focused in thought for a moment, "I just met one, right? When I used the air to lift the stone, the height I got it to was as high as it would let me."

Resken nodded, "Yes, in this case, that was a material limit. I was expecting you to guess that. Now, come outside. Let us try fireballs and similar spells. Fireballs are useful offensive spells, especially due to the large range of sizes one can have. In fact, it is often a favorite method of attack by mages. Destructive and rather easy to cast."

Dane allowed the rock to drift back to the ground, then began to follow Resken to the patch of ground where Rilyn had been summoned only a few weeks prior, "Will I be only doing this with the frozen ash rod?"

"You will be doing it with the frozen ash, yes. But also as a mage, so that you can understand," Resken gestured at a series of targets, "Hit one with a small fireball. Using magecraft, first."

"Is there a certain incantation you want?"

"No. Make one of your own."

Dane turned to the targets and raised a hand, "*Negdir ve hed nive tred gre vered ko O gre erel hasi O hofroen,*" at Dane's words, a flame appeared in the palm of his hand, quickly growing to become a small, but lively, ball of fire that twisted and raged. Dane gazed at the flames. Something about them…

"Dane," Dane started, turning to Resken. As he did so, the fire in his hand remained unchanged by its caster's distraction.

"Huh?"

"You did not hear me."

"Forgive me, Master. I was… thinking."

"Thinking," Resken's voice was plain, without a hint of passion, "I see. As much as that can be useful, I asked for you to attack the targets with the fireball, not stare at it and contemplate over it. Now, attack the targets."

"Yes, Master," Dane hefted the weightless flames, then flung them with all the grace of a novice, nearly falling over from trying to throw them with force. Even as Dane struggled to avoid falling over, an explosion erupted in front of him, causing him to stagger back and nearly fall over again. When he finally looked up, he was greeted by a chaotic sight.

His fireball had, in fact, hit the target. Or rather, targets. The explosion had decimated most of the targets, with the few that had survived were tilted at an angle and on fire. Resken gazed at the destruction before sighing.

"You lost focus. Your spell also did not restrict the explosion."

"I didn't mention explosions at all."

The shaman nodded, gesturing to the destruction, "Yes. That is how fire is. When you confine such a strong flame into such a small area, it will explode. Had you mentioned the explosion, you could have restricted it. Instead, you caused this."

"I… I didn't mean to. I…"

Resken shook his head, "Do not misunderstand me. You are a novice and are still learning. Mistakes like this are inevitable. But you grow and become more powerful should you learn from that mistake."

Dane stared at Resken for a few moments, then gave concise nod, "That sounds like something my father once told me, 'You learn the most from when you fail than when you succeed.'"

The shaman gave no noticeable reaction to Dane's word, instead replying with, "Words well spoken. Now, take up the frozen ash rod. I want you to create another fireball. Without such an explosion, if you could."

Chapter 12

Questions

Vreena stopped outside the hut that had been given to Dane almost a week prior. In the several months he had been here, he had been busy. In spite of his studies, he still found the time to offer help to the villagers. And the half-elf had to admit, though many of the villagers did not trust him, he was surprisingly effective at convincing them to allow him to help. He'd even managed to earn some respect from the Quel'meg by joining in some of their beffula hunts, even managing to bring one down. Of course, Dane rightfully insisted that he had no clue what he had been doing. Regardless of what Dane insisted, Chief Nesik nevertheless insisted on granting him a more permanent hut. Whispering and comments, their words natural when directed towards an outsider, voiced many a concern over the decision. However, none openly opposed the chief's choice. None but one, anyways.

She glanced to the side, then sighed. There he was, as always. Jascor, one of the tribe's strongest, was watching Dane's hut. Ever since Dane had arrived, Jascor had been watching him almost unceasingly. Almost, anyways. It was as if he expected Dane to do something.

Vreena shook her head and began to turn back to Dane's door, only to be startled when a rumbling voice sounded, "Vreena. What brings you here?" Lying to the side and mostly behind Dane's hut was Draco. Since their arrival, Draco had grown quite a bit. Now he was a little taller than Vreena at his shoulder. Big, but the hut was bigger. Along with his size, Draco's voice had grown deeper. Now, it was more akin to a rumble that sounded like words, as opposed to actual speaking.

"Ove adegran neh."

"Just a greeting? I remember more from elves," Draco commented, sounding smug, arrogant, and teasing all at once. It was a tone that only creatures of absolute authority could manage. The likes of dragons and cats, if they could speak. At least, Vreena assumed so.

"Just a greeting. I am very much different from an elf, as you can no doubt see."

"Aye, that you are. But I digress. Why are you here? My guess is you wish to speak with Dane?"

Vreena gave a nod, sweeping her hand to make a broad gesture at the door, "He is here, no?"

"No, he isn't. He left to do something or other. I would wonder if he ever slept, except that he is very strict about his sleep."

Vreena nodded again, perfectly aware why Dane liked his sleep. Perfectly aware, indeed, "It matters not. I can speak with you until Dane's return."

Almost as soon as Vreena had spoken, a voice floated from behind her. It was just a little mocking and a lot amused, "Then you may have to wait for some time. I am awfully busy, standing here and waiting for you two to end your conversation," Vreena spun around to see Dane watching them with his lips curled in amusement.

Draco huffed a sigh, "Are you sneaking around again? You are far too good at following people and watching them without anyone knowing. Will you ever tell me the reason?"

"No. It's my secret and I want to keep it. Besides, I like to keep my skills honed and sneaking up on you is just as good as the dogs back at home."

"Don't compare me to a dog!" Draco grumbled, his eyes locked into a momentary glare, "Talk as you two wish, I'm going to rest. It takes far too much energy to fly around and hunt in this blasted wind. Not that there is much to hunt."

Dane gave a short chuckle and strolled past Vreena. He pushed his door open and gestured, offering to hold the door for the half-elf. With nothing better to do, she allowed herself to be guided inside his hut.

The inside of the hut was very spartan in design. There was a mat to sleep on and a small platform with a drawer that served as a desk. There was a small pile of broken wood in the corner. Another corner held a bag holding his other possessions. Dane stepped into roughly the center of the space and sat on the floor. With a wave of his hand, he offered Vreena the mat.

"I would offer you the stool, but it isn't really intact right now," Dane nodded at the broken wood pile, "Resken has me using magic to break and fix it over and over. I grew too tired and strained and left it like that."

"Then your studies are going apace, yes?"

"Fairly. But you didn't come to ask about that. What did you wish to see me about?"

Vreena frowned and lightly shook her head, "A little direct. Were I an elf, you would seem too hasty, but no matter. You will not stay much longer, no?"

"Here, you mean? No, not really. Resken has been noting Draco's size and keeps mentioning that he has taught me the basics and that the rest can be learned alone. Rilyn also has been claiming that not everything can be taught. That you must experience it. And she has been talking about her home a lot. I think she's homesick. Finally, there is you, who has been repeating the same facts to me for the past week… Also, Draco has little to do but sleep and hunt now that he is too big to comfortably view my studies. Says he is not going to stick his head in a hut like some trained animal," Dane admitted, then added,

"He insists that we shouldn't wait too much longer. That we've burned too much time already."

"'Repeating the same facts?'"

"Yes," Dane grabbed the small pile of parchment that was his notes from his desk and showed her some of the top pages, "See, I have written just about everything you said about each topic and here are the pages I've written for the past week," Dane showed some pages to her. To her dismay, he was right. They were all exceedingly similar, "They are basically repeating the same information about the legends of the dragonborn. Just said in slightly different ways."

"They are. My apologies. I have been a little distracted as of late," Vreena agreed. Her gaze was not on Dane or his notes, but on to a random spot off to the right.

Dane frowned, his head slightly tilted as he considered her statement, "I know you have. You've ignored my questions this past week. I'm not sure you've heard me at all. But why?"

"Why do you want to know?" Vreena snapped, an edge appearing in her voice. As quickly as it appeared, it vanished as she sighed, "You actually do deserve to know, since it is about you."

Dane blinked and momentarily recoiled, "Me?"

"Yes, you. I have wanted to ask you a question this past week, but every means I could think of seemed too ridiculous and uncertain. I suppose just asking is the best…"

"A-and that question is?"

Vreena glanced at Dane and gave an amused smile. The human attempted to shake off the connotation of such a smile as Vreena gave her reply, "My question is simply this: Will you permit me to accompany you to *Arun Fril*?"

Dane gave a small, nervous smile, "Y-you want to come with us? I guess, but I have no clue why you'd want to," Dane silently cursed to himself. He had to go and get the wrong idea and make a fool of himself, *But she could have taken care to not make it sound so... so...*

"Why I want to? That, I will keep to myself," Vreena replied, startling Dane out of his thoughts. Silently berating himself for being a fool, Dane swiftly came froth with a reply.

"As I said, I suppose you can come with us, but I have no clue if Draco would approve of it and I don't really like the prospect of travelling with an angry dragon... Angrier than normal, anyways. But that reminds me, I have a question for you."

"Yes?"

"Should a dragon like Draco grow to a size like that in... three months?"

"No, he shouldn't. It likely has something to do with the... black dragon, was it?" Dane offered a nod in response to Vreena's query. To which Vreena nodded in turn and continued her prior thought, "Yes, it likely has to do with the black dragon and its mysterious spell. But let me deal with Draco, I can convince him," Vreena gave a soft smile, "Dragons aren't very hard to deal with, as long as you know what you're doing."

"They aren't? I don't think you've talked with Draco much. He's more convoluted than Akrazek's Knot and seems to try to put you as off balance as much as he possibly can."

Vreena gave a soft laugh, shaking her head in what seemed to be derision, "So he seems, but he *is* a dragon, no? I will have no trouble," Vreena said as she left the hut. Leaving Dane to gaze after her in minor dismay. He could only look after her and hope she knew what she was getting herself into.

Vreena let her smile fade as the door settled close behind her. Dragons were easy. They were greedy, proud, and vain, and loved gathering wealth, for some reason. But they were very susceptible to flattery. All she had to do was convince him that she could go with them. Easy.

As she drew near to where the dragon was lying, her footsteps woke Draco. Rather than simply rise, he barely cracked one eye to see Vreena approaching, *What could she want?* was the thought that crossed the dragon's mind, but he opted against moving or giving any sign he was awake. Vreena stopped barely five feet away, waiting.

Neither moved as the minutes slowly ticked past. Vreena wondering whether she should wake Draco or continue to wait, Draco wondering what Vreena was going to do. Finally, Vreena seemed to make a decision. She spoke, "Draco? Wake up, please. I must speak with you."

Draco didn't move, suddenly wanting to see what she'd do. He watched her, amused, as she stood there for about half a minute before speaking again, "Draco. Wake up! I cannot believe you would sleep through me being here. Dragons aren't that heavy of sleepers. Especially as you were awake but moments ago!"

Draco did nothing. This was starting to get interesting as Vreena glared at the "sleeping" dragon. Vreena huffed a sigh and muttered something about 'rumors of lazy dragons.'

"I must speak with you, Draco! If I have to, I will wake you up myself!" Vreena all but exploded as she began to stalk closer. As she did, Draco finally gave a visible reaction.

"Mmm? Oh, greetings, Vreena," Draco murmured as he gave a fake- yet astonishingly realistic- yawn.

"Greeting, Draco. You were very tired, yes? You didn't wake until I was about to wake you myself."

Draco began to laugh, "Ha ha! Ooh, no. I was awake since you approached. It was quite enjoyable to see you get... flustered? Is that the word? It was enjoyable to see you get flustered at me."

Vreena's eyes widened, then her gaze tightened into a glare that was directed at Draco, "Enjoyable?! You were awake and let me believe otherwise!"

"Aye. But enough of that, you wished to speak with me?"

Vreena almost growled. She took a single step towards the dragon, then stopped. She took a deep breath, then, much to Draco's surprise, spoke in a voice that perfectly hid anything but pleasant emotions, "You and Dane are leaving soon, no? Then you believe you two are able to deal with any danger, yes?"

"Both are correct. Dane and I are both capable of caring for ourselves. That is, if Dane doesn't starve to death first," Draco replied. Suspicion sat in his gaze as he eyed the half-elf, as though he was demanding she reveal her secrets.

"Perhaps. I have no doubt that a dragon like yourself and a warrior as skilled as Dane can hold your own against anything you might encounter, but-"

"Enough. If you have something to say, I would rather you speak your thoughts aloud and straight without all the unnecessary flattery," Draco interrupted, "I've always hated flattery. Useless... words. That aside, what is it you actually want to say?"

Vreena blinked, momentarily stunned at the dragon's easy dismissal. It would seem that she should have taken Dane's words more seriously. "Ah, well... Alright. Will you allow me to travel with you to *Arun Fril*?"

"Answer me this question first: Why do you wish to go?"

"I wish to see the lake. Such a thing. A lake shining with light… It must truly be beautiful. I wish to witness such a… a phenomenon first hand,' Vreena replied wistfully, "A beautiful sight."

"A rather shallow reason. Tell me more."

Vreena froze. For a moment, her mind rushed to find an acceptable excuse. Then it just… stopped, "I… suppose it would not hurt. I am something of an artist. My wish is to travel, to view beautiful sights and capture them with whatever grace my skills can provide.

"Hmm. Very well, as long as Dane does not object, neither shall I."

Vreena started, she had expected more resistance. But then again, she had expected Draco to be much more like other dragons than he was. Convoluted indeed!

At that moment, Dane appeared from within his hut. He pulled the door closed, then seemed to notice the expression on Vreena's face. As he did so, the human couldn't help but erupt into laughter, "Ah ha ha! I told you! He is not simple, not at all," Vreena glared at him. Her eyes almost seemed to be hurling daggers at the laughing warrior, but Dane didn't seem to notice.

"Of course. I am a dragon, after all," Draco replied smugly, "Is that all, Vreena?" Vreena's glare turned towards Draco, but much like Dane, it had no effect.

"Yes. I think it is," She stalked off, muttering something under her breath. Draco believed the word 'fools' might have been used. He took a few moments to watch her go before turning to Dane, "She already asked you, I would assume," when Dane nodded, he continued, "Very well. I would also assume you said yes… But, since today seems to be the day for such things, I have a few questions for you, Dane. Questions I have been meaning to ask for a while now."

Dane nodded in response, but offered no actual words. Even so, the dragon noted Dane's face bore the unmistakable signs of nervousness. Rather than spend time questioning this, Draco chose to press on with his questions first, "You followed me without question. Why?"

Dane gave a light laugh that held a note of relief within it, "Not without question, but yes. I followed you because I do not hate dragons and I felt I could trust you."

"... You killed people, yet don't seem to care. I have seen many humans kill and only those who are cruel or heartless are not affected."

Dane paused, then murmured, "You didn't actually ask a question, but I've... killed before. I've found my own way to live with it... Somewhat..."

"Somewhat?"

"Trust me, it isn't the best way, but it works for me... It has to."

"Hmm. What are you hiding from me?" Draco asked, his words and tone could have been used as a mace.

"What do you mean?"

"What are you hiding from me? You are carrying a secret that you refuse to share with me. Tell me now."

"I-I cannot. It is not mine to give," Dane said, his voice quiet. He was not looking at the dragon.

Draco eyed Dane, expecting to see the lie upon his face. Even with the human looking away from him, the dragon could only conclude that his human companion had been sincere, "Whose is it?"

"Rilyn's."

"Rilyn... Then tell me. Tell me the other secret."

"The other secret?" Dane glanced at Draco, his expression clearly hesitant.

"Aye. You met Rilyn only recently. I speak of the secret you have hidden from me since the day our journey began. The one you refuse to speak of. The 'curse' you muttered to yourself before we encountered that strange dead wolf."

"My… curse. My curse. It doesn't-," Dane cut himself off, chiding himself with a shake of the head, "Well, if it doesn't matter, then it shouldn't hurt to tell you. I am unlucky. Misfortune follows me like an assassin. As well, my previous encounter with a direwolf has left me unsavory to wolves. Does that answer your question?"

"Unlucky? Misfortune? I have yet to see it. Though most wolves are not fond of direwolves, I do not see how one encounter would make them hate you."

"The direwolf bit me," Dane pulled up his right sleeve, then the left leg of his breeches. Upon his right forearm and left thigh were very clear bite-shaped scars, "Perhaps that is why. But the misfortune *is* a curse. I can't go through a normal life without something happening every day."

"Hmm. Then what of your healing powers?"

"Healing powers? I don't have any healing powers," Dane responded, a look on his face speaking volumes of his surprise. There was no questioning that Dane had no idea what Draco meant. It was as clear as day.

Upon hearing this and seeing the human's truthfulness, Draco found himself unable to decide on what to say. The two stood there, neither speaking. If there had been a clock present, the two would have been able to note how time ticked on inexorably. Despite being aware of this, neither moved. It was after roughly five minutes that Draco finally broke the silence, "You did not lie, and yet you spoke of it to yourself," Draco's comment was accompanied by rather intense scrutiny on the dragon's part.

Dane looked away from Draco, though not because of how Draco was studying him. He was torn on what to say. It would simplify so much if he just told Draco, but… Dane just couldn't bring himself to tell the dragon. It went well with Rilyn and Vreena, but they had been risks he judged as either safe or necessary. This was not, "I have no power for healing, but I do heal quickly. Quickly enough to be something of an interest."

Draco, still having not moved from his spot, sighed and laid his head upon his paws, *Dane is too hesitant. He is acting as though he has something to hide. Yet, as far as it seems, he is telling the truth… I hate it when my own mind tricks are turned against me. Assuming it is a trick. But that's the golden question. Is it a trick? Is Dane really speaking the truth?*

"Draco? Can I ask you a question?" Dane interrupted Draco's pondering. The dragon fixed his gaze on Dane and grunted.

"Just one?"

"Just one."

"Very well. Ask," Draco sighed, his tail tip rising for a moment, then striking ground. The sharp sound nicely punctuated his words, "But do so quickly, please. I tire of this."

"Do you trust me?"

Draco stared at Dane, *Do I trust him? I… I'm not sure. Dane is… he is clearly secretive. A number of things about him do not line up. Too many… And yet… He's done nothing worth my distrust. He saved my life twice over. If anything, he has earned… Earned my trust. Yet I am still suspicious of him… Secrets he may have, but he is trustworthy,* Draco finally decided.

"Aye. I trust you."

Dane nodded and offered a smile, "Then trust me when I say that my secrets will not hurt you. Many people have secrets that are harmless to others. Mine are nothing you need fear."

"Hmm. Very well. Unless I see otherwise, I will allow you to indulge in your secrets."

"Thank you, Draco," Dane said, maintaining his smile, though now it was accompanied by an expression of relief, "I meant it, though. My secrets are not something you need to worry over."

Draco sighed, shaking his head. His tail twitched as he spoke, "All secrets are dangerous in some way. Worth the worry. But enough, away with you."

Dane's smile held firm at Draco's response, "This is my hut you are lying next to. But I understand. I think I will look at one of those spell books Resken gave me."

Draco gave a low growl as Dane meandered back into his hut, "You have a silver tongue, Dane," he muttered to himself, after Dane had disappeared, "But make no mistake. You will tell me those secrets you defend so vigorously, else I would endanger myself. Not now, perhaps. You are too cautious, but you will certainly tell me."

Chapter 13

A Double-Edged Gift

Dane lowered himself into a crouch and drew his sword, watching the two wolves that had appeared from the forest around him. They stalked towards him, one on either side. He prepared himself for an attack, his blade defensively in front of him. Sure enough, one of the wolves leapt for him. Much to his surprise, it never made it. Instead, the other wolf leapt at it, sending the two beasts into a struggle against each other.

Dane watched as the two wolves fought, still not lowering his guard nor his blade. What was happening? Did they both want him, but couldn't agree on something? It didn't escape his notice that shadows seemed to cling to them like a cloak.

It also didn't escape notice that one wolf seemed to be getting bigger and more powerful. When the fight had begun, they were the same size. However, as the fight wore on, one wolf was clearly now larger and starting to dominate the fight more. Dane raised his sword, his face taking a grim expression. If they were what he thought they were, then he needed to strike first. If he didn't…

But when the warrior raised his sword, something happened. Something he hadn't been expecting. His vision broke, shattering into four parts. It was as if he was looking through four eyes and seeing each of their views individually, yet at the same time. Unsure as to what was happening, Dane shook his head. He couldn't let this stop him. He couldn't where these wolves were concerned. Dane swung and his four gazes were met with four swords coming down. Then, with the shock of a flash flood, a torrent of sights broke in, shattering rational thought.

His sword bit a wolf's neck, slaying it. His sword struck a wolf's side, killing it. His sword struck and slayed one wolf, then, at his decree, it bore down upon the other. His sword lowered, its edge unbloodied. A wolf pounced on him. A wolf lowered itself in submission before him. A wolf laid dead. The ground, bloody from battle and death. The ground, soaked by blood. His blood. A wolf's blood. Both wolves' blood. No blood at all. Death. Life. Spared. Slain.

It was too much. Too many things at once. He cried out, howling his confusion and the emptiness, the loss and betrayal. Too many emotions, too many things, But nothing to understand. The world seemed to shake from the force of his howling, his vision turning to an incomprehensible collage of disagreeing imagery.

Dane's eyes shot open and he rocketed into a sitting position, only to headbutt something and fall back.

"Ow!" Vreena exclaimed as she leaned back, pressing a hand to her mouth and nose. Nothing felt broken to her, but a little blood, likely from her nose, was on her hand when she pulled it away, "What was-?" she broke off when she noticed that Dane had sat up again and was breathing heavily, staring about wildly and completely disregarding her presence.

"The wolves. Where are the wolves?" he demanded as soon as he realized Vreena was there. Vreena blinked and opened her mouth, no doubt to question the human. He didn't give her a chance to speak, however, but began ranting, "One wolf, two wolves, no wolves. Wolves alive, wolves dead. Wolves fighting, wolves attacking, wolves submitting. And nothing. It makes no sense, I don't understand! Tell me what it means!" Dane was shouting by the end of his tirade of nonsense.

"Dane! Calm yourself!" The hut shook from the force of Draco's roar. As if that sound had been a salve, Dane's raving gradually subsided. He blinked and looked around. He was in his hut, with Vreena, Chief Nesik, and Resken watching him. Outside, Draco had an eye peering through the building's single window to glare at him.

"Are you okay?" Chief Nesik asked after waiting a moment. No doubt to ensure that Dane was in his right mind, "Your yelling woke the entire village and, for a moment, you sounded like a madman."

"I-I saw wolves. Nothing made sense. There were only two, and yet… more. I saw so many things happen to too many wolves. It was too much. Too much at once."

"Hmm. Perhaps a warning of what will be?" Vreena wondered, as she dabbed at her nose, then pulled back her hand to inspect the slightly bloody result.

"I don't know. It was too much…"

"I see. Hmm," Nesik seemed lost in thought. After a few moments, he nodded and turned to Resken, "Tell the rest of the village that everything had been taken care off," at the chief's words, the shaman gave a nod and swiftly exited the hut.

After the shaman was gone, Nesik turned back to Dane, "I cannot say what any of that means, but you should get prepared. You are leaving and the village has a surprise for you."

Dane, distracted by his own apprehension, offered a slow yet non-committal nod. The chief turned and left the hut, gesturing for Vreena to follow. The half-elf didn't say a word as she followed Nesik's order. Not that it would have mattered if she had spoken. Dane didn't even notice the pair leave.

Rising, Dane grabbed his bag and checked through it. He stopped partway through, realizing that he couldn't recall what he had just looked at. Shaking his head in a vain attempt to push the thoughts out of his head, he began perusing through the bag a second time. This time, he found everything where he had expected it. Heaving a sigh, Dane took a moment to ensure his armor and weapons were in good condition. He lifted his hauberk, noting with satisfaction that no rust had formed on it. Similarly rust-free were his weapons. As expected, *Verachodairgin* was in immaculate condition. However, it pleased Dane to see that his other weapons were still in good shape. Tucking away the weapons and belting *Verachodairgin*, Dane swung his bag over his shoulder and made his way to the hut's door.

As he stepped outside, he found the old woman from when he had arrived waiting for him, "I would warn you."

"Of what?"

"Of the dangers of ancient places," she said, pointing a finger at him, "There are many things in the world, and not all of them are friendly."

"Thank you for the warning, then."

"Watch for rabbits as well. Vicious little things, they are."

"Erm, right," Dane considered questioning the odd comment. Though he didn't have the chance as the woman went on her way. Her big, strange cat followed her a moment after, "I'm not sure strange begins to describe her."

"Eh, I would say crazy or mad, but I've seen those already," Draco said as he wandered over from next to Dane's hut, "The entire village is meeting in the center. Might as well see why?"

"Might as well. Nesik said the village had a surprise, for some reason."

Much like when they had first arrived, the village was arrayed in a circle, with Nesik in the center and occupying the only chair. Among the assembled villagers was, of course, Jascor. The Quel'meg villager had his expected glower painted across his face upon seeing Dane and Draco. He wasn't the only one at first. Many among the village had announced their distrust of Dane in a variety of ways. However, Jascor was usually the loudest and with the darkest expression.

"Dane of Verious. You came under suspicion and in dark company, or so we had thought. Yet you showed sincerity in your actions and proved that not everything is as one thinks. In the interest of my tribe, I thank you and would offer you a gift," at this, Nesik gestured to a man holding a large box. It was a long box, yet slender. The man brought it forward and handed it to the chief, who had risen from his chair. He opened the box before looking up at Dane.

"The strength of the winds here makes archery a difficult skill to learn. Those few who try use heavy bows, like this one," Nesik removed a massive bow from the box. The bow was unstrung and featured a spike on one end. It also dwarfed Dane, "Of course, they usually use much smaller ones. This is one of our great bows. It takes a strong man to draw these bows. Perhaps you would try?"

Taking the proffered bow and its string, Dane began to try to string it. Attaching the string to the lower arm, Dane stepped through, putting the arm behind his left foot, but in front of his right shin. With some effort, he bent the upper arm. It certainly wasn't easy, but now that it was somewhat bent, Dane was able to attach the other end of the string. Dane blinked as he stared at the ready bow. Even strung, it was still a good seven feet tall.

Nesik held up one of the bow's enormous arrows, "The arrows are heavier than ones you are likely familiar with. It helps with the wind," Nesik pointed it at a target that had been set up while he had been explaining about the bow.

Dane took the arrow and nodded. He turned to the target and hefted the bow. Pausing upon doing so, he nodded, then planted the bows spike in the ground. Nocking the arrow to string, he began to draw the string. To his embarrassment, he could only pull it back to about half draw. Refraining from releasing a sigh, Dane noticed that, with the arrow in its proper place, it was level to his shoulder. He couldn't sight down the shaft like this. An odd notch was put in the bow level with his head. Perhaps for aiming? Not able to hold the bow drawn for long, he used that notch to try to aim, then released his grip upon both arrow and string. He started when the arrow practically disappeared from the bow and reappeared halfway through the target. The shot may have hit the very edge of the target, but it didn't matter. That kind of blow would have at least staggered anyone and done great damage besides. Dane looked at the bow, *That was an easy 50 yards at half draw! Just what is this bow?*

Nesik spoke up, "Impressive, no? The bow is very difficult to use properly, especially the first time. In fact, I'm surprised you are strong enough to draw it that much. We rarely use bows, especially that kind, but we hold stories of when bows like those were given to dragon riders in ancient times. As we had deemed them capable enough, of course."

"Dra-Dragon riders? But I'm not a dragon rider!"

Nesik nodded, "That may be true, but you and Draco… The way you two act around each other speaks of a strong companionship."

"It does?"

The chief chuckled and offered another nod, "Yes. It is said that dragon riders and their dragons treat each other more like family than companions. I wouldn't say you are family, but Draco treats you differently to other humans. It is very clear."

"Er… but I… That's just… I-I'm just…"

Draco sighed and rose to his feet. As he did, he loosed a growl, drawing the eyes of everyone present, "Enough, Dane. Let's get going," without waiting for a response, the dragon turned tail and began to leave. The villagers quickly parted, getting out of Draco's way as he stalked past.

"Ah, sure. Let's do that," Dane quickly jumped on the dragon's words, following the retreating figure of his draconic companion. The box that contained the tribe's gift was securely under his arm. Vreena watched them go for a moment, then shook her head and began to follow.

The chief nodded, "Ah, yes. You are leaving as well, Vreena."

"I am."

"Then I wish you good fortune and farewell." the chief called as the trio left, heading eastward. Dane noticed Vreena was sporting a bag of her own that had a bundle of shaved branched lashed to the side of her bag. She was also easily keeping pace with both Dane and Draco. As they passed the villagers, the village began to echo with farewells. That being said, Dane did notice that Jascor still just stood and glared at them.

Dane raised his hand, "Good fortune to you all. Farewell,"

"*Neh ve frojeg lesir*!" Vreena bid, her voice smooth and rather pleasant to hear.

As the distance between them in the villagers steadily grew, the trio maintained a mutual silence amidst the growing noise of the winds. At least, they did until they were well away from the Quel'meg, when Draco loosed a low rumble. Dane glanced at Draco, then shook his head when the dragon continued to stare forward.

"He lied," Draco was still looking forward as he suddenly spoke. Dane jumped, startled by the dragon's sudden desire to speak.

"What do you mean?"

"You are no dragon rider. I am no servant. Simple as that."

"S-Servant?"

"That is exactly what a dragon is to its rider. A servant."

"I won't agree with that, but that is not all Nesik did not tell you…" Vreena surprised Dane by speaking up, "That bow… This is the first I've seen of its like."

"They didn't exist?"

"No. They did… But they have not made one in all the time I lived there. And not only that, those particular bows, the great bows, were made specifically for dragonslayers. Perhaps some were made for the odd rider, but it was slayers who more prevalently took them up. According to legend, there was once a time were dragons and humans fought, and it was the great bows of the Quel'meg that turned the battle in the human's favor. Later, upon the birth of an order of dragon riders, most of those great bows were given to warriors for protection in case a dragon or its rider got too caught up in their power. It is no coincidence that the very place where these bows were made was the preferred place to find future dragon riders."

There was silence for a long while. No one seemed willing to bring it up, until Draco spoke again, his voice disdainful and even hateful, "Get rid of it. The dragonslayer's bow."

Vreena glanced at Draco, her expression sharp, "That bow could be useful. Not all dragons we meet will be as 'friendly and nice' as you. If it comes to battle-"

"You will not beguile me with words. He does not need a bow like that. Its size alone makes it a hassle to travel with."

Vreena nodded, "True… But it would be better to moan about it and have it than to not have it and regret it. A similar thing can be said for travelling with armor that one is not wearing."

Draco growled in response, his tail lashing from side to side, "I can deal with any dragons we meet. There is no reason to keep the bow. Unless you don't trust me?"

Vreena shook her head, "I trust you to do that, but-"

"Enough," Dane said, interrupting Vreena. He turned to Draco and shook his head, "Do you really want me to get rid of it? It could be useful in the event you cannot protect me. And it was a gift."

"They gave it to you, so it's yours to do with as you please. But you don't need it. Any need you might have for it, I can do. The only other reason would be as a weapon against me…"

Dane paused, considering what Draco had said. Then he offered a nod, "I see… I'd never use it against you, but I will do as you ask," he held out the box and set it on the ground, "Feel free to destroy it, if you want."

"My pleasure," Draco took a breath, then loosed a stream of fire that bathed the boxed weapon. When the dragon's jaws snapped close, the box, its contents, and a fair amount of the grass around it, had been reduced to ashes, "Ah, that felt good."

Vreena sighed in obvious disapproval, "Never throw away anything that could have a good future use. But it is too late now," she shook her head and continued moving. Dane gazed after her, then, after sparing a moment to nod at Draco, began to jog after her. Fortunately, she was going no faster than a walk, allowing Dane to easily catch up to her. Even as he did so, she spoke. Though what she said was more of a demand, "Why?"

"The bow obviously made Draco uncomfortable. He was worried that I would use it. If it can help keep his trust by letting him destroy it, I don't see why not."

"It could have been very useful."

"That it could have, but I don't think we'll need it."

Vreena sighed and shook her head again, but acquiesced, "Fine."

Dane glanced at her, "You don't trust him. You think he will backstab us."

She huffed and gave another sigh, then turned her gaze back to the fore, "Not at all. Humans think that, not elves. I worry about what might happen when we do not have Draco with us."

Dane nodded slowly, as though pondering her words, "I see…I think it is better to have Draco's trust while we are with him. Either way, we will have to do without the bow. There could very well be a time we are without him. There probably will be. But I think we should be fine. After all, I've been fine without him."

"Life won't be the same. It never is," Dane didn't reply to Vreena's statement. He couldn't think of anything to say. A sentiment shared by Vreena as the pair continued onward. After being joined by Draco, who caught up to the pair, they still did not speak. The trio travelled onwards through the steadily growing wind, towards whatever fortune, or misfortune, awaited them. In silence.

Chapter 14

Sanctuary's Ruin

"This wind is so strong, I think I'm walking sideways!" Dane yelled out. He held no illusions that his voice would be heard over the roaring winds, and thus took care to augment his words with gestures. Whether or not his companions understood what he meant, the movements were enough to get Vreena's attention.

Vreena nodded and appeared to begin muttering to herself. She might have been talking in a normal voice, of course. Dane wouldn't have been able to hear one way or the other. At least, not until a few moments later, when the wind was suddenly no longer quite as strong. As though it had suddenly decided to no longer put as much effort assaulting the trio. The change was so sudden that Dane very nearly fell on his face. He saved himself at the last moment.

"There," Vreena gasped. She shook her head, as though steadying herself, then added, "That spell should divert some of the wind away from us. We should be able to talk as well, if we stay close."

"That's a relief," Draco muttered. Fortunately for the others, the dragon was more than loud enough to hear, "I felt like the wind was going to catch my wings if I didn't hold them close."

Dane glanced at him and said, his voice just a little too coy, "Like it did a few months ago?"

Draco glared at him. His wings rustled as they ever so slightly rose, "Don't bring that up. Don't you *dare* bring that up."

Vreena chuckled, the sound soft enough to barely rise above the noise of the wind, "I suppose I cannot ask about it, then?"

"No, you can't."

Vreena nodded, then looked to Dane. She offered the human a mockingly bashful expression as she asked, "Will you tell me if I did ask?"

Dane glanced at Draco, then shook his head. However, he did so with a cheeky grin on his face, "If the look on Draco's face says anything, I might get eaten if I do. Probably would still be worth it."

Draco growled in obvious frustration. As he spoke, his tail lashed with more than enough force to strike the ground with an faintly audible thud, "I'll do worse than eat you if you say anything about it."

Dane chuckled before gazing around at the empty plain around them, "It's rather empty out here... I hope we actually find something at the center."

Vreena also gave a sweeping look, something akin to melancholy touching her visage, "Supposedly, there is some sort of ruin there that the Quel'meg hold sacred. I've never seen it myself."

Dane almost stopped walking, instead turning to Vreena, his eyes glittering with curiosity, "Really?"

Vreena nodded, a faint smile tugging at her lips, "Each Quel'meg shaman must make it there without using magic to prove that they are strong enough. It is very difficult. In fact, it wasn't uncommon for there to be long times where the Quel'meg were without a shaman."

"I can imagine why... I'm not sure I could even do that," Dane noted, looking around at the empty plains. He felt newfound appreciation for Resken well up as his gaze found nothing but flattened grass and the occasional boulders. To think the old man was once capable of traversing this. Without magic, too. Venerable though he is now, Dane found himself wondering what kind of figure Resken used to be.

The trio continued their travels, mostly in silence, though due to a lack of conversation topics rather than a lack of companionship, or so Dane believed. With a dragon like Draco, it was rather hard to tell. After several minutes, Dane decided he'd had enough of silently walking when he had other people with him. As Vreena was the newest, he turned to her.

"Vreena?"

"Yes?"

"You're a half-elf. How did you come to live in a human village in a place like this?" To complement his question, Dane made a large, sweeping motion with his hands.

"My mother was from this village."

"She was human?"

"Yes. It is the main reason I appear so human. My father is an elf, but he was an interesting one. He preferred to roam, rather than stay in the forests, and absolutely loved to find beautiful views of landscapes and animals," Vreena smiled as she spoke, her words soft and almost seeming to be filled with warmth.

"Sounds like a great guy."

"He is. He visited the Quel'meg village on a tip from another elf. It was there that he met my mother and fell in love with her."

"That simple?"

"No. At first, he had only eyes for the tranquil, endless landscapes. He once told me that he never noticed my mother until he was about to paint a picture of the land and she accidently walked in front of him. She realized what she had done and tried to apologize, only to have my father tell her to stay where she was."

Dane chuckled at that, "Really? She gets in the way, but he wants her to stay there?"

"He said that she completed the view, that she added a sort of beauty that the landscape needed. When he finished, he showed it to her. It was a very good painting, but it was my father that said she made it better… I never let you into my hut or you might have seen the painting yourself. No matter. After then, she began helping him with his paintings and would often travel with him, though they frequently returned to the village. Both out of it being my mother's home and my father's love of the landscape. They fell in love and would eventually have me."

"Did I meet them?"

"No. My mother died four years ago and my father never stayed in the village for very long amounts of time, even before she died. He is often traveling for more inspirations, though he used to bring me some of the paintings he'd made. The places he showed me with them were beautiful. Ever since, I'd also wanted to go with him… But that is not important. I've seen him… only half of a dozen times since my mother died."

"I'm sorry."

"It is nothing. I am already grown, it doesn't bother me. It is enough that he still comes by," Vreena replied, her voice smooth and without blame. Dane couldn't imagine being happy with his own father only showing up once in a while, yet the half-elf's expression bore only contentment. However, that was not what he had meant.

"I meant your mother," Dane replied, a little worried that he offended her.

"Thank you… But please, do not bring it up again…" Vreena hadn't looked at him while she spoke, instead gazing forward where they were going.

Dane turned his gaze away, a slight bit ashamed of his prying, "My apologies."

"You did not know. I hold no ill will towards you."

"Thank you... I'll tell you something... about me, if you wish," Dane's gaze was fixed on the ground as he spoke, his voice hesitant and ever so subtly warning.

"No. I don't need to know anything. I already know enough. Far more than I believe I truly needed to know or that you wished to tell me. I do appreciate the offer," Vreena grew quiet, as did Dane.

Draco, who had been gazing forward during the entire conversation and generally ignoring them, grunted, "Do you see that?" he flicked his tail to point roughly to the trio's southeast.

Dane followed Draco's gaze to see what appeared, at first, to be more rocks. Except there were far too many and they didn't quite seem like random boulders, "Are those... buildings? They have to be the ruins."

Vreena gazed at the sight, her gaze and voice displaying an emotion that lay somewhere around excitement, "Then we have nearly made it. Let's keep moving."

Dane and Vreena seemed to have the same idea, as both hurried their pace. For a moment, this caught Draco off-guard. Especially when the pair passed him and left him staring after their backs. Naturally, he increased his own gait. As the trio approached the distant ruins, it gradually grew in their visions. While the dragon saw nothing unusual, Vreena and Dane both noted the size of the ruin, even from this distance. It had to be unusually tall, especially to appear as it did. Moreover, upon reaching what could be guessed as a few hundred meters out the wind abruptly stopped.

"The wind. Then this is the center, if the stories are to be believed," Dane noted, receiving a nod from Vreena.

When the group eventually arrived at what seemed to be the outermost edge, the remains of the wall before them was far taller than even Draco. But that proved to be far and away from the most peculiar sight. The ruins were made of stone and possessed architecture that was unfamiliar to Dane. What he guessed were the city walls appeared to have once looked like they were covered in scales. Many of the buildings seemed to have a vaguely similar styling, but some also appeared like they were just boulders thrown together. That being said, some more buildings seemed to have different styles entirely, making everything seem mismatched. Almost as if there had no consistent or definite plan on appearance when the ruins had been originally constructed. The hollow silence, devoid even of the sound of a howling wind, lent an eeriness to the locale, but the strongest feeling Dane found himself experiencing was sadness. Sorrow at the crumbled buildings and their once grand shells. Melancholy at the streets that must have once held a cacophony of citizenry. Perhaps a once beautiful place, now long lost to time.

Dane ran a hand over a crumbled building, feeling the pebbles that broke off to rest in his hand, "What is this place?"

Vreena shook her head, "I don't know. The only mention of this place I know of are Quel'meg's stories. But even they have no idea who made it."

Draco studied a wall for a moment, then turned away with an almost callous dismissal, "These look like scales… But that is not what we are here for. Let's keep moving."

Dane nodded in agreement, "So this the center of the Plain of the Winds. I hadn't expected this."

"That is quite obvious, Dane. Thank you for stating as much," Draco replied, sarcasm coloring his voice, "Now let's move. I want to see if we wasted our time here or not."

"Yfel mægðmann sý hæfde dôð forwrecan, yonder êow hwettan sê frignes," a voice called out.

"What was that? Who said that? What did you say?" Dane had stopped dead in his tracks, his gaze sweeping about in vain to find the speaker.

"Ah, I see. Ye do not speak the olden tongue. I should know better by now, but still I try and hope. I said that I may have thine answer, if ye would provide the question," the voice replied, speaking slowly and with a strange accent. It reminded Dane of the time he heard a wolfear speak. They had been hesitant and slow. Even when they hadn't done either, like Draco, their words had still held a bestial accent that oddly distorted the words.

"What? Who are you?!" Draco snapped, eyes darting from shadow to shadow.

"Who am I? … I was known by several names. Sanctuary's Peace. The Fallen King. The Hope of the Dying. But my favorite is Forgotten Arbiter."

Draco growled, his claws crushing bits of rubbles further into dust, "That answers nothing. Who are you?"

"I am not alone, dear dragon. My friend is a dragon, as much as thee. Though he claimeth many years more. Several centuries more, in truth. Not as many as myself, but many nonetheless."

Another voice broke in. This voice was much deeper and far more bestial. Not too unlike Draco's own, "Get on with it. Gods, you still like to ramble."

"I am old! Of course, I do! Asides, he is known as the Great Bulwark, the Master of the Skies, and the Elder Watcher. But ye may call him the Arbiter's Seat."

A rumbling growl shook the ruins, "You just love to joke with me," the voice was laced with sarcasm and just a tinge of a threat.

"But of course! Must old, wise men be mirthless?"

"I would prefer you were sometimes."

Laughter echoed through the ruins. When it had ended, the voice continued, "Ye wish to know where you are, do you not?"

"No," Draco's reply was quite blunt. It was also quite ignored.

"Ye stand within the ruins that are the center of the Plain of the Winds. These ruins are the ruins of an ancient city of which I was king. It was called Sanctuary. Lying to the side of Sanctuary is a very special lake. The Lake of Light, or, as it is known to elves and dragons, *Arun ko Fril*. I suppose that is thy query?"

Draco rumbled a warning growl. More rubble was crushed to powder beneath his claws as he replied, "It is, but, and I will ask this only this once more, who are you?"

"Ye truly wish to know? It has been some time... I am a near dracon by the name of Leonidas. A pleasure to make thine acquaintance, though ye have yet to offer names of thine own," with those words, a figure stepped into view. He was tall and armored in blue scales. Rather obviously attached to his back was a pair of wings, as well as a pointed tail that swung lazily behind him. His clothing was only a simple, white tunic that reached his mid-thighs and was belted at the waist with a leather belt.

"My companion here- step on out- is Argrex. He is my dragon, I am his rider," At the dracon's insistence, a huge, black dragon stepped into view. He clearly dwarfed Draco with his shoulder height being half again Draco's own. More noticeably, Argrex possessed only one pair of wings. Below his off-white, backward-facing horns, the black dragon had frills that covered the sides of his head. Upon sight of his black scales, Dane and Vreena's hands leapt to their weapons as Draco dropped into a slightly more aggressive stance, "Do not be so quick to draw blades. Argrex is quite friendly. If ye anger him not, of course. Asides, the two of us together are known as the Guardians of the Ruins. Rather, that is what the Quel'meg prefer to name us."

Argrex glared at the trio, his jet-black eyes seeming deep as the void, and spoke. His voice had morphed to be even deeper and greatly threatening,

"Now… Stay where you are and be judged. Elsewise, you shall be turned away on pain of being eaten."

Chapter 15

Shine, O Darkness

"Eaten?!" came Dane's response, his face making it very clear that he didn't like the idea of that, "Could we possibly not do that?"

The black-scaled dragon sighed, barely looking at the three newcomers, "How shall we do it this time, Leonidas? … Leonidas?" The creature in question was not paying attention to the dragon, instead choosing to examine Dane. At the dracon's lack of a response, Argrex turned to look at Leonidas, the faintest hint of concern drifting on his voice, "Leonidas? What ails you?"

"The water," Leonidas suddenly spoke, causing Argrex's head to jerk back in very clear surprise. He glanced at the dragon before turning his gaze to the trio of travellers, "Follow me."

Leonidas turned and began making his way through the rubble, leading the trio through the ruins. He didn't say a word, though neither did anyone else. After a few minutes of silent maneuvering through the broken building, Vreena decided she'd had enough of there being no sound save for the crunching of stone on stone.

"You called yourself a dracon. I wasn't aware that your kind existed. I'd only heard of them in legends."

"To be precise, I am a near dracon."

Dane frowned faintly, curiosity welling up in his voice, "What's a near dracon? I've heard of dracon, but are there certain kinds?"

"Aye. Near dracon, that is we, are… a special kind of dracon. Similar to other dracon, yet very different. Thou couldst compare it to the similarities and differences between draconians, dragonborn, and dracon."

Vreena frowned at that point, "They are the same, no?"

"Nay. They are draconic humanoids all, but are certainly different. Dragonborn are ancient. They are very similar to dragons and are said to have existed nearly as long, often likened to cousins. Perhaps they were born alongside the dragons, if some legends are true. I have my doubts that any exist. Like as not, they were all slain long ago. Draconians were created from, and by, dragons through magic. They are not dragons anymore, but are descended of them. Mostly, they serve as servants or slaves, often dependent upon the dragon. And dracon are cursed dragons. We are dragons, yet not true dragons. Unlike draconians, who are a rather young race, we dracon are old. Not as old as dragons and dragonborn, but old still," Leonidas replied, "I have heard that, if the legends surrounding our origins are true, our existence is a mark on dragonkind, yet once was the symbol of its salvation. That dragons shan't die so long as the dracon remain. Or so it is said."

Vreena nodded slowly, one finger tapping her other hand, "And there are different kinds of dracon?"

"Aye. Winged, tailed, scaled, breath, and near. Each with our own ways and strengths. And customs, in fact. It would not be wrong to say that even our very cultures differ from community to community. As though each of the dracon were a greatly different people. A pity it was. I would explain more, but here we are."

Leonidas slipped around the edge of a ruined building, more a pile of rubble than a building, and urged them to follow. Dane followed and found himself shocked as the view of a lake revealed itself before him. The lake was crystal clear and looked flawless, as though it was an unbroken mirror, but there was one thing wrong about it.

"This is *Arun Fril*? Where's the light?" Draco snapped, his glare sweeping from the lightless lake to Leonidas.

The dracon offered what could be interpreted as a pointless smile while he studied the group. Of course, like any reptile, he could not actually smile. At least, it looked to Dane as though he couldn't. The best the dracon seemed to manage was a parting and very slight pull back of his scaly, somewhat peculiar, lips. This naturally made him look to be hissing without actually hissing, though his still amicable eyes certainly helped make him seem less threatening.

A moment after Dane put these thoughts together, Leonidas gestured at the human, "Thou canst see it… Dane, did the dragon not calleth thee? Thou knowest how to see it, dost thou not?" he gestured towards the lake, "Thou art versed with nature, no? Thine eyes can see of which I speak.

Dane nodded, his words stolen from him. At first, he thought Leonidas was a touch lost in the head. At least, until he remembered something Rilyn had said. That someone had, 'blessed another lake to shine like Sehero,' With that thought in mind, and Leonidas's own words about being, "versed with nature," he decided to use what he had come to call his "Druid Sight," despite Rilyn's displeasure at the name. Closing his eyes, he allowed himself to relax. To feel the pulse beneath the ground. When he had opened them… It was an amazing sight.

This… This is the Lake of Light… Even if we have no reason to be here… No reason to seek this place out… This sight alone was worth it…

The lake shone. It shone and danced with a soft, calming, *promising* light. Like a diamond glittering in the Sehero's light, but after Sehero had long retreated beneath the ground. The sight made Dane calm just by looking at it.

He hadn't felt like this in years, not since… But, either way, he loved it. He could see why a city had once been built here. Why it had been called Sanctuary. The lake seemed to promise protection. Safety. Peace.

"Thou seest it." Leonidas smiled. Dane could only bring himself to nod again, "That is why it is called *Arun Fril*. The Lake of Light. That is why."

"What?" Draco questioned, his words bearing the weight of his confusion.

"Thou shouldst not worry thyself over it," Leonidas smiled that same not-quite-a-smile-but-as-close-as-the-dracon-could-get expression from before, and gestured to the lake, "Come. Ye shall prove yourself upon the blessed shores."

"'Blessed shores.' Of course. Why would it be called anything else?" Draco's words were stained harsh by scorn and painted cruel with derision. Dane found himself stopping on the spot at the dragon's tone. A nudge from the larger black dragon behind him prompted the human to continue following Leonidas.

"Thou hast much hatred towards the blessed, dost thou not? Perhaps born of a wrong long past?"

Draco snorted, his eyes shadowed by wariness, "What I think of gods and their so-called blessings is none of your concern."

"So thou sayest. Know well that much that seemeth to be the concern of but one may truly be the concern of many," Leonidas's retort didn't have much time to sink in as the dracon's clawed foot-paws struck the lakeshore, "Asides, we have arrived. I am certain that thee hast noticed this, of course. It is time for our trial…" the dracon paused for a long moment, then made his slightly off-putting smile-like expression, "Fear not, it is quite simple. Touch the water."

"Touch the water," Draco repeated in disbelief. He stared at Leonidas, as though he expected the dracon to correct himself.

"Touch the water."

"That's it?"

"Aye."

Draco laughed, disdain soaking the sound, "Easy!" he sauntered up to the shore, pride apparent in even the slightest movement, and plunged his paw in the water, "That good enough?"

Leonidas studied Draco's paw as the dragon pulled it free of the lake, "Yes… Thou art well… Next?" Vreena glanced at Dane and offered a shrug before stepping forward. While nary a moment more of hesitation, she submerged her hand into the near crystal-clear water.

"Show thy hand," Vreena removed her hand from the lake and offered him her palm, which Leonidas studied for a moment, "Thou art well," He nodded to himself before he turned to Dane. The movement was somewhat slow, as though the dracon regretted the action, "Thy may now do so, also."

Dane drew near the water, then could help but hesitate, *A monster, like me, touching the Lake of Light? This can't go well… It can't…* Though his thoughts were undeniable, Dane ignored them and plunged his hand into the lake before his hesitation seemed too suspicious. He winced as his hand was immediately struck by a burning pain and tugged it free. A gasp escaped his lips as the spike of pain truly made itself known. It was like he had plunged his hand into a pot of boiling water. Without hesitating for a moment, he began to shake it rather violently, trying to get the water off. As quickly as he had begun, he stopped. He couldn't prevent himself from making a second gasp as his eyes widened.

A cloud of darkness swirled around his hand. Dane didn't even need his Druid Sight to see it. It snaked and coiled around the human with the wispy smoke of a dying fire. Ever so slowly, Dane looked at everyone, one hand clutching the other. His voice very faintly shook as he managed to say, "I know what you see, but-"

"It looks like you have been lying to me, Dane," Draco cut in, his voice a low, threatening rumble. Dane winced as he heard it. It was unlike any sound the golden dragon had yet made, "What are you?"

"I haven't lied to you at all, I promise. But please, listen-"

"I don't care about your excuses," Draco growled, the fury that had been hiding in his last sentence dancing into view now, "What. Are. You."

Dane winced again at those words. He had no choice now. He had to tell him. Still, he hesitated with answering the dragon, "What am I? I... Forgive me, if you can, but... I am a dire werewolf... I think..."

Dane's proclamation hung in the air. For just a few moments, nothing broke the silence that followed, saved for the lapping of the waves. Then, with a fury only barely held back by reasons unknown, Draco roared, "A WEREWOLF? You are a werewolf?! A murderous, unadulterated beast?! I should kill you now, beast!"

Dane's expression changed, becoming almost malleable as it shifted from fear and pain to anger, then sadness in a blink of an eye, "Yes, I am a werewolf. I am a monster... with no one. I had hoped... but no. You are like everyone else. Just like them..." Dane's hand swept to his sword. Draco's stance dropped, as though to pounce, but he didn't get the chance. Instead of drawing it, the human removed it from his belt, "Here, you need to find yourself a real hero, not a monster like me," with no care for ceremony, he flung *Verachodairgin* to the ground at Draco's paws.

Shaking his head, perhaps to hide the mask of sorrow that overtook his face, Dane turned his back to the dragon. However, he paused as Draco's voice seemed to shoot into his ear, "Where do you think you're going?"

Dane didn't turn around. He merely shook his head before replying, his voice drifting back at the dragon, "Away. Don't try to stop me."

Draco growled at Dane's back, one paw crashing forward in a thunderous pawfall, "And what, exactly, makes you think I would let a monstrosity like you just walk away?"

It was Dane's next response, blunt as an ironbound club, that brought even Draco to a halt, "Nothing. Because I am a monster… and the monster always dies," with that, Dane stepped forward, walking away from the stunned silence behind him. Vanishing amongst the ruins, no one saw the human look back.

Chapter 16

A Clash of Night and Shadow

"No."

"Draco, stop being stubborn! He's your friend!"

"He is not. He never was. I am not friends with murderous beasts," Draco glared at Vreena as he made quite clear his feelings on the matter about Dane.

"Who has he murdered? Dane hasn't hurt anyone that hasn't tried to kill him!" The half-elf snapped back.

"And why, then, does Dane claim that he has found his own way to deal with the pain of killing others? His way is that he revels in it. He has no regrets over it."

"Not true…" Leonidas strolled over. The dracon seemed to be almost unusually at ease with the situation, "Dane appeareth quite the opposite. He seemeth quite tormented. I would go as far to say that Dane feareth or, mayhaps, even hateth himself over it."

Draco fixed the ancient dracon with a withering glare that was promptly ignored, "Stay out of this. Dane isn't the person you've spent months with, only to find out he is what you hate most."

"Why do you hate werewolves? It's not like they're a threat to you. Not a major one, at least," Vreena demanded, her expression somewhere between anger and exasperation.

Draco glared at her. He was doing quite a lot of glaring, not that he minded. It did quite well with getting his point across, "You'll find your answer when your 'friend' is your murderer."

Vreena sighed as she looked over the dragon, "Dane is not a murderer. Not from what I've seen of him."

Draco scoffed, "What you've seen of him. And what you haven't seen of him?"

"If you're thinking of his wolf self, I have seen him in that form and talked to him in that form. He did not hurt me. He was afraid that he'd hurt me, but he did not. Moreover, he was of his own mind while within that form."

Draco paused for a few seconds, then shook his head and gave a growl, "Enough. I am not going to find Dane and that's final."

"You might have to," Argrex startled Draco and Vreena by speaking. Throughout the argument, it had become progressively clear that Argrex had not been interested in saying anything. Yet now he spoke, "Whether Dane is a murderous monster or a good-hearted person doesn't change the fact that we need to keep track of him. If he is a monster, then we can kill him and prevent him from hurting anyone. If he isn't, then it still doesn't hurt to know where he is. He could be a useful ally."

Leonidas nodded, his gaze turning to Draco and Vreena, "Argrex is right. We do not need another threat, but another set of hands, or paws, as it were, could be useful."

"Another threat?"

Argrex shook his head, "That is something we can explain once Dane has been dealt with," the black-scaled dragon's words were accompanied by Leonidas nodding in agreement.

Draco sighed, aggression firmly planted in the sound, "Fine. But he could be anywhere in these ruins. We should split up and look for him."

Leonidas studied the dragon for a moment before he stated, "Thou wishest to do so in order to kill him without interference."

Draco scowled, turning away from the dracon, "Say what you will, but we will never find him if we search as one big group," the dragon announced before he began to stalk off. Quite clearly from his bodily language, he had begun his search. Vreena watched him go with dismay.

"He's just going to kill Dane."

"Then we need to find Dane first," Leonidas replied.

"Agreed. Let's go! We have no time to lose."

ΩΩΩΩΩΩΩΩΩΩΩΩΩΩΩΩΩΩΩΩΩΩΩΩΩΩΩΩΩΩΩΩΩΩΩΩΩΩΩΩΩΩΩΩ ΩΩΩΩΩΩΩΩΩΩΩ

It had been several hours since Draco had last seen Dane. Several hours since he started this pointless search. Still there was no sign of Dane. With night fast approaching, Draco found himself growing ever more irritated.

"Trust the damned beast to make life harder for everyone," he muttered, then glanced up at the sky. His eyes narrowed and he found himself heaving a sigh, "The greater moon lies full. The werewolf will be loose," this perturbed him more than it should have. It must have been the feeling. That something was watching him. Something had to be. Yet, when he looked, he saw nothing.

Draco sighed again, shaking his head in a vain attempt to rid himself of the eerie sensation, "Fool. What made him think I would like to be friends with a *werewolf*?"

"Look, Brother," Draco froze as a voice sounded. The dragon released a low growl as he glanced over to see a pair of humans studying him, "Is that he?"

"It is."

Draco studied the pair of humans, *Where did they come from? No one was there a moment ago... Where are they from? Their manner of speech is peculiar, let alone their appearance. Black hair and ashen skin. Unusual for a human. And their bearing... Assured, yet cruel. Even so... they are blank-faced and hard-eyed... Hard-eyed with glowing red eyes. Just like that accursed dragon... Ha. They have drawn blades, too. Do they truly expect those to pierce a dragon's hide? They are overconfident fools... Though, I suppose it would do to learn who they are. Perhaps there are more like them. Grrr, brandying words with negligent fools I should be killing. Just like Seven... That beast.*

"Who are you?" Draco growled, shaking his head to turn his attention back to the topic at hand. He punctuated his question with a threatening glare.

"The Conflicted is absent. Will that be an issue?"

"This one believes not. The mission was him."

"I asked-" Draco started, only to be promptly cut off.

"These are aware of his question. These have chosen not to answer it."

"Indeed. It has no import to Truth."

Draco's glare grew sharper as he made a deep rumbling growl. These humans were proving to be so very irritating. So much so that he felt that he needed to show them why dragons were too often feared, "Perhaps I should enlighten you as to why you should have answered me."

One of the humans gave a sigh that sounded like an elder disappointed in a youngster, "Must he struggle? Do as these command, and he will have his life. He will know Truth."

"I'd eat my tail, first."

"Then these have no choice. Prepare for annihilation."

Before anyone could move, a growl broke the air and it wasn't Draco's. The rapid beating of something striking the ground erupted, attracting the attention of all three disputers. A fair distance to their left, a large wolf was charging across the empty ruins. The trio barely had a moment to acknowledge the creature's presence before it lunged forward, thoroughly placing itself between Draco and the strange humans. Its fur was rather normal for a wolf, a mixture of black, grey and white fur eventually fading to a white along the belly. Despite its quite normal fur colors, a glance told Draco that this beast was far too big for a regular wolf. It could only be a direwolf. Not that this knowledge pleased the dragon.

It also managed to fail to please the humans, "It is the Conflicted."

"Yes," one of the strange humans turned to address the direwolf, "Conflicted. Stand aside. This is not of his concern."

"Did they not include the Conflicted?"

"They did. But these are not to carry it out. These are here for him."

The direwolf gave another growl. It seemed distinctly uninterested in doing what the humans had said. In fact, the wolf's eyes seemed to sport a wild, barely restrained rage while its lips were pulled back, baring its fangs. Its pelt bristled, making it appear just a little larger, even despite the crouch it had put itself in. If Draco didn't already despise the fact that the creature was present, he might have been impressed. Though probably not.

"The Conflicted will not move. It assumed a threatening posture. These are not to cause it harm, truth?"

"Not truth. These are not to supply lethal force to the Conflicted."

"These may fight?"

"These may."

The direwolf took that phrase poorly. It lunged at the nearest human with an almost startling ferocity. It failed to land a blow as the two humans leapt back with near inhuman reactions.

"Conflict!"

"Battle ensues."

Eerily, the humans each attacked the direwolf at the same time, as though this was nothing more than a rehearsed script. One lunged forward in a stab while the other slashed. The wolf leapt back in turn, then lunged at the human who had slashed. Its teeth sank into the human's leg, but it quickly released the human to pull away, attempting to avoid the twin swords of its foes. The wolf yelped as one sword carved a long gash along its left flank, though it fortunately avoided the other strike.

"Pain shall not interfere."

"Cease aggression."

The wolf completely ignored them, charging forward, only to twist and dart past the humans. It spun and nipped at the backs of their legs. The first it missed, but on the second, its mark was too slow and the wolf's fangs caught flesh. The human it bit didn't howl in pain, but they did collapse. A hand swept to the back of the human's knee as the two humans paused.

"Brother, this one is crippled."

"Is his usefulness at an end?"

"Such is truth."

The uninjured human raised its blade, "His end is found," before anyone could move or even place what was going on, the blade fell. The injured human's head hit the ground first, followed moments later by the body.

Draco cursed. He was struggling to keep up with or even place what was happening. Also with finding an opening to scorch the humans with fire, though he blamed that on the direwolf. The wolf, meanwhile, needed no time for any of that as it took advantage of the moment to lunge at the remaining human. It proved to be ineffective as the human dodged. The human studied the wolf, leveling its sword at it.

"This one goes on. The mission must not fail."

The human lunged forward, sword arcing. The wolf twisted to avoid the blow and lunged forward to repeat how it had injured the other human. However, the human seemed to expect that and struck back. The wolf gave a yelp of pain as its foe's blade sank deep into its shoulder.

"The Conflicted is outmatched. Cease aggression," the human stated, withdrawing its blade. The wolf only growled again and lunged at its arm, fangs digging into the forearm of the human. Their hand spasmed, causing its blade to fall to the ground. The human stared at the wolf, its eyes wide.

"Truth is… bested… No…" it murmured, right before the direwolf released its bite and lunged again, this time going for the throat. The human didn't move to stop it. Neither did Draco, who found himself watching, his face expressionless, as the wolf's fangs struck with unerring accuracy. The human did not last much longer.

"Hmm… I wonder, what did they want with me?"

The direwolf seemed to study the fallen humans for a few moments, before turning and beginning to limp off into the ruins. Noting this, Draco began to follow the beast. He wasn't about to let his mysterious helper just wander off. Especially since it was a direwolf. As what could only be considered natural, the wolf immediately noticed him. However, it made no indication that it was interested in stopping him. It just kept moving, though it was slowed by its injury. Nonetheless, after a short trek, weaving through the crumbling, once grand buildings, the wolf vanished into one. Finding the gap big enough even for his frame, Draco followed.

The inside of the ruined building was quite big. Big enough that Draco could easily find a place to sleep if he wanted. The direwolf, meanwhile, had already picked a spot in a smallish nook and, after circling a few times, had curled up there. It watched Draco for several moments before laying its head down and seemingly going to sleep. Draco watched it as well.

"Why did you help me? What did you get out of it?" Draco mused to himself. The wolf shifted, and even opened its eyes for a moment, but gave no indication that it had understood Draco. The dragon eyed the wolf for a few moments more, then sighed, "Wolves… Why am I constantly plagued by wolves?"

Draco shook his head and just laid down where he was. It was comfortable enough. But even as he did so, he continued to watch the now sleeping direwolf, *It doesn't add up. It's a direwolf. What does it get from helping me, a dragon? And how the humans talked to it… They knew something about it. They called it, 'The Conflicted,' Why? Why is it conflicted and what do they want with it? … So many questions and no answers. Damn wolves…* Draco decided to put the thought to rest. At least, for the night. Mostly because even he needed to sleep. After all, the search for Dane would continue in the morning, *Besides, Dane in his werewolf form would no doubt be much more difficult… Yes, it would be easier to deal with him as a human.*

Chapter 17

The Monster's Plea

Dane frowned, gazing at the sleeping Draco. He had no idea what foolishness he was thinking, being here with the more than hostile dragon, yet here he was. With the dragon, *I must be exceedingly foolish…*

Sighing internally, so as to not wake Draco, of course, Dane crept around the dragon. No point staying if he was only going to cause problems. If he was only going to play the monster. At least, that was what Dane thought. However, the matter was decided for him when a golden tail slammed down in the way of his only path out. The sound of scraping announced the tail's owner moving, his scales dragging across the stony floor.

"So here you are, beast. Sneaking around instead of directly confronting me," Draco sounded derogatory and extremely aggressive, not at all interested in fixing a broken companionship. Not that Dane expected anything different, "Hardly the best way to dispose of old 'friends.'"

Dane sighed, shaking his head in a rather sorrowful manner, "I was hoping to avoid a confrontation like this."

Draco glanced around the ruined building, then returned his gaze to Dane. The draconic eyes were narrowed in suspicion and anger, "I see you've done away with the direwolf that helped me."

Dane nodded, "He's gone, yes. But only for now… Only for now."

"Where is he? What have you done to him? I have more to do with him."

"He is nearby, but I have done nothing to him. What you should ask is what he's done to me."

Draco growled. He brought a paw up, then sent it crashing down just before he spoke, "Speak clearly, beast. What have you done with the direwolf?"

"Nothing. That is my fate, unfortunately. To fight, but inevitably do nothing."

"I said, speak clearly."

"Stop this meandering conversation. What do you want of me, Draco?"

"You know exactly what I want. Your death, beast."

Dane gave a hollow smile, "My name is Dane, if you remember," the human's eyes were devoid of the mirth his empty smile tried in vain to convey.

"I could care less."

"So you could. But you don't."

Draco growled yet again, not at all interested in Dane's weak attempts at light-hearted antics, "You must want to die," Dane said nothing as the dragon continued, "If you want dying words, let them be clear and unmistakable. And actually pertain to your death."

"Fine. Finish me."

Draco paused, surprise seeming to emanate from him at the sudden phrase, "What?"

"Finish me. Kill me. End me. However you want to say it, just do it," Dane drew his sword, which Draco thought he recognized, from his belt. Draco growled, but that was all he had time to do before the sword clattered to the ground by his paws, "Once more, my blade lies at your paws. I am defenseless."

Draco eyed Dane, his wings rustling as he moved them in his new-found discomfort, "What are you trying to pull?"

"Nothing. Just kill me. End the misery and torment."

Draco scowled, "If you say so," rising to his feet, Draco lifted his head high. Then lashed out with a paw. To his surprise, he hit and sent Dane sprawling. Of course, he hadn't hit the warrior that hard, but he hadn't expected to hit him to begin with. Even so, Draco had avoided striking Dane with his claws. Though that was more on accident than actual purpose.

"Ow! If you're going to kill me, then do so. Don't maim me," Dane pushed himself to his feet.

"Silence," Draco growled and rose again to attack. But before he lunged down to end the defenseless warrior's life, he couldn't help but look at Dane again. Dane had not moved since standing. Not in the slightest, even though he knew Draco's intentions. He was gazing unflinchingly at the dragon. Draco found himself hesitating. It was unnerving and made him uncomfortable with the proceedings. He had made it clear that he was not above hurting Dane, yet Dane still stood there… Accepting? No… No, Dane's face was… It was a challenge. Draco didn't like it. But this was a werewolf. He had to die. Draco lunged forward.

And stopped. His fangs hung a few inches from Dane, but moved no closer. This felt wrong. He pulled back and asked, "Why are you just standing there?"

"Why do you think?" Dane asked, his voice neutral, though it did sound slightly weary, as though he was tired about something, "I'm waiting for you to make your move."

Draco growled and slammed his tail against the ground, "Fight back! Do something other than stand there and look pathetic!"

"I… am pathetic. I am a beast… No, I'm not even that. I am not human, nor am I a beast. I'm a person who can create and love, yet I am a creature of instinct devoid of the concepts. I am both, yet neither. I've taken the lives of innocents and have said nothing as to their fate. Why should I fight? I don't deserve the honor."

Draco growled, however, his growl seemed slightly uncertain. Ever so slightly weak. Though that might have just been Dane's imagination, "Fight back. If you are as you said, then something must be pushing for you to defend yourself. Even monsters fight. Don't just stand there…"

"Why? A monster like me doesn't deserve to fight. After all, in all the legends, it's the monster that always dies. Whether I fight or not, I die. So I will make it easy and just die."

Draco growled, but it sounded more like a whine this time. Not that the dragon noticed, "Just fight back already. You are about to die!" Draco paused, then heaved a heavy sigh, "I can't do it otherwise… It feels wrong… Like I'm not killing a monster… Like I'm doing nothing more than just murdering someone… I can't stand the thought… … Fight back," Draco finally begged.

Dane responded with a chuckle that was both rueful and forlorn, "Why? As I said, I don't deserve it. I'm nothing. I have been for 11 years. Innocent blood is on my hands- no… not hands… paws. Claws. It doesn't really matter, does it? I have killed innocent people. I… I have fed on them. I'm a monster. A murderous beast. A creature worth nothing but the retribution for the lives I've taken. I deserve death. You were right."

Draco still found himself hesitating. No, not hesitating. Frozen. He couldn't move, couldn't bring his own body to strike and end this pathetic human before him, *What am I doing? This is a werewolf, not a human. It… He does not deserve mercy. He deserves death, he's said so himself… Yet I can't do it*, the dragon sighed, his thoughts continuing to dance in his head as if to a confusing, broken tune, "What an… impasse is the word? Aye, an impasse… I can't bring myself to kill you because I… I just can't do it. Yet you will not fight back because you believe you do not deserve the honor… How pathetic…"

Dane sighed as well as he lowered himself to a seated position, "Indeed we are… If we are to remain in this impasse, should I tell you a story?"

"A story?"

"The truth of how I became the monster I am. Of the innocents I've slain… Of the blood on my… Whatever you wish to call them."

Draco studied Dane again. He seemed… sad. Regretful, even, "Very well… Perhaps you might just convince me to kill you yet… Beast…"

Dane shook his head, that same empty smile touching his lips again, "What a bargain. I'd better do my best, then,"

Draco didn't laugh, though it did please him that Dane sounded a little less depressed. He immediately began to regret it as it made him feel even more uneasy about killing Dane.

"My tale begins 11 years ago…"

ΩΩΩΩΩΩΩΩΩΩΩΩΩΩΩΩΩΩΩΩΩΩΩΩΩΩΩΩΩΩΩΩΩΩΩΩΩΩΩΩΩΩΩ
ΩΩΩΩΩΩΩΩΩΩ

"Leonidas!"

The ancient dracon turned to see the half-elf, Vreena, approaching. In her hands, she held the sheathed *Verachodairgin*. He nodded and raised a clawed hand to greet her, "Greetings, Vreena. Hast thou found Dane?"

"No, I was going to ask you the same."

Leonidas shook his head, his tail gently swaying from one side to the other, "I see. Perhaps Argrex has found him."

"Perhaps… What about Draco? Have you seen him?"

"Nay. Again, we will have to go see what Argrex has to say."

"Leonidas. Vreena. Come with me," Almost as though their speaking his name had called him, Argrex came gliding in, landing next to the pair with a rather heavy thump, "I found them."

"Them? As in, Dane and Draco together?" Vreena asked, her expression one of shock.

"Correct. And Dane is still alive."

"Where? We have to help him!"

"We will not. This is a delicate time," the black-scaled dragon replied, his voice sharp as a blade, "Intervention would be dangerous."

Vreena frowned, confusion painting itself across her face, "What do you mean?"

"They are talking. If we intervene, we may well get Dane killed. I will show you where they are, but we listen without acting unless it is certain that Dane will die otherwise."

Leonidas nodded at this. Vreena sighed, but nevertheless gave her reply, "Fine. Show us where Dane and Draco are."

"Vow to do as I say."

Vreena huffed, "You don't trust me?"

"No."

Leonidas chuckled at the dragon's response, "There is a reason he has lived long enough to hold the title of 'The Elder Watcher.'"

Vreena sighed again, then gave Argrex a displeased look, "I vow to not intervene with Draco and Dane unless it becomes clear that Dane may die."

Argrex nodded. Whether or not Vreena's vow pleased him was impossible to tell. He looked as expressive as a stone wall, "Good. This way."

The pair followed Argrex as he began to weave his way through the ruins. As they walked, the stone crunching underfoot, Vreena began to notice a few things about the ruins around her. A few buildings seemed mostly intact, but the majority seemed as if they'd merely fallen apart due to age. But not all. Many of the buildings looked almost like they'd been destroyed by something.

It also didn't escape the half-elf that the buildings, despite their similar styles, bore noticeable architectural differences that led her to believe that they were built at different times. Not unlike some human buildings, "Leonidas, you said you were once a king of Sanctuary?"

"Not a king. The king. There has been one king of Sanctuary, and that was I."

Vreena paused, noting this, then began to gesture at the ruins about her, "Then you know why these buildings look a little different. See that building? It looks similar to this one here, but that one must have been built some time after this one. It looks older."

Leonidas gave a slow nod as he approached the wall of the second building Vreena had indicated and ran a clawed hand along it. His scaly, draconic face displayed little emotion, but, with how his scales pressed against each other and his eye ridges' positions, the dracon appeared sad. He heaves a gentle sigh before answering the half-elf's query.

"It was… Thou hadst no knowledge of this, but the second building thou speaketh of was built long ago, during the first Sanctuary… the first building was built during the third, and last, Sanctuary."

"There were three Sanctuaries?"

"Indeed… Each was built upon this land… Each was built for the same purpose… Each was attacked and destroyed… Each had a dracon, mine own self, upon its 'throne…' And it was each time, I was spared… Whether I wished it or not…"

"That sounds horrible."

"Aye, it was."

"Hush! We are here," Argrex broke in, then swung his head to roughly point towards a building missing most of a roof, "They are in there. Approach with caution and listen."

Vreena gave a subtle nod and crept forward, taking care to avoid causing the ground to crunch beneath her feet. This proved to be effective, as her footsteps were near silent compared to either Leonidas's or Argrex's. As they drew near to the building, they began to hear voices that unmistakably belonged to Draco and Dane.

"Indeed we are… If we are to remain in this impasse, should I tell you a story?"

"A story?"

"The truth of how I became the monster I am. Of the innocents I've slain… Of the blood on my… Whatever you wish to call them."

"Very well… Perhaps you might just convince me to kill you yet… Beast…"

"What a bargain. I'd better do my best, then… My tale begins 11 years ago…"

Chapter 18
Birth of Darkness: Draconic Summons

Dane swung his wooden sword, only for a blade of wood to intercept in a resounding clack. He quickly swung again, only to stop in a feint and slash somewhere else. It's only achievement was another blocked blow and another clack.

"Come now, Dane. You must be faster and make it more difficult to tell what you are doing!" His father, Sir Firrik, chided the young swordsman-in-training. Firrik's iron-gray gaze sat piercingly below his heavy brow and dark locks of hair. The man towered above Dane, his muscled form seeming to reach far into the sky. With the man presently lacking a shirt, Dane was able to see a number of scars that traced along his father's torso and arms.

Firrik casually swung his practice blade back and forth as he continued speaking, drawing Dane's attention to the lesson again, "Try again. As I said earlier, we will not stop unless you mark me or I say otherwise."

"Yes, sir!" Dane replied. Remembering previous lessons, he lunged forward into a quick stab. When his father inevitably parried, Dane leapt back, then dashed forward, swinging his wooden blade low. With his father being much taller than himself, attacking low would inevitably be an advantage. Except that his father was expecting it and knocked aside the attempted attack, leaving Dane wide open for Firrik to deliver a swift smack.

"Predictions are necessary in battle, but act on them with caution. Some predictions will be false. Others will be true, but your opponent will know of them and know how to counter them. Always be ready to act in the event that something goes wrong. Never allow yourself to become complacent in perceived victory. Now, try again."

Dane took his place as his father stood there, sword at his side, rather than raised. The experienced knight watched his son for a moment, then raised an eyebrow.

"Sword arm up. Remember, always be ready to block or parry an enemy attack," Firrik chided. Dane winced as he realized that his own sword was at his side. He quickly raised his sword to position it in a defensive diagonal across his body, "Good. Now, have at it. Try to hit me."

Dane frowned, his brow furrowing in concentration. He and his father had been going at this for nearly 15 minutes. There was something he was missing. There had to be. He swung at his father, only for his father to block the strike, just like before. Except that, finally, Dane believed that he saw what his father wanted him to see. His father had blocked again. He was not dodging. Come to think of it, Dane was certain he hadn't moved at all. While blocking was useful in combat, so, too, was dodging and moving in general. In fact, if his father was not going to move, then Dane could see a way he could try to hit his father. Sure, it would be a risk, but a risk he had to take if he was finally going to catch his father off guard.

The young warrior made to strike again, then, just as he was about to swing, dived to the side. Dane had intended to roll and come up swinging, but the nine-year-old had no experience with this particular maneuver. So, naturally, he messed it up and made a fool of himself.

When Dane dived, instead of rolling, he fell and hit the ground. Realizing his mistake, he scrambled to rise to his knees as Firrik turned. Hoping it might help, Dane made a wild slash as he rose. He held no hope that such a desperate attempt would even come close to succeeding. Then there was a thwack and everything seemed to go still. Dane froze in disbelief, blade still outstretched. He wasn't looking, not yet, but… a wooden sword on a wooden sword wouldn't have made the sound he had heard. He was sure of it.

His head moving at a speed that would have made cattle scoff, Dane slowly looked over to see his sword touching his father's leg. Firrik was studying him, seemingly unaffected by a wooden sword to the shin.

"Sloppy. Very sloppy. But a good plan. A little harder and you might have hurt me, even momentarily disabled me. But you did mark me, as requested. Well done," Dane felt a rush of pride at the praise. He had done it! "We will have to do this more, so as to ensure you learn to see an enemy's weakness and swiftly devise a method to take advantage of it. Just remember, never stand still in a fight, like I just did. You will *always* be defeated by any competent opponent if you do. Further, be wary of such reckless actions. Had this been a proper battle, I would have taken your life right there. Understood?"

"Yes, sir!"

"Now, let's work on your defense… After we see what Gil over there has to tell me," Firrik said, his gaze turning to view the man in question as he approached the pair.

Gil was a sandy-haired, blue-eyed human with a lithe runner's body. As he was commonly called the Swift, he was, of course, a fleet-footed runner and made for an excellent messenger. When he had to, he also excelled as a scout. Seeing the runner present did not particularly surprise Firrik, though it was easy to guess why he was here. There was presently little need for a scout and Gil the Swift was the Royal Messenger. He was no doubt delivering a message for the king. Of course, there were few people in Verious that were likely to receive a message from the king himself. In fact, Firrik could only think of one such person. Himself.

"Sir Firrik!"

"Well, if it isn't the royal messenger! Slippery Gil, how are you?"

Gil seemed out of breath, but that certainly didn't stop him from delivering his message. Never seemed to, "King Aridor has requested your immediate presence in Fainendor Castle," If this was a battlefield, Firrik would have been on alert immediately. It was unusual for the king to request an immediate audience. Even more so if it was important enough that Gil didn't react to his old nickname. Gil had never liked that nickname.

"Hmm, did he say anything else?"

"Only to bring your son, Dane."

Firrik frowned in thought, mystified at the request. The king knew of Dane, of course, but what could possibly be important enough to demand the presence of a nine-year-old boy immediately? "Bring Dane? But why, I wonder…"

"I have no idea, but you might want to hurry it along. The king seemed very anxious when he told me the message."

"Was he? When His Majesty becomes anxious, something is inevitably wrong. Potentially of his own doing… Very well. I'll get going. You should rest before you head out again, Gil."

"Can't. Said he wanted to know your response as soon as he could."

Firrik scowled, worry now taking over his features, "He knows what my answer is. If he needs reassurance on something he knows… Hmm, in any case, tell me that you at least rode a horse here."

"No."

"Of course not," Firrik sighed, shaking his head, "Still don't trust a horse since you slid off one's back."

"It threw me off!"

"It didn't move," Firrik replied with a faint smile, then glanced over at Dane, "Dane, go get the horses ready. We are going to Fainendor Castle. As for you, Gil, you had better get moving, especially since you aren't going to let yourself be bothered by resting. Besides, I'll end up beating you there if you don't get a head start."

"Because you're riding horses. You know you can't win in a footrace."

"I know I can't. You've proven that to me more than enough times. Now, get moving. You have a league to run."

ΩΩΩΩΩΩΩΩΩΩΩΩΩΩΩΩΩΩΩΩΩΩΩΩΩΩΩΩΩΩΩΩΩΩΩΩΩΩΩΩΩΩΩΩ ΩΩΩΩΩΩΩΩΩΩ

Firrik, with Dane by his side, strided into the throne room of Fainendor Castle. The ride here had been uneventful. Not that it was supposed to be, it *was* only a league, after all. Even so, Firrik found himself to be marginally surprised to discover that Gil had indeed beaten them to the castle. And they had only given him a quarter hour of a head start.

Said head start would have been shorter, but Firrik had decided that Dane should try to saddle the horses himself. As the knight had expected, Dane managed his own horse easily enough, but had difficulty getting Firrik's horse to listen. Eventually, before they wasted too much time, Firrik was forced to intervene when the horse foiled Dane for the third time.

As Firrik approached the throne, he was greeted by the man sitting upon it. King Aridor. The king did not appear especially muscular, but he wasn't lanky, either. In all truthfulness, he was well-balanced, if on the shorter side. Above his brown hair sat a glittering crown. It was rather simple, an engraved band of gold with only three gemstones, a diamond flanked by two rubies, that sat above the king's eyes. Beneath the golden shine lay his ever-so-slightly angular face. It bore a stern expression that, normally, would have been nearly ruined by the kind twinkle in his grey eyes. But that twinkle was nowhere to be seen at the present…

"Firrik."

"Your Majesty," Firrik knelt at the foot of the throne, a gesture swiftly replicated by Dane.

"Rise, Firrik. I have much to discuss," Firrik nodded and rose, his expression reserved and ever so slightly grim, "Firrik, you were the one I sent to Adrian."

"That I was."

"According to your own words, you did not see a dragon while there."

"I did not. There were scales and one or two claws, but no dragons as a whole."

Aridor tapped the armrest of his throne with a scarred finger. The finger scarred by the very man before him, "Still, of my knights, you have the most experience with the creatures."

"If you say so, your Majesty."

Aridor gave a weary smile at the knight's response, "Enough with the formalities, Firrik. We've known each other long enough. We are alone, save for your son. Speak to me as the friend and brother-in-arms you are."

Firrik inclined his head for a moment, then offered a nod, "Very well. In my honest opinion, I have little to no experience with them. No more than any other knight would."

"I would disagree, but fair enough. Even so, I have to send someone…" Aridor sighed.

"Send someone?"

"Yes. I have received a report that the citizenry of Diadal has spotted a dragon."

"Hmm… I would not expect a dragon to be so bold. To show itself and refrain from laying assault to the village," Firrik commented.

"Neither would I. I was told that this dragon has black scales and seems to be frequenting the lands north of the village."

"That's mostly forest for leagues, until it opens up to hills, then the Sidatial Mountains."

Aridor nodded, the crown upon his head glittering as it moved, "Indeed. The dragon was last seen heading towards the Sidatial Mountains."

"You want me to go after it."

"I want you to investigate the threat. I do not wish for a scorched corpse. Or corpses, I should say."

Firrik considered the order for a moment, then turned a knowing gaze to the king, "Very well. But why is it that you requested Dane be present today? You surely do not mean that he comes along?"

"I mean that exactly."

Firrik nodded. His head was slow to move, akin to a man deep in thought, "Forgive me, your Majesty, but I must disagree. Dane is not ready for any such mission. He is not properly trained. Not yet."

Aridor was ready with a reply of his own, "He would not be alone. Such would be foolish of me. I am also sending my son, Prince Jairend, with you."

"Not only my son, but the Prince of the Crown? Aridor, you risk much with this venture. You yourself have already told me of the dragon. Our sons would be mercilessly slaughtered by such a beast. Precious few are those who could challenge it and survive."

"I have told you of a report based on claims. None of the soldiers I sent to guard the village have seen the beast. It might not exist at all. Moreover, I'm not asking you to deal with it. I wish for you to merely investigate the claims. In either case, it will do Jairend and Dane good to learn from each other. Was that not so for us?"

Firrik nodded reluctantly, "You speak truly… Still, it does not sit well with me. Do not forget how near we both came to death when we were young."

"Fear not, Firrik. I will never forget. I still bear the scars," the king held forth his hand, displaying the scarred fingers, "Yes, I remember quite well. But surely they would be safe together, surrounded by forty soldiers, a fair number also being knights. And I am sure you would take all due precautions. Am I not right, my friend?"

Firrik sighed, his next words an agreement. However, his tone made clear that it was only so because of the sensibility of the king's words. And, perhaps more importantly, who Aridor was, "I suppose you are right. Very well. We will march as soon as the men have gathered."

"Good. Before you go, I wish to speak with you, Dane."

Dane jumped at being addressed. He had been kneeling this whole time and began to believe that he would be until he and his father left, "Yes, your Majesty?"

"Are you still kneeling? Well, I suppose I did only specify your father… Rise, Dane," Dane rose as he was commanded, "Dane, I know well that you heard everything we talked about. Do you have a blade?"

"Not a proper one, your Majesty."

"No need to add 'Your Majesty,' to everything. Your father must have taught you that… Is that not so, Firrik?" the king did not wait for a response. He did not need one, " Hmm… I see that you are using the sword I had made for you, my friend. What of the one you had?"

Firrik allowed a hand to drift down and rest upon the weapon's pummel, "I believe that one is in your armory. A gift for a gift, however poor in comparison."

"Ah, yes. Dane," the king addressed the young warrior, "Before you and your father leave here, you are to meet my son, Jairend. He will doubtless know where to find the sword… and I believe it will do you both well to meet. That is all. You may leave."

Chapter 19

Birth of Darkness: The Wolf's Night

"Hmm, a knight, huh? I still like being a prince," a rather young boy with brown hair and a circlet made of silver replied to Dane's question, "Who would want to give up something like being Prince of the Crown?"

Dane shrugged, "I guess you have a point, but, if you were a knight, your subjects would grow to respect you more. They would become loyal not just because you are their prince and eventual king, but because you are a strong knight who cares for and protects his people. Who fought for them. They would come to care for you as much as you them."

The prince gave a rather elegant wave of his hand, though it was accompanied by a faint grin, "I know. You're right… and I know my father did that, alongside yours, when he was a prince… I'll have to think about it…"

Dane chuckled, "Fine with me. But, while we're waiting for Father to gather the men, would you like to spar?"

The young prince shook his head, "No, thank you. Right now, I'm just fine waiting and talking. Some days, it feels like I get no rest from my studies, so I'd rather enjoy this while I can."

Dane nodded, a grin of his own appearing on his face, "Father makes it feel about the same. Some days, when he had nothing in particular to do and after we're done, I can't wait to just go to bed… Not that I actually remember getting to the bed."

"You and I are alike in that… Dane? A question."

"What is it?"

"How do you know what would make me a better prince and king? Usually, such knowledge is privy only to the king himself."

"I wouldn't say that, but the answer is my father. He is King Aridor's closest friend, after all."

The boy shrugged, but offered Dane a nod, "You do have a point… Again… I'm going to have to think harder around you, aren't I?"

Dane shrugged as well, chuckling again, "Maybe. Father is always pushing me to be the best I can. Sometimes, I can't help but wonder if he's trying to make me like him."

The prince gave a chuckle and shook his head, his circlet glittered in the light, "Okay, my father isn't that harsh on me. You win."

"I win? What, exactly?"

"Hmm, I don't know. The harshest father?"

Dane laughed, shaking his head, "Thanks, I guess."

"You are most welcome," the boy grinned and joined Dane in laughing.

At that moment, drawn by the minor commotion, Firrik turned a nearby corner and began to approach the pair, "Jairend. Dane. There you two are. The men are assembled. You are aware of what is expected of you?"

The two nodded, though Jairend spoke, "We are to follow your orders and must stick together in the unlikely chance that we leave the rest of the soldiers. While we are off, I am to be no one more important than a knight's squire, with as much rank and privilege. Unless otherwise necessary. And my name is Jeff."

Firrik glanced at the prince, but gave an affirming nod, "Exactly. Keep that in mind. Now, come with me. We are setting out. We will march to Diadal, assess the situation, then continue north until we reach the Sidatial

Mountains. Unless we find proof of the dragon, in which case, we turn back and deliver our report to King Aridor. Do you both understand?"

Jairend nodded in agreement, while Dane responded by pounding a fist against his chest and announcing, "Yes, sir!" When he got nothing else, Firrik looked back to Jairend.

"Jeff?"

"Yes, sir."

"Good."

ΩΩΩΩΩΩΩΩΩΩΩΩΩΩΩΩΩΩΩΩΩΩΩΩΩΩΩΩΩΩΩΩΩΩΩΩΩΩΩΩΩΩΩΩΩΩΩΩ ΩΩΩΩΩΩΩΩΩ

While Firrik had said march, the journey to Diadal was a ride. Still, even with horses, it was lengthy and tiring, especially since Firrik had the group ride for long periods of time. He did make allowances for the two younger members, but otherwise, they rode.

When the forest-encircled village of Diadal finally began to draw near, the group was greeted to the sight of a kindly-looking old man waiting at the village's edge. He smiled beneath his long, grey beard and managed to wave the knights over quite well, in spite of his bent and tired shoulders, "Greetings, good knights! You come from King Aridor?"

Firrik, who rode at the front of the group, naturally spoke for them, "We are. I am Sir Firrik of Verious. We were told that a dragon had been sighted nearby."

The old man bobbed his head, "Indeed, good sir. The dragon was seen north of town. It flew around for a bit, then continued farther north still. We don't know where it went after that."

Firrik raised an eyebrow, then turned his gaze to the north. The raised eyebrow sank into a shallow scowl as the knight drifted into thought, "Hmm… Likely towards the Sidatial Mountains. Just as his Majesty was reported… Hmm… What is your name?

"Rayn, sir."

"Rayn. It has grown late. We will remain outside the village and leave come dawn. We will not require anything from the village. I thank you for your assistance."

"No, my lord. It is I who should thank you!"

Firrik nodded his acknowledgement, then turned to his men, "Alright. Set up camp over there, beyond the fields. I want men patrolling at all times, we will be next to a forest and I do not want a midnight slaughter."

"Yes, sir!" came the response as the men began to set about their work. As they did, Dane urged his horse over to his father, prompting the man to frown.

"What are you doing, Dane?"

"I want to take part in patrolling the camp."

Firrik seemed to think for a few moments, then nodded in agreement, "Yes… And Jeff shall as well… However! You will be following one of the other men. You are not at a point where it is safe for you to be alone patrolling."

"I am fine with that."

"Good. Now, come along. We must help set up camp."

"Yes, sir!"

ΩΩΩΩΩΩΩΩΩΩΩΩΩΩΩΩΩΩΩΩΩΩΩΩΩΩΩΩΩΩΩΩΩΩΩΩΩΩΩΩΩΩ ΩΩΩΩΩΩΩΩΩΩ

Dane swung his gaze about the darkened landscape. His nighttime patrol was, as per his father's orders, accompanied by Sir Aaron of Skyrock, a rather jovial, thin man with a long and well cared for black mustache that framed his mouth. As a matter of course, the young warrior began to learn about his new companion. Amongst other bits of tidbits, Aaron had a fondness for water. No doubt due to living in the coastal Skyrock. The man even carried a small, sealed jar containing sea water from the Boundless Sea. Aaron, as it turned out, rarely got a chance to return to a remote town like Skyrock, so he'd turn to the water jar whenever he felt homesick.

As it happened, Aaron was carrying the jar at that moment while the two made their rounds. He was studying the jar as he talked to Dane, who was both listening to the knight and continuing his vigil over his surroundings, "A few days before the harvest festival, every man with a boat goes out to collect fish. Then we bring them back, prepare them, and have a feast. Whatever isn't prepared for the feast is spread amongst the townsfolk."

"That sounds good," Dane found himself replying in a somewhat wistful tone. He couldn't think of a time that he'd been to such an event.

"It's more than good. The festival is a symbol of perseverance, community, and hope! In no small way, it holds the town together. What with the different races living there. Only place in Havmare where wolfear and humans live so close to each other in something like harmony, you know."

Dane nodded. As he acknowledged this, another guard began to approach, on a route that crossed with Aaron and Dane's. The newly-arriving and slightly underweight guard raised a hand in greeting.

"Aaron. Dane. How was your patrol?"

Aaron raised a hand, returning the greeting, "Ours was fine. How about yours, Frein?"

"Nothing of note. Aside from a squirrel," he glanced at Aaron's hands and chuckled, "You've got your jar again."

"Yes, I do."

Frein shook his head, a smile creeping across his face, "You and that jar. You take that thing everywhere."

"You know why."

"Of course, still-"

Before Frein could finish his sentence, growling and snarling began to erupt from the nearby woods. Frein and Aaron didn't seem to be slightly startled, instead immediately drawing their blades and moving towards the source of the sound. While doing this, Aaron still found the time to slip his jar onto his belt and raise the shield strapped to his arm. Dane imitated them, drawing his blade while slowly following along behind.

The forest, rather pleasant in the light of day, took a much darker, more evil atmosphere in the dead of night. Trees seemed as though they were reaching out, looking to tear skin from bones. Or, perhaps, reaching out in desperation as the darkness consumed them. Dane found himself set on edge. These woods had seemed so hospitable before, but now… The change was jarring.

Much to the relief of all three, they soon made their way into a clearing. Their relief faded rapidly when they just as swiftly discovered that they weren't alone in the clearing. The clearing happened to be the location of the sources of the sounds. And they definitely did *not* seem nice.

Battling it out in the middle of the clearing were two wolves. One was much bigger than the other, but both seemed bent on tearing the other apart. They fought with a savage ferocity, clawing and biting, ripping and tearing. They may have well been all over the clearing, such was the two wolves' ferocity. Blood was splattered throughout the clearing, giving everything a wet, macabre shine. Neither beast seemed to care in the slightest.

Aaron's eyes widened in shock, then morphed into fear, "By all the gods! A wolf and direwolf! We have to alert the camp," Aaron was whispering, his voice as rushed as it could be. Dane and Frein could only offer nods in response. Aaron's caution was in vain, however. Easily hearing Aaron's desperate whisperings, both wolves spun to look at the new arrivals, their feud seemingly forgotten.

Frein took a step back and hefted his blade "Aaron… Have you fought a wolf before?"

"Never."

"You're about to learn," Frein murmured, staring at the two wolves who stalked steadily closer. The direwolf was slowly beginning to circle Aaron, while Frein stood across from the smaller, normal wolf. Dane stood behind the others, watching in shock. While he still held his blade, it was with an uncertain and very loose grip.

Frein spoke softly, eyes never leaving the beast before him, "Dane, run. Go, get help now before-," whatever else he had wanted to say all of a sudden no longer mattered as the wolf charged at him. Frein darted to the side. He seemed wary of the wolves and was seeking to keep it from getting behind him. As the wolf got too close, the knight swung at the beast, momentarily driving it back. The wolf, not giving him a chance to breathe, darted to the side and slightly forward in an attempt to get at the knight's booted legs. Just to Frein's right, Aaron had his shield raised, attempting to use it to protect him from the direwolf's attack. When the creature's circling carried it too close, he jabbed his blade forward. The strike was resoundingly ineffective as the direwolf dodged easily. Just as swiftly as it had dodged, the beast slammed into Aaron's shield, knocking him over. With the direwolf now on top of his shield, the knight found himself firmly pinned. Beneath the shield and the beast's weight, his sword was equally pinned. Unfortunately, this meant that there was nothing he could do to stop the direwolf's next, ultimately fatal move. The lunge for the throat.

Dane's breath caught and his eyes widened in shock at the sight. Aaron was lying there. Not moving with blood welling up from his throat. The knight's water jar had been smashed, the seawater mixing with the blood beginning to soak the ground around him. But Dane didn't have the time to pay any more attention, nor even acknowledge that Aaron was truly dead. The direwolf was now focusing on him. And he was far less skilled than Aaron.

The direwolf, muzzle now painted red, charged at him. It must have evaluated him as of little threat, for it lunged, going straight for the throat. Dane swung his blade, panic spurring his strike. As it was, that very panic drove the swing far from its mark, missing the beast. The attack did, however, put his arm up just as the direwolf reached him. Dane fell back and cried out as its fangs sank into his arm, his hand releasing his sword. However, even as before he and his blade struck the ground, Dane's left hand was scrabbling for his lost weapon.

Perhaps fortune smiled upon him, for his hand seized his fallen sword. Newly armed, Dane swung the blade, desperation giving it strength. Luck once again saw him through as the poor slash became an accidental stab that pierced the direwolf's eye. The beast collapsed almost instantly, its weight dragging the young boy's arm down. Still caught fully in the throes of panic, Dane dropped his sword again and grabbed the head of the dead direwolf, trying to pull its fangs free. But, with only one hand, he found his struggles to be in vain. To make an already horrible situation worse, the wolf that had been attacking Frein suddenly spun and rocketed towards the bleeding and downed boy.

With the corpse latched onto his arm, Dane couldn't get up. His only option was to kick at the approaching wolf and hope he hit it on the nose. The wolf could have seen the kick coming from a mile away and dodged with almost pathetic ease. Dane barely had a chance to acknowledge the wolf's action as it lunged, mouth gaping. There was nothing Dane could do as the beast's fang dug into his left thigh. Dane cried out again and, managing to seize his fallen blade, wildly lashed out with his sword. It failed to find its mark as the wolf released him and darted back to avoid what could have been something of a painful blow. It snarled and prepared to lunge at Dane again, this time trying to finish Dane off.

Just as it was about to leap, the wolf gave a strangled yelp and collapsed. Or would have, for it was held in a vaguely standing posture by a sword that had run it through. Frein grunted as he tugged his blade free from the beast's back. He seemed tired and just a little bit worn, but unharmed. He staggered over and, with the help of Dane's good hand, pried the fallen direwolf's fangs free, "We need to get to camp. Let Firrik know what happened."

"Frein? Aaron? Dane?" Frein and Dane looked over as Firrik pushed into the clearing. His eyes alighted on the dead wolves, Aaron, and the injured Dane, "Frein, what happened here?"

"Sir? Why are you here?"

"You three failed to cross paths with Semyer and Hast. They alerted me. It wasn't difficult to guess where you'd be, especially with the sounds of snarling and panicked yells to guide me. Now, what happened here?"

"We also heard snarling and went to check it out. A wolf and direwolf were trying to kill each other, then they turned on us. Aaron was killed quite swiftly and Dane got bit by both. Thigh and arm."

Firrik knelt next to Dane, his face etched with worry, "I see. Help me get Dane back to camp so Aversa can look at those bites. Hast should be waiting just upon the edge of the forest. We'll have him come here to watch over Aaron until we get back."

"Yes, sir."

Chapter 20

Curse of the Wolf

"We went back to the camp and Aversa took a look, bound my wounds, then said that, barring magic, I wouldn't be healed enough to continue. So Father sent me, Sir Frein, and Prince Jairend back with a message for the king."

Draco studied Dane, his ever expressionless face set to being firmly impassive, "And how does that explain anything?"

"I'm not finished. For a while, nothing of particular note happened. Father returned without discovering a dragon or any trace of a dragon. I recovered from my injuries. He went back to training me. Everything was fine. Then about… three weeks, maybe? Three weeks after the event, something happened. I went to bed and had a strange dream, one where I rapidly started craving meat and hunting and companionship. Next thing I knew, I woke up as a direwolf. At the time, I had no idea what had happened, but I didn't want Father to see me and I… well… I was a little hungry. So, I managed to slip out of the house and fled to the nearby forest, where I went hunting. It was… unfamiliar, yet strangely enjoyable. And… And natural. After a while, I managed to get back home and into my room. It wasn't long before sunrise, yet, all of a sudden, I felt very tired. I went to sleep, and woke up, at sunrise, my normal self. This happened again the next night, and the next, and continued for about a month. Around that time, my scar began to glow a color like an amber stone. Just like the eyes I bear when I walk as a wolf. It's usually not easy to notice in the daylight. I was able to conceal it for a month…"

"Then Firrik found out," Draco stated, guessing at what seemed obvious to him.

Dane heaved a sigh, then offered a nod, "Father found out. He wanted to start waking me early, to get me used to it. A knight should be prepared to be called upon at any hour, after all. But he came in before sunrise, before I fell asleep. He found me, as a direwolf, and believed that I, the wolf, had done something to me, Dane. So he started to attack me- he had a wooden training sword, no doubt if I failed to rise. Even so, I refused to bite at him. I wanted to. I really wanted to. Well, *I* didn't, but another part of me did. A bestial, wolf will that fought to take over, to control me and act as a wolf should. I was able to stop it and Father eventually realized that I wasn't attacking. I was able to stall him until sunrise, when I changed back to my normal self. Mind you, I prefer to change while asleep, it is incredibly painful when I'm awake. Yet painless while asleep... Anyways, after he realized what had happened, Father... Father didn't do as I had thought he would. He began helping me figure out what I was, if I could free myself- which we found to be not possible- and help me tolerate it... I'd thought he would have ran me off or tried to kill me."

"So that's it?" Draco finished, only to receive a firm shake of the head from Dane.

"No. About half a year later, I was in distress. The source was a rather mean boy known as Eric who loved to make himself seem like the best. Naturally, he proved that by harassing me, the son of the only knight in Verious. I probably could have stopped him, before my... You know what I mean. Afterward, I didn't want to risk the wolf somehow showing itself. This time, however, Eric went too far. He'd attacked me and chased me into the forest. I tried to fight back, but I didn't want to push it. Didn't want to risk it. I'd... Father and I had found out that I had to be careful when I transformed and attacked him while sparring. Father stopped me before I caused a problem then, but… But Eric wouldn't stop. And I felt it. The beast, wanting to take over. To fight back. Anger. Fear. Hatred. I struggled against it, but there was naught I could do, not with Eric refusing to back down, despite my warnings. I… I changed, there and then, and… And… And attacked. Tore Eric apart. There was nothing I could do. The wave of emotions empowered it and I had lost all chance of regaining control. It was by fortune alone that I didn't end up in Verious like that. I regained myself and, after a while, returned to my true self. I went to Father, told him what had happened… Since then, I've worked to master my emotions and will, to keep the beast in check… … There… That's it… The tale of a murderous monster."

Draco watched Dane, who seemed noticeably unwilling to look at the dragon. He seemed nervous and ashamed. For the first time in his relatively short life, Draco found himself feeling actual pity for another creature. The human was just so pathetic, "Dane. You told me your tale. Shall I tell you mine? Why I hate werewolves as I do."

Dane nodded, but didn't speak. Draco sighed as he walked the painful road of memories, "It would have been… eight and twenty years ago that it happened. I was traveling with a… a fellow traveler, an elf named Recere, looking for another traveling companion of our, this being a human called Seven. I never learned his real name, we just called him Seven because he was the seventh of his siblings."

"A seventh son," Dane guessed, still not looking at the dragon.

"You are correct… We were looking for him, to little success. We had been about to give up, then he just walked out of the forest. He was a little tired and beat up, but perfectly fine. Much like you, nothing happened for a while. We traveled and did what we normally did. Then, about a month later, Seven began getting anxious. He kept trying to get away, but we wouldn't let him. He kept trying to convince us to let him go do something or other for about a week. We wouldn't listen. He seemed too suspicious. Much like you. We told him it was safer for him to not wander off again. Then it happened. One night, the greater moon, which you know as Ephala, rose full in the sky. Seven changed before our eyes, going from the 'friendly' human we knew to a bloodthirsty monstrous beast, a wolf mockingly shaped like a man. With no warning, he attacked. Recere stood no chance. I was able to fight Seven off, but I don't believe I killed him... Not that I didn't try... But Recere... There was nothing I could do. He died there. By his own accursed friend's hand. I was angry. I hated that Seven never told us. That he killed Recere. I took what remained of Recere back to his people and vowed that I would never let that happen again. Since that day, I've been the dragon I am. And I've hated werewolves."

Dane winced, yet still managed to say, "I had no idea. I'm sorry... Though I now understand your hatred of me."

"... Perhaps I was a little harsh on you. After all, you didn't kill Recere... I... I might have been wrong about you, actually..."

Dane shook his head, "I would deserve it. I'm all but a murderer."

Draco sighed, "No... you're not. Maybe not safe or... pure, I suppose. Not that, but not a murderer or as monstrous as I'd said. Vreena told me as much, yet I refused to listen..."

"As a dragon does, I suppose."

Draco chuckled, his tail tip drifting from side to side in a rather pleasant manner, "Aye, as we do. I've been told I am arrogant, but now I see why."

"Took you long enough."

"Don't start. I only just changed my mind about you, don't make me change it back... But that direwolf... That was you, wasn't it?"

"Of course it was. I'm surprised you didn't realize that immediately," Dane replied, one eyebrow rising slightly at the dragon's question.

"Enough of that! I'd never seen your wolf form. I didn't know you were an actual direwolf and not a wolf-man... what do you call a cross between two things?"

"A hybrid?"

Draco nodded at the words, an action that he accompanied with a light rustle of his wings, "Aye, that's it. A hybrid. I thought you'd be a wolf-man hybrid, not an actual direwolf. You can't blame me for not realizing it... Another question. When you fled yesterday, you said something about thinking I'd be different."

"I... I hide my true nature. You know why, but... I was hoping that you would be different. That, when I finally worked up the courage to tell you, you would understand and remain a friend to me... It was why I followed you in the first place. You weren't human, perhaps you wouldn't care about a werewolf... That you'd be my first friend who I couldn't scare away with what I am or risk tearing apart..."

Draco thought quietly for a moment before replying, his voice soft in an odd, even downright strange, way, "I see... You didn't so much as try to harm me while a wolf. You helped me, to be honest. Perhaps, then, I might be able to see past the werewolf part. Enough to work with you, at least."

"I guess that's all I can ask for. I thank you, Draco."

"Don't thank me yet," Draco watched as Dane knelt and recovered the sword he had tossed on the ground, "That sword. It was your father's."

"Once, yes. Now it's mine."

"I see."

As Draco acknowledged Dane's statement, Vreena, Leonidas, and Argrex took that moment to enter, with the half-elf announcing their entrance with a question, "So you aren't going to kill each other? That's quite the relief. I was worried that I'd have to jump in and stop you."

Draco gave the half-elf a deadpan look, not at all impressed, "You were… ah, what's the word? When you listen to a conversation you're not meant to hear?"

Dane raised an eyebrow again, chuckling as he responded, "Eavesdropping?"

"That's it… Gah, I've spoken Human for quite some time, yet I still have difficulty. That aside, you were eavesdropping, Vreena."

Vreena shrugged, "And you know why," even as she spoke to Draco, she offered the sheathed *Verachodairgin* to Dane, who accepted the blade quietly.

"... Aye, I do. Enough of this. There are more important matters to discuss. Leonidas. Argrex. Dane and I fought a pair of strange-looking humans."

Leonidas nodded, his head moving at a steady, yet slow rate, "Ashen of skin, black of hair, and red of eye?"

"You know of them?"

Argrex gave a low grunt, his expression something akin to being grim. Or as grim as a dragon's rather rigid face could be, "They are the other problem we mentioned. They are called, 'The Corrupted.'"

Leonidas smoothly picked up the conversation, almost like they were of one mind, "Indeed. We believe that these unfortunate creatures ventured to a vile place known as *Dedran ko Ivfrofril*. The Cave of Darkness. We know not what lies within, nor how the Corrupted came to become the creatures they are… But…"

"We dare not enter," Argrex sighed, shaking his head in an undulating motion unique to dragons and snakes, "There is far too much that we don't know about *Dedran ko Ivfrofril*. It is not worth the risk if we do not know what the danger is."

Draco scowled and even gave a soft growl, one he stopped immediately when everyone looked at him, "Those are the words of cowards. You cannot learn the danger if you do not take risks."

Leonidas sighed, "What we mean is that we dare not risk the danger to me in leaving *Arun Fril*. I… I was cursed with a crippling illness many centuries ago. If not for the restorative waters of *Arun Fril*, I would already be dead."

"Restorative waters?" Dane asked, curiosity staining his voice.

Leonidas offered a nod, waving his clawed hand in a gesture towards the lake, "Aye. Water from *Arun Fril* can cure nigh any illness and break nigh any curse upon being drank. Those illnesses and curses it cannot cure, such like mine, will have the suffering they cause be relieved for a time. If ye are injured, soaking thine injury in the water will speed the healing by tenfold."

"It can do all that?" Dane's voice was that of the awestruck, his amazement evident.

"Indeed. But I would advise against trying for thyself. The water eats away at darkness. For a creature of such to drink, it is certain death."

"I will remember that," Dane replied, dread filling his thoughts, *The water did hurt when I touched it… Then I'm… really a dark creature? Am I destined to be evil?*

Draco scoffed, but didn't refute them, "I suppose that's an explanation. Even so, I find it cowardly. But these… Corrupted. What else do you know of them?"

"Very little," was Leonidas's reply, "They act in most peculiar manners. They refer to themselves as 'this one,' and others as it, he, she, or they. To each other, they are brother and sister. They also speak of a truth, whatever they mean by it. It is most peculiar… But ye seek to assault *Dedran ko Ivfrofril*, do ye not?"

Draco shook his head at the question, "Not originally. I'm far more interested in the dragon with black scales and red eyes that assaulted me at Adrian. That said, I am curious about these Corrupted and if they have anything to do with *Dedran ko Ivfrofril*, then that is where I will go. Perhaps I will find the dragon there."

"Then allow us to prepare you for it. Whatever is there will no doubt be a trial. It would be best to prepare thyself."

Dane shrugged, turning his gaze over to his draconic companion, "He does have a point, Draco. We could use the help. I mean, I could only learn so much from Resken and Vreena. If they're as old as they say, they might know something that could help."

"I doubt we need it."

"True, but it's much better to have it. 'The truly strongest are nigh always the most prepared,' Another lesson from my father."

Draco sighed, but acquiesced, "I suppose. Fine. Let us learn… Though I doubt I have much more to learn from them…" he added in a low mutter.

Leonidas chuckled and offered a nod, "Good. First, however, I must know something. Thou claimest thou art a dire werewolf. If thou art truly, then thou art the deadliest creature in these ruins."

Dane stepped back in shock, "I-I am?"

Rather than saying yes or no, Leonidas replied with, "Tell me of thine abilities."

"I turn into a direwolf upon Merani's rise each night or if a particularly strong emotion causes me to lose control. As my wolf self, I can somewhat remain in control of myself, but it is easy for me to lose it. Very, very easy…"

"Canst thou change at will?"

"No."

"... Thou art unique. As is normal, shapechangers that take the form of a wolf or wolf-man are either werewolves or lycanthropes."

Vreena frowned at this and gestured to get Leonidas's attention, "Are werewolves and lycanthropes not two names for the same thing?"

"Nay. Werewolves are men, elves, and dwarves 'neath the watchful eyes of Sehero, but become bloodthirsty, ruthless monsters when Ephala looks fully on the world below. Lycanthropes, however, are men, elves, and dwarves most of the time, but can, at their whim, take their wolf form. In this form, they are more rational and can retain a sense of self. However, it is but a cracked mask, ready to fall apart when strong emotion strikes. Then they become unbounded hunters, smart and clever. Nigh unstoppable by normal men… Though a lucky hit could do them in."

"It could? I thought werewolves were only vulnerable to silver," Draco said, interest seeping into his voice.

"Werewolves and lycanthropes are vulnerable to moon-blessed silver, that is true. That is, silver that is enchanted with a specific ritual during a night when Ephala, Merani, and Neranha walk the skies together. Thou doubtless knowest this well, but this must be near to dawn or dusk, due to Neranha. Still, werewolf and lycanthropes can be harmed by regular weapons, moon-blessed silver simply has the greatest effect."

"But what of the dire werewolves?" Dane pressed, "Am I not one?"

"No. Thou must understand, dire werewolf is a term for two types of creatures. Were-direwolves and true dire werewolves. Were-direwolves are exactly the same as a normal werewolf, save for that they are larger and more aggressive. They never give up a chase unless they have completely lost the trail or Ephala sets before they finish the hunt. But they are not truly dire werewolves. A true dire werewolf is little more than a bloodthirsty monster bent on naught but pure destruction. They could kill a dragon in single combat with little difficulty."

Dane's face blanched. The warrior, face now as white as snow, took a step back, "No... I'm not... I wouldn't..."

"Thou art not a dire werewolf. If thou were, thou wouldst change like a werewolf, but, upon completing thy transformation, thou wouldst be a mindless beast of wanton destruction. Thou wouldst not just kill anything in thy path, thou wouldst destroy everything as well. No building, no person, no *anything* could stop thee. Thy hide would be resilient, most normal objects cannot pierce it. And even those that could do so would do little. Dire werewolves heal at an extraordinary rate. While werewolves and lycanthropes heal at a rate that is most unnatural, dire werewolves can heal from almost any injury nigh upon instantly. The only thing that could hurt a dire werewolf and not immediately have the damage it causeth rendered worthless would be moon-blessed silver. And even with that, victory would be long and arduous. Far from guaranteed. So dangerous and difficult they are, of the four dire werewolves known to ever have existed, only one was ever slain. And her death was due only to determination, great sacrifice, and more than a small portion of luck. To further their danger, they cannot die from age. Even as their normal selves, dire werewolves are uncannily strong, heal extraordinarily fast- so fast that their body doth not suffer the ravages of age- and are exceedingly difficult to kill with even a proper blow. They heal too fast and, most abnormally and what makes dire werewolves unique among werewolves, they are not vulnerable to moon-blessed silver. Aye, their regular forms are *not* vulnerable to moon-blessed silver, like their wolf forms are."

Dane's face was still a near white, with little color having returned during Leonidas's speech, "You mean... They are at their most vulnerable... when they are at their most dangerous?"

"Exactly so. And, if I am correct, thou canst get hurt, no? If so, then thou canst not possibly be a dire werewolf. Thou couldst not be harmed otherwise. Furthermore, dire werewolves only shift when Ephala is full. Thou dost not. Thou changest upon Merani's rising. Thou art very different from any werewolf or lycanthrope."

"Then, what am I?"

Leonidas paused. When he spoke again, his voice carried an edge of uncertainty, "I… I am not sure. Thou art unlike any kind of werebeast or therianthrope I know of…"

"Therianthrope? Werebeast?"

"Lycanthropes are therianthropes. Werewolves are werebeasts. They are the names used for such creatures, allowing for beasts other than wolves. Such afflictions are rare, but far from not existing."

Dane hesitated, then managed to nod, "I see…"

Leonidas eyed the human for a few moments, then gestured, "Come. Let us go to the ruins of the Temple of Dairgingarad."

Draco scoffed, "The supposed 'Father of Dragons?' Why are we going there?"

"Because it is the least damaged building in the city. Though it is and was the temple of a different god, those who attacked Sanctuary did not dare harm it more than was necessary, for fear of Dairgingarad's wrath. Dane, come. Thy training shall continue there."

Chapter 21

Blade of an Ancient

Leonidas, about to begin leading Dane, paused to add, "Draco. Thou wilt go with Argrex. He shall begin thy training."

"Why should I?" Draco challenged, aggression causing his tail to flick to the side.

Argrex gave a low rumble that almost made it seem like the earth was shaking, "As you should well know, there is a distinct difference in the physical capabilities of humans and dragons. We would know them."

Draco growled, "Aye, I do. Fine. Let's just get this over with," the dragon followed Argrex away from the temple ruins as Leonidas gestured for Dane to enter.

"We shall start with combat. Dairgingarad's Temple was one of the places weapons used to be stored in Sanctuary."

"In a temple?"

Leonidas nodded. He paused to look over the ruins of the grand building before him, then began to explain, "Dairgingarad is, to dragons and dracon, called the Son of Chaos. He was known for his chaotic personality and unpredictable mood swings. It is said that dragons get their more chaotic tendencies from him. Because of this, he is heavily associated with battle and combat, among other things. Thus, his temple additionally serves as an armory. And a good one. If thou wouldst recall, attacking a god's temple, even if his people do not call him a god, is a dangerous action."

"For fear of the god's wrath," Dane finished for Leonidas, "Even if Dairgingarad's temple was full of powerful weapons and artifacts, it would be risky to attack it, making those items safer."

"As thou sayest. Now, I am getting some of those weapons. They will look strange to thee, but I shall explain. Come."

Dane didn't respond as Leonidas led him to a side room. Inside, the dracon stopped at several racks to collect some of the aforementioned weapons and set them on a stone table. Three of the weapons had oval-shaped crossguards, and leather wrapped handles that seemed to be somewhere between a one-handed and a hand-and-a-half in length, leading Dane to believe that they were swords. If so, they were odd ones. They had meter-long curved blades that were very broad, rather thick, and featured a single edge. Their shapes reminded Dane of an axe. Of the three weapons, two had a curious hook about 20 cm up the blade, leaving a hollow that the haft of a weapon could easily fit in. Further, two of the three weapons, including the one without the hook-like hollow in the blade, had a chain attached to the pummel. This chain was roughly six feet long and sported a heavy metal ball at the end. The blade without a chain had a spike for its pummel. All three of these weapons looked very heavy, unwieldy. While Dane pondered the blades before him, Leonidas put one more weapon on the table. This weapon was a triangular-bladed rondel dagger with a chain attached to the pummel. The thing on the end of this weapon's chain resembled three fishing hooks attached back-to-back. Or shank-to-shank, if Dane recalled his fishing hooks right.

Leonidas gestured to the three broad-bladed weapons, "These are the traditional weapons of the dracon. They are collectively called *veragdairginas*, or 'dragonwings,' a name they get from their shape. They were originally created by breath dracon as a means of combating other kinds of dracon," he reached out and tapped the *veragdairgin* that had both the hollow and a chain, "This was the one they created. They called it *veragdairgin letrago*, which means-"

"'Chained dragonwing,'" Dane said, studying the weapon, "Because of the ball and chain on it?"

"Aye. Thou wilt notice that this one does not have the ball and chain. That one was wielded by winged dracon and is called *veragdairgin hebrago*, 'Spiked dragonwing,' Quite clearly, the name came from the spiked pummel. The reason for the lack of a ball and chain is due to a lack of need. The ball and chain was primarily used to strike at low-flying winged dracon. As would be expected, the winged dracon did not need to strike down the other dracon and the ball and chain weighed them down. Thus, the chain was replaced with a spike," Leonidas reached out and laid a clawed hand upon the next weapon, "And this is *veragdairgin gegred*. 'True dragonwing.' These were wielded by the tailed dracon. They were forged without the tailcatch like the others for a sole reason. The tailcatch was, as its name suggesteth, forged into the blade so that one could catch an opponent's tail."

"'Tailcatch?' Are those the hollows?"

Leonidas nodded and swung his tail around, "Look to where my tail starts to change into the endspike. That point is where the tail is the thinnest," he then lifted a blade and carefully fitted the hook-like hollow around the spot he had indicated on his tail, "As thou canst see, that point fits in the tailcatch. A very skilled or lucky warrior could catch it mid-battle and gain the advantage. By simply jerking the blade around, enemy attacks can be interrupted and enemies can be knocked off balance, both great advantages in battle," he gave a light tug in emphasis, "It can also be used to catch other things, such as the chains of *veragdairginas*."

"Okay… But what of that one?" Dane pointed at the fish-hook-and-dagger, "That's the scaled dracon one, right?"

"Aye. *Ehelk vefrogegred* were originally the weapon of the scaled dracon."

"'Lying Serpent?' Why that name?"

"Its shape. Seest how it isn't the same as the rest? It is a chain, one end having a dagger meant for piercing and the other has a tri-pointed hook. Tell me, canst thou think of how the scaled dracon used this?"

Dane pondered Leonidas's question for a moment, "The dagger is triangular… It would be good for thrusting and piercing armor and scales. Then there is the chain… meant for winged dragons. And the tailcatch was for tailed dragons, so the hook is for them?"

"Exactly so. The hook can also be used like a grappling hook. However, thou mayst wonder why the scaled dracon didn't use a *veragdairgin*."

Dane nodded, studying the blades, "You mentioned the tailed dracon's didn't have the tailcatch because it's meant to deal with tails. Just like the chains are meant for the winged dracon… Is the shape of *veragdairginas* used to deal with scaled dracon's scales?"

"Thou art correct. Dracon would use the weight of *veragdairgin* to pass by the tough scales of the scaled dracon. Dracon are quite strong compared to humans. They could use these with much less difficulty."

Dane tapped one of the weapons, glancing over to the dracon, "Can you wield these?"

"All four, though I favor *veragdairgin letrago* over the others. But enough of me," Leonidas offered another *veragdairgin*. This one had no chain and was made of wood, "This is *rederal veragdairgin hebrago*. A spiked dragonwing used for training. Take it."

Dane did as the old dracon asked and took the wooden weapon. It felt unbalanced and heavy, not that Dane was surprised. It would make a terrible sword, but Leonidas had said… "You want me to practice with it," he concluded, turning the wooden blade over in his hand, considering the thought that had come to mind.

"Nay. I want thee to spar with me," Leonidas hefted a wooden *veragdairgin letrago*. The wooden weapon featured a rope in place of a chain, "Come. There is a part of the temple where the roof collapsed. Once a dining hall for the servants of Dairgingarad, it is now an excellent place to spar. Unstable footing, uneven ground. Even unpredictable conditions, if the weather should happen to be disagreeable."

Dane did as the elder bade, following him through the once-proud temple. The ornate, yet simple decorations gave the ruined structure a sort of complex simplicity, as though the place was easy to understand, yet all the more convoluted because of it. However, Dane did not get to see much, as the collapsed dining hall proved very close. As Leonidas had said, the room was open to the sky, with large chunks of stone littering the floor. What space wasn't filled with this stone was cluttered with old, long-rotted wood from ancient furnishings. Gold filigree and broken decorations gave faint indications to the room's former grandeur. Leonidas made his way through the quiet, yet somber scene.

"Come, Dane. Let us begin this clash of ours," the ancient dracon lowered himself into a peculiar stance. His right foot was extended with his left foot back and angled to the left, the leg bent as though it was bearing his weight. His wooden blade was raised across his body, the edge down and perpendicular to the ground, displaying the flat of the weapon to Dane. His right hand was near his side, loosely holding the rope, the wooden ball dangling, "Come."

Dane nodded, his face becoming blank. He dropped into his own stance, but imitated Leonidas on the position of the blade, though with the edge facing up. It was wide enough to be used as a makeshift shield, albeit a small one. Still, the blade was unfamiliar and still felt unyieldingly blade-heavy to him, requiring him to use both hands to begin to approach a comfortable grip. And its shape nagged at Dane's mind. Surely…

For several long moments, the two warriors squared off with each other, neither willing to move in this treacherous landscape. Finally, Dane made the first move, charging while keeping low to the ground to make himself a smaller target should Leonidas attempt to use the ball and rope.

Leonidas remained motionless, letting Dane come, then leapt sideways, using his wings to aid him. Dane scowled in momentary frustration as Leonidas alighted on a chunk of rubble. He had forgotten that Leonidas had wings and a tail. He couldn't do that again.

"What is thy next move? I have the high ground. Attempting to climb opens thyself to attack. Of course, thou couldst strike at my legs, but my tail is an option for defense… What wilt thou do?"

Dane backed off. If he stayed close, Leonidas would still be able to strike him with the ball. As he did so, Dane snagged a small chunk of rubble and hefted it. Leonidas chuckled at the sight.

"I see. Thou backest away to distant thyself from me whilst collecting something to use as a weapon. Thou art clever in the art of war. Perhaps I should end this clash now?"

Dane scowled, then flung the rubble at Leonidas. As he expected, Leonidas dodged the "attack." However, Leonidas surprised Dane by leaping up and forward, using his wings to gain extra height. The maneuver, which included a somersault that Dane would have deemed unnecessary, if he had time to think about it, allowed Leonidas to drop expertly behind Dane, putting them almost back to back.

Dane spun, almost unconsciously swinging his weapon in a diagonal cleave. The momentum carried the weight of *veragdairgin* quite well, prompting a spark of pride to rush through Dane. He was right.

That pride vanished as it seemed Leonidas was prepared for this. The ancient dracon spun as well, crouching low and lashing out with a leg as he did. Leonidas's leg struck Dane's, taking out his legs and knocking him to the ground. Leonidas was quick to take advantage, hacking downward with his blade, only to be surprised when Dane wasn't as stunned as he had expected. The dracon's weapon met with the flat of Dane's own. Beneath the weapon, the warrior used the palm of his hand to support the block, putting his full strength behind his defense. He was quick to display the advantages of this by giving a shove, tilting his blade and causing the dracon's weapon to harmlessly skate to the side.

Rolling to the other side, Dane rose to a kneeling position in time to deflect another strike from Leonidas. Dane grunted as he did. The blade's weight and width compared to the much slimmer and lighter arming sword he was familiar with made his usual quick maneuvers difficult to manage. Leonidas's comment about the dracon's strength was no idle boast. They must be quite strong and full of stamina to wield such weapons regularly.

Pushing himself to his feet, Dane tried to jab the end of the weapon into the dracon's gut. When that strike was dodged, Dane quickly transitioned into another diagonal hack, which Leonidas deflected before striking back with a backhanded strike. Dane leaned back, avoiding the stroke, when he gave a cry of shock as his legs were once more kicked out from underneath him. This time, when Leonidas went for him, Dane was too slow to protect himself.

Leonidas's blade stopped, hovering above Dane's neck, "I claim victory, Dane. Dost thou object?"

Dane held perfectly still before murmuring, "No…"

The aged dracon nodded and rose, offering a clawed hand to Dane, of which the beaten warrior accepted, "Thou showest promise, thy skills art well honed."

"You practically controlled the entire fight… Aren't we continuing?" Dane asked after he noted that the dracon hadn't made a move to return to his original position.

"No. Simply thy form in handling an unfamiliar blade and thy tactics in facing a disadvantage reveal a base to build from. Aside, I harbor a distaste for battle. It hath cost me much and much more… Despite the sword upon thy side, thou art versed in the axe."

The human nodded, displaying his *veragdairgin*, "I noticed its shape is like an axe and you mentioned that the dracon used the weapon's weight against scaled dracon. It would be difficult to impossible to wield it like a sword, but like an axe? It's practically made for that."

"Thou art quick-witted. All this is true. Moreover, the scales of the dracon, even those who are not scaled dracon, are quite effective a deterrent against slashes. Hacking and smashing achieveth better results."

Dane appeared to think for a few moments, but soon nodded before asking, "If I may ask you a question about that leaping attack you did. Where did you learn to perform it? I've never seen its like."

"Thou wilt recall that I spoke of Argrex as my dragon and I, his rider. While not true in the entirety of it, it is true enough. We are the last remaining members of *Orsas ko Firtess*."

"'They of the Watch?'"

"Aye. Peasants, however, saw warriors riding and controlling dragons. As such, we became known as Dragon Riders."

"But… you said you are the last of They of the Watch. What happened to them? I've never heard of them."

Leonidas nodded, his eyes softening, "To no surprise, I assure thee. They of the Watch died out many centuries ago, well before the fall of the kingdom of the wolfear. They were made out of a greed for power, were turned into a force of peace, then died to disagreement, superstition, and fear… I fear my presence marked the end of their time."

Leonidas sighed and sat down on some rubble, his tail sprawling out behind him. He glanced over to Dane, then patted the rubble, "Come, sit with me," Dane did as the dracon asked, finding a semi-comfortable spot on a pile of stone to Leonidas's left. Idly, Dane noticed that the collapsed roof had to have been a thing to see, given the amount of rubble.

"Where to start?" Leonidas began, face upturned to gaze at the sky above, "Hrmm… Surely, thou knowest that I am quite the unusual creature for the common human to meet. Mine assumption is correct?" Dane offered a nod, "Good. I had gone to *Orsas ko Firtess* in search of purpose. They had become noble and honorable since I had first heard of them… To be truthful, I had once fought against them. Back then, they were little more than a rabble of mercenaries. Powerful mercenaries, what with dragons amongst their ranks, but mercenaries nevertheless. Of course, when I met them for the first time outside of battle, I harbored no ill will towards them and was able to prove mine intentions. For a time, I was an Initiate until a clutch hatched. Thou must understand, when a clutch of dragon eggs began to hatch, it evoked a sort of celebration called a Hatching. The celebration culminated with the Bonding, when the newly hatched dragons would either find a person that it favored, for some reason or another, or it would refuse everyone and live on its own. I was present at three Hatchings before Argrex chose me."

"'Chose you?' As a hatchling?"

"Aye. Hatchlings are not entirely helpless, unlike many creatures of youth. Upon his choosing of me, we were left alone for a time. This was to allow us to bond and understand one another."

"This sounds a lot like *Feminatenas Gerato*," Dane mused, recalling the words of Kathernirin.

"The entire concept of 'Fated Companion' is naught but a fabrication… Perhap not all of it, but much of what is said about it. *Orsas ko Firtess* created it to prevent thieves from attempting to make off with a dragon egg. After all, if it is well known and believed that the dragon within is only meant for a very certain person, of whom they don't know, then the egg is next to worthless. Perhaps only marginally useful only as a curiosity or a pet."

Dane blinked, considering the explanation, then offered a nod, "That makes a lot of sense, actually. Then what of Draco's ability to talk to me without speaking?"

"Some people are known to possess abilities most unusual. Perhaps it could be that Draco is one of such. I wouldn't know. But shall I finish my tale? Or dost thou have another question?"

Dane shook his head, adding, "No," just to be sure.

"I raised Argrex, as was the tradition… Or, perhaps, it would be better to say that he grew up alongside me. He… was a challenging task. Of all the hatchlings, wherever there was trouble, Argrex was inevitably there. And I with him, trying to convince him to behave… Eventually, he gained a maturity that helped with such issues, but Argrex the Troublemaker is far from dead, I assure thee… Or would doom thee be the better? Asides, we became members in full, but twas this very thing that sparked the order's fall. Those we protected grew to fear and despise me as a monster. This weight carried to the order as accepting monstrosities within its ranks. The order began to turn on itself and, encouraged by some dragons' dislike of the existence of 'riders,' dissolved from infighting. Argrex and I kept track of the various members, both enemies and allies alike... We used to, anyhow. Now, of course, we are the last."

"I'm sorry," Dane bowed his head slightly, only for Leonidas to wave the action away.

"It is of no consequence. Twas long ago... Show me thy sword. The one thou casted aside when thou first fled."

Dane blinked in surprise at the sudden shift of topic. Still, he drew *Verachodairgin*, the blade shining as it caught the light, then spun it, offering the hilt of the weapon to Leonidas. Gingerly accepting the blade, the ancient dracon studied it, running a claw along the decorations of the hilt, "The flame-branded blade and draconic hilt... There is no doubt, I have heard tell of this blade. *Orsvehed ko Fril*. Bringer of Light."

"*Orsvehed Fril*? I was told that its name is-"

"*Verachodairgin*? A name given to it by those who believed it failed the purpose for which twas forged... Though they are not wrong, if the story is told one way."

"What do you me-?" Dane was cut off by a crash that was swiftly followed by a roar which seemed to echo amidst the ruins. Leonidas sighed, though whether or not in disappointment was unclear to Dane.

"I suspected as much. Draco beareth far too great a pride. Come, Dane. Let us seek him out and discover the truth," Leonidas rose from his spot, returning *Orsvehed Fril* to Dane as he did so. He began padding off in what sounded like the direction of the origin of the sound, beckoning to the human as he did so. Dane wasted no time following him.

Chapter 22

Scales on the Wind

Leonidas, about to begin leading Dane, paused to add, "Draco. Thou wilt go with Argrex. He shall begin thy training."

"Why should I?" Draco challenged, aggression causing his tail to flick to the side.

Argrex gave a low rumble that almost made it seem like the earth was shaking, "As you should well know, there is a distinct difference in the physical capabilities of humans and dragons. We would know them."

Draco growled, "Aye, I do. Fine. Let's just get this over with," the dragon followed Argrex away from the temple ruins as Leonidas gestured for Dane to enter.

After the pair of dragons had put a fair distance between themselves and the ruined temple, Draco stopped and scoffed, "Right, now what do you want?"

"I wish to begin your training, as Leonidas stated previously."

Draco snorted, his tail lashing to the side, "I have no interest in your lies. You do not know me. I have no interest nor need for your supposed 'training.'"

Argrex simply sighed, "What have I done to you to warrant such a response? Stop this foolishness befitting a hatchling and come. Allow me to train you."

Draco, most obviously, did not move. Instead, he glared at Argrex, "And why should I? What makes you believe that I have anything to learn from you? I know all I need to survive and more. Pretend to teach me if you wish, but you know nothing about me. I will not fall to your fool's game."

Argrex heaved a second sigh, then closed his eyes, "What is your name, Draco?"

Draco stared at Argrex, incredulous, "What?"

"Your name. Offer it, if you would."

"You know my name well enough," Draco scoffed, "Enough of this. You claim to want to teach me. I am not as easily fooled or convinced as Dane. Say whatever you will, I shall stay no longer!" With that proclamation, Draco spread his wings and charged. Argrex, despite being directly in Draco's path, did not move. Instead, he watched as Draco drew closer and closer. Just as it seemed that Draco had gone too far, the younger dragon pushed against the ground, simultaneously pumping his wings. The two actions sent Draco airborne, allowing him to just skim over Argrex's back.

Argrex, for his part, still hadn't moved. Instead, he gave the now flying dragon an irritated glare, "Disrespect me? Is that the type of hatchling you are? So be it. Fly and be a nuisance all you want. The smart hunter knows better."

Draco soon found himself well above the ground, the wind rushing over his scales and wings. Oh, what a feeling! The dragon allowed his eyes to drift close, if only for a moment. Yes, this is what it meant to be a dragon. No lessons or 'learning,' Dragons didn't need that nonsense. Dragons were creatures of fire and air. Instinct and furiosity. The air was their home, where they were the true masters.

Draco's eyes flashed open as he tilted to the side, sending himself into a sharp turn. He allowed the turn to continue, morphing it into a tight spiral. If Draco had a human face, he would have smiled for what was next. Nevertheless, the dragon found his spiral becoming tighter and tighter. Soon enough, Draco was practically plummeting headfirst while rapidly spinning on the spot. If a human had seen him, they would have thought he was in some sort of death spiral. Indeed, on the ground below, such was what crossed Vreena's mind as she watched the dragon. However, Draco was not feeling the terror that normally would have accompanied such a situation. After all, this was no death spiral. This was a favorite trick of Draco and proof of his mastery over flight.

With nothing but joy practically radiating through him, Draco suddenly twisted. With a flare of his wing, then an almighty flap, the dragon pulled out of the breakneck, spiraled dive with only a few dozen feet separating himself and the ground. After a momentary glide, the dragon's wings began to beat, propelling him skyward once more. Draco tilted again, his upward climb now also taking the form of a very large spiral. If the dragon had bothered to look below, he would have seen that he was circling the lake.

Rather than level out, Draco decided that he was going to further show off his aerial supremacy. With that decision in mind, the dragon spiralled higher and higher, the lake below dwindling in size. When the lake below began to resemble a large blue coin, Draco finally leveled over once more. Rather than immediately performing another trick, he allowed himself to lazy drift in circles and gaze at the lands surrounding himself. The long stretch that was the Plain of the Winds. The mountains far to the north and east that the humans named the Sidatial Mountains. The ruins that encircled the western and southern parts of the lake below. Most importantly... Even the occasional specks that sat far away, in the skies above the Sidatial Mountains. Unless one was flying like Draco was now, those specks were far too deep in the mountains to be seen... None of those specks dared trespass into human lands. Not with what humans tended to do...

"Cowards, the lot of them," Draco scoffed. He had long since stopped caring about the rest of his kind. They were mighty, but spineless. Cowardly. They weren't worth Draco's time, "And that includes that fool down below."

Draco snorted, then twisted about. Without preamble, the dragon turned his lazy circling into a large, vertical loop. At the apex of the loop, Draco felt himself slow. Rather than cut his losses and transition into a dive, Draco continued. However, with his forward momentum gone, the dragon found himself plummeting out of the sky. And with his belly to the sun, no less!

Once again, if Draco had human features, he would have smiled. After allowing himself to plummet a fair distance, the wind rushing past him, the dragon's wings seemed to flutter. And with that flutter, the dragon began to turn in the air. In what the dragon was ever so proud of as being a feat of aerial maneuverability, the dragon was no longer plummeting. No, now he was diving. With a flare of the wings, Draco swooped back into a levelled flight, pleased almost to an excessive degree with himself.

"Impressive. Very impressive!" Draco started, surprised in whole as Argrex seemed to appear from the air next to him, "You are quite the skilled flier."

"What are you doing here?!" Draco snapped, glaring at the black dragon for a moment.

"If you refuse your lessons on land, then I shall give chase to you within the air. Now, will you offer your name?"

"Leave me be!" Draco tilted, peeling away from the older dragon. Argrex smoothly tilted as well, following Draco. The golden dragon noticed this easily, "Leave! Let me fly in peace!"

"You wish to escape me? Then show to me your mastery of the skies and outfly me!" With that proclamation, Argrex suddenly pumped his wing, pushing himself higher into the sky. Draco snarled, pushing himself higher as well.

"Fine! You want your damned trick of a lesson?! Then catch me, if you dare to match my skills upon the wing!" Draco tilted and suddenly sent himself into a steep dive. The ground grew rapidly closer, the air ripping past Draco's scaled muzzle. When the ground became so close that he could clearly see every bit of rubble below, Draco pulled out of the dive. He smoothly transitioned into a spiralled climb, his eyes flicking about in order to spot the no doubt approaching Argrex.

Unfortunately, Draco did this too late. He managed to catch sight of Argrex as the black dragon slammed into Draco's side, sending both dragons into the ground. An almighty crash broke out as Draco slammed into an already broken building, Argrex on top of him. Draco loosed a furious roar and struggled to push his elder off, only to freeze when several claws pressed down on his neck.

"And I have won," Draco growled at Argrex's words, but was unable to speak before the black dragon did, "Do you see? I had no need to match your skills. I had only need to try your patience and overcome your expectations."

Draco snarled, eyes locked on those of the black dragon that was pinning him, "Let go of me!"

Chapter 23

A Dragon's Name

The pair of Dane and Leonidas found Draco rather easily. It was quite hard to miss the young-ish dragon who was pinned to the ground beneath his elder's paw in the midst of rubble.

"Let go of me!"

"I simply asked of you your name, but you chose to be quite rude. Dragons may not be 'civilized,' or even all that orderly, but don't you think we can be a little courteous?"

"You know my name, you lackwitted fool! Draco!"

Argrex sighed, his head and tail both swinging from side to side in a slow, almost mournful arc, "I do not mean the name you call yourself. I meant *your* name. I assumed you knew it. Are all you younglings like this?"

"How wouldn't I know it? And cease with your 'younglings!' I am over two and thirty years old!"

"'Tis but a drop to a lake to me… Enough of this foolery. You claim to know your name. Tell me it, and perhaps I shall return it upon you."

"Let me up and I might," Draco spat back.

"Very well," the black dragon removed his paw slowly and stepped back. With an air resembling that of disinterest, Argrex pressed, "Well?"

Draco's lip curled up, a low rumble emanating from them as he got to his feet, "I'm getting up."

Dane, who had been watching quietly up to this point, slightly turned his head to speak to Leonidas, "Draco seems so hostile towards Argrex."

"Aye. 'Tis nothing of thy concern, so long as Argrex stayeth his claws. Dragons are territorial by nature and oft act aggressive within another's presence. The number of times I had to step between Argrex and another is proof enough."

Dane nodded slowly, his face sloping into a slight frown of thought, "Yes, but dragons respect elders of greater strength, right? Argrex is obviously stronger than Draco."

"Thou speakest truly. Yet thou missest the most notable fact. Argrex has yet to return Draco's aggression. He appeareth as though Draco is not but a nuisance, a sure way to bolster the fires of any dragon."

That thread of conversation was stopped as Draco snarled, which Argrex almost seemed to reply to with a low rumble and a vague wave of the claw.

"What-?"

Leonidas interrupted Dane, smoothly answering his unasked question, "Draco is about to tell Argrex his name. Be silent and listen."

Draco began a semi-long chain of what seemed to be just growling, rumbling, and other noises, "Grrrraalllrallgggrrrrraaallllkkkrraaallll-" would be Dane's best description of what Draco sounded like and even then it was a poor, almost pathetic imitation of the feral, almost threatening nature of the noise. And incomplete, as Draco seemed to go on for nearly a minute. Of course, it was not merely sound alone. Draco at first stood proud, his head high, wings spread to bear them to all, and his tail raised. That changed over the course of Draco's sounds. A shift in the head here. A rustle of wings there. Even a smack of the tail against the ground. All of it made no sense to Dane.

"Was that his name?"

Leonidas nodded, his tail flicking to the side, "Aye."

"I-"

"Don't understand? Dragons, as thou art well acquainted with, can speak in tongues other creatures better understand. With the help of a little magic, of course. While useful, many dragons still favor their own guttural methods of communicating. Draconic humanoids do the same, but not the same as that of dragons. Nevertheless, as thou canst surely see, that method relies as much on movement and the body as it does sound. Enough that near purely vocal languages, such as thy kind's, can be much less tiresome. Nonetheless, I could tell thee of what twas that Draco said."

"You could?"

"Aye. The name of a dragon is always preceded by every brood it is of descent, save for occasions where a long introduction is risky. Of course, they do not include Dairginheras. It is quite uncertain as to whether or not Dairginheras was a dragon and a given. They rarely include which of Dairginheras's daughters from which they descend. Their bodies prove that well enough."

"Dairginheras?"

"The Mother of Dragons. Mate of Dairgingarad. She mayeth not have been a dragon, but her daughters were. They numbered four, with each inspiring a brood. Ephala, the Elder Dragon, mother of the strongest and most powerful dragons. Argrex is of her brood. Seest thou how he has but a single pair of wings to the three pairs of Draco? The second was Neranha, the Northern Dragon, mother of all who claim not the might of fire. Then there is Merani, the Southern Dragon, the common mother. Draco's appearance maketh well clear that he is of her descent. And, lastly, Rederada, the Lost Dragon, claimed to be the mother of the twisted and least dragon of the dragons."

"Mothers? Do dragons trace their brood through the females?"

Leonidas nodded in approval, "Thou art sharp of mind. Dragons place great weight in the mother and female. Ah, but willst thou be silent for but a few moments more? Argrex is to speak."

Argrex, who had been considering what Draco had said, nodded, then began his reply. The sounds were just as incomprehensible to Dane as Draco's were, though his stance was somewhat more impressive. Argrex's neck was triumphantly arched, his wings spread wide to cover a fair distance. Argrex's tail curled towards his right side. Surprisingly, he finished faster than Draco had, despite seeming to move about much more during his name than Draco did.

"He didn't take as long. Is his mother closer related to Ephala?"

"Correct."

Draco didn't give Dane a chance to say anything else before exclaiming, "Aniora? But she only took one mate."

"Aeriol, oft known as Lord of the Skies," Argrex stated, seeming pleased, "I had not expected you to know such."

"Why would I not? None before or since possesses his skill in the sky. Even myself, and I was as well known for my skills as… I was well known for my skills in the sky."

"True, but you are not without your own names of interest. Belga of the Southern Badlands. One of the fiercest dragons known to spawn a brood and also one who took a single mate. Fierce enough that she alone lives amongst the sands of the Vast Unknown."

Draco inclined his head, pride taking over his voice, "*The* fiercest. She only accepted my grandfather after she barely managed to overpower him. No one else has come close."

Argrex bobbed his head, "Perhaps. There are those who would argue… What say you, Leonidas?"

"What say I? I say ye are both dragons of fair blood. Perhaps ye can agree on that?"

Argrex's gaze turned to Draco, his tail idly drifting to the side, "Sage advice. You agree, Draco, do you not?"

"I suppose I do. Why did you care about my name?"

Leonidas began to chuckle, as did Argrex as he said, "I was curious. You clearly have little of a sense of humor, yet the name you use, 'Draco,' means 'dragon' in a tongue that hailed from a distant and dead land."

Dane blinked in surprise before stifling a laugh. After a few moments to control himself, he managed to say, "So, if I were to call him Draco the Dragon…"

Argrex bobbed his head once more, a glint in his eye, "Then you would also be calling him Dragon the Dragon."

Dane began to laugh. In truth, it wasn't that funny, but Draco's expression, mixed with the absurdity of what his name means, just set him off. And not only him, it would seem, as Argrex began making a rolling rumble-like sound. Being a dragon, Draco didn't really have much in the way of expressions, as far as humans were concerned. Still, it was enough, as Draco seemed to be attempting to be surprised or angry, Maybe both at the same time. His eye ridges were raised, but his lips were pulled back and just barely revealing his teeth, not unlike what a wolf would do.

"Stop that," Draco spat, his expression morphing to what was certainly anger, "Or I will make sure you do."

Dane nodded, but was distinctly unable to respond as he heaved in a breath. Fortunately for Draco, he had stopped laughing nonetheless. That still didn't change his name, but it was close enough.

"If you intend to teach us, tell me more about this *Dedran ko Ivfrofril*, Leonidas," Draco growled. His eagerness to put the conversation to something other than his name was easily apparent in his voice, "Most importantly, what is it?"

The dracon sighed, "An apt question. I regret to tell you that we ourselves do not have the answer to it. The name itself makes it clear that it is the 'Cave of Darkness,' but we are unsure what it means by this. Perhaps there is something like *Arun Fril* there, but it could just as easily be for some other reason that we do not know. Even so, if such a thing doth exist, it will be dangerous beyond doubt. Which is why we seek to teach you what we can whilst you are still here. We are quite old beings with ancient knowledge."

"So far, you've failed to teach me anything of value," Draco snapped.

"Does that include your name, Dragon?" Argrex asked, his posture reminiscent of a person making idle conversation, though there was nothing idle about the question.

"Aye, it does," Draco snapped again, "Do you have anything useful to say?"

Argrex nodded his head, neck doing its normal undulations, though his posture remained relaxed, "Yes. Have you heard of *Arun Ivfrofril*?"

"No."

"I expected as much," the older dragon looked over to Dane, only for the human to shake his head, "Not you, either? No surprise to me. It is a rather uncommon topic. *Arun Ivfrofril* is supposedly, as the name makes clear, a lake of darkness. Despite Leonidas's oh-so-lovely theatrics in dodging around his knowledge, we do know *Arun Fril* was created because of it and that it was made by evil humans, but outside of that, we know very little about it. Including where it is."

Draco promptly began grumbling, his gaze sharpening into a glare, "Of course, you don't. Why would you?"

Leonidas didn't seem to take offense to Draco's words. In fact, what might pass as a smile touched the dracon's lips, "Ah. Argrex, dost thou still recall Master Arenel?"

"I do. He never seemed to have the answer we were looking for. Always had some other answer that would prove useful to a later question, but never the one we needed at the time."

Draco's glare remained on the two as he spat, "What does that have to do with anything?"

"You'd be surprised," Argrex chuckled, "The answers with no questions can oft be the most important ones."

Draco scoffed, "I have no interest in this rambling. Can you actually teach us anything at all?"

"We can teach thee much, if thou wilt listen," Leonidas replied, his voice sharp, "Such as this: Dost thou know the true nature of Dane's blade?"

"*Verachodairgin?*"

Leonidas shook his head, "No. Properly, the blade is known as *Orsvehed ko Fril*. Twas forged long ago to battle against dark foes. Demons, if I have heard right. The blade is remarkable in its make. Tis supposed unbreakable and forged of silver blessed by the three moons. Bathed in light and warmed by fire, or so twas I heard. The name *Verachodairgin* was born from anger."

"Anger and dragons," Draco huffed, "What is with humans and their insistent ideas that dragons are related to anger?"

"Tis not an unfounded reasoning. Even so, twas also not humans who gave this blade the name. At the time, twas believed that dragons were to blame for the demons. As it were, one was. Nevertheless, the warrior who wielded *Orsvehed Fril* failed to save those who depended upon them and twas the blade that bore that failure."

Draco huffed yet again, "And we care why?"

Much to the surprise of Draco, it was Dane who spoke. He slowly drew *Orsvehed Fril* from its place on his hip, before murmuring, "Because, for one, I had no idea this blade was moon-blessed. Now that I do know… I think it will be far, far more useful than it already is."

Turning his gaze to the human, Draco was quickly in his reply, "Not on yourself, I hope. I didn't consider overlooking what you are for you to die by your own hand."

Dane shook his head, still studying the glittering weapon, "I'd never. Father once told me that a knight's duty is all that should matter. Honor comes next, then glory last. But always duty first. And my duty, as it is now, is to aid you. To that end, I must live."

"Good."

"Make no mistake, Draco. I have no illusions regarding what I am. I am a monster. I know what I am and what will one day come. After all, the monster always dies. But until that day comes, I will live as I can and be of use to someone."

Draco scoffed and began grumbling, "You humans and your devotion to the future. Gives me conniptions…" the dragon heaved a sigh, then added, "But, so long as I wake each morning to a *living* Dane, you may say what you will. No doubt you will find that you are speaking nonsense."

Dane just shrugged, "I suppose I might. Anyways, you were saying, Master?"

The dracon shook his head, his eyes gaining a hint of a hollow look to them, "Thou mayst call me Leonidas. I deserve not the title of Master or King. Not now…"

"Understood, Leonidas," Dane nodded, his hand still tracing the sword's blade, "This battle you spoke of. Could you tell us more?"

Leonidas nodded, though Dane felt as though he wasn't paying attention, "Hmm… I should have known better. To build a city when dracon were yet feared… No less than a month later, the Flaming City-"

"Leonidas, you are walking amongst a different time again," Argrex called out, "Wake up."

"Hmm? Ah, forgive you me. I was… elsewhere. What was it thou askest of me?"

"I was interested in that legend you spoke of. You mention demons were part of the battle. Are they anything like the Corrupted?"

The dracon seemed to think for a moment before cautiously replying, "I do not believe so. If I have heard rightly, demons are denizens of Unmeino Fukasa. A place they are mostly restricted to, with a few exceptions. These Corrupted, as far as the two of us are aware, are entirely creatures of Anevike Protaodrakos. While certainly demonic, the Corrupted are not demons. As far as we know, of course… Ah, but come. See? Clouds approacheth and shall soon cloak the sky. Let us retire to a building with an intact roof lest we stand amidst the rain."

Chapter 24

The Face of the Accursed

Draco paused as he padded through the ancient ruins, his gaze turning to lock onto the lake. It sparkled with Sehero's fading light as he crept towards the world's edge. Draco watched the lake for a moment, then snorted. If the humans were to be believed, Sehero was chasing the little moon, which they called Merani, who would be rising very soon. Superstitious fools.

However, his thoughts were soon turned away from Sehero and the moon as he spotted a humanoid shape, wielding a blade and framed by the light of Sehero, upon the beach. He watched as it stabbed, darted about, and made swift, short swipes that didn't seem like they could do any real damage. After watching for a few more moments, curiosity began to overtake Draco as he began to approach the figure.

As he grew closer, the figure became clearer as the light became less of an issue. Standing upon the beach, wielding a slender blade, was Dane. The warrior was practically dancing on the beach, his movements seemed more elegant and nimble than normal. At least, Draco thought so.

"Is that sword what was in the long bundle strapped to your pack?"

Dane started at Draco's voice. Glancing over at the dragon, Dane smiled and gestured with the sword, "Yeah. It... was a gift. It's a rapier."

"Why do you need it? I understand your father's sword, you had it before the healer gave you... it was *Orsvehed Fril*, wasn't it? Aye, I understand that, but why the rapier?"

Dane nodded, staring at the blade, the gemstones on its hilt glittering in the sunset. It occured to Draco that the sword must have some monetary value, "Why, indeed? As I said… it was a gift. From… a friend."

"I thought I was your first friend?" Draco asked, his query doubling as a challenge.

Dane sighed and shook his head, "You are the first one who I'm certain I can't badly hurt, but you are hardly my first friend."

"I see. And who gave you that blade?"

"Jairend," Dane studied the weapon, running a finger over its ornate, woven-basket-like handguard, "He taught me how to use it. He was my first real friend. And the first to truly understand…"

Draco raised an eye ridge as Dane returned the blade to its sheathe, "By, 'taught you to use it,' you mean all that stabbing?"

"Rapiers are most suited for thrusting… But come, night's approaching and I believe you wanted to witness me… shift, I think Leonidas called it."

The dragon looked Dane over, "Hmph. So you do want me to see that. I've seen a werewolf shifting, you don't have to show me."

"It would be best if you witness it, that way you aren't surprised if it should happen sometime."

"Again, I have seen it before, but very well. Let us go," despite his own words, Draco didn't move. He looked Dane over, his gaze seeming restless to the warrior.

"What is it, Draco?"

"… Nothing of importance. It is proving surprisingly difficult to see you as just my companion and not also a potential enemy. I have seen werewolves as a whole as a… a personal foe for so long, having one as anything but an enemy…"

Dane offered a thin smile and shallow nod, "I see. Well, that's something else my shifting could *maybe* help with. Maybe. So long as you don't attack me on sight, I'll count it as successful."

"Hmph. Think of it as you will. Let's go," Draco began padding away, then paused as he realized that Dane had yet to start moving again, "Well? You are the one doing the shifting. Go on ahead."

Dane gave the dragon a nod before leading him back towards the ruins. Weaving his way through the crumbling building, Dane would occasionally stop to gaze at a building. It was one of these moments that Dane was about to start walking again when he froze and knelt, something on the ground catching his eye.

"Why have you stopped this time?"

"This," Dane stood and showed Draco what he had picked up. In his hand was a black feather.

"That's a feather. What's so special about a feather?"

Dane shook his head and tapped the base of the feather, "It's a quill, actually. And, more importantly, it's made from the feather of a crow."

"So?"

"I carry a quill with me in case I have a need for it. But I made mine from a goose feather. And Vreena's quills, including the one she gave me, are made from the feathers of hawks. Neither of us have crow feather quills."

Draco grunted, "I get it. You doubt that this quill has survived since this place was destroyed last."

"Exactly... Though it could be Leonidas's. Except I haven't seen him use one yet... Nor have I seen any crows here. Meaning it would be hard to replace it..."

"Enough. I'm as interested as you but we don't have the time. You *are* going to shift soon, are you not?"

Dane nodded and tucked the quill away, "Right. Come on. Quickly."

"Finally," Draco grumbled as he followed Dane. Fortunately for both the dragon and human, the structure Dane used as his bed wasn't too far away. It was a mostly intact building that Leonidas claimed once was a library, though what books and scrolls that hadn't been plundered or damaged had been moved by the dracon long ago, leaving the ruin empty. However, Dane held no interest in the history of the building at the present moment. Even as Draco watched, the human tugged his tunic over his head.

"You are unclothing yourself. Are humans not embarrassed by doing such in front of others?"

"Yes. But if I didn't, I might unnecessarily damage my clothes upon shifting. Of course, I've no particular interest in clothing, unlike some nobles, but this is all I have. I'd rather not destroy them," even as he spoke, Dane began tugging his breeches off, revealing a loincloth beneath.

"I see. I suppose I understand the embarrassment, as well. Younglings going through molt often are embarrassed."

"Molt?"

Draco sighed and turned his face away, "Aye. It normally happens several times in our first five or six years, though anytime a dragon grows rapidly causes it. Our scales can't keep up and fall off in large numbers. This leaves us looking patchy and leaves gaps in our armor… And no, I have no idea why I haven't molted yet. I should have, given the unnatural speed I've grown. I'm almost the size I was back when I'd claimed my third year."

Dane nodded to himself, his expression somewhat ponderous, "If you do, let me know. Maybe I can help or something. Anyways, I'm just going to lay down. Keep watch on me."

"What of the… whatever you humans call what you are wearing?"

"A loincloth. I have some extra cloth for that, so I keep it on. Usually, I'm lucky enough that it will still be intact," Dane grinned before laying himself down on his sleeping mat, "It will happen as Merani rises. Just keep watch," he added before closing his eyes. Before the dragon could manage a response, Dane's breathing had already evened. The human was asleep.

Draco blinked, catching notice of how still Dane had become, "Dane? Dane? Are you asleep?" After Dane gave no answer, for obvious reasons, Draco twisted about and peered out of the ruins as he huffed, "You just fell asleep. In an instant. How have you managed that?"

Even as the dragon spoke, he noted that the smaller moon began to crest the horizon. Turning back to Dane, he witnessed a sight he had, unfortunately, seen before. A black cloud began to drift off the sleeping human's skin. Draco watched, his face even more expressionless than it already was, as the black fog-like cloud began to obscure Dane entirely. The cloud writhed and shifted, as though the cloud was alive. Of course, Draco found no interest in the cloud, other than its presence. He was much more interested in what would come out. What Dane could look like. Even so, he couldn't help but be concerned with the cracking sound that occasionally erupted from the Dane-concealing cloud.

Before long, no more than a minute, the black cloud began collapsing in on itself. As a result, the cloud faded into nonexistence, finally revealing a large wolf with grey fur and a pale, off-white belly lying next to a strange, meaty mass of… something. Even as Draco watched, the wolf's eyes drifted open. With a huff of what seemed to be displeasure, the wolf pushed himself to his feet. Taking a moment to extract its back end from the cloth that enshrouded it, the wolf then nodded towards Draco, holding still to give the dragon a good look.

"Hmph. So this is your hidden face… What is that?" Draco turned his attention to the fleshy, slightly pulsating mass. The mass smelled strongly of Dane, giving him no doubts that this had to do with a werewolf's shifting. Still, that didn't answer what it actually was.

The wolf proved no help as he simply shook his head and began to walk away from it. Draco huffed, but began to follow him anyways, leaving the fleshy mass behind, "Can you speak? I'd assume not, but you might be different. You *are* different from the normal werewolf, after all," the wolf stopped and looked back at Draco. However, he did not speak, instead shaking his head, "Of course not. Why would it be that easy?" the dragon grumbled as he followed the wolf, only for the wolf to not move and continue staring at him, "What do you want?"

The wolf began to walk in a circle before lying down, staring pointedly at the dragon. He remained like that, staring at Draco while the latter returned the stare, "What do you want?" Draco snapped, starting to get irritated at the wolf for not moving.

The wolf huffed what seemed to be a sigh before laying his head down and pretending to sleep before looking pointedly back at the dragon. Fortunately for the wolf, Draco didn't take long to figure out what he was saying.

"What? I should go to sleep?" the wolf nodded, "And I suppose you won't need any sleep for yourself?" the wolf shook his head, "Of course not," Draco heaved a sigh of his own and turned away from the beast before him, "Alright fine. I was getting tired anyways. You go do… whatever you do at night," the response he got was yet another nod.

The dragon just shook his head and began to walk away, leaving the wolf to stare after him, "Damn wolves."

ΩΩΩΩΩΩΩΩΩΩΩΩΩΩΩΩΩΩΩΩΩΩΩΩΩΩΩΩΩΩΩΩΩΩΩΩΩΩΩΩΩΩΩΩΩΩΩΩΩΩ
ΩΩΩΩΩΩΩΩΩΩ

The wolf gazed after Draco, watching the dragon disappear into the former library. Almost as soon as the dragon's tail tip had vanished, he turned and practically threw himself into an all-out run through the silent, broken city. He had to. He had to do something. It took far more effort than Draco would have believed for the wolf to simply stand there and tell the dragon to go to sleep. Even now, even now… He had to run. Had to run. He had to do something and running was the easiest. He just had to.

The wolf practically tore through the ruins. Pebbles and small stones clattered in his wake as they were flung into the mismatched walls of the dilapidated buildings. The wolf didn't care. He didn't notice the sounds. He couldn't notice the sounds. He barely even felt the pounding of his paw pads against the rubble-specked ground. No, all he could feel was the rush. The force, the will, that was pressuring him. He knew what it wanted. But he didn't have to know. He could feel it. It wanted to chase, to stalk. It wanted a feast and a hunt. It wanted blood. And, as it always, always did, it didn't care what the prey was.

This will was powerful. Oh, so powerful. It took all the willpower the wolf could muster to fight it. Even then, without the mindless running, he wasn't sure he could have contained it. He was never sure. At least, until the moment when the will just gave up. No warning, not even the slightest hint, then it just stopped. It slinked away, like a whipped dog, leaving the wolf alone in his thoughts. Almost. Even beaten, it was still there. Almost like a whisper that was felt. *Blood. Hunt. Feast.* As urgent as could be, yet was undesired as a rabid beast. Still, now that the will had resigned itself to a background position for a little while, the wolf could slow his breakneck sprint and become aware of his surroundings once more. And it was this newfound awareness that allowed him to pick up a faint sound. Gazing around himself, the wolf was able to recognize his location at last. The crumbled building he was next to, according to Leonidas, was once the city's equivalent of a palace. Even in its heyday, the building didn't look as though it was anything special. Regardless, the sounds seemed to be coming from within.

As he approached, he was able to identify the sounds as a voice, "No… N-No… I can't… I-I can't… Not him… Please, not him…"

With the pleas in his ears, the wolf began picking his way through the ruin. Stones shifted and crumbled as he put his weight down, sometimes meriting a cautious change in footing. Still, the wolf was deft enough to make it through the rubble. He followed the whimpers and half-sobbing cries through a broken hall and around a corner. There, lying amidst the rubble, was Argrex and Leonidas. The dracon was fast asleep, while the dragon was watching him, a glittering that might have been worry in his eyes. Even as the wolf drew closer, Leonidas twisted in his sleep, his face contorting, "Stop… Not him… Please, stop… He knowest naught… No. No. No! Argrex!"

Much to the wolf's surprise, the dragon responded, "Shh. Calm yourself, Leonidas. I'm right here. I'm fine," the dragon whispered, or, rather, cooed, lightly running the flatter part of his tail tip along the dracon's winged back, "We are both fine. Hear you me? I'm not hurt. Nothing's wrong."

The dracon pressed himself closer to Argrex, still quite asleep, as far as the wolf could tell. Even so, Leonidas began clutching onto the draconic leg that he had been somewhat laying on, "Argrex… Dost not leave me… Never go… Never die…"

In an almost practiced voice, Argrex replied smoothly, as though he was talking to a scared child, instead of a sleeping elder, "I never will. I swore as much. You know the oath we made, 'We are as one. Our bond is unshakeable, our hearts unbreakable. United we stand and together we fall. So I swear, now and unto our death.'"

Even as Argrex spoke, Leonidas began to mumble along with him, "... as one… unshakeable… hearts… united… fall… I swear… unto our death…"

The wolf could only stare, incredulous, as the dracon's writhing calmed in response to speaking the oath. His twisted grimace faded into a peaceful expression, his face looking no different than it always did. Argrex, watching the events with the care of a patient father, nodded to himself. Then, almost like he had been waiting to do so, the dragon's head swung around to lock his gaze on the wolf.

"I thought heard something approach, Dane," Argrex rumbled in what could pass as a dragon's whisper, "He has done this quite a lot. Some nights, he is plagued by nightmares of past memories and future fears. Those few where I am amidst his dreams, I can calm him. But many, such as each time Sanctuary has fallen, seemingly in spite of him, I cannot do aught for him… He is beyond my words and reach," Argrex sighed, eyes returning to the sleeping dracon, "Not that I do not try, but… it pains me. We have stood together for so long, yet my ability to help him is miniscule compared to his to do the same to me. It is maddening… and truly pathetic."

The wolf only stared at him, being, of course, unable to speak. However, the wolf's lowered ears and downcast eyes told the ancient dragon all he needed to know. Argrex shook his head, his eyes softening as he did so.

"Do not concern yourself with it. He has had these nightmares for as long as I have known him. Doubtless longer. Heh, it used to scare me to no end when I was younger. I once thought he was dying in his sleep… Still, there is naught you can do for him. Though, if you happen to know or come across a way to help… Ah, no matter. Pay me no mind. Go, do whatever it is you do these nights. Leonidas will be no different than he always is come morning."

The wolf continued to stand there, to which Argrex only shook his head a second time, "Do as you will, but I will return to sleep. Remember, I am to meet with you tomorrow," the wolf gave him a little head bob before the dragon relaxed, laying his head down and allowing himself to drift off to sleep.

The wolf watched him for several moments more. After assuring himself that both the dragon and dracon walked the realms of sleep, he turned and padded his way back through the ruined "palace," With nothing else to do, the wolf began his nightly routine. Which was little more than roaming around the area, keeping guard for his sleeping companions. Of course, he had to be careful but it was nothing like he was used to, as there were no wolf packs that claimed this area as their territory, judging from the lack of scent markers. That, and there were no unexpected people to be afraid of.

The wolf heaved a sigh as the thought crossed his mind. Wolf packs. He almost longed for the one back home. That one occasionally helped him so long as he helped them in return. Only because they knew they were no match for him, but it was still something. Creatures who somewhat went through the same things he did… But now was not the time for his mind to wander. Especially as a wolf, but more because he caught a scent upon the wind. It smelled human, but bore other scents as well. Ink. Parchment. A scholar, most likely. But why here, of all places? Most scholars stayed in or near libraries. He noted that he also caught the scent of a wolf, but not. He couldn't describe it, but it was like another wolf's, yet it was different.

The wolf shook his head. Not only was there now an expected person's scent, but there was a wolf-like not-wolf scent. More things for the wolf to inevitably ruin and be attacked over. Even so, with nothing better to do and a lot of questions, he began to follow the human scent, noting as he went that he passed where the crow feather quill had been found. Perhaps the scent's owner also owned the quill? Whether or not that was the case, the wolf had to know who. If they were a threat and, more importantly, if he had to taste blood tonight.

The wolf cringed as the thought passed through his head. *Blood. Taste. Feast.* The will began to pressure him again, forcing him to turn tail and run. Run like always. Run from, yet with, his problems. Run and hope his willpower didn't falter. Hope that his strength of mind was enough.

Chapter 25

House of Darkness

Draco groaned as he began to wake. Not of his own volition, of course, as it was most certainly not even dawn. No, he woke to something incessantly pressing, rubbing, and hitting his side. Not that it took much for the dragon to guess who the offending beast was. The dragon groggily loosed a low growl as he raised his head to glare at the direwolf at his side, "What do you want?"

The wolf padded over to the other side of the ruin, where a pile of cloth, as well as the pulsating mass of mystery meat, were waiting. The wolf paused and took a few moments to nose at the fleshy mass before beginning to pad in a circle. He completed several of these circles before lying down, his amber eyes glittering in the half-light of twilight.

Draco, who had been glaring at the wolf since he had been awakened, groaned and began grumbling, "Damned wolves. Making me wake up to see this again. It isn't dawn yet," still he continued to gaze at the grey-furred beast, "Well?"

The wolf made no movements to acknowledge Draco, instead simply closing his eyes. The dragon, anger within his gaze, watched as the wolf fell fast asleep in mere moments. The dragon opted to glare at the wolf for a moment more. Were Draco a basilisk, the wolf would have been dead there and then. Unfortunately, the dragon was, in fact, a dragon. Heaving a sigh of obvious discontentment, Draco rose to his feet and padded past the sleeping wolf to gaze at the skies from a crumbled wall. Dawn was fast approaching, leaving the world in a grey, quiet twilight. For just a moment, Draco felt a measure of peace steal into him. He may usually be asleep at this time, but that didn't mean the dragon didn't like this time of day. It was a beautiful, quiet, and peaceful time. Too bad it was followed by the hectic dawn.

Speaking of dawn, Sehero was beginning to rise, peering over the edge of the distant land. Draco, pausing a moment to release a massive, toothy yawn, made his way back to where the direwolf slept. Draco paused for a moment before stepping into view. He was greeted with the sight of the wolf becoming encased in that mysterious black fog. And not just the wolf, but also that fleshy mass. Before long, Draco couldn't see either of them, but he didn't have to as a cracking sound erupted from the shadowy form. Returning to the spot he had been sleeping in only a short time ago, Draco allowed himself to drop heavily. The impact made a satisfying thud. Pleased with himself with the action, the dragon turned his attention back to the enshrouded wolf. Or former wolf, as was the case when the black fog began to fade. Where the wolf had been was now Dane, entirely naked. The pulsating mass was nowhere to be seen.

Even as the dragon noted the disappearance of the fleshy mass, Dane's eyes fluttered open to the accompaniment of a long, world-weary groan. The newly restored warrior laid for a few moments, then heaved a heavy-sounding sigh. The human pushed himself into a seated position as he muttered, "I *hate* nights like that. I really do."

"Nights like what?"

Dane glanced over at Draco while he reached over and snagged the cloth next to him, "Nights when that will is particularly active and bloodthirsty and there is nothing to sate it with. All I can do is drive myself crazy trying to keep it in check."

Draco huffed, eyes stained with the weight of suspicion, "I don't understand what you mean."

Dane nodded as he began to wrap the cloth around his waist, deftly making a serviceable loincloth, "I'm not surprised at that. At night, when I walk in the form of a direwolf, there's this will. I don't know where it comes from or what it is. I call it the Wolf's Will. Nonetheless, it's there and it pressures me. To do all sorts of normal wolf things, but… beyond what is normal. Hunt just to kill. Fight just to revel in bloodshed… Mate just to feel the pleasure… You understand what I mean?" Dane asked as he finished making the loincloth. He paused for a moment to look at the dragon before reaching for the next bit of clothing.

"I understand. I suppose… Mate?"

Dane froze, his cheeks turning red just before they vanished behind his tunic as he began to pull it on, "Yes. It is so hard to resist the Wolf's Will. Fortunate, then, that it requires two… But enough of my moaning and groaning. Have you any other questions? Before everything begins for the day."

Draco chuckled to himself, amusement coloring the sound. That didn't stop him pressing the question most on his mind, "That pile of flesh and meat. What was that supposed to be?"

"A pile of flesh and meat."

"Oh, how funny you are," Draco snapped at Dane's reply, his mirth evaporating and his voice practically a waterfall of sarcasm, "What is it?"

"What I said it is. A pile of flesh and meat. Neither I nor my father know anything else about it. All we could find out is that something like it appears any time a shapeshifter- which I would be one- shifts to a form that is smaller than their current one. It is consumed when and if they shift from the smaller form to a larger one near it."

"Is that so?"

Dane shrugged as he began to pull a boot on, "So the book we found says. As it seems to work like that, I'd assume that must be it. But we have very little idea where it comes from or why. My father assumes it must be whatever parts of my body that are not used to make my wolf form, but I don't see why it doesn't just disappear instead of forming that grotesque mass."

Draco shook his head. Were he human, his expression might have resembled exasperation, "Why does it matter? So long as it isn't killing you, there is no need to care what its purpose is."

Dane rose to his feet, pondering Draco's words as he set about attaching the sheathed *Orsvehed Fril* to his belt, "That makes sense, coming from someone like you."

"What is that supposed to mean?"

Dane waved the question away, "Nothing important," he offered the dragon a smile and brushed away a bit of dust that had already formed on his tunic. Of course, in a ruin like Sanctuary, the gesture was an exercise in futility, "We should go. Argrex and Leonidas are expecting us."

"They always are. Every day. As though we have nothing better to do."

"We *have* nothing better to do, dear Draco," Dane gave Draco another small smile, which the dragon returned with a venomous glare, "Our only plans are to attack where we know the Corrupted are coming from. As we have no idea where *Dedran ko Ivfrofril* actually is, we have nothing to do until we can find out. Normally."

"Normally?"

Dane nodded slowly, speaking almost in time with his own thoughts, "Last night, I caught the smell of someone unfamiliar. Someone with the smell of a scholar. If I'm right, there is someone here other than us. Probably a scholar interested in the ruins or lake. There was also the smell of a wolf-not-wolf."

Draco raised an eye ridge ever so slightly, his wing rustling as he shifted them, "'Wolf-not-wolf?'"

Dane gave the dragon a helpless shrug, "That's the best way I can describe it… I think I know the smell. But I'm not sure where from."

Draco huffed, grumbling, "More damned wolves. I'm starting to regret bringing you with me. All it seems to be is wolf after wolf after wolf ever since I met you."

"Including me?"

"Especially you."

Dane surprised Draco by laughing, a foolish grin stretching across his face. Draco just stared at him, "What's so funny?"

Dane shook his head in dismissal, still grinning, "No idea. It just seemed funny, is all. That aside," his grin faded into a more serious expression, "I am curious what scholar is out here, and who or what is the source of that strange scent. Moreover, how dangerous are they to our current goals."

"Then let us find out. I'm tired of listening to the two anyways. Knowledgeable though they are, they have shared little useful knowledge."

Dane chuckled, stepping around the dragon to make his way out of the ruined library, "To you. To me, much of what they share is useful. Such as the temperament of dragons."

"I could have told you that," Draco snapped as he began to follow his much smaller companion.

"True. But they do know things you don't or seem to have no interest in sharing with me."

"Like what, exactly?"

Dane surprised the dragon again by turning and tapping him on the chest scales, "For one, the chest and upper torso muscles of dragons are denser, stronger, and are very specifically positioned so that you can fly and still use your front legs. Dracon, like Leonidas, as well as dragonborn are the same. It's why they are so strong. The disadvantage is if those muscles are damaged too much- and it doesn't take much, according to Argrex- you could easily lose the use of both your front legs and your front wings," the human gave Draco's chest scales another firm tap, "They also told me that dragons have organs that fill with air to make it easier to fly. As it turns out, Leonidas does not have them, hence why he can only glide and hope for the best. That aside, if those were to be punctured, you wouldn't be able to fly without extensive magic use. Even with them, some dragons need to use magic. Aside from those organs, there is also the gland at the back of your throat that you can use to produce a mist that burns on contact with the air. This 'liquid dragonfire,' as it is called, can be harvested and is apparently safe so long as it is in large amounts and not exposed to too much air."

"Can we stop with the lessons?" Draco began grumbling, "I get enough of this nonsense from those senile old fools. If we are going somewhere, then let us go."

Dane offered a nod as he sighed, "Alright, alright. But you're explaining to Leonidas and Argrex... If I'm remembering this right, the scent went... towards the southside of *Arun Fril*."

Draco bobbed his head and began padding forward, "You lead the way, then."

The pair began weaving through the ruins, trying to simultaneously find the source of the mysterious scent and not cause too much damage. Draco had already found out the hard way that some of the "intact" buildings were not very intact. Or stable.

Rounding a broken pillar, Dane carefully stepped over some rubble and stopped. Turning his head, he waved at Draco, "Hey, take a look!"

"What?"

"Some parchment," Dane snagged the article of note and held it up, "It looks like it's some scholar's notes… Hmm…" he added after studying the pages for a moment or two.

"Is it about anything of use to us?"

"Nothing too interesting. For you, I'd think. They seem to be about the ships that inexplicably go missing around the Triad."

"What ships?"

Dane turned his gaze to Draco and shrugged, "There's a legend that ships who sail too close to the Triad run the risk of vanishing without a trace… Huh," the human frowned slightly as he returned his attention to the parchment.

"What is it now?" Draco huffed, disinterest in Dane's discovery permeating his every word and flick of the tail.

"The scholar who wrote this apparently had an idea what was causing the ships to disappear. It seems they surmised that some kind of sea serpent may be responsible."

Draco shook his head as he stepped over a collapsed wall. His tail swung to the side and knocked a crumbling pillar into yet another pile of rubble, "Great. We can ignore that while looking for the scholar."

Dane chuckled as a thought came to him, "You are quite the vexed dragon, aren't you?"

"I wouldn't be if you would stop getting sidetracked!" Draco snapped, his golden, reptilian eyes rather clearly conveying his irritation to the cheerful-faced human.

"Hey, getting sidetracked can be useful," Dane stepped around what looked to be the weathered, draconic head of an old statue, "I once ended a clan of bandits because I happened to visit a blacksmith's shop I had no reason going to. Heard that he was quite the skilled blacksmith and felt like seeing him at his craft."

Draco eyed Dane, then managed to surprise the human by heaving a sigh and conceding, "You think that will tell us about the scholar we're looking for, then?"

Dane shrugged, "If it is by them, then yes. It could give us an idea on how to negotiate with them and avoid needless deaths."

"I expect that you mean the scholar's death. I severely doubt a scholar will be much of a threat," Draco remarked, his gaze drifting across the ruins. It halted on a lone spot amidst the crumbled masonry, "Speaking of that, look. That must be him."

Dane followed the dragon's gaze to see a human-shaped figure seated on some rubble, fiddling with something in front of him. Whatever it was hidden by the figure's back. Regardless of the object's identity, the figure seemed to be engrossed by it.

Dane glanced at Draco before resting his hand on the hilt of his sword. With slow steps tempered by caution, the warrior began making his way towards the figure. As he drew closer, Dane was able to identify a few things. One was that the figure was, in fact, also a human with brown hair. Secondly was the figure's garb. Rather than the robe that most scholars preferred, he was dressed in the tunic and breeches of a commoner, though his were dyed black. Despite this, what looked to be a black cloak was folded and lying nearby. Finally, they seemingly had moved chunks of masonry to create a makeshift desk on which books and scrolls were scattered about.

In addition to those observations, Dane was now in an angle that allowed him to see what it was that the stranger was doing. The human was gazing at the lake and writing something on a piece of parchment. Occasionally, he would consult one of the books or scrolls, then write something else on his parchment.

While Dane found himself unsure how to best get the stranger's attention, his draconic companion held no such reservations. Draco scowled as he watched the human. Without so much as a glance at Dane, Draco opened his mouth to speak.

"Please, don't say anything," Dane and Draco started as the human paused in his writing and spoke, "If you were to speak, dragon, you might very well blow some of my scrolls away. These are quite rare and valuable to my work and I'd rather not chase them here and there. Or watch them be blown into the water."

Dane looked at Draco, then spoke himself before the dragon got too indignant over the comment, "Our apologies. We just saw you here and-"

"I know. I saw you, too. On the west shore of *Arun ko Fril*. Yesterday evening, you were training with a rapier."

Dane nodded, his hand warily caressing the hilt of his sword, "Yes… I was… Who are you?"

The human raised his head. Turning about, he fixed his hazel eyes onto Dane, "I am Kohlen. I am a scholar studying the paranormal and the cryptic."

"The what?" Draco, having moved his head so as to comfortably speak without sending Kohlen's scrolls flying, asked.

"The paranormal and the cryptic. Ghosts and disappearing ships, to give an example."

"Then this is yours?" Dane offered the paper he had picked up earlier. Kohlen accepted, then gave Dane a nod after taking a moment to look at it.

"It is. I hadn't realized I'd lost it. Thank you."

Dane nodded, then made a vague gesture, really just a wave of the hand, at the paper, "You think there really is a sea monster near the Triad?"

"Potentially. There are signs that may be pointing to its existence. The disappearing ships, sailor's legends, and a few recent sightings of something near that area. Some claim it to be a dragon that had been seen, though just as many disagree as, after all, dragons aren't aquatic creatures."

Draco huffed, still avoiding the scholar's scrolls, "I have no interest in your nonsense. What I do have interest in is what you are doing here."

"I am looking into *Arun ko Fril*. Legends are widespread of this lake, but few scholars have taken it upon themselves to legitimize these tales. As is obviously apparent, I sought to do exactly that."

Dane peered at the papers Kohlen had before him, "'The Spirits of the Lightbound Lake?'"

The scholar nodded, his light brown hair barely seeming to catch the light, "Yes. Some refer to *Arun ko Fril* as the Lightbound Lake. But it is my belief that the lake may potentially be inhabited by spirits of some kind. And it is not idle speculation, as I have had some say. Rather rudely, mind you… Nevertheless, the lake does things that do not befit simple enchanted water. For one, it defends itself. Were I to suddenly attack the lake with a spell of some sort, the spell would be consumed before a counterattack consisting primarily of a ray of light would be used against me. It was quite the impressive sight. Still, if this is indeed part of the lake's enchantments…" Kohlen paused, then snagged his quill, which Dane was able to notice was a crow's feather, and began to write on the parchment before him, "The lake would have the ability to kill evil creatures, banish darkness, heal injuries, cure poisons and diseases, absorb magic, *and* attack threatening individuals. Such an enchantment is exceedingly difficult. The sheer magic prowess needed to create it would put even gods to shame. It makes more sense that something is protecting the lake. Most likely a nature spirit of some kind. I would suspect a naiad is responsible, except naiads have an affinity for fresh water, not light."

Draco snorted, "And that matters why? We know what the lake does, that's enough."

"Is it?" Kohlen challenged the dragon, pointing the tip of his quill at the scaled beast, "And what if that spirit not only exists as I believe, but wasn't friendly and suddenly attacked? If you don't know what you are opposing, you are doomed to failure from the start. Knowing is half the battle, after all."

Draco huffed, dissatisfied. Even so, he didn't refute the scholar, "Enough of this. If this spirit of yours exists and I have to fight it, I'll-"

Dane glanced between the two before suddenly stepping forward, interrupting the dragon, "Draco, could I ask him something before you continue your rant?"

"What is it?" Draco snapped, his voice both annoyed and curious.

Dane looked over to Kohlen, who was gazing at him expectantly, "Do you know about *Dedran ko Ivfrofril* or *Arun Ivfrofril*? Or anything about the creatures called Corrupted?"

The scholar nodded almost immediately, "Yes. I do. But I can't say it will necessarily do you much good... you haven't given me your name."

"I haven't. I am Dane, son of Sir Firrik. The dragon with me is-"

"Draco. You said his name just a few moments ago," the scholar gave a pause, before a small grin drifted onto his face, "You do know what the name 'Draco' means, Draco?" the dragon's only response was a low, threatening growl, "I see you do. It's quite the generic name, you know. So generic it's unusual," the scholar began to chuckle.

"Enough. Tell us what you know."

Kohlen, still grinning from his chuckling, offered a second nod, "Absolutely. Let's see… *Dedran ko Ivfrofril*, the Cave of Darkness, has quite the reputation. It has been, in order, the home of a clan of vampires, the lair of a necromancer who died attempting to control those vampires, the den of a particularly brutal pack of werewolves who were wiped out by the vampires, the lair of a lich who used to be the necromancer and managed to control the vampires this time, and the den of a second pack of werewolves who destroyed the lich and the vampires before turning on each other due to the influence of a sorcerer known as Akrazek. Beyond that, nothing is particularly known about it. No one has noted anything about what is inside. Not even Akrazek, despite there being definitive proof that he did, in fact, go there."

Draco gave the scholar a rather narrow-eyed look, his tail drifting from side to side in a slightly twitchy manner, "That's it?"

Kohlen offered a shrug and made a sweeping gesture with his hands, "Sorry. I've found nothing else about the place. If I did, I'd have already said it. Though I do know its location. Do you have a map? I'll mark the location on it," Dane nodded and extracted a worn sheet of parchment from his belt, a gesture Kohlen nodded approvingly of, "You choose to always have it on hand. Good choice. And it's well used, too," the scholar added before taking the parchment, marking a small 'x' in the Sidatial Mountains southwest of a forest marked as the Forests of Fae.

Dane accepted the map and took a moment to note where Kohlen had marked before returning it to his belt. As he did so, Dane noticed that Draco's tail had started to twitch more aggressively and decided to quickly step in with another question, "What about *Arun Ivfrofril*?"

The scholar offered another shrug, "Not much. *Arun ko Ivfrofril*, the Lake of Darkness, is as mysterious as *Arun ko Fril*. Legend claims it was created by some dark spellcasters in a past age. A group of five spellcasters- a mage, wizard, sorcerer, druid, and dark mage, ironically- bent on conquering the world. Fortunately, they were quite incompetent. When they corrupted the lake that would become *Arun ko Ivfrofril*, all of them, save for the wizard, died. Of course, that is where legends get hazy. None actually agree on the wizard's fate. All we know is that part of the legend is true."

"Which part?" Dane pressed.

"The creation of the lake. We have found several records where past scholars mentioned the corrupting of the lake by a group of evil spellcasters. However, they clearly were written with the idea that one already knew where the lake was. They include its original name, 'Dangelo Follia,' but not where it was. Equally unfortunate is that no known map has the lake's location. Maps from before the lake was corrupted are quite damaged and do not have it labelled anywhere. Or if they did, it was either too damaged or faded for anyone to realize it. In addition the location was either lost or it was, at some time, forbidden to mark the lake's location on a map, as no recent maps name the lake. There is a theory that the reputation of *Dedran ko Ivfrofril* is, in part, due to *Arun ko Ivfrofril* lying within the cave, but, of course, there is no proof whatsoever to back this claim. If anything, the claim is likely more false than true."

Draco surprised Dane by not immediately scoffing at the scholar, "I thought so. Even us dragons don't know of such a lake. *Arun Ivfrofril*, I mean to say. Dangelo Follia is a name I've heard before."

Kohlen blinked for a moment, then his face seemed to light up at the dragon's words, "Truly? Perhaps you would be so kind as to share?"

Draco shrugged, "I've not been to the place. It's exact location was lost to all but a few ancients. Even they claim that, unless it was too late, you would never find the lake. Don't ask me what that means."

"A few ancients, hmm? Perhaps I should speak to the dragon here. Argrex was his name?"

"You know of him?" Dane asked, his eyebrows raising in a clear gesture of surprise.

"Indeed. None may approach *Arun ko Fril* without their blessing, after all… Well, you can, but you'd be hounded by them the entire way."

Dane nodded before continuing, "Good point… We had one more question, if you would."

"Indeed, you did. What do I know of the Corrupted? The answer is nothing. I've never heard of the creatures," Kohlen snagged a rather thick book from next to him and offered it to Dane, "That's a bestiary. It details most known creatures. I've been working on it as I learn of more creatures. Even so, it is woefully incomplete. But, were you to look, it does not mention these Corrupted. Nor have I found anything regarding them in any book, scroll, or tome I've had the fortune of getting my hands on."

Draco's eyes began to narrow as his tail resumed its previous twitching, "You're saying we lied?"

"Not at all. I'm saying that these Corrupted have not, to my knowledge, ever been documented. To that end, I'd like you to tell me what you know of them. Perhaps they go by another name?"

Dane allowed his head to somewhat bend, his expression mirroring that of a thoughtbound scholar, "The two we saw appeared to be humans with ashen skin, black hair, and red eyes that glowed. They spoke in a very unusual manner and acted almost as one…"

Draco continued for the warrior as he paused in uncertainty, "According to Leonidas, the Corrupted once went to *Dedran ko Ivfrofril*," Dane nodded in agreement as Kohlen seemed to ponder the words.

"Is that so? Hmm… That is quite the useful bit of information," Kohlen grabbed a sheet of parchment and began to write, his quill darting from letter to letter, "If the Corrupted were regular people, then *Dedran ko Ivfrofril* is quite dangerous… However, this only adds to its mysteries. I wonder just how many it has. And what they are… Yes, I think…" the scholar continued to mumble to himself, his words becoming quieter and quieter until they were entirely incomprehensible. None too surprisingly, the scholar had also begun to ignore Dane and Draco.

Dane blinked, surprised at the scholar's sudden change in pace. It was moments later that he realized he was holding the bestiary Kohlen had offered. He went to place the book on a nearby rock, only for the engrossed scholar to interrupt.

"Keep the bestiary. I've another one. I find it useful to be able to consult such books when I uncover something new. After all, it might not be so new."

Dane nodded and looked over the book, "I think I've seen this book before."

Kohlen paused in his documenting to focus his gaze on Dane, "Have you? Are you a scholar as well? Or, perhaps, a noble? Most others would not have one…" the scholar paused for a moment, then continued as a realization seemed to touch him, "You called your father Sir Firrik. So you are a knight's son. But not just that. Your father, if I am right, is also a Whisperedge, trained to mastery upon the Eye, and Royal Knight of King Aridor. It is no wonder you know of the book."

Draco glanced between the two, then gave a rumble, "Dane, we have no need to be here any longer."

Dane turned his gaze to the dragon, then nodded in agreement. Instead of immediately leaving, he chose to offer a bow to Kohlen, "I would thank you for your aid, Kohlen."

The scholar chuckled as he began to turn his attention back to his papers and scrolls, "It was no effort on my part. I quite enjoyed our little talk. Perhaps we can meet again?"

"I would like that. Have you ever been by Verious?"

"Once or twice. If I have the chance, I might stop by sometime. I feel that you might provide more intriguing insights," the scholar waved a hand at them, "Enough for the day. I have research to do and you have somewhere to be, no?"

Dane chuckled and dipped his head towards Kohlen, "That we do. Farewell, Kohlen."

"Fare thee well, Dane. Draco," the scholar waved them away again, his attention locking back onto the books and scrolls before him.

It was Draco who moved first, not questioning or arguing with the now totally engrossed scholar. The dragon simply turned and began padding westward, back towards where Leonidas and Argrex awaited them.

Even as the pair trekked their way back through the rubble, Draco was surprisingly slow to start speaking. Dane had expected him to start immediately, "Do you think that Leonidas and Argrex might know more than they told us?"

"They could, but why would they not share it?"

Draco scoffed, shaking his head in a weary manner, "Why would they? We have no reason to trust them or the scholar."

Dane nodded as he stepped around a scaled stone hand, "True. We don't have any reason at all. Then again, I had no reason to trust you when we first met, but I did. Now look at us. Give them a chance."

The dragon awarded Dane with a scathing glare, "Then tell me. If they happen to know more about *Dedran ko Ivfrofril* and the Corrupted, why have they said nothing?"

"Well, it could be that they actually don't know anything else. But if they do…" Dane gave it a few moments of thought, then added, "If they do, then they could simply be waiting for the right time… Or hiding it and waiting for us to march to our deaths. Who's to say?"

The dragon just huffed as they drew near the part of the ruins they were more familiar with. Before he had a chance to give Dane the stinging reply he had planned, Vreena appeared from behind a crumbling wall. The half elf ran towards them, her steps as fast as she could make them and light as a bee's touch.

"Dane. Draco. With me, now."

"What is it?" Dane asked, but his question was immediately struck down.

"Just come!" With those words, Vreena took off back towards where the ruins of the city's palace were. Dane began to run after her, the heavy footfalls of Draco striking the ground behind him.

Chapter 26

Corruption's Mark

As the trio hurried through the ancient ruins of the long-dead city, it did not take long for Draco to loose a growl in annoyance, "Damn all this rubble. You two continue on foot, I'll follow in the air."

"Yes, do that!" Vreena assented. The dragon wasted no time at all getting himself airborne. If he wasn't too busy following Vreena, who was rushing at a very rapid pace, Dane would have commented on the dragon. He hadn't seen Draco move that fast since the pair had first met.

Of course, Dane was much too busy hurrying after Vreena, dodging a bit of rubble himself as she jumped over a fallen statue, "Where are we going? What happened?"

"Corrupted. They showed up and began attacking Leonidas and Argrex. I was sent to find you while they kept the Corrupted busy."

"Corrupted? Did they say why?"

Vreena leapt over another bit of rubble, the minor display of athleticism hardly even interrupting her ability to speak, "Not at all. They just appeared, yelled, 'Battle commences,' and attacked. But, more importantly, is that they are elves."

"Corrupted Elves?"

"Yes. But enough talk, we must hurry!"

Dane nodded and began to redouble his efforts, dashing through the ruins with an agility that would have been a bit too reminiscent of a wolf for his liking had he noticed. As the pair drew ever closer to the ruined palace, the sounds of battle began to drift over the silent ruin. Vreena momentarily disappeared from Dane's sight as she rounded a more-or-less intact wall. When Dane followed her, he came to see the source of the sounds.

Four human-like creatures were engaged in battle with Argrex and Leonidas. Three bore narrow, slender swords- not unlike Vreena's- while the remaining one wielded a flat, leaf-shaped spear, and all looked to be female. They were quite tall, but thin. Their bodies were fairly angular, yet had an elegant air around it. What caught Dane's eye was how smooth and well-cared for they looked. It was as if someone had meticulously cleaned and groomed them from head to toe. If not for their ashen-skin, red eyes, and black hair, he would have called them beautiful. Whatever the human thought of them, the ashen skin and red eyes made it abundantly clear that they were Corrupted and thus the elves Vreena had spoken of. If they were, Dane decided that he wouldn't mind meeting non-Corrupted ones.

More important than their looks, however, was their speed. It practically stopped Dane in his tracks, though that was entirely from surprise. The Corrupted flitted about the dragon and dracon like hummingbirds, never in one place too long. It made Dane, albeit momentarily, wonder how his father could ever even come close to matching them.

A clang rang out, bringing the human back to the task at hand. A Corrupted elf dueled with the weaponless Leonidas while Argrex had his claws full keeping track of his three opponents. Dane charged as he pulled his blade from its sheath. Despite the difference in speed and his lack of a weapon, it seemed that Leonidas was more than capable enough to hold his own, prompting Dane to turn his assistance to Argrex.

Dane swung his blade in a lethal arc towards one of the elves' necks, hoping to catch the spear-wielding Corrupted off guard. At first, it seemed as though he actually was going to hit the elf. Then, in the blink of an eye, it turned and spun its weapon, knocking the warrior's blade aside.

"Begone, Conflicted. This is not of his concern," even as the Corrupted spoke, she whipped the spear into a level position, then lunged forward with a speed that defied Dane's sight. The human warrior only just managed to dodge the thrust, the spearpoint even managing to catch on his tunic as it shot past.

"Take heed, Dane!" Leonidas called as he batted away a sword swing, "Their speed is unparalleled and beyond natural, but limited t-" the dracon broke off with a grunt as his foe's blade slashed across his side. Instead of finishing the sentence, the aged warrior chose to counterattack, forcing his foe to dodge back. The dracon tried to press his advantage, only to find himself surprised when the elf he had been fighting swiftly pivoted and began engaging the newly arrived Vreena. At the same time, one of the remaining elves harassing Argrex suddenly darted towards Leonidas, forcing the ancient king into backpedaling to avoid her lethal stab.

His backpedal carried him past Vreena as she darted back to avoid her own opponent's thrust. She darted forward just as fast, countering her foe's thrust with an upward slash. The corrupted elf didn't allow the slash to succeed, deflecting it off her own blade before slashing at Vreena with a swift diagonal strike. Vreena leaned to the side, allowing her foe's blade to slash only the air by her head. Even as this happened, a cry rang out, but it wasn't from Vreena.

Dane staggered back, his empty hand pressing against the shoulder of his sword arm. He didn't get to do much more than that as his opponent, the remaining sword-wielding elf who had been engaged with Argrex only a handful of moments ago, charged at him again. Dane dodged to the side, narrowly avoiding the deadly blade, before delivering a backhanded slash. The blow never landed as he stopped mid-swing, turning his feint into a stab. Much to his surprise, the elf proved to be unprepared for the tactic and was, to his momentary shock, too slow to stop the strike. *Orsvehed Fril* sank into the Corrupted elf's shoulder, the mere act of getting injured seemed to stun the elf. Dane didn't take a chance to question it as he used his- now bloody- free hand to shove the Corrupted away. The elf staggered back, then recovered and darted forward, blade sweeping low towards Dane's legs. The human saw through the elf's recklessness and leapt forward, stepping past the elf. Taking advantage of the position, Dane swiftly spun about, bringing his blade into a stab as he did. The elf failed to react in time, allowing the human's blade to grant the ashen-skinned creature a certain death and Dane a few moments' reprieve. Pulling his blade free- and wincing at just how easy the task had been- the warrior turned his gaze to see the spear-wielding elf he had been fighting just a few moments ago was keeping Argrex busy.

Argrex loosed a roar, slamming his paw down. His roar turned into an annoyed growl as the spear-wielding elf dodged with a mockingly stylish roll. The elf kept going, turning the defensive maneuver into an attack by thrusting upward. The spearhead shot past Argrex's head as he simply shifted his neck; the dragon having fully expected the move. He allowed a breath to fill his lungs, preparing to end this foolery with a single devastating breath. Unfortunately, he didn't expect the elf to leap to her feet and suddenly pull the spear back. With a burst of that unnatural speed the elves seemed to be wielding like weapons, the Corrupted plunged the spear into Argrex's eye.

Argrex gave out another roar, though now one of pain as he recoiled from the strike. The elf took her movement in stride, gracefully darting backwards while tugging her weapon free. The action only prompted the dragon to loose yet another pained roar, leaving him unable to notice the elf's next, obvious movements. The elf swept to the side, bringing the dragon's remaining eye, his left, into view with her spear poised to throw.

Just as she was about to fling the spear, the ground beneath her feet shook, born of some great force behind her. The elf spun about, bringing her spear to bear, only to freeze and go rigid as what appeared to be a diamond-shaped, golden blade erupted from her back. Draco sneered, his gaze laden with disgust as he gazed at the elf lodged upon his tail tip, "Filthy vermin," the dragon spat before whipping his tail to the side, flinging the dying elf into a nearby ruin. The aged stones collapsed on top of the body, kicking up a cloud of dust in the process.

The dragon ignored the now-ruined ruin and turned his gaze to his companions, about to come to their aid, when he saw that there was no need. Vreena disarmed her foe at that very moment, her blade flashing in the midday sun as she quickly turned the disarm into a stab, putting the newly-unarmed Corrupted elf down.

At the same time, the remaining elf fought a hopeless battle against the combined strength of Leonidas and Dane. The elf swung its blade in a horizontal backhand, seeking a blow against Dane. Leonidas didn't allow it, stepping between the pair and catching the blade with his bare claws. Unable to tug the weapon free, the elf had no means of preventing Dane's next strike, a lethal strike to the Corrupted creature's exposed neck. The human warrior heaved a sigh of relief as the elf's body fell upon the broken cobblestone.

For several moments, no one made a sound as each tried to understand what had happened. Then, with a grunt, Draco turned his gaze to Argrex, "How are you, old one?"

The older dragon shook his head, his face bound by a mask of pain, "Better than I could be, much worse than I want to be…"

Draco grunted, then turned his gaze to their smaller compatriots, "Dane?"

"We're fine," the human called while wrapping a strip of cloth about his upper arm, "How are you, Leonidas? You got hit in the ribs, did you not?"

The dracon waved the question away, "I am uninjured. Fragile though they are, my scales were enough to shield me from receiving anything more than simple bruises. Argrex is in much more need of medical treatment than I. Seest thou to him."

Vreena waved Dane away when she heard Leonidas's words, "Allow me. I am no master, but I do know some healing magicks."

The dracon chuckled, prompting the remaining two humanoids to turn and stare at him, "Dost thou truly? Ah, what irony those words haveth to mine ears."

"Irony?"

"Hmm, indeed. I was once told that twas priests and those of faith who haveth alone the right to heal. Others are but a mockery. I always found the notion unfathomable."

Vreena shook her head, "It is a common notion that the potency of healing magic is tied to one's faith. Not everyone believes this, of course. Though some of the strongest healers are known to be priests. It is quite the mystery… No matter. Let me see to that injury of yours, Argrex."

"Very well," the dragon groaned as he lowered himself to the ground. He laid his head before the half-elf, a grimace strewn across it. Blood streamed down the right side of his face, pooling about the black-scaled muzzle. Much to the surprise of Dane, the dragon's remaining good eye was watering, as though his usual stoic personality was threatening to break.

"*Arkelw ve froehrain,*" Vreena murmured as she reached out to lay a hand upon the dragon's wound. Argrex didn't move as to not disturb the half-elf, though Dane noticed the dragon's eye ridge twitching. As she did so, a warm glow began to radiate from Vreena's hand, filling the air with an odd, yet comforting feeling. Dane found himself attempting to both smile and grimace. The air itself felt soothing, despite him not being the one getting healed, yet it somehow also tinged him with a hint of anxiety. He couldn't quite decide which felt right.

Even as Dane puzzled over this odd conundrum, Vreena continued her spell until Argrex heaved a heavy sigh, though this one of relief, "Thank you, Vreena. This may come as a surprise to you, but I am very sensitive to pain. It is not often that I am injured, you see," when the dragon pulled back, Dane blinked, startled when he saw that the missing eye hadn't returned. Instead, there was a dark, empty socket where it should have been, albeit not bleeding.

"Your eye," the human managed to say, before turning his gaze to Vreena, "You didn't heal his eye?"

She shook her head, "I would have, if I had the knowledge and strength to. I am far from weak in magic. Even so, compared to most elves, I am not a very skilled spellcaster, nor are what spells I know all that powerful. This was all I could do," she waved towards the dragon's face, then turned her head to gaze at Argrex herself, "You might be a little hungry after that. Go get something to eat, if you would."

"Yes. I will do that," Argrex paused, almost as though he was thinking, then bobbed his head, "You have my gratitude, Vreena."

"Go. Eat. Gratitude will not fill your belly. But it is noted," at the half-elf's words, Argrex gave a moment's chuckle before taking to the sky, the wind from his wings scattering dust all over the place and everyone present.

Leonidas coughed, then gave a short growl, "He knoweth well that I hate that. Thrice-Blasted dragon."

Draco watched Argrex fly off for only a moment, then turned his gaze to the ancient king, "Tell me, where did these-" he nudged one of the fallen elves with the bloody tip of his tail, "-come from?"

Leonidas awarded the dragon's inquiry with a shrug, "It is as likely as not that you know more than I. They simply appeared and attacked. Nonetheless, it concerns me well that they would enact so bold a plan."

Draco grunted, then turned his gaze to Dane, "Remember the Corrupted that attacked us when you were a wolf? They mentioned something about a… well, a 'They,' If we can find this 'They…'"

Vreena was studying one of the fallen elves for a moment, listening to Draco, when she suddenly jumped back, a curse falling from her lips, "Dane! Draco! Leonidas! Look! The bodies!" Vreena didn't know if the pair reacted to her words. She was far too focused on the body, which were changing. Their black hair were the most obvious change, turning to blondes and pale reds. The one whose eyes remained open had them turn from glowing red to a rather pretty blue. Even their skin went from ashen to an eerie, yet beautiful alabaster color. Dane, observing the elves himself, wasn't certain if beautiful fit the description. Radiant, perhaps?

Beauty to Dane aside, Vreena found herself at a loss. A loss she chose to voice to her companions, "They've… changed. How? And why? They've gone from Corrupted elf to true elf…"

"True elf?" Dane inquired as the half-elf seemingly couldn't tear her eyes away from what was before her.

Vreena offered a shrug and shook her head, "Elves… Let us simply say that elves are quite driven towards beauty. Quite. But that is not what is important. More important is that these elves, in appearance, have had their mysterious corruption purged from them after their deaths. If I were to guess, I'd say the corruption is not permanent. It must be able to be undone."

Leonidas, who had knelt next to the nearest elf, rose and offered Vreena a nod, "Aye, I would agree with thee… I don't recall seeing such a thing, though I must admit that the few Corrupted we encountered escaped with their dead whenever it was that we fought."

Dane nodded, then looked over to Draco, "Draco?"

"What is it?"

The human paused for a moment, his gaze turning back to the bodies, before he finally convinced himself to speak, "We know where to find *Dedran ko Ivfrofril*, don't we? What do you say to seeking the place out?"

The dragon huffed, eyeing his human companion, "Are you expecting me to say no? I'd rather you tell me when we are going and what took you so long to ask."

Dane awarded Draco with a grin, "As soon as possible and because I wasn't quite sure. If these Corrupted are truly coming from *Dedran ko Ivfrofril*, then it must be dealt with. The longer we wait, the more of these Corrupted are created and are able to do… whatever it is that they have been doing," even as he said this, Leonidas turned and began to walk off. It was almost as if he didn't care what they were saying.

Paying Leonidas little mind, Vreena stepped forward at Dane's words, "We have no idea on how many Corrupted there are, or what kinds. We know of human and elven ones. Perhaps there are dwarven or even dragon Corrupted."

"That's fine by me… If need be, we can… We can wait until nightfall…"

"When you shift," Draco said, his gaze wary and almost poisonous, "I thought you disliked that."

"Right… I don't want to, but I am smaller and faster in that form… But I hate the idea of it, yes… Even so, if I have to use it… No matter. You and I should prepare ourselves to march east."

Vreena stepped forward, drawing Dane's attention towards her, "You and Draco? What of me?"

"I would offer you to come-" Dane started, then paused for a moment. After a moment to collect his thoughts, Dane shook his head and started again, "I do want you to come, but we aren't planning to attack the place. Draco and I are going to scout out the place. Make sure we know what is happening there. That way we don't charge to our deaths when we do attack it. Draco can fly to escape any danger while I... I should be fine. Does that make sense to you, Vreena?"

The half-elf gave a pause, her gaze at first locked on Dane, then drifting to gaze at the rubble-strewn ground. Her hand began to fiddle with the hilt of her sword, as a mask of doubt held firm upon her face, "... Very well. I'll speak with you later then."

"Huh?"

"I should go check on Argrex. To make sure he is okay. Losing an eye will be disorienting for a time," she murmured, walking off.

Dane watched her go, then gave a sigh, "She seemed disappointed."

"Yes, she did."

Dane shook his head, then picked up a small piece of rubble, "I wonder why... Could she have wanted to go there for a reason? Other than to help us?" Dane ran his thumb along the jagged chunk of stone. On one side of it, the chunk resembled a piece of a scale. The rest of it may as well be a regular piece of rock one could find in any mountain range. He ran his thumb about the flat, scale-like part while Draco silently watched him. The dragon seemed to show no interest in answering the question Dane had posed.

The two remained like this, locked in silent observation, for only a few minutes, when Dane suddenly spoke again, "Draco?"

"What is it?"

"The dragon you fought at Adrian. It was black with red eyes, wasn't it?"

The gold dragon bobbed his head, realizing Dane's query as soon as the human had finished his question, "You believe there might be Corrupted dragons."

"There's a possibility."

"Like as not, the possibility is very real," Dane glanced over to see the speaker, Leonidas, standing to the side and watching the pair, evidently having just returned. In his clawed hands was the arming sword that was once Dane's father's. Leonidas offered the weapon to Dane, "If it is thy wish to seekest *Dedran ko Ivfrofril*, I ask that thou leavest *Orsvehed Fril* here. This blade of thine ought to suffice."

"And why would he do that? *Orsvehed Fril* is a better weapon," Draco contested, "Dragons don't need weapons, but even *I* can see that. Why would he use an inferior blade?"

Leonidas nodded, but did not pull back his offer, "Thou art not wrong, but think thee in a different way. Ye go upon this scouting mission because ye have no knowledge as to your foes' numbers, nor their capabilities. If the worst should come to pass and ye are discovered and hopelessly outmatched, it would be better to lose a blade lacking special power such as this rather than *Orsvehed Fril*, would it not? When ye have returned with your knowledge on our foes, and when it is that we march upon them, then it is safer to bring *Orsvehed Fril*."

"I get it," Dane chimed in, "If we know what to expect, then we are not risking powerful weapons falling into enemy hands as easily."

"Exactly so. If thou wishest to take thy blade, I would not oppose thee. Even so, givest thou my words a moment's thought."

Dane reached down in response and unbuckled *Orsvehed Fril* from his belt and offered the sheathed weapon to Leonidas, "I think you have a fair point. Keep an eye on this, would you? I'm going to need it."

"Indeed," was Leonidas's reply as he both took the blade and gave Dane the other arming sword, "I promise to thee that I shall take care of it well."

"Thank you."

"What I believe more important is thy preparations. For what remains of the day, gather what it is you shall need in this endeavor. Your quest shall begin on the following day. Is this sufficient for you?"

Dane nodded and glanced over to Draco. The dragon eyed the blade in Leonidas's hands, but sighed as he acquiesced, "Very well. We should begin."

"Agreed. Let's go."

Chapter 27

Eyes of an Artist

Dane gave a nod, his eyes scanning the inside of his pack. Assured to himself that his pack was ready, the human set about tying it closed. As he did this, he couldn't help but sweep his gaze about the ruined city. Oddly, the crumbling stone seemed to glimmer in the light of the early morning. Odd though it was, Dane found the sight comforting. It was like the city was wishing him good luck.

As Dane acknowledged the beauty of his surroundings, Draco stalked over. His pawfalls seemed to ring about the empty ruin with every step he took, "Are you ready?" The dragon grumbled.

"Almost. I'm packed and ready, but there is one more thing. Do you know where Vreena is?"

Draco grunted and jerked his head towards the west, "She was over there somewhere. I don't know what she was doing."

Dane chuckled, "You don't care, do you?"

"So long as she doesn't interfere, then you are right. I don't care what she does. But if you must, go."

Dane gave the dragon a small smile before walking off into the ruins. Just like before, the ruins glittered in Sehero's light, except that the glittering now danced about as Dane moved. Now, rather than wish him good luck, the city seemed as though it was celebrating him. Dane found himself disliking the thought. He wasn't anyone to celebrate. If anything, he was better off being reviled. Much better off…

It was in such a terrible mindset that Dane continued through the ruins, his gaze sweeping across what was once a city to pick out Vreena. For a time, he couldn't find her. All he saw was rubble, broken buildings, shadows, and some loose scales that likely belonged to Argrex and Leonidas, given their colors. Dane had an eerie thought that it was just the place for a monster to live. Dane shook the thought away- though not in its entirety- and kept walking.

He continued to find absolutely nothing. Nothing but rocks and rubble until he rounded a building with a caved-in roof that used to be the barracks and finally saw Vreena. She was positioned on a small, gradual hillock that overlooked *Arun Fril*. She had some barkless branches Dane recognized set up to make a makeshift easel. On that easel was a small wood-framed canvas that Vreena appeared to be painting on.

Dane approached and watched her paint, his movements leaving no sound to hear. The painting Vreena was making was a near-detail perfect depiction of Arun Fril. In fact, Dane found himself wondering if she was a better painter than King Aridor's royal painter. Despite how impressive the painting looked, Dane couldn't help but notice the odd shapes. Laced through the lake were pale yellow ovals, meanwhile wherever there was sunlight there were these little transparent green diamonds. For a painting of a landscape, they seemed like they should be out of place. However, Dane found that he didn't dislike them. In fact, he found himself thinking that the way Vreena portrayed the shapes added a very unique, even elegant, aspect to the painting.

"That's beautiful, Vreena. I love how well you captured the lake and the sunlight," Dane said, studying the painting. As he spoke, Vreena jumped and made a noise that sounded like a cross between a yelp and a cry. She spun around with a wild expression that seemed to fade even as she turned. She paintbrush lowered from the defensive position she had it in as she recognized Dane.

"Dane. What are you doing here?"

"I would ask the same of you, but I can see what you are doing. It's very good," Dane countered, "Though… is this supposed to be a landscape painting?"

"Yes."

Dane nodded slowly, then pointed at a yellow oval, "Then what are these shapes? I don't see them."

"I do…"

"Where?"

Vreena shifted uncomfortably, her gaze locked on her painting, "Everywhere… No one else sees them. That I know of, anyways. I've always been able to see them."

"Really? What are they?"

Vreena gave a short chuckle, more a bark, then shook her head, "Sorry. I explained that terribly. They aren't anything. Real, anyways. They're all in my head, if you will. They appear when I look at things and hear sounds."

"Look at things and hear sounds? What do you mean?"

Vreena chuckled again, this time more fully, as if she were relaxing, "Exactly that. When I look at something, shapes start to appear in my vision. When I hear something, the shapes are colored. Or that's how I think it works…" she paused for a moment, then, seeing that Dane still possessed a confused expression, added, "When I look at the lake, I see ovals. When I hear the lake, the ovals turn yellow. Because the lake is so far away, I can only just hear it, so the yellow is very faint. If I were right next to it, with the sounds of the lake at their loudest, the yellow would probably be very vivid."

Dane blinked, his expression still uncertain, "So, does everything have a color and shape?"

"Yes. And they can mix depending on what I see and hear. It's quite peculiar when I see multiple things and hear multiple things… But, yes. Everything has a shape and color to me. You yourself are a deep purple star."

"Deep purple star?"

Vreena nodded, a little reluctant, then offered a shrug, "I can't control what I see. Your voice is a deep purple, and the sight of you invokes stars… But you weren't looking for me to talk about my strange visions. Did you need me for something?"

Dane nodded a bit too fast, saying, "Yeah. Yesterday, you seemed upset with Draco and I when we decided we were going to *Dedran ko Ivfrofril* without you. I just wanted to make sure you were well before we leave."

Vreena smiled at Dane's words, shaking her head, "I will be fine. I'm just deeply concerned about whatever is causing the creation of these Corrupted. It is not easy to catch an elf, yet we just fought four who had been corrupted."

"There are human ones, too."

"Yes… There is something of a poem known well amongst elven children. Of course, it was human-made and not exactly good, but it is very fitting:

> *The dwarves are strong and durable*
> *The humans, crafty and cunning*
> *Try as they might*
> *They'll never catch*
> *The nimble, agile elf.*"

Dane frowned slightly, his eyes locked on Vreena for a few moments before he shrugged, "I'm not sure what your point is with that."

"My point is that elves are exceedingly difficult to catch. Even if one was losing a fight, they could simply run and there'd be little anyone could do about it, save another elf. Or if they had the elf surrounded. Yet, somehow, those four were Corrupted."

Dane blinked, his head slowly nodding as he considered the half-elf's words, "Meaning they must have been captured. Somehow."

"That is possible. It could be that they were Corrupted willingly. Or somewhat willingly. In either case, it concerns me."

Dane's face once again fell into a thoughtful expression, "I see. Then we both are after the same thing. We want to know what's happening."

Vreena paused, mouth slightly open, then pointed her brush at him. Her voice was ever so slightly condescending as she huffed, "That much was obvious from the start."

"Yes, but now I know why. Draco was curious as well. Somewhat."

"He didn't care, did he?"

Dane sighed and shook his head at the question, "No. As long as you aren't interfering, he doesn't care what you do."

Vreena sighed as well, her gaze drawn towards the ruins, "What a charmer he is."

Dane chuckled, "Heh, you get used to him."

"I'll take your word for it. But you understand why I wish to come, no?"

"I do, but I'd rather you stayed here. Three people are more noticeable than two. Argrex also just lost an eye. He has Leonidas, but I'd rather someone with the ability to heal be nearby," Dane gave Vreena a light, yet pointed, look, "You understand?"

Vreena heaved another sigh and shook her head, "I suppose I do, to some extent. I'd rather that I came. I am quite a bit more stealthy than Draco, but so be it."

Dane smiled, catching Vreena off-guard, and chuckled for a second time, "Oh, I know you would, but Draco can't heal and with Argrex getting used to having one eye, no one could stop him from coming. But you have my thanks, Vreena."

"You'd better come back, though. Or I will hunt the pair of you down, beat the scales off of Draco, and strip you of your fur to make a cloak," Vreena pointed her paintbrush at Dane and jabbed it towards him like a blade, "And you being what you are isn't going to get you out of the snare this time."

"'Strip me of my fur,' hmm? Alright. We will. I can't speak for Draco, of course, but I'll be sure to be careful."

"Good. Now, go. Draco's probably waiting and getting annoyed that you are wasting time."

Dane grinned at Vreena's verbal jab, offering her a chuckle in response, "Heh heh heh, he almost certainly is. Farewell."

"And you, also," was Vreena's reply as Dane offered a nod, then left. His trek back through the ruins was uneventful, which was relieving for the human. Uneventful was how he preferred it. What wasn't uneventful was his arrival at the lakeshore. There stood Draco, grumbling to himself as he so often did. The moment he caught sight of Dane, he raised his voice.

"What kept you?"

"Talking to and finding Vreena. Not in that order."

Draco scoffed, "Enough of her. Are we to leave?"

Dane shook his head and pointed at the dragon, "You need to relax. She's a friend."

"So says she."

"So says I. She's a companion of ours and an ally."

"Enough. You and I are not changing each other's mind on this… ah, what is the word? Sur? Suj? Sub?"

"Subject?"

The dragon huffed, but awarded Dane with a slight nod, "Aye. Subject. No matter. Are we going or do you wish to continue prattling about here?"

"No. I'm good to go," was Dane's response as he snagged his pack, "Let us away, Dragon."

"You know my name. Use it."

"I did, Dragon," Dane shrugged, a grin twitching onto his lips. He began to step forth, eyes locked to the east. However, if his ears had been those of a wolf's, they would have been perked. And for good reason.

"My name is Draco, you rotten-scaled, flame-lacking fool. Call me 'Dragon' again and I swear; I will tear your furless hide to slivers," the dragon harumphed, which Dane hadn't known Draco could do, then proceeded to grumble more, "Damned werewolves and their damned insistence on making a fool of me. And my nose! Damn you, Dane. You must have ran all over this blasted ruin. The smell of wolf is everywhere."

Chapter 28

Trust

The winds rushed past the pair as they marched eastward, ever at their backs and spurring them to travel onward. They had already traveled some distance from *Arun Fril*, which came as both an annoyance and a relief to the pair of travelers. The wind, of course, was so strong that it practically blew Dane off his feet and made communication, aside from Draco's mysterious telepathy, generally impossible. However, the further east they traveled, the more the wind gradually grew weaker. Looking forward to being able to hear something other than the rushing winds, the two pressed onward.

Draco, his head swinging from side to side in an effort to make sure he wasn't caught off guard, jumped when Dane suddenly approached his left flank and pounded on it. The dragon fixed his diminutive companion with a stare, *What do you want?*

The human began to wave his hands about. He brought them together in front of himself, brought them closer, then had them separate as they approached his chest. He then tapped his ears and looked pointedly at Draco, as if expecting that the dragon understood.

The dragon, to put it bluntly, did not understand, *Whatever that was, it was meaningless to me.*

The human awarded his friend's ignorance with what appeared to be a huff, then began to speak. That is, Draco assumed that was what Dane was doing, because his mouth began to move. Draco stopped walking and watched his silent companion speak without speaking for a few moments, when the wind decreased from rip-roaring gale to a mere steady wind without so much as a 'this is happening.' Dane sighed as soon as the wind was no longer preventing him from being heard.

"That's better. I remembered Vreena doing this on our trek to Sanctuary. I was able to convince her to teach me how she did it. Thought it might be useful."

Draco's gaze swung about himself, his eye ridges rising as though he were pleased about something. The sound of the strong winds wasn't gone, but now it was a bit farther away and a lot lessened. Far enough that the dragon felt reasonably comfortable, "Finally, you do something useful."

"I've been plenty useful."

"So says you and you alone," Draco snapped, then shook his head, "Enough of this. Useful as it was, we continue onwards."

Dane offered a nod, as though he was agreeing with the dragon's want to press forth. His words, however, were anything but, "You need to take a few moments to relax, Draco. You've been high-strung and touchy about everything since I met you. I understand that this is a pressing matter. I know it is. But we won't get anywhere with you constantly leaping at my throat."

The dragon swung its head about to give Dane a scathing glare. The words that followed were sharp and stinging, "I'm leaping at nothing. We met a few months ago. I consider you an ally, but not a friend. And I don't want you attempting to worm your way into some sort of affection like you are."

"Just an ally? You couldn't bring yourself to kill me."

"Because I loathe killing people who don't deserve it. Werewolf though you are, you clearly are not like any other werewolf. In other words, you've done nothing worth killing you over. That doesn't make you a friend of mine. Especially that you are a werewolf."

Dane shook his head, heaving a disgruntled sigh, "You just said I'm different."

"You are. And that's why I have no interest in being your friend. I told you before that I trust you. And that is still so. I trust *you*. But *you* are not the wolf. You said as much with your rambling about your 'wolf's will.' That, I don't trust. I believe you understand me?"

Dane sighed a second time, but offered the dragon a nod. One hand playing with the blade at his belt, he nodded again, "Yeah. I get you. You're worried that you won't be able to kill me like Seven."

"I never said anything about Seven."

"You tried to kill Seven. Even though he was your friend, you would have killed him if you could have because there was no other way to stop him. Because he was a monster. A brutal werewolf that would tear anything to shreds without remorse. I'm not the same. I can more or less control myself. But not always. And that makes you afraid. You're afraid that you'll have to kill me because of what the Wolf's Will is doing. Unlike Seven, who was an uncontrollable beast when Ephala hunted full, there is no guarantee that I cannot regain myself. You-"

"Don't want the weight of killing a friend for no reason on my conscience. Aye, you're right," Draco sighed, then shook his head. His eyes drifted back to Dane before the dragon gave a low grunt, "Enough. You understand now. More than I had intended, I might add... No matter, let us go. To the Cave."

Dane reached down and tugged the worn sheet of parchment from his belt and opened it for the dragon to see. He tapped a small labeled dot on the map, "I want to go to Sei. It's just southwest of our destination, according to Kohlen. Perhaps they will have knowledge of use before we walk into something we are not prepared for."

Draco wasted no time whatsoever. Almost as soon as Dane had finished speaking, the dragon started walking again, "Then let us go. We have not the time to waste."

"I suppose. Are you flying or continuing on foot?"

"Wind is too strong to stay near you. On foot."

Dane nodded, though he enhanced the action by adding a chuckle and a short statement, "You don't want a repeat of a few months ago? When we were on our way to the Quel'meg and you-"

"If this conversation continues, I'm eating you like the beast you are."

Dane raised his hands in surrender, a smile touching his lips, "Alright. Alright. We can walk on in silence. After we consider what it is we shall do about the Ekasor."

"What of it?"

"I will have to cross the river at some point. I'm curious as to whether you have an idea as to what to do."

Draco grunted, his tail flicking to the side in what was best described as a highly agitated manner, "No. That will be a problem that *you* shall handle."

"Will you carry me?"

"No."

Dane smirked, then shrugged, "Well, it'll be faster that way, but if you want to take longer, then complain about it..."

"You will cross it on your own. I will not carry you."

"What will you do if that isn't possible?"

Draco continued to stalk forward, his posture screaming his displeasure, "I will watch you flounder and flail impotently until you do. Now, silence."

"Alright-" Dane began, a mischievous smile crossing his face.

"That is not silence."

ΩΩΩΩΩΩΩΩΩΩΩΩΩΩΩΩΩΩΩΩΩΩΩΩΩΩΩΩΩΩΩΩΩΩΩΩΩΩΩΩΩΩΩΩΩΩ
ΩΩΩΩΩΩΩΩΩΩΩ

The walking in silence did not last very long, in Draco's opinion. In reality, Dane kept silent for a good two to three hours. Still, the dragon would have much preferred it if Dane had been thoughtful enough to stay silent all the way to Sei. The human asked too many difficult questions.

"Draco. Could I ask you something?"

"No."

"Heh. Very funny," Dane offered the dragon a grin before continuing his question, "I wanted to know what your life was like."

"I've told you enough about me."

"You have. But what about friends? Other than Seven and Recere, did you have any?"

"Why should I tell you?"

Dane rolled his eyes, though he coupled it with a knowing grin, "Can we just skip past the stubborn dragon part and get to where you reluctantly answer my question? I understand you don't want to be all that close to me, but-"

"But nothing. I will say no more."

"Fine, fine. No more out of you, I get it… Draco, I have another question. This one has nothing to do with the last one."

"Doesn't matter to me if it did or did not, but you're going to ask anyways."

Dane nodded with a hesitant grin, then loosed a low sigh, "You have me there… Draco, how do you question a certainty?"

The dragon paused, his gaze straight forward. Then his head swung round, locking onto his human companion, "What do you mean by that?"

"If you know something for certain, how do you question it?"

"You understand I realize that you are hiding your real question behind a thin veil."

"I do," Dane squeezed one of his hands before shaking his head, "But how would you question it? How do you question something that is certain?"

"You don't," was Draco's blunt reply, "If you know it is certain, then there is no questioning it. It is absolute. Unless you are not sure of its certainty."

"I'm… I don't know… I think it is certain."

"Then don't question it. You humans always ask far too many questions. Far too many."

"That we do… that we most certainly do," Dane murmured, his gaze drifting off. As it drifted north, the Sidatial mountains loomed before him. He sighed as he made to turn his gaze back to Draco, then froze. His eyes were locked to the east, his finger soon followed, "Draco. Look. Do you see it?"

The dragon squinted, suspicion momentarily reigning in his mind before he turned his gaze. Dane's finger pointed just south of the Sidatial mountains. There, nestled amongst the foothills was a small human village. Its stoic grey buildings seemed to stand resolute, as though to challenge the mountains to the north. Draco eyed it, then huffed an indecipherable sigh, "Sei, I take it?"

"It has to be. Which means," Dane turned his gaze north of the village, "that *Dedran ko Ivfrofril* is somewhere over there."

"Yes. Now that is established, to Sei. Come."

Dane's grin, dancing with a mischief that the dragon found himself ever so annoyed by, reappeared as Dane teased the dragon, "What? Not going to be difficult and insist we go directly to *Dedran ko Ivfrofril?*"

"I am not difficult. You are the difficult one. Even so, no. It is better if we go to Sei first. A thought has come to mind and I do not enjoy entertaining it."

"What thought?"

"No more questions. We move," the dragon huffed and turned away from Dane. One heavy footstep followed another as the dragon began to make his way towards the village. Dane watched him for several moments before beginning to follow. Beneath their feet, the pebbles born of the mountains crunched like the bones of forgotten lives.

Chapter 29

Questions for an Empty Village

Despite being able to see the village from the banks of the Ekasor, it was still quite a distance away. Even worse for Dane was the foothills that sat between the human and the village. It wasn't completely terrible, in the human's opinion. Draco had opted to continue walking with Dane even though the pair had long left the Plain of the Winds. They had done so mostly in silence, but Dane found that he didn't mind it. It was… nice to have someone walking beside him. In spite of knowing what he was. It was encouraging.

As the human crested one of the hills, granting himself another view of Sei, he was surprised by Draco suddenly speaking, "Dane. I have a suspicion."

"What is it?"

"The village. What will we find when we get there? Will it be a lively place or will the Corrupted have already brought it to heel?"

Dane frowned as he thought the question over, "Hmm, that's a fair question. I can't think of a reason they'd leave a vulnerable village so close to the Cave alone. Assuming they are in the Cave like we think."

Draco huffed, his tail twitching and wings rustling as he stared at the village, "Then we should be prepared to defend ourselves. We are just as likely to find friends as we are foes."

"Almost certainly. Let's just hope that the Corrupted don't care about a small village situated very close to their home."

"Right, like that would happen."

"You can hope even if it is hopeless."

The dragon decided to not deign that response with a proper answer. Instead, he settled the conversation with an ill-content grunt and continued to pad towards Sei. Dane found himself giving a sad chuckle in response before following Draco.

The hills leading up to Sei were surprisingly gentle for foothills. Even so, every step seemed slow and laborious. Despite his prior words, Dane couldn't help but worry that Draco had been right about Sei. What would they find? Would it be empty or full of the Corrupted?

The pair soon had their answer as they crested yet another hill to reveal the village before them. It was far from a large place, boasting only a couple dozen quaint stone buildings. The small structures, each topped by a thatch roof, sat in a haphazard sprawl about the relatively flat plateau that housed the village. Dane's gaze slid along the place, taking in points of interest. A road that did not leave the village. A rather large building that appeared to be a trading post. A central green that was anything but green. And absolutely no people whatsoever.

"No one's here."

Draco spared a droll glance at Dane before shaking his head, "Quite obviously... I don't smell anyone, either," the dragon's tail was still, occasionally twitching from one side to the other, "I'm going to take a look."

Dane didn't respond, instead stepping forward into the village proper. He paused next to one of the houses, looking it over. Draco eyed his companion for a moment, then padded into the village himself. The dragon had barely begun to look at anything when Dane called out, "Draco, look at this!" Draco just sighed before padding his way over to Dane, who was knelt next to the door. Dane looked up for a moment before gesturing at the door, "What do you see?"

"A wooden door."

"A wooden door with dents in it. Something hit the door and it either hit hard or was heavy."

Draco studied the door for a moment, then shook his head, "It could have been something wrong or it could have just been a rock thrown at the door."

"Then why is the latchstring not out?"

"Latchstring?"

Dane tapped a small hole on the right side of the door, "On the other side of the door is a latch that keeps it closed. A cord or string, called a latchstring, is tied to that latch and fed through a hole like this, allowing you to open the door even from the other side of the latch. However, the latchstring is missing, meaning it's been pulled inside. The door can't be opened from our side without the latchstring."

Draco studied the hole for a moment, then eyed Dane, "You are saying that someone has to be inside to open the door?"

"I'm saying someone *is* inside. The latchstring has been pulled in, but look," Dane pressed his hands upon the door and pushed. The door started to move with him, but was almost immediately stopped, "The latch is stopping the door from opening. Unless someone latched the door, then fed the latchstring back through the hole when they were leaving, this door was closed from the inside."

"I see," Draco's gaze returned to the slightly dented, innocent wooden door, "In that case, how about I get the door open?"

Dane frowned, his brow furrowing as he pondered the dragon's question, "'You get the door open?' But I just said the latchstring was pulled in. Not that-" the human broke off as something came to mind. He was quick to follow up, however, "No! Let's not break down the door. If someone is in there, all that will do is make them think we're enemies."

"'Break down the door?' Now, when did I say I was going to do that, hmm? No, I'm going to do *this*," at his words, Draco gave what Dane could only describe as the dragon's version of a cock-eyed look. As he did so, his tail began to snake its way through the nearby window. As it did, there was promptly a crashing sound.

"Knocked something over. Couldn't see it," Draco muttered. Dane raised an eyebrow, but didn't comment. However, he couldn't help but notice that the dragon spoke almost at the very same instant that the sound had been heard.

Before Dane could follow up on that thought, a scraping sound erupted from the wall in front of them, "Found the wall," more scraping announced that Draco was moving his tail. Fortunately for the pair, nothing interrupted the dragon's actions until there was the thump of his tail striking the doorframe, "There we are. Now, there should be…"

Scraping sounded from the door as Draco dragged his tail along it. After several long, noisy moments, the noise stopped, "There it is. Now, lift up," more scraping came from the door, "Dane, push the door open."

Dane did the dragon's bidding, giving the door a push. As it swung open, Dane was just able to see Draco's tail slither back, letting the wooden bar of the latch fall back down. Dane shook his head and found himself turning to look at Draco.

"Where did you learn to do that? That is absolutely not a normal thing for a dragon to know how to do."

The dragon in question offered Dane his odd, starting-to-kneel-but-not-really motion that passed as a shrug, "I don't really care. I can use my tail how I wish. I'd be a fool to waste a useful tool," when Dane didn't immediately respond, Draco glanced over at him. He was rewarded with the human grinning at him, "Can you stop leering at me?"

"Leering at you? I just found it amusing that you repeated something someone else told you."

"I repeated nothing."

Dane shook his head, his smile still gracing his lips, "Draco, you cannot be telling me that that last sentence was your own, 'I'd be a fool to waste a useful tool?' Your tail, a tool? Those were not your words. They couldn't have been."

"They are. Now, that's enough. Go see if anyone's in there," Dane shook his head, clearly not believing the dragon for a moment. As he pushed his way inside, Dane was just able to catch Draco grumbling again, "Damned wolf and his damned nonsense."

Dane didn't respond to the dragon's grumping. He was far more interested in the sight before him. The stone home was a mess. The remnants of wooden furnishings laid likely where they were broken. Trinkets, tools, and similar objects, no doubt the belongings of whoever lived here, were scattered about the structure's singular room. Dane couldn't help the scowl that touched his visage as he began to sift through the mess. He found an ornate silver candelabrum that was undoubtedly the most valuable object in the house buried under a small pile of cloth and wooden splinters, but nothing else. Pushing aside a small curtain revealed the small portion of the home that served as the sleeping area. Much like the rest of the building, the area was a mess of bedding and belongings. Dane sighed as he picked up a small carved dragon. Probably meant as a child's toy, the dragon was badly damaged, missing a wing, the tip of its tail, and its entire head. Dane could only give another sigh as he put the toy down. As he made his way back through the door, he found Draco waiting for him.

"Well?" Dane just shook his head, to which Draco nodded expectantly, "So no one is there. I doubt we have to look through the rest. We already know the answer."

Dane studied the other buildings for a moment, then gave a nod of his own. His voice sounded somewhat hollow, "Right. All we can do is seek out *Dedran ko Ivfrofril*. And hope that we just have an empty village."

Draco eyed his companion for a moment, then huffed, "Why hope for that? We both know that they're Corrupted. Better to hope that there aren't too many Corrupted."

"Because not everyone is as pessimistic as you?"

Draco huffed again, "Not going to pretend I know what that word means. What I am going to say is I'm realistic."

"And I'm not?"

"No. No, you are not. You are very much imaginative. Speaking of, if you start fighting imaginary enemies, I'll just leave you there to flounder in your insanity."

Dane cracked a thin smile, mirth glittering ever so slightly in his eyes, "Glad to know that you have my back. Nonetheless, we should get moving. The cave should be to the north and east. And Draco?"

"Mm?"

"If you can manage it, we need to be stealthy. I may be hoping that the Corrupted are thin in numbers, but that won't change that they could very well be hundreds strong. If we can avoid it, I'd rather not get caught."

The dragon heaved a sigh as he turned his gaze first to Dane, then northeast to the mountains. His tail gave an agitated twitch as he muttered, "Tell the dragon to be stealthy. Yeah, tell him. He's the big bulky thing that clearly has no idea how to move unseen and unheard."

"All I did was advise that we be cautious and stealthy."

"And this is coming from the human who found it entertaining to sneak up on dogs," Draco's voice was very nearly a monotone-like drone, "You and I both know who that statement was meant for."

"Even if you are right, does it matter? We have a cave to investigate," Dane gestured to the northeast, then began to walk that way himself. A piece of stone made a grinding sound as Dane's foot fell upon it. It didn't impede the human's movement in any way, but it did seem to add a punctuation- albeit belated- to Dane's statement.

It wasn't long before the faded grinding sound was replaced by the heavy footfalls of the dragon. Dane chose not to acknowledge Draco's decision to move, nor did he acknowledge when the dragon started his practically signature grumbling, "Damned human and his damned self-righteousness. Can't be a dragon around him without him poking his damned fun. Can't even be right without him being righteous and overlording. I wonder how righteous he'll feel when he remembers who is both stronger and not a squishy little walking lunch," Dane may have been refusing to acknowledge the dragon's grumbling, but that didn't stop him from wondering if this was simply an act by Draco. Or if it was all real...

Chapter 30

One with the Dark

Dane crouched by a boulder, his eyes locked on the gaping cave that sat directly before him. By his side stood Draco, the golden dragon doing the best he could to not look like someone had spilled a chest of treasure on the mountain side.

The trek through the mountains had been quiet. Far, far too quiet for Dane's liking. If this cave was in fact the home of the Corrupted, then there should have been something. Anything at all. Guards. Scouts. Even disgruntled outcasts or exiles would have relieved Dane's suspicion. However, their short trek had been no different than any other.

His voice low to avoid attracting undue attention, Dane murmured, "You certain you didn't smell anything on the way here? Absolutely certain?"

"I've already told you, yes. All I smelled was wolf. Why don't you check for yourself?"

"I don't have the sense of smell you do. Not as myself."

The dragon rewarded Dane's response with a huff and sharp response, "Then stop questioning me and just accept that I didn't smell anything. Can you do that?"

Dane found himself grimacing as he sighed, "Fine, fine. You didn't smell anything. That being the case, where are the Corrupted? Or anyone, for that matter. Someone or something had to be responsible for Sei, yet there is nothing and no one. No people, no animals. If it wasn't for the grass, moss, and the odd scraggly plant, this place would be barren."

"The scraggly plants are called tinderbrush. They're good for digestion," Draco muttered. When his comment didn't get a response, he tilted his head so as to see Dane's face. Dane, as it were, was staring at him in what Draco could only describe as a mixture between surprise and incredulousness, "What? I'm two and thirty years old. I know well enough what is good for me and what is not. Tinderbrush is good for digestion. Has a very odd taste, but not exactly unpleasant. Some of the more ancient dragons eat the stuff with practically everything," Draco's voice drifted off into the quiet musing, which was still more than loud enough for Dane to hear, "Speaking of, I should probably snag one on the way back. Might help with those cramps I've been getting."

Dane blinked at hearing the rather idle-sounding statement, then softly cleared his throat, again taking care to make sure that Draco and Draco alone could hear him, "When you are done mumbling whatever it is to yourself, I've got an idea. We need to know what is in that cave. But trying to enter it will almost certainly just result in us being attacked if the Corrupted are here."

"Obviously."

"Yes. My plan is that I masquerade as one of the Corrupted, then use the opportunity to infiltrate the cave and see what I can find. Meanwhile," Dane continued, preventing Draco from even getting a chance to complain, "You will remain hidden and wait. That way, you don't have to worry about the fact that you shine like a kingdom's treasury and are ready to go if I come running out with a mob of angry ashen assailants. Speaking of, how interested are you with having a rider?"

The moment Dane said the word, Draco's eye- the one the human could see- suddenly flared up, "No. I am not some animal for you to hop on and ride off merrily into the sunset. I will not accept a rider, do you hear me!?"

"Keep your voice down. What I mean is, if chance has it that I have to flee, can I count on you to allow me onto your back? That way you can fly rather than the both of us attempting to flee on foot."

Dane's explanation was met by a long, drawn-out silence as the dragon glared daggers at his much smaller companion. The silence held out for so long, Dane found himself wandering if Draco ever planned on answering. Or, perhaps, the human's reasoning had somehow struck Draco dumb. Eventually, however, both thoughts were proven wrong as Draco heaved a rather aggressive sigh and turned his head to gaze at the cave, "So be it. If, and only *if*, you are fleeing for your life because you messed up your sneaky nonsense, I shall carry you away. But only for this one reason and I will be carrying you. No riding. Don't expect me to offer this again! Ever!"

"Keep your voice down. Anyways, thank you. Now, to find the materials to make a passable disguise. With some dirt and ashes, I think I can mimic their skin color, but the red eyes are going to be the hard part. Draco, do you-?"

Draco, still disgruntled at being forced to allow Dane to use him like some beast of burden, didn't immediately notice anything. A few moments later, however, it crossed his mind that Dane had said his name. With the realization, the dragon found himself getting annoyed. Again, "Dane, I am not interested in your games. If you are going to say my name-" as he spoke, Draco swung his head about to glare at the human. His voice promptly drifted off in shock as he found Dane being held with a blade at his throat by an ashen-skinned human.

The Corrupted cautiously reached down and relieved Dane of his sword. Dane felt a tinged of concern, but dared not make a move against the creature, "The Conflicted has come. Stay quiet."

Draco's lips peeled back into a clear snarl. The gesture was accompanied by a growl just before the dragon spoke, his voice rumbling like an incoming flame, "Put that splinter of a weapon down and back away from the human. Now, or I show you just what a dragon is capable of."

"Cease hostilities. He is outmatched. This is Truth."

"Draco, look around," Dane murmured, his eyes flicking back and forth.

"At what? There is-" Draco swung his gaze about to see a few dozen Corrupted. Not including the pair of black-scaled dragons watching him. For a moment, Draco took a step back, then rectified himself and snorted, "What makes you think this will stop me, hm? Let the human go."

"Draco, don't," Dane spoke, eyeing the collection of foes, "You cannot fight two of your kind at once, let alone two and this many Corrupted."

"Dane, I-"

"Unbend your pride, you damned dragon!" Dane erupted, shocking his companion, "You cannot win this! Attempting to fight will result in your death and your death alone!"

Dane's eyes were panes of anger, but Draco found himself surprised to see that they were not directed at him. Instead, the human's eyes were locked onto the gathering of darkened figures. Moreover, Dane's eyes... Draco wasn't afraid of the little human, but the feral look in his eyes caught the dragon off guard. It was a look that didn't belong on Dane's face, yet it somehow didn't seem alien. The thought left Draco confused about the entire situation. It all felt exceedingly strange.

"Surrender, Draco. You can't win this fight," Dane growled. His voice held an animalistic edge that sounded so wrong, yet even more normal than his regular voice.

Draco's gaze swept along the stoic Corrupted. Not one moved or even seemed to be more than a host of peculiar, realistic-looking statues, *Damn these bastard beasts. Dane's right... I don't stand a chance in fighting all of them... I...* Draco heaved a sigh, then lowered his head, "Alright, fine. You win."

At Draco's words, several of the Corrupted stepped forward. Each held a chain in hand, "He will stay still. Movement shall make surrender difficult," one called out before they began to throw their chains. The metal-link ropes arced over Draco, only to be caught by even more Corrupted on the other side. With the chains in hand, they ran in unison, darting under Draco. Each step perfectly in time with their fellows, the Corrupted emerged from beneath Draco and lunged up, hooking the chain to the chains themselves and firmly pinning Draco's wings.

Draco wasn't focused on them, however. He was focused on the Corrupted elf that had darted forward and, with agile movements that Draco couldn't even begin to track, wrapped a chain about the dragon's muzzle and horns, all but locking his mouth closed. Quite naturally, this immediately spun the dragon into near rip-and-tearing levels of anger.

Any action the dragon planned on doing was cut short when Dane glared at Draco and rebuked the dragon's anger with a very quick, "Draco, no."

Draco didn't have a chance to react to the rebuke for, at almost the exact same moment, a Corrupted elf practically flung itself onto his back and pressed a blade to the underside of the scales on the back of his neck, "He shall begin movement forward. Attempts to the contrary shall be met with severe injury. This is Truth."

Reluctance dogged the dragon's footsteps as he obeyed. As much as he wanted to forgo the act and just rampage on the Corrupted here, Dane was still here and now unarmed. He was far, far too easy for the Corrupted to kill like this. And as much as the human irritated him. Draco still needed Dane. With no other option, Draco resorted to glaring at his captors.

The pair were marching into the cave. The stony walls appeared to be made of a black rock that did nothing to improve visibility. And visibility there was not. Dane and Draco had barely been led about a dozen dozen meters into the cave and it was already near black. It wasn't long before Dane no longer knew which way they had come from or even if they were still going in a straight line.

The darkness was almost weighted. As though it was pressing in from all directions. Dane found himself breathing a little heavier. It was as though he was walking in his own personal box. A box without sides, yet that pressed in from all angles, *It's so dark. So dark. So small. I... I need to get out! I can't stay. I can't! I must get out! I have to get out!*

Just as it began to cross Dane's mind to do something more than merely panic and actually escape the all-confining darkness, a faint light caught his eye. Coming from directly ahead, it resembled the flickering of firelight. Dane didn't care. It promised a way out of the pressing darkness. It may not be a good way out, but it helped settle his mind. Just a little.

As the last dregs of panic faded from Dane, the Corrupted marched him and Draco through what resembled a rough-hewn gateway. What waited on the other side was a large rotunda. Its size could only be comparable to that of a wealthy cathedral in a kingdom's capital. The black stone walls, contrary to the several passageways leading in, were expertly shaped and bore many elegant carvings. The flaming torches that sat in their meticulously crafted sconces sent shadows that danced amidst the darkness and seemed to imbue the carvings with a sinister aura. One the far side of the rotunda from where Dane and Draco entered, the floor vanished into a near semicircle of water.

As eye-catching as the dark room was, it was the many Corrupted that waited within that drew Dane and Draco's attention. There had to be at least two dozen present, each standing near a wall. And they were of all different kinds. Elves, humans, and dragons. The short, squat, bearded, and muscular dwarves. The human-shaped wolves known as wolfear. All were present. Eerily, the gaze of each of the Corrupted seemed to be locked on Dane and Draco. Barely blinking and without the twitching of a person trying to look at two objects at once.

The Corrupted escorting Dane and Draco continued to march the pair forward, through the center of the rotunda. As this happened, more Corrupted began to appear from the passageways. They gradually began filling the room behind the captives, leaving no space for escape. Still, it wasn't the numerous Corrupted appearing out of the shadows that called Dane's attention. It was the pair of Corrupted that stood on the bank of the pool of water.

These two were also staring at the two captives, but their gazes were studious, as opposed to eerie. One of the two was a rather large, black-scaled dragon. The other was a human that wore a twisted crown that appeared to have been forged from a black metal. He was garbed in a black robe reinforced from beneath by black metal plates on his shoulders, thighs, forearms, shins, chest, and back. Hanging around his neck, in front of his black garb, was a gold chain upon which hung a small green orb. The human loosely held a unique-looking spear. The over two meter weapon shone like silver from its haft to point. The spearhead was long and edged, almost exactly like a sword blade, and sported a wide, sharp-looking crossguard. Curiously, the blade-like spearhead did not have flats, but instead seemed to meet into two more, broader edges. Idly, Dane noted that anything stabbed by the weapon would likely end up with a rhombus-shaped hole in it.

Dane and Draco were marched up to the pair of Corrupted, then stopped as one of their captor's voices rang out with a sharp, "Halt! Cease march!" As this happened, the crowned human gave a hollow smile and spread its arms.

"Welcome to this place, Dane. Welcome to this place, Draco. Welcome to the home of the seekers of truth. Welcome to *Dedran ko Ivfrofril*. I, the Black Iron King, humbly welcome such distinguished figures. It is truly an honor for it to be that such pivotal figures would offer their aid."

Draco gave a low snarl, conscious of how outnumbered they were, "We offered nothing."

"Oh, but you did, indeed!" the Black Iron King began to laugh. It was steady and full-throated, but held an edge of… something. A note that delved deep into the depths of the mind. That place where no man should dwell, "Ha ha ha! Ah, ha ha! You agreed the moment my ambush claimed you. Yes, indeed. You will drink from the water of the lake," he swung his hand towards the pool in a grandiose manner, "It will be your death. It will be your rebirth. It will expunge the lies that cloud you. It will guide you to Truth."

"This is Truth," the voices of the innumerable Corrupted rang out.

"And if we refuse?" Dane asked, his voice possessing an element of passiveness and calmness that caused Draco to start looking at him in sheer surprise.

"You cannot. Your choice has been made by myself. You may fight, but it will only result in failure and your death. A pointless thing, death. Why allow the inevitable to be inevitable? Deny it by your actions now and let the inevitable fade," at the king's words, several of the nearby Corrupted directed their weapons towards Dane and Draco, "You are not convinced? It seems you do not understand. I am the Black Iron King. I am the night. I am the Truth. I am the chosen light and dark. I am the one who bears the change of the lost from the shadows of the forgotten. I am the heart of gold and the heart of black. I… I am the needed future of a world consumed!"

Dane scowled, not even attempting to disguise his distrust. Even so, he didn't grace the king with a response. Well, a response with words. Dane's arm swung up and back, elbowing the face of the Corrupted standing directly behind him. Without skipping a beat, the warrior twisted about. One hand caught hold of his opponent's sword hand while his left seized the Corrupted's sheathed dagger. Before the dark-bound soldier even knew what had happened, Dane plunged the stolen dagger into the ashen hand, forcing it to release its blade. With the sword now uncontested as his, Dane swiftly brought it up, then thrust it into the disarmed Corrupted's throat. Pulling the weapon free, Dane turned again, then gave a yelp as he dodged to the side. The shimmering head of a warhammer came crashing down, pulverizing the ground where Dane had been.

Dane glared at the Corrupted before him. The human gradually lifted its hammer again, clearly struggling, then blankly stared at Dane. The Black Iron King began to chuckle, "Impressive, no? We call it Duskfall. The falling curtain of the hem of the dress of dusk. The hammer is forged from the metal of a fallen star and blessed beneath the triplet moon. It is unfathomably heavy, yet the bane of all things by virtue of weight and blessing."

Dane didn't give the Corrupted king's words a second thought. He charged the hammer-wielding warrior. Just as they went to send the murderous weapon crashing down, Dane darted to the side. As the massive hammer pulverized another spot of floor, Dane leapt at its wielder, sending both crashing to the ground. The momentary stillness that followed was swiftly broken as Dane rose, swinging his sword around to level it at the Black Iron King. His left hand equally brought the dagger, still held in a reverse grip, to bear. The fallen Corrupted did not so much as move.

The king didn't even slightly look shaken. In fact, he began to smile, "Feisty, are you? And certainly quick upon your feet. But you are deluding yourself, Conflicted One. You were trained by your father primarily on the use of the sword and shield. You are inexperienced at best with paired blades. Come now, be rational. This is for the best of all, especially yourself."

Dane gave a grim smile, "I wonder where you got such madness from. Let me enlighten you, King of Black."

A deep rumbling erupted. Its source was quick to identify as the Corrupted dragon that laid behind the Black Iron King spoke, "*Foolishness. Foolishness. Foolishness. You are grave fools,*" the dragon spoke strangely. Its first word sounded rather normal for a dragon, but the ones that followed were rushed and discordant, "*You stand alone amongst a vast number. Any action you choose shall come at fatal cost. Cost. Cost. It shall cost your lives.*"

As the dark dragon spoke, Draco started. His eyes seemed to bore into the other dragon as he exclaimed, "YOU! You were the one! The dragon I fought at Adrian!"

Chuckling erupted from the Corrupted dragon, "*Yes. Yes. Yes. You are most correct. I am He of the Night-Black Scales. Destroyer and All-Breaker. You may call me Master. Master. Master. You are mine.*"

Draco began to growl, low and threatening. He didn't get the chance as Dane surprised everyone. The human charged, weapon already swinging.

Dane's blade scythed through the air, seeking the neck of the Black Iron King. There was a resounding clang as the weapon struck the king's swordspear. The king smiled, "Nice tr- Huh!" the Black Iron King darted back as the point of Dane's stolen dagger thrusted forward. The bloody blade narrowly missed the king's neck.

Dane was quick to follow, stepping forward. Before the Black Iron King had a chance to react, Dane's dagger swept about and caught the crossguard of the king's weapon. Tugging it to the side, Dane's sword shot backwards, his intention on spearing his Corrupted foe and ending him right there abundantly clear. An intention he would have made reality if the voice of the dark dragon still behind the Black Iron King hadn't rung out, "*Finish the strike and the dragon dies.* **Dies.** *Dies. His life shall be forfeit.*"

Dane froze, prompting the king to chuckle, "How easy the fires of fury fade. Yes, as the foremost of my dear subjects stated rather bluntly, one of my subjects still rides the dragon. It would take but a push of the blade. I must admit, you display a skill with paired blades that surpasses my expectations. Very much practiced. But of matterless nature. You will put down your weapons or face our wrath."

The warrior sighed, then lowered his weapons and slowly put them on the ground, "I was hoping to slay you before anyone could react."

"Quite obviously. Indeed, such you nearly did. Your skill with the blades are unusual. How did you come by them? Your father did not teach you them."

Dane's response was rather cordial, "My father was always worried that some spy or another was watching us. Rightly so, as it would seem. My specialty has always been the paired blades, but only in secret. As far as anyone knows, I wield a sword and shield while on foot, like a traditional knight."

"You are quite forthcoming with information that you once hid. It is refreshing, yet born of discomfort."

"No point hiding it when I've already shown my skills. But what do you plan to do with us?"

The Black Iron King offered a faint smile. There was an edge to the smile, a crazed uncertainty, "I have stated the Truth already. You will drink from the waters of *Arun ko Ivfrofril*. You shall embrace vassalage to the Truth. You shall join a brotherhood of darkness to sweep the world and save the light."

"To the Abyss with you before we do," Draco snarled.

"You have no choice, Dragonslayer Draco," Dane started at the king's words, but the action was ignored, "Now, step forth and drink. Do so of your own will or let those who know guide you. The choice is yours."

"That is no choice!"

The Black Iron King smiled again. It was an empty smile, no feeling or will behind it, "Of course, there is a choice. But that is of no consequence. Decide, Kinslayer," Dane did not react this time, but found himself curious, *What is that supposed to mean? Dragonslayer and Kinslayer? Does he truly mean-? No, those words must be meant to confuse and surprise, nothing more.*

Before Dane could consider much else, one of the Corrupted dragons began to push Draco forward. Draco was barely able to react when a second Corrupted dragon stepped forward and began to do the same. They were firm, yet oddly gentle. Almost as if they were guiding a youngling, rather than a nearly grown dragon. The Corrupted dragon known as the Master shuffled to the side, giving Draco a clear path directly to the pool of water.

Draco snarled, and attempted to pull back, but then stopped. He was unable to fight against two Corrupted dragons, especially with another Corrupted still poised to deliver a fatal strike to his neck. As much as he wanted to fight, he couldn't. Not yet. So, with resigned steps, Draco slowly trudged forward.

The pair of dark dragons led Draco to the pool's edge. He stared at the water for a moment. It looked just like normal water. Was this really the legendary *Arun Ivfrofril*? He was broken out of his thoughts when a voice called out, "Don't drink! Draco, don't drink!" It was Dane… From the sounds of it, Dane was struggling against something. As Draco realized this, he also noticed three things. The Corrupted was no longer on his back, one of the Corrupted dragons had stepped further forward, and the paw of that dragon had begun to press on Draco's head.

Draco barely had time to react to this knowledge as the Corrupted dragon pressed down. Draco heard one last cry of, "Draco!" from Dane, then his head went under. Dane, meanwhile, continued to attempt to free himself from the grasp of the two Corrupted dwarves that had grabbed and firmly secured him while he had been confused by the Black Iron King's words. For all his struggles, all Dane was able to do was watch. Not that there was much to watch. Draco was writhing and futilely attempting to escape from the clutches of his captor. Draco's struggles were accompanied by splashing and pointless bubbles. Then, without warning or preamble, the golden dragon went limp. All was still, even Dane, as the Corrupted dragon that was previously pinning Draco's head beneath the water pulled the limp dragon free.

Dane's eyes were locked on the collapsed form of Draco, ignorant of all else. So much so, he didn't notice when the Corrupted dragons had left Draco lying alone. Dane also didn't notice that the Corrupted holding him were dragging him forward. All Dane saw was Draco slowly rise.

"Draco?" Dane's question was hollow and lonely, yet seemed to be the loudest thing in the room. The golden dragon froze, then opened his eyes. His red eyes. They locked onto Dane, the look behind them was confused and disoriented. Not that Dane got much of a chance to see them as his head was plunged beneath the water's surface.

Dane renewed his struggles, desperation now fueling his strength. He *had* to escape. For Draco, if nothing else. In spite of his efforts, the Corrupted dwarves held fast. Dane could not even shift them the slightest bit. It was as though he was trying to push boulders with his hands bound behind him. He tried to push his head back up, but found the hand of the back of his head negating all of his pitiful attempts. Even worse, he had been caught by surprise and hadn't the time to take a breath. His lungs were already pleading for air, leaving Dane with little options. That didn't stop the drowning human from continuing his attempts. Jerking his shoulders back and forth, attempting to kick one of the dwarves. Anything!

In the end, it was futile. His strength fading and lungs all but tearing themselves free of his chest in search of air, Dane had no choice. His lips pryed themselves apart, whether or not of his own will being a moot point. The water rushed in and Dane's awareness of the world was gone.

Chapter 31

The Starless Night

Hunger…

Rage…

Fear…

The werewolf's eyes opened, greeting it to a black stone room. The creature paid no mind to the darkness, rising to its feet. Its two feet. The werewolf only momentarily regarded this… unfamiliar feeling before sweeping its gaze about the room. It was empty and the only entrance was a lonely passageway. The beast paused again… It was dark, yet the beast found no difficulty viewing its surroundings… No, not viewing. Its eyes did nothing. Its ears and nose made up the difference.

The beast shifted. Everything that happened was entirely natural, yet… Something was discomforted. Not the beast itself, no… Something or someone else… The beast shook its head. No matter. It was time for them to rest, after so long. The beast was awake and it- Whatever else crossed the werewolf's mind fled as the urges reminded the creature of their existence. Hunger. Rage. Fear. The beast's lips curled back, the fur of its hackles rising. Yes, it was time to hunt.

All hesitation the werewolf had vanished as it flung itself towards the room's singular portal. It didn't bother remaining on two legs, instead dropping to all fours. As it did, it noted that odd feeling of fear. It had grown. The thought discomforted the beast. What was there to fear? And was that fear its own or theirs?

Even as these peculiarities brought themselves forth, the werewolf did not stop its charge. The passageway it entered was as black as the room it had left. It was also just as deserted, with nothing of interest for dozens of meters. The passage began to gently curve just before the beast noticed the telltale sounds and smells of another passageway… and a living thing. The creature didn't bother identifying whatever it was approaching, instead opting to lunge at the unknown being.

The Corrupted didn't have the time to even react when a hand-like paw seized him and dragged him well within range of the werewolf. The ashen-skinned human found its gaze dominated by the soulless eyes of the beast.

"It is not a Brother. It has come from the nowhere. It shuns the Truth!" the Corrupted managed to say before the werewolf slammed his prey into the ground. One paw came down and dug into the Corrupted's exposed chest, pulling free large chunks of flesh and splatters of blood. A second paw dug in as the Corrupted screamed, this time anchoring onto something within the darkened human. When the werewolf pulled its claws back, the Corrupted was dragged with them, slamming his head rather brutally against the nearby wall. The beast seemed to be without mercy as it rammed the Corrupted against the floor again. A crunch sound and the ashen-skinned human went limp, much to the werewolf's dismay. It had hoped to exact more torment on the despicable violator. The beast was quick to rally, however. There would be more violators.

The werewolf charged forward, leaving the Corrupted's body to vanish into the darkness. It didn't really care which way it was going. As the beast came upon points where multiple passages converged, it would hurtle down whichever path was the closest to straight forward. Or led to something alive. Indeed, the path it was currently charging down held the scent of living creatures. That was all the werewolf needed to know, frankly. It didn't care if the scent meant multiple enemies or what kinds of enemies. All it wanted was to find something to tear apart.

And find something it did. The beast's path carried it directly into a collection of Corrupted. A short and stout dwarf, a lithe and slender elf, and a pair of average, every-day, red-eyed humans. The elf was the first to react, drawing her long, slender blade.

"This beast is an enemy of Truth. Begin assault," the elf stated, advancing on the werewolf. The elf barely managed to take two steps before the beast flung itself at the group. It barrelled into one of the humans before they had a chance to react. With little hesitation or even thought, the werewolf seized the human it had catapulted itself into and promptly flung him into the nearest wall. The Corrupted's fate was announced with an echoing crunch.

The dwarf and the remaining human drew their own weapons, a spiked mace and an axe respectively. Unfortunately, neither got the chance to engage the werewolf. The werewolf engaged all three of the Corrupted by seeming to flail at them with its claws. Seeming to, for each slash was astonishingly well placed. One across the human's leg, bringing the pale-skinned man to his knees. Another scoring the elf's sword hand, forcing her to drop her blade. Yet another slash tore across the dwarf's upper body. Much to the dismay of the dwarf's comrades, that slash also ripped the fighter's neck open. With the dwarf now collapsed and dying in her own blood, the remaining Corrupted managed to counter. The elf reclaimed her fallen sword while the human managed to swing his axe up, then send it meteoring down onto the werewolf's side.

The werewolf loosed a snarl as the human's axe crashed into its side, then seized the human by the head, its claws digging in. It completely ignored the elf, even though she was using her newly-recovered blade to open a gash across the beast's upper arm. The werewolf slammed the human into the wall, then managed to do so a second time before it felt the human spasm. The reason for the spasm was rather obvious, given the werewolf's claws were deep within the human's brain. A ruthless jerk of an arm movement sent the now-limp body crashing into the elf. The elf, the last of the four Corrupted, found herself pinned beneath the body as the werewolf began to approach.

The beast seized the slain human and flung the body aside. The elf, even with her superior speed, didn't have a chance to avoid the werewolf. A furry hand-like paw clamped onto the downed Corrupted and jerked her into a roughly standing position. Roughly, for the elf's feet were no longer touching the floor. The elf got a moment to stare at the soulless eyes before being bodily flung into the wall. The Corrupted grunted as her back slammed against the black stone, her blade still clutched in her uninjured hand. The elf managed to looked up at the beast again as the werewolf flung itself at the disoriented elf. If there had been anyone else there to see the spectacle, they would have witnessed the beast turn a once-living elf into a mass of blood and meat.

The blood-splattered werewolf stood there for a moment, its breath heavy and wounds already faded. It should have felt pleasure and pride at a successful hunt, or so it would have thought. Instead, it had a rather mysterious feeling. What was this feeling? Fear? No… Disgust? Not quite… Satisfaction? Perhaps… The beast shook its head. Their feelings didn't matter. Not now. Not right now… Or did they? The beast shook its head for a second time, their tail held still in alarm. Why? Why weren't they resting? They hated what the werewolf was doing. Yet they insisted on watching… So, why? Why?

The werewolf shook its head yet again before charging down the corridor. Unfortunately for the beast, they met nothing else as they hurtled down black stone corridor after black stone corridor. Only to happen across a surprise. Whether by chance, fate, or design, the werewolf emerged into the same rotunda where the violation took place. Unlike then, no one was here. It was quiet, save for the gentle lap of that vile water. The beast's gaze swept across the massive space, but found nothing save for a massive hammer.

The werewolf was about to charge towards the opening that led outside, when it got a feeling again. However, this one was easy to understand. The hammer… The beast felt like it should take the hammer. There was no reason to. The weapon would be nothing more than a burden to the werewolf. And yet…

The beast approached the hammer and wrapped a paw around the weapon's handle. When it attempted to pull the weapon up, however, the werewolf found that it was a struggle. So much so that the beast was forced to use both paws to lift the hammer. It was unreasonable how heavy the weapon was, yet it was gratifying for the beast to find that it could lift the weapon. With the almighty hammer settled over the werewolf's shoulder, it began to stalk towards the exit.

The long hallway out of the black cave was surprisingly empty. Well, not surprising to the beast, of course. It couldn't care less that no one was there. But the werewolf did have this feeling. That feeling was unease, though the beast was certain the feeling did not belong to itself. They were uneasy, not it. Still, the feeling nagged at the beast. Why were they still not resting? Why did they insist on this? They hated this, truly hated it. They hated the werewolf and what the werewolf did. They feared the dark, enclosed spaces that the beast was so indifferent towards. So why? Why did they yet pursue their own self-torment?

The beast didn't consider the odd feelings much longer as the light of the outside world revealed itself. Finally, escape was close at hand. Again, however, the werewolf found that odd feeling. It wanted to leave, but they wanted to turn back. Something was missing. The beast shook its head. No. No, it could not go back. Not there. Death waited there. The werewolf shook its head again as the feeling grew more insistent. Death was nothing to fear, but it could not die yet. They had too much to do. Too much to die here.

With determination and no small amount of willpower, the beast erupted from the cave's entrance. It momentarily drew to a stop, confusion evident upon its muzzle. There had been light, yet the darkness revealed that it was night. Where, then, was the light?

"Ha. Ha ha ha. Ha ha ha ha!" Laughter suddenly emerging from behind caused the werewolf to spin about. Stepping out the cave's entrance were the all-too-familiar forms of the violators. The Black Iron King and the Master. The Corrupted king offered a bow, his hand comfortably holding his swordspear, "I had both expected and not expected you to try to escape, but how easy do you abandon your dear friend! And look at you! A beast through and through. It suits you well, just as well as anyone else as it was, but that is what it is."

The werewolf lowered itself into a much more combat ready stance. Its lip drew back into a visibly and audibly clear snarl. In spite of the clear threat the beast was offering, the king was rather passive. In fact, he was smiling.

"Ah, the instincts of the beast. Yes, you are just as I thought and just as I am. You are of darkness born and black of heart. You are as a brother to me. And, like a brother, shall I offer forgiveness that is not deserved, yet given still. Look around," the king gestured skyward, as he gradually made his way down in front of the cave's entrance, "See the emptiness? There are no stars tonight and Ephala is new. Even Merani has hidden away. The night is starless. This night is the night of strength and hope for those of our ilk. No light dissuades us. No light binds us. The starless night of Ephala's new hunt.

The darkest of dark nights. It is our time, you and I. This is when we truly thrive. Now, come. Let us return. Let us be as we are."

The king turned his gaze back to the beast before him. The werewolf didn't give him a chance to continue his meaningless monologuing. The beast flung itself at the Black Iron King. While the Master opted to not move at all, the king swiftly flung himself out of the way of the charging werewolf while bringing his weapon to bear. The ground almost seemed to shake as the werewolf's hammer came crashing down. The beast didn't bother holding onto the weapon as the king gave a grin while righting himself, "Know you my weapon? An elegant weapon forged of thrice-blessed silver that I have declared as being named Heroes' Ruination. But enough. You have chosen battle, to my regret. Though it is what it is, no? So be it. Deny yourself the Truth and face a brother's blade!" Following his announcement, the king swept his swordspear in a large arc, forcing the werewolf to refrain from charging again. At least, immediately. The beast flung itself forward as soon as the king's swing had finished, only to snarl in frustration as the king danced back.

"Come now. Surely you can try a little harder to not fail a simple task. Or not so simple, as it would well be," the king commented as he darted to the side, avoiding a brutal swipe from the werewolf and putting himself as the beast's side. With the grace of a master, the Black Iron King thrusted his swordspear forth, digging the blade into the beast's side, drawing forth a grunt of pain. The king swiftly backstepped, narrowly avoiding the werewolf's retaliatiatory swipe. Conveniently, the king had also freed his weapon.

"Come now, come now. Surely you can muster more than that? Or perhaps you can't. But I ramble nonsensically. Muster your strength, my bad beast, for the Truth is before you! Your king!" The Black Iron King quickly realized that he shouldn't have been postulating. The beast flung itself at him, seized him by his armored robes, then bodily flung him into the nearest mountainous wall. The king slumped to the ground, a stunned look on his face.

"Now THAT is what I was looking for! Yes, indeed! But all good things come to end, did you know? And so I must end it with a heavy heart. But it was to be my bad, bad beastly abomination. For I am sure you know, but I shall say here: Abominations are fated to perish!" the king smiled and he rose, then began to blur. The werewolf took a step back, spooked by the oddity before it. The king's form had become indistinct. It was hard to tell where the king's body ended and the world around him began. The werewolf took a step forward, sniffing. Much to its surprise, the king's scent smelled strange. Almost as though the Black Iron King had left, his scent was becoming that of a person who was there, but is no longer.

The beast staggered as something struck its right side, scything a wound just below its ribs. Before the werewolf had a chance to comprehend what had just happened, it was struck again. This time, a slash was opened along its left side. The beast didn't see anything, feel anything. It was as if the air itself had struck it. However, the werewolf didn't have time to react to this knowledge as another blow was struck, opening a long wound down its chest. But that proved to be what it needed. The beast was able to see the source of the blow this time. A blur had appeared into front of it and, with a speed that impossibly defied all physical limits, had swung a glittering object. The werewolf tried to reach forward, to seize its attacker, then froze. The beast's body went rigid as the blade of the Black Iron King's swordspear erupted from its stomach. From behind the beast, the king laughed, then planted his boot on the small of the werewolf's back, kicking the beast off Heroes' Ruination. The beast was sent sprawling on the ground as the king strolled close, raising his blade.

"A pity. You are a dangerous foe and were to be quite the useful tool and friend… But it is not to be. Your darkness is held back, your light is suppressed. You are a walker of shadowed twilight. A wild card that will spell many things. Tell me, if you can. Do you feel a strange sadness? You are a being of twilight, of shadows. Of dawn and dusk. Of the time when our world intercepts that of the spirits who bear lingering regrets. Do you feel the loneliness that pervades the hour of twilight?" the king smiles grimly, "Perhaps, perhaps not. No matter to me or you or anyone. The time has come. Lights out!"

Even as the king finished speaking and had raised his weapon for the final blow, he was interrupted by a hollow voice, "Majesty. This one's Brother has awakened."

The Master turned his gaze to the speaker, a Corrupted wolfear, and spoke, "*Thank you. You may go.* **Go.** *Go. Go and begone,*" at the dragon's words, the wolfear left without another word.

The Black Iron King nodded, "It would seem that I must go. Best to meet such a special Brother in person. Farewell, Beast of the Dark," the king turned, his robe swirling about his legs, and stalked into the cave, followed by the Master.

The werewolf, now alone, slowly dragged itself to its foot-paws. It hurt. So much pain… And this feeling. The feeling was something like sympathy… no, the feeling *was* sympathy. They were being sympathetic? But why? They hated the werewolf. No matter. The beast dragged itself over to its abandoned hammer and took hold of the weapon. There was no reason to claim the weapon, but it couldn't help itself. Was it the sympathy that convinced it? Perhaps…

Dragging mighty weapon behind it, the werewolf began trying to put as much distance as it could between itself and the cave. It knew when it was beaten… but where to go? Another thought invaded the beast's head. The lake. The broken den beside the lake. Without any hesitation, the werewolf turned itself to the west and began to slowly make its way towards the lake. It had to get there. It had to.

Chapter 32

Dreaded Tidings

Vreena rolled her eyes, her expression anything but calm. Across a small gap from her, Leonidas sat on a piece of rubble, a passive expression marking his inscrutable reptilian face. With a sigh, Vreena responded to the dracon, "Yes, I suppose. But that still doesn't answer the question. They were going on a scouting mission. They shouldn't be gone *this* long. It has been far too close to two weeks. Where are they?"

"Peace, Vreena. They have not returned, but trust in them. Thou art merely worked up from doing nothing and having nothing to do," Leonidas's tail drifted to the side, displacing a small amount of stones and dust, "They shall return. And we shall wait for them. A war is won by spies, scouts, and sabotage as much as blades, warriors, and battles."

Vreena shook her head, then picked up a rock, inspected it, then idly tossed it against a broken wall, "I know. I know. But it doesn't feel right. They are capable, but… I'm uncertain about Draco. He is almost certain to lead Dane to some sort of trouble. Perhaps not willingly, but they are prone to trouble, especially Draco."

"True enough. True enough," Leonidas shrugged, then tilted his head, "Listen. Argrex approacheth… His gait is hurried, he beareth news."

Sure enough, at Leonidas's prediction, Argrex rounded a ruined home. The black dragon paused for a moment, then turned his lone eye on Leonidas and Vreena, "Eastward. We have an arrival."

Vreena was first to react, "Dane and Draco?"

"No, I don't think so. They are alone and of human shape. Yet they stand larger than Dane. If you are going to meet them, I would recommend caution."

The half-elf nodded, her expression stony and resolute, "If the Corrupted think such an obvious ploy will take us, I'll prove them wrong."

Leonidas, now rising from his seated position, shook his head, "No. Thou must stay thine anger. We know not if this creature is a foe or friend of the Corrupted. It could very well be that they are an ally of ours made by Dane and Draco."

Vreena scowled, then turned her attention to Argrex, "Can you describe the newcomer better?"

"No… My eyesight suffered greatly due to the loss of my better eye. I could tell the figure was furred or wearing furs and dragging something long behind them, but nothing more."

Vreena nodded a second time, mostly to herself. With a determined set to her shoulders, Vreena began to stride forward, "No matter who they are, we had best meet them. Are you coming with me, Argrex? Leonidas?"

The dracon's wings rustled as he shifted them into a more comfortable position, "Of course, I shall come. Let us away."

Argrex rolled his single eye, "Don't bother to ask me, will you? Just assume that I am coming with you. Sure. Do that."

Leonidas glanced over his shoulder as he passed the stationary dragon, a glint appearing in his eyes, "Thou art staying?"

"Of course not. What do you take me for?" Argrex sniped back, his voice lighthearted and far friendlier than the words themselves seemed.

"Then we had best hurry," Leonidas extended an arm in the direction of Vreena, who was already a fair distance away, "Vreena seems to careth not if we are behind her," with that announcement, Leonidas began to pad after her. The thumps echoing behind him made it clear that Argrex was following behind.

Rather expectedly, the trek to where Argrex had seen the mysterious arrival proved to be secure. No strangers, no unexpected encounters. Not even an unplanned bit of rubble clattering, almost as though everything was holding its breath. Almost as though everything was waiting for something that was about to happen. Vreena had just noticed this herself as a crash erupted from farther in front of her. Without so much as a moment's hesitation, the half-elf charged forward. When she got to the site of the sound, what she saw was not what she expected.

Sprawled in a pile of rubble was a werewolf. It's fur would have been an expected mixture of grey, white, and black with a white belly. Would have been, for it was right now matted and colored red with blood. Several wounds, including a large, rhombus-like one in the midst of its belly, marred the unfortunate creature. Lying next to the fallen beast was a large warhammer that the wolf's lithe, even sleek form did not look to be physically able to wield. Of course, the hammer was strange. It's head was a massive block of some extraordinarily reflective, bluish-silver metal. The only thing that marred the mirror-like surface was an etching of a sun exploding.

The werewolf managed to raise its head, locking a feeble gaze onto Vreena. The half-elf sneered, pulling her blade from its sheath. The slender blade glimmered as it caught the light. Vreena stepped forward, only to be surprised when the werewolf *whimpered*. The armed half-elf found herself pulled to a stopped, shock etched upon her face. The werewolf continued to stare at her, then whimpered again. Vreena shook her head, so as to attempt to be sure she wasn't mistaken. A werewolf, the beasts known for their destruction, rampages, and hatred of all that was, was whimpering. It was so pathetic, it brought to mind the dogs that humans kept. Of when they were injured or lost. Of when, in desperation, they sought help from their master, however beloved or not.

As Vreena was musing over this oddity, Leonidas and Argrex finally managed to catch up to her, prompting the half-elf to wave the draconic pair over, "Leonidas. Argrex. Come here. Look what I've found…" at her behest, the two drew closer, clearly seeing the injured werewolf before them, "It's a werewolf."

"Perhaps," Leonidas mused, "Perhaps it is a lycanthrope who hast come too close to death to shift," as if to punctuate the dracon's words, the injured beast began to whimper again, once more seeming to conjure up thought of an injured and lost dog, "Vreena."

The half-elf hesitantly turned her gaze over to look at Leonidas, "What is it?"

"Wilt thou heal the poor creature? I believe it is of no danger to us, most certainly due to those very same injuries," as Vreena's confused look, the dracon elaborated, "Whether werewolf or lycanthrope, those injuries should have healed without assistance. A weapon of moon-blessed silver was no doubt the cause. If such was the case, a werewolf would have struck with furious abandon, even when it lay dying. Most like, this is a lycanthrope and a friend. Heal them."

Vreena sighed, but acquiesced, "Very well. Whoever you are, hold still," she knelt next to the fallen beast and laid a hand on the wound that had been run through it, "*Arkelw ve froehrain.*"

Like the last time she had used this spell, a warm glow began to radiate from her hand. The beast, who was closely watching Vreena, winced and gave a long, drawn-out whine. It began to shiver, prompting the half-elf to glare at it, "Stop moving."

The beast began to whimper again. Even as he did so, a black fog began to emanate from the creature. Vreena jerked back as the fog became so thick that it obscured the beast in its entirety. Unpleasant creaking and cracking sounds began to erupt from the fog. Following the cracks and creaks were whimpers of pain, moans of distress, and groans of suffering. Vreena found herself only able to stare at the all-obscuring fog, accompanied by the nauseating sounds. Then, the sounds stopped. The fog began to dissipate. And Vreena found herself gasping.

Lying where the beast had been, next to a newly formed fleshy blob, lay Dane. The badly injured human blinked, then slowly looked up at Vreena. She was surprised to see Dane's eyes were overflowing with tears.

"I-It's all m-my fault…" Dane moaned, "D-Draco… Draco… I-I'm so s-sorry… I-I…"

Vreena was about to interrupt the sobbing human when Leonidas tossed a tunic over top of Dane. The half-elf spared the dracon a glance, only for him- still clothed himself- to shrug, "I carry an extra one. Humans prefer to be covered in some capacity and thou wouldst be surprised as to the number that have appeared before me unclothed."

Vreena sighed with a shake of her head, then turned back to Dane, "Dane. What happened to Draco?"

"Draco… They w-were waiting… Th-They expected us… D-Draco was… Corrupted… I-I'm so s-sorry…" silence prevailed over the present gathering, aside from Dane's continued sobs. What was there to say? So the four remained as Sehero began to creep over the horizon, bringing a dawn laden with the promises of darkness.

Kuritik ko Metol

-as - Plural (Suffix)

-lun - Were

-o - Past (Suffix)

Adegran - Greet

Akron - Sword

Al - With

Arkelw - Mark/Scar/Wound

Arun - Lake

Dairgin - Dragon

Dedran - Cave

Deret - Him/Her

Ehelk - Serpent/Snake

Ehrain - Open

Erel - Ball

Eren - Am/Are

Feminaten - Companion

Firtess - Look/Watch

Fril - Light

Fro - Not/No

Garad - Father

Gegred - True

Gerat - Fate

Gre - In

Groir - Hear

Hasi - That

Hebrag - Spike

Hed - Come/Gather/Bring

Heras - Mother

Hofroen - Throw

Iar - To
Ireak - Foe
Iv - Be
Jeg - Go
Jel - Land
Karak - Dire
Kens - Let
Ketik - This
Kevis - Talk/Speak
Kior - Die
Kirin - Before
Ko - Of
Kuritik - Language
Lesir - Well
Letrag - Chain
Metol - Magic
Negdir - Fire
Neh - You
Nelg - Stone
Ner - Wind
Nerk - Hurt
Neverin - Promise
Ni - And
O - I
Ors - It
Rederal - Wood
Reils - Yet
Rekilek - Curse
Rotese - What
Sekel - Truth
Seres - Use/Purpose

Sir - Air
Sirit - Ever
Telsier - Ready
Ti - Like
Tikelo - Known
Tolkest - Speak
Tred - Hold/Stay
Ve - Do
Ven - Lift/Rise
Verach - Forge
Verag - Wing
Vered - Hand/Grasper
Verich - Wolf
Wetkrek - Spark
Zesul - Sane